A QUEST OF EARTH & MAGIC

OTHER TITLES BY S. USHER EVANS

THE SEOD CROI CHRONICLES
A Quest of Blood and Stone
A Quest of Earth and Magic
A Quest of Sea and Soil
A Quest of Aether and Dust

PRINCESS VIGILANTE
The City of Veils
The Veil of Ashes
The Veil of Trust
The Queen of Veils

THE LEXIE CARRIGAN CHRONICLES
Spells and Sorcery
Magic and Mayhem
Dawn and Devilry
Illusion and Indemnity

**For a full list of published works,
including adult and cozy fantasy titles,
visit susherevans.com**

A QUEST OF EARTH & MAGIC

THE SEOD CROI CHRONICLES

BOOK 2

S. USHER EVANS

Sun's Golden Ray
Publishing

PENSACOLA, FL

Version Date: 10/7/25

ISBN: 978-1945438523

Cover Design by Bianca Bordianu | www.bbordianudesign.com
Cover Typography by Sun's Golden Ray Publishing
Map Designed by Frederick Kroner with Stardust Book Services
Line Editing by Danielle Fine, By Definition Editing
Proofreading by Lisa Henson, Capitol Editing

Sun's Golden Ray Publishing
Pensacola, FL
www.sgr-pub.com

For ordering information, please visit
www.sgr-pub.com/orders

THE FAE REALM
PENNLAN
KONEVELL
SUDAEMOR
DRIWANIA
NESURIA
N

Chapter One

Ayla

"I banish you."

I turned the Pennlan stone gently in the sunlight, searching for any sign of power hidden in its shiny depths. It was such a small thing—much smaller than I'd thought. For centuries, it had rested in a crest above the throne room until it had been stolen—

Not stolen, taken for safekeeping.

By Leandra, my father's wife. After she'd murdered—

Compelled via magic.

I exhaled loudly, glancing at the ceiling. It had been six months since the world had turned on its head, when Eoghan, the wizard who'd all but raised me, had shown his true colors. Since I'd made the mistake of banishing him instead of ending his life. And now—

"I say, are you listening?"

I jumped, staring into the wrinkled, disgruntled face of Lord Galliford. The envoy from Konevell had arrived in a cloud of misery, and it hadn't gotten any better when we'd sat down to dine. He had a complaint about everything thus far, from the state of the castle to the greeting he'd received. I could only assume he was now complaining about something else—perhaps this before-dinner wine and chocolate selection—so I plastered a sweet smile onto my face and cleared my throat.

"I'm so sorry. What were you saying?" I asked, trying my best to look interested. "Something about your rooms not being to your liking?"

He made a noise and took a long sip of wine before examining it. "This vintage… Is it fae?"

"No," I said, glancing at the red liquid in my own glass. "Though we've been sent a shipment, if you would like to try it."

"I don't eat fae food. Don't trust it."

That makes two of us. "The Erlking is very interested in rebuilding our trade alliance. I doubt he would've sent me poisoned wine."

He bristled. "You may have forgiven the fae, but that doesn't mean the rest of us trust them."

Forgiven was a strong word. It was more like…a tepid reopening of conversation. "In any case, this is, I believe, an old vintage from Konevell. I thought it a good choice, considering."

He inspected the wine and took another sip. "Must've been a bad year. Or like so many things in this kingdom, *poorly kept.*"

It was hard to keep a smile on my face. Galliford's thinly veiled insults had made it clear he preferred the previous occupant of my chair —and I didn't mean my late father.

"Well, we all wish Eoghan hadn't done…what he did," I said. "None more than me."

"Do you truly believe the fae were innocent victims?" Galliford asked with an incredulous smile. "That Eoghan concocted this elaborate plan to marry you to gain access to the Pennlan stone?"

As many times as I'd had this conversation over the past six months, it was still incredibly unsettling to discuss. I pressed my lips into a thin line. "Yes. He planned to marry me during my coronation."

"Until he found your sister."

Half-sister. I pushed the wine glass a few inches across the table as my pulse quickened. "Yes."

"And she's of your blood? You're sure?"

I idly thumbed the stone hanging from my neck, remembering the moment she'd appeared in Eoghan's chambers. Like looking in a dead-eyed, raven-haired mirror.

"She wouldn't have been able to wield the stone otherwise," I said, hoping we could get off the topic quickly.

He chuckled. "The Erlking certainly kept that under wraps, didn't he? I wonder what other secrets might be revealed in due time."

I bit my lip instead of responding. The biggest secret of all was one Riona herself had spilled to Eoghan. That this stone wasn't the *seod croí*, the most powerful magical object in existence, but merely a piece of it. That the real stone had been broken into quarters and hidden away.

One to the humans in Pennlan, one to the mountains, one to the sea, and one to be buried in the aether.

And had I done the *right thing* and just ended Eoghan's life instead of sparing it, the other three stones could've continued their eternal rest. But no, I'd been too soft. A decision I hated myself for every day as I waited for our scouts to return with news.

"As I said, there's no one who wishes things were different more than me," I said, quietly. "But we must press on and try to find some sort of normalcy." I tilted my head. "Especially at the border. I've been told very little has been allowed to pass through to Konevell in a little over a month."

"Indeed," was all my taciturn companion said.

"I suppose I'm just confused. You've had no problem accepting Pennlan goods before."

He took a long sip of his wine and helped himself to another of the assorted chocolates lying before him. "Queen Ramira has grave concerns about how much of what comes from Pennlan is truly Pennlan's and not...tainted with fae magic."

"Everything sitting on the border now is from Pennlan," I said. "Hence my concern—it's starting to go bad."

"How can we be sure there isn't anything *magical* hidden amongst the contents?"

I swallowed. "The border with the fae may be open, but...we aren't exactly trading with them."

Not for lack of trying on the Erlking's part, either. He'd sent three letters asking if I would meet with a member of his court. So far, I'd declined, citing busyness. Sooner or later, I'd have to come clean. But the thought of inviting a fae into my castle still made me uneasy.

"I see."

"Which is why," I continued, "I was happy to receive such a gracious envoy from Konevell. I hope we can fix whatever issues have arisen between our nations and come to some resolution, so that Pennlan goods can move again."

His mouth twisted into a patronizing smile. "And we would love to come to a resolution as well."

"Excellent," I said, a real smile finally coming to my lips.

"But Queen Ramira needs more assurances."

I blinked. "Assurances? Of what?"

He put his hands into his lap and lifted one gray brow. "I'll be frank: the prevailing theory is that the fae have bewitched or confused you into believing they can be trusted." I bit my tongue before responding, allowing him to finish. "So Queen Ramira wants to place one of her own people here to ensure our best interests are being considered."

I narrowed my eyes. "A permanent ambassador?"

"Of sorts." His gaze dropped to the stone hanging from my neck. "She proposes a match with one of her sons."

I sighed. Of course, this conversation again. I'd thought, perhaps naively, that the subject of my marriage would fall by the wayside once Eoghan was gone. But every envoy who'd crossed my doorstep had the idea. I was the most eligible woman in the human world, it seemed.

"Did you have someone in mind?" I asked, humoring him.

"Prince Manfrid would make an excellent partner for you."

I opened and closed my mouth, surprise loosening a nervous laugh. "Manfrid is…a child, isn't he? Seven?"

"Eight, Your Majesty. He would come with a guardian, of course, one who could report back to Queen Ramira that the fae have not bewitched you as we have heard. And, of course, with the understanding that the second heir you produce would be returned to Konevell."

My head spun. They wanted to send a child here, one I would marry in a decade, and were already making plans for hypothetical children we'd bear together? This was a new level of desperation—one that sent anger to the depths of my heart.

"Absolutely not," I said with a fire that bordered on disrespectful. "I won't allow you to whore a young boy like that."

"It's not…" He bristled. "This is tradition for the royal family. You were merely unaware because—"

"Because I was also being groomed and prepared for a marriage with a much older person so they could gain access to the stone," I snapped. "It didn't endear me to the tradition."

"This isn't about—"

"Spare me," I said with a wave of my hand. "You didn't waste any time telling me that a second child—of my blood, which means the ability to wield the stone—would be sent back to Konevell."

He opened his mouth to argue, but I was faster.

"It is not up for discussion," I said. "Now, what other option do you have for us to resolve this impasse?"

"There…are no other options," he said, folding his napkin and tossing it on the table as he rose. "If Her Majesty is not willing to even entertain this offer from Queen Ramira, I suppose there's nothing more to discuss. I will head back to Konevell in the morning."

"Wait, Lord Gall—"

Before I could even finish saying his name, he was gone. His words rang in my ear, mingled with a phantom chuckle from Eoghan.

I sat back in my chair. The room was oddly silent now, a stark reminder that the *one* purpose of this meeting with the envoy was to negotiate the full opening of the border, and somehow…somehow I'd failed at even keeping him here for more than one night.

I fought back tears, reminding myself that queens shouldn't

blubber, and grabbed the wine bottle, filling my glass to the brim. I sucked it down without tasting much then poured the rest of it. This time I held the goblet between my hands, staring into the murky depths as the alcohol soothed my fury. Soon, shame and fear overtook anger, and I began to regret my words—especially considering the visit with Galliford was one of the last chances to normalize relations with our biggest trade partner.

Once the dust had settled after Eoghan's treachery, I finally understood just how bad a shape he'd left the kingdom in. He'd spent the past nearly two decades spending our gold on lavish gifts and empty promises to the other kingdoms, running huge trade deficits he promised would be paid for by Cade, Eoghan's apprentice, or my hand in marriage.

Of course, he hadn't planned on making good on those promises. From his journals, it was clear that Pennlan was merely the first conquest in a vision that spanned one end of the continent to the other. In his mind, whatever debts Pennlan had amassed would be wiped clean when he became supreme ruler of all.

Those debts, unfortunately, remained even though the wizard had been banished. And with Cade otherwise occupied in the fae realm, the only thing left to pay for them was my hand. But I couldn't be split between four countries, and I wanted to exhaust every possible option before giving up my last bit of freedom.

I took another sip of wine and picked up the stone that hung from a dainty chain around my neck. So much scheming for such an... unimpressive-looking object. I had bigger gems in my official crown, and the jagged edges made it look like a piece of glass broken on the floor. But perhaps I was just looking for imperfections, hopeful that the magic I'd seen had been a dream. Because I hadn't been able to even conjure a spark since banishing Eoghan.

I'd tried. I'd spent hours in my room staring into the blue depths, imagining a flash of magic or those voices that had urged me on when it had been activated. But there was nothing. Luckily, no one had asked for a demonstration because I would be exposed for the fraud I was.

As I stared into my glass, unsure what to do next, the familiar ache of missing my mentor, my friend, my Eoghan rose up like blood in water. I could picture him, the version with no plans to destroy kingdoms, the one who wiped my tears and guided my hand and taught me everything I knew.

Except...

After six months as queen, it had become apparent just how woefully inadequate that teaching had been. While my tutor had drilled me on history, economy, sciences—there had been nothing on how to decide what was best for my country. Why bother teaching a girl to be sovereign if she was never meant to be one?

And just like that, my heart broke again. I was truly and wholly alone atop my throne.

"Your Majesty?" Bronwen, my attendant, stood in the kitchen entrance, her hands folded. A few years older than me, she had pale skin, mousy brown hair, and a kind smile. She was one of the few people Eoghan had allowed to get close to me, and I was grateful she stayed after his banishment.

I cleared my throat. "Yes?"

"Will you still be having dinner this evening?" She paused, swallowing. "Alone?"

"I... No," I said with a small smile. "No, I think I'm going to go for a walk."

Chapter Two

Ward

The sky was starting to turn pink as the sun set, but I wanted to get as much out of my soldiers as I could. The days were growing shorter, and with an evil wizard lurking outside our borders, I wanted to be as prepared as possible.

I paced the green, stopping to offer suggestions where I could and praise where it was warranted. But it was getting hard to see, so I brought my fingers to my lips and whistled.

"Good work today," I said. "Dismissed."

They saluted then dispersed to the barracks. Two hung behind, waiting for me. Rutley was on the shorter side but built like a rock with ruddy skin and an even ruddier beard that came in patches. Small and sinewy, Elodia had rich ebony skin and wore her black hair in long rope braids that she kept tied at the base of her neck. They'd arrived from the same town a couple of months ago—hand-picked by Captain Gabhann, as I'd been—and since we were the youngest soldiers by at least a decade, we'd formed something of a friendship, even though I was their commander.

"I hear there's a festival in the village this weekend," Elodia said, wagging her brows at me. "Traveling circus or something. Will *the boss* let us go?"

"The boss might," I said. "To work."

"Boo!" Rutley said with a frown. "You're no fun."

"You'll get to see the show," I said with a light punch to his shoulder. "Just while making sure to keep the drunkards in line."

"But what if I want to be one of the drunkards?" Elodia asked.

"Next time," I said, clapping her on the back.

"Why don't you send Platt's men?" Rutley asked. "They don't do half the work around here we do."

I grimaced. Platt had been the second-in-command for years and hadn't taken very well to my abrupt promotion. And it hadn't helped that I seemed to be a more adept commander than he was. I had a feeling Gabhann had asked me to watch the festival because she trusted me more.

"We have our orders," I said, after a moment. "Now get to the barracks. We have an early morning."

"Are you headed up to the castle?" Rutley asked with wagging eyebrows. "Off to see your lady love?"

"Knock it off," I said with a low growl. "There's nothing going on between Ayla and me."

And I wanted to keep it that way. Ayla and I had spent hours one-on-one together, but the conversations were about things like the state of the soldiers, whether I'd heard from our scouts looking for the other three stones, what I thought of a particular decision that had far too many moving parts for me to understand. Our brief moment in the garden six months ago seemed to be an aberration. As much as my heart wished otherwise.

"C'mon, you know you've always wanted to be a king," Elodia said. "We can be your courtesans."

"I believe that means you'd be my whores," I said with a wry smile.

She blanched, looking at Rutley, who shrugged and said, "I'm game if you are."

"I'll pass." Movement at the front of the castle caught my eye. Ayla stood under the portico, looking forlorn and lost. Her dinner with Whatshisname from whatever country must've gone poorly.

"Duty calls," Elodia said, patting me on the back. "I'm sure you can cheer up our queen."

"If she invites you to dinner, get me one of the good rolls," Rutley said.

"Ooh, yeah, smothered in butter," Elodia added.

"I'll do my best on both counts." I waved them off. "Now get to bed. We're up bright and early in the morning to run the grounds."

That earned me a groan from both—neither were fast runners—but also got them to leave me be. I waited until there was no one left on the green to watch before making my way across to Ayla. Up close, she looked even more distraught, and there was a faint smell of wine on her breath.

"So…" I began slowly. "How'd it go?"

"He wanted me to marry an eight-year-old prince," she said with a glare. "Provided, of course, I send our second child back to Konevell."

"Of course," I said with a half-smile. "Should we ring the wedding bells?"

"Not funny." She sighed. "Walk with me?"

I offered my arm, and she took it silently. I let her lead the way, keeping my tongue until she'd gathered her thoughts to speak.

"An eight-year-old." She shook her head. "They're getting desperate. All for a stupid little stone."

I might've reminded her what Eoghan had done, but that wouldn't have gone well.

"Even worse, he said that was the *only* way Queen Ramira would fully open the border again," she said, looking at me as if I knew what she was talking about.

"I'm sure he'll come around."

"He's leaving tomorrow," she said. "That was the only card he was allowed to play, it seems."

I opened and closed my mouth. "Well, can we trade…with someone else?"

"Ward." She turned to look at me, a little impatience in her gaze.

"Lord Galliford came from Konevell."

I should've known what that meant, but I was at a loss.

She sighed, and spoke as if I were a naughty student. "The Adleh River splits the continent and forms the border between Pennlan and Sudaemor in the east and Konevell to the west. It ends in the city of Orapus on the far southwest side of Pennlan, which is essentially shared between our kingdoms. *Everything* goes through Orapus—and nothing goes beyond if Konevell doesn't say so."

I vaguely knew that. "And they aren't saying so?"

"Not very often." She chewed her lip. "I think they're just trying to leverage the only thing they have to force me into marriage."

I snorted. "Why in the world would they shut down a border just to force you into a marriage? Because you're just that pretty?"

"I don't flatter myself to think they're falling over themselves for my face," she said with a sly look. "They want to marry me because when they do, they'll have access to the Pennlan stone. And all its power." She paused, flashing me a mischievous grin. "But thank you for saying I'm pretty."

My face warmed, and I scrambled to change the subject. "I'm sure you can think of something else Konevell might want."

"Nothing like the stone."

"They have a pretty narrow view if that's all they're after," I said. "They'd really shut down all trade with their northern neighbor because you won't marry a kid?"

She grew quiet, slowing her gait.

"You said everything goes through Orapus in the south, right?" I said. "So why not just send stuff north to the fae? The gate's open, isn't it? I'm sure they'd be eager to get it."

She worked her jaw, saying nothing.

"I thought—"

"Trading with the fae won't solve the problem," she said, a little heatedly. "We have goods sitting in Orapus. They need to be able to go through. Once we solve that problem, then maybe…" She smoothed her hands on her dress. "Maybe we'll think about moving goods north."

"You know the fae have magic, right? Cade, even, could probably move whatever needs moving in a snap. Or Riona."

She flinched at the sound of her sister's name but hid it quickly. "Cade would be the better option, *if* he were available. But he studies in the morning and trains with fae in the afternoons. And in the evenings, he scours the Erlking's library for books on the stones."

"I'm sure he could take time away to help you."

"The way he tells it…" She softened a little. "He says they've made it clear they expect him to protect the realm should…should the worst happen."

"No pressure." I glanced at the jewel hanging around her neck. "But you're more than enough to protect Pennlan against him."

"Unless Eoghan gets the other three. Then…" She licked her lips. "Then I don't know what we'll do."

I didn't think Cade would be able to handle a wizard with three pieces of the *seod croí*, but I kept that particular comment to myself. "For all we know, you banished Eoghan to another continent. Perhaps he can't get back to cause trouble."

She nodded but didn't look convinced. "No wonder Ramira thinks I'm a weak queen."

"Nobody thinks you're weak. On the contrary, they seem to want a piece of your strength," I said. "And that you can decide who gets it— that's the true power."

She lifted a shoulder.

"Look," I said, turning to her, "I think if you show Konevell you're capable of making alliances with other kingdoms, especially others who have gold, like the fae, then they might be more willing to bend on some things. And if they don't, well…you've got a new trading partner, don't you?"

She picked up the stone from the chain around her neck. "I can't believe Queen Ramira could be so…cavalier with her own child. But I suppose the promise of power is tempting."

"If one wanted such a thing," I said.

"You wouldn't want it?" she asked, something unreadable in her gaze.

"I don't think I need it," I said with a shrug. "I have my sword."

"And what use is a sword against a wizard?" she asked.

"I used it plenty against Cade—and Eoghan," I said with a little smirk. "Besides that, I have you. Why would I need anything more than that?"

Her lips parted into a small 'o' as she turned to me. There was something innocent in her gaze, those vibrant green eyes surrounded by dark lashes. It was moments like this that I wished she wasn't a queen, and I wasn't a simple guard.

"I suppose," she said, after a moment. "Because if you were to want this power, you'd have to marry me."

It was my turn to be speechless, and my heart did somersaults in my chest. She'd captured me in her gaze, almost daring me to contradict her. The problem was…I needed to.

"Or find another of the three stones," I said, my throat constricted. "Do you think they have the same caveats?"

She turned away, lifting her shoulders and shielding her reaction from me. "One would hope there'd be some kind of protection on them so a wizard like Eoghan wouldn't be able to walk in and take them."

"One would hope."

We stood in silence for a bit longer, and I wished again that I were a little more reckless. Her lips were stained from the wine, a dark red that picked up the auburn in her hair. If I kissed them, would I taste the vintage? And if I did kiss her, what would happen next?

But I couldn't continue that train of thought.

Perhaps she was thinking the same, because she finally broke my gaze. "I suppose I should go to bed," she whispered. "Maybe in the morning, I'll be struck with a brilliant idea of how to solve this problem."

"Write to Cade."

"I told you—"

"There's more magic people than just him up there, and you said yourself that they want to trade with us."

"It won't work."

There was something in her voice that told me she was digging in her heels, so I shrugged. "Suit yourself. But if I were a queen with closed borders to the south and a willing trading partner to the north, I might let go of whatever hangups I had and take the outstretched hand. At least for now."

She watched me for a moment, and I could see the war in her eyes. But after a long pause, her shoulders dropped and I knew I'd won.

"I suppose it wouldn't hurt to *ask*." She smiled, though it was a little less emphatic than before. "Good night, Ward."

I bowed. "Good night, Your Majesty."

"Ward…" She smiled at me over her shoulder. "We've talked about this."

"Very well." I bowed again. "Good night, Ayla."

"Much better."

I remained where I was in the hallway, even long after she'd turned the corner and disappeared, the sound of her name on my tongue echoing in my ears.

Chapter Three

Cade

I stared down my opponent, showing no signs of weakness or fear. The long, wooden staff in my hand was alive with magic, crackling and sparkling green as I prepared myself for the next volley. The fae, Darragh, was formidable, one of the strongest I'd faced so far. His clay-colored skin was lightly sheened with sweat as he tied up his long, silky black hair and prepared himself to strike again.

"Begin," called the old, wizened voice to my left.

Darragh gathered magic in his hands and I shifted, planting my feet. His magic took the form of sparrows—a little disconcerting at first, but now that I'd seen it a few times, I was better prepared. I just didn't know where the attack would come from.

I saw it out of the corner of my eye and constructed a magical shield on my left flank. The sparrows came from the ground, smashing into my barrier with all the force of a storm. But my magic held fast, and—

Too late, I missed the second attack from the front, and the force of fae magic landed squarely in my stomach, sending me skidding backward. I was able to keep my feet and launch a spell of my own. The fae easily dismissed it.

"You can do better than that, wizard," he chided.

I could, but it was hard to catch my breath. "I…will get you for that…"

The old voice called out, "Heal yourself and resume."

I glanced to my right where an older fae woman stood watching the fight with a pensive look on her face. I kicked myself for not remembering; I'd spent two whole days last week learning new techniques for casting quick healing spells on myself in preparation for this fight.

But there wasn't time to ruminate. This time, the birds came from above, from the right, then right between my legs. I jumped out of the way of the last one, but the barrage didn't give me enough time to cast a healing spell on myself—perhaps the point. As Clíodhna had made abundantly clear, when I faced Eoghan again, I wouldn't have the benefit of taking a break.

Again, I saw the next attack before it hit, and was able to deflect and fire off one of my own. The distraction was enough, and I healed my stomach, easing the pain immediately and allowing me to draw a deep breath for the first time in a few minutes. My opponent recovered from my attack, ready to fight again, but I was back to full strength.

I blocked three spells, at the same time gathering magic in my staff for an attack spell. And in the brief moment between his attacks, I cast one of my own, sending him flying back into the wall. He slumped down, eyes closed, and my heart sank.

"Darragh! Are you all right?" I said, running toward him.

But Clíodhna was faster, waving her hand over his body and rousing him. He blinked heavily and allowed her to help him to stand.

"Good show," he said, rubbing his head. "You got me good with that last one."

"I must've put too much on it," I said with a half-smile. "Sorry."

"You'll need that sort of effort when you face the wizard," Clíodhna said, nodding to the other fae. "I only gave you a rousing spell. You should visit the healers just to make sure."

Darragh nodded, shook my hand, then limped away. I watched with more than a little guilt—these matches weren't supposed to result in injuries—but also a little pride that I'd managed to overpower such a strong opponent.

"That was slow," Clíodhna said with a frown. "You think too much."

"So you've said," I replied with a half-smile. "But I did all right, didn't I?"

She snorted. "If you want to defeat your former master, you will need to be better than all right."

"Unless Ayla uses the stone on him," I said. "Killing him this time."

Clíodhna gnashed her teeth, saying nothing. But I was already acutely aware of how she felt about Ayla's missed chance to rid us of Eoghan once and for all. Clíodhna and the fae didn't understand why she'd merely banished him.

I did. Even six months later, it was hard to wrap my head around just how deeply he'd betrayed us. He'd taken me from my home, an island hundreds of miles south of Pennlan, when I was a boy. I'd been told my people had gifted me to receive the best training from a fellow wizard. That my existence was a miracle, as only one wizard was born per generation. Eoghan had raised me as his own and had imparted all his knowledge.

Or so I'd thought.

Now, everything I knew about myself was on shaky ground. Eoghan had a master plan nearly twenty years in the making, and my own part was still a mystery. I couldn't even be sure he'd trained me for any other purpose than to venture into the fae realm and attempt to take the stone for him. I still had nightmares about him destroying the staff he'd given me.

But in place of my master's betrayal had been the most surprising of friendships. Clíodhna, the queen of the *sidheog* people to the north, had taken a special liking to me. When wizards had been more plentiful in this realm, they'd come to the Erlking's castle to learn to hone their magic. Now, I was the only wizard left, but Clíodhna had restarted the tradition.

"That will be all for today," Clíodhna said, and before I could respond, she was gone in a puff of snowflakes. But that was her way.

I made my way back to my room—a large, welcoming space with a sitting area and separate bedchamber—but I wasn't planning to stay long. While my mornings were dedicated to studying and afternoons to practical training, my evenings were taken by research into the *seod croí*. The Erlking had no knowledge of where the pieces of the stone might've gone, but he'd given me free rein in his library to scour the thousands of old books that might offer some clue.

Six months and a few hundred books later, I was no closer than when I'd started. But there were millions more at my fingertips, and I'd only scratched the surface, even using magic to help me speed-read through tomes as thick as my arm.

The current stack was ready to return to the library, but I stopped short. A small chest on my desk was glowing a soft white. The magical box was Clíodhna's idea, as post between the fae and human realms hadn't yet been established. I approached it with a smile, quickly unlatching the top to reveal a sealed letter addressed to me. I pulled it out, holding it gently and wishing I was holding the writer instead.

Ayla's loopy handwriting was so familiar, and the ache for home roared to the forefront. We'd been exchanging letters every couple of days, and I found myself eager to see what she'd written, hopeful for good news. I'd told Clíodhna that the moment we heard the stones had been found, I would be returning to help.

But as I scanned the letter, I found more of the same. Ayla had met with an envoy, it had gone poorly, and it seemed she was just in need of a friendly ear. Or eyes, as it were. I read it two or three times, hoping for something about the stones, but there was nothing. Ah well. At least she'd chosen to complain to me, instead of leaning on Ward. In fact, she barely mentioned him—giving me hope their relationship didn't hold a candle to hers and mine.

There was, however, a postscript that left me a little concerned. Ayla wanted me to request an audience with the Erlking to discuss moving goods. Since my arrival, I'd seen Birch exactly zero times, and I wasn't sure he'd even agree to an audience. I didn't think I was in a position to ask him anything. But Ayla seemed eager to use me as her go-between, so I'd have to come up with something.

Dearest Ayla,

I'm sorry to hear your meeting with Lord Galliford went so poorly. I'm sure, in time, Queen Ramira will come around.

The fae continue to treat me exceptionally well, and I'm pleased to report that today I sent Darragh to the infirmary. He should make a full recovery, but I daresay he may think twice about volunteering to train me again. Clíodhna seems to think I'm making excellent progress, though she'd never say it out loud.

I will take your concerns to the Erlking and report back as soon as I can.

All my love,

Cade

I sealed the letter and placed it back in the box, tapping it in a rhythmic motion to release the spell. The box glowed brighter for a moment then went dull. When I opened the box, it was empty.

>⊷ >⊷ >⊷ >⊷

With the stack of books floating behind me, I walked the corridors to the library. Everything in this castle was alive—statues often sprang to life and walked to another part of the castle, and paintings changed their subject matter all the time. The first few weeks I'd been here, I'd had to use a locator spell just to find my way before I learned to use the floor tiles as markers.

A pair of wart-covered lesser fae who only came up to my knees walked down the hall, deep in conversation. They stopped to stare at me, and I nodded to them. I'd become accustomed to seeing all manner of creatures here. They all seemed to know who I was—then again, my staff and rounded ears gave me away—and kept their distance, for the most part.

I turned the corner to the library, and allowed the full view to wash over me. I'd thought Eoghan had an impressive collection of books, but it was nothing compared to the Erlking's. I could live a thousand lifetimes and never get through even half the books here. I doubted even the librarian Finnegan knew what he had on his hands.

He was one of the more peculiar-looking fae—wrinkled, tanned skin pulled taut over a bony skeleton and snow-white hair that seemed so brittle it would break at the slightest touch. His ears were pointed, but long and folded over like a dog's, and his nose was short and almost pig-like.

"Hullo," I said. "Do you know—"

"She's putting books away." He pointed one bony finger toward the shelves.

"Thanks," I said, pushing the stack of books onto his desk. "More for her to work on."

He surveyed the books with golden eyes. "She's still working on yesterday's."

Still? I thanked him for his help and headed in the direction he'd pointed.

I walked until I found her atop a tall ladder. Riona wasn't shelving, though; she was reading, twirling a lock of her hair as she perched precariously on the top shelf. I recognized it as one I'd quickly parsed through a couple days ago.

"Anything I missed in there?"

She screamed, falling backward off the shelf. When she didn't use magic to stop herself, I stepped in, casting to gently place her upright on the ground. She turned to me, fire in her green eyes, and gave me an annoyed look not unlike her half-sister's.

"Don't scare me like that," Riona barked.

"Sorry," I said. "What are you doing?"

"What does it look like?" she said, grabbing another thick book and walking up the ladder. "Putting away your books."

"Looked like you were taking a break," I said with a smile. "Why don't you just magic them away?"

"That would defeat the purpose of my punishment," she muttered. "Which is to fritter away in this dreadful place until I die of old age. Or boredom."

I smiled, sighing a little. Riona's punishment was due to the fact that she'd run away from the Erlking's castle to assist me and Ward on our search for the Pennlan stone. I would've thought that being entranced by an evil wizard and made to almost kill everyone was punishment enough, but clearly the Erlking had other plans.

She brushed her hands on her shirt. "What do you want? Just to say hi?"

"I heard from Ayla," I said. "She'd like me to get an audience with the Erlking. Do you know how I could make that happen?"

Her scowl evaporated. "Ayla? What did she want? I can take you. Let's go!"

"Don't you have to work?"

But she grabbed my hand and dragged me toward the library exit.

CHAPTER FOUR

RIONA

Helping Cade meet with the Erlking was far more interesting than hanging around the stacks, and I was eager for a change in scenery. It had been a while since I'd deviated from the well-worn path between the library and my bedchambers. Besides that, I was looking forward to seeing the looks on my relatives' faces when I showed up with a wizard in tow.

The throne room was audible before we even reached it, and the wizard seemed surprised to see a room full of fae creatures, all jostling for an audience with the Erlking. The sound was deafening, a hundred conversations overlapping one another.

"What are all these people doing here?" Cade asked.

"You don't think you're the only one who seeks an audience with him?" I asked. "C'mon."

I pushed and shoved my way through, carving a path for him to follow and earning complaints from every fae I walked in front of.

"I've been here for three days!"

"I've been here a month!"

I ignored them—if they couldn't see how things worked around here, I wasn't going to help them. The wizard opened his mouth to argue but wisely decided against it.

Finally, we reached the front, where a few of the Erlking's other children were waiting to be heard. There was no way I could usurp them; from here, we'd have to wait. But King Birch was in sight, meaning our chances were good he would see us and ask us to step forward.

"So what now?" Cade asked, looking around warily at the collection of fae creatures pressing in around him.

"We wait."

He craned his neck. "There's a pair of fae staring at us."

"At you, most likely."

"No…" He turned to me. "Staring at you."

I chanced a look at who he was talking about—a pair of second cousins to the Erlking. They were a little older than I was, wearing looks of derision. The wizard was right about the object of their scorn, but I shifted and turned away from them.

"Ignore them."

The wizard gripped his staff and leaned forward, squinting. "What is he talking with?"

I couldn't see exactly, until the creature's wings glinted in the light. "Looks like a brownie."

"Brownie?"

"Small creatures that live in the cupboards of fae," I said. "Amazing that she was seen at all, but she must've had something important to ask him."

He nodded, seemingly more questions on his tongue, but he held them as the Erlking stood and held up his hands. Magic shimmered across my skin, and the room went silent.

"Hear me, fae creatures all. Any fae who mistreats a brownie in their service will have their tongues permanently twisted in their mouths."

Another shimmer of magic rustled my skin, this time at the hair behind my neck.

The wizard rubbed the back of his head, blinking curiously. "What was that?"

"It's an edict," I whispered back. "We're right here, so we feel it. Other fae outside this room don't, but they're bound to it, same as us.

They'll get a warning feeling, plus the burning on the back of their neck." I shrugged. "Sometimes it's a guessing game as to what rule you're breaking before something bad happens."

"Wow… All from those words?" Cade breathed. "He has such power. How?"

"It was given to him by the queens and kings of the other peoples by virtue of his role as the Erlking," I replied. "Old magic. Very old." I shifted as the Erlking sat back down. "C'mon, now's our—"

The room exploded in a hundred voices, each of them screaming at the Erlking to see them next. I began frantically waving my hands, gesturing to the wizard, my voice joining the others. Birch gazed out across the room, taking time to see those close in and those far out.

And just when I thought we wouldn't be noticed, the Erlking's gaze locked with mine, and he smiled. "Riona. Come."

The fae in front of us parted, though not of their own volition, and Cade and I walked forward. Although the Erlking had silenced the air around us, I could still feel mocking words of anger from those gathered. I tried to ignore the glare from the pair of cousins, knowing what they were saying about me.

"Wizard," Birch said, sitting down. "What news of the stones?"

"Nothing, I'm afraid," he said, casting a bewildered look around. "Why can't…I hear anyone else?"

"I've enchanted the air," he said with an amused smile. "All conversations with the Erlking are private."

He turned back, a little tongue tied as he mouthed for a minute, so I stepped forward to help. "Your Majesty, the wizard comes with a request from Her Majesty, Queen Ayla of Pennlan."

"Does he now?" the Erlking asked. "I've sent many a letter these past six months. None have been answered."

Cade actually looked nervous. "I'm sure there's…a reasonable explanation for that."

"Indeed." He didn't look convinced. "What does the young queen want from me?"

"There's a backlog of goods at the southern border—produce, various perishable items, along with some craftsman-made items," Cade said. "Her Majesty would like to know if the fae would be interested in purchasing those goods to relieve some of the pressure."

"We would, but the southern border is a long way away," Birch replied.

Cade opened and closed his mouth, as if he wasn't quite sure what to ask. "Would it be possible for you to magically move goods from the human borders to the fae realm?"

"Me? Not without much effort," he said with a hearty laugh. "And as much as I'd like to help your queen, my time is better served elsewhere."

Cade's face fell, but I elbowed him in the ribs. Something in the Erlking's tone told me he wasn't finished.

"However, *you*, wizard, might be able to help."

"I don't—"

"You and Clío can discuss it tomorrow during your studies," he said.

Cade's hand flew to the back of his neck as the edict was made. I bowed, grabbing the wizard's arm to yank him backward, but before we got two steps, the Erlking spoke again.

"Can I have a few moments alone with my granddaughter?"

➤➤ ➤➤ ➤➤ ➤➤

I hadn't a clue where Birch would lead me, but when we took a left toward the ash tree gardens, my pulse quickened. No one ventured into those gardens except the Erlking, so whatever he wanted to say, he didn't want to risk lip-readers.

The ash trees had always scared me growing up. Someone—perhaps one of my cousins—had told me the trees held the spirits of dead fae, and that was the source of magic wizards tapped into. I'd learned, of course, that wasn't even remotely true. But even now, I swore I could hear whispers in the branches as the Erlking and I made our rounds through the courtyard.

"So," I said, breaking the tension when I could take no more of it, "what do you want to speak with me about?"

"Your wizard friend seems to be making good progress," he said, nodding to the empty space where the tree that had become Cade's staff had been. "Clíodhna reports he has taken to his new staff like a fish to water."

"Will he be returning to Pennlan?"

"He still has much to learn, and there's no pressing need for him back there, so I gather. You and he have become friends these past few months, haven't you?"

I nodded. When I'd first met him, Cade thought me a monster, a treacherous liar, and a dangerous murderer. But when the wool was pulled from his eyes, and he saw the world for how it really was, his initial suspicions of me had all but disappeared. Six months of living in the fae world, eating from the fae tables, and being housed under a fae roof had also softened his attitude.

"Did you really drag me out here to discuss Cade?" I asked.

He looked down at me, curiosity in his gaze. "You speak so freely, Riona. You should have more respect for your Erlking."

I should, but as we passed close to a large ash tree, something ghostly almost reaching out to me, my desire to get out of the wood was more pressing than decorum.

"It's come to my attention that you're refusing to use magic. Finnegan says you've been putting the books away by hand. He asked me if you had any magic at all." He tilted his head in my direction. "Why?"

I gripped my hands behind my back. "I didn't realize my magic was something that needed your attention." *Considering you never let me use it before.*

My grandfather seemed torn between chiding me for my borderline attitude and amusement. "You didn't answer my question."

Because I didn't want to. Even thinking about it was enough to bring sickness to my throat. "Because I was never taught how," I said, after a minute. It was close enough to the truth to be believable, but my tongue still burned as I skirted close to an untruth.

"Your tutors taught you simple spells. Glamour, transfiguration. You should know how to move objects, at least."

Heat crept up my neck as I searched for another lie he would believe. "They weren't as thorough as you'd hoped, I guess."

"Hm." Whether he believed me or not, I couldn't tell. "Have you ever understood why I never allowed you to learn magic with your peers?"

Because I'm an abomination. "No."

"Your mother was the daughter of the Erlking and queen of the *sidheog,*" he said. "Unintended, of course."

Gross. "I know."

"Even as a child, Leandra had powers neither Clíodhna nor I thought possible. It was thought she would usurp the throne, in fact." He looked down upon me like I was his prized possession. "And you, my dear, have that same magic. I feared if you were given a seat with your cousins, you might demonstrate enough proficiency to garner attention you weren't ready to handle."

I'd garnered it regardless. My lineage had been a closely guarded secret, though rumors had swirled my entire life. The events six months ago had cleared the air for anyone who'd had their doubts, and now it was common knowledge—bringing with it a new level of disgust from everyone I passed.

But it had nothing to do with my mother, and everything to do with my father.

"I'm half-fae," I said softly, almost like it was a curse. "Even if I have some of Leandra's magic, it's diluted by my human blood."

"Your father wasn't just any human," he said. "Why do you think the Pennlan royal line was chosen as the stewards of the stone?" he asked. "Theirs is a unique bloodline, full of latent magic that can only be tapped by the stone. You share that blood."

I frowned. "Only if I have it."

"Perhaps." He closed his hands behind his back. "But it's time that you learn how to harness the power in your blood. To take your rightful spot among the rest of my children and grandchildren."

I could scarcely believe my ears. "You want me to…what?"

"Up until now, I have kept you at arm's length to protect you. But it was clear after your display with Eoghan that you need no such protection."

The sound of that monster's name was like a bell. Another whisper of otherness slid over my skin, but this was a memory. The ghost of someone else in my mind, controlling my magic. A violation of the most intimate sort, a filth that no amount of scrubbing could clean. Even the simplest spell felt tainted, as if the wizard still held my soul in his hands.

The Erlking was still talking, oblivious to the storm churning in my soul. "Your grandmother has graciously offered to allow you to learn alongside the wizard."

I nodded, sickness growing in my stomach. This wasn't a request—it was an order. "Yes, Erlking."

"And Aldrick will oversee your practical training."

My heart sank to my stomach. "Aldrick? He'll…" I shook my head. *He'll kill me.*

"He has been given his orders. And now, you have as well. It is decreed."

The magic burned the back of my neck, and it was all I could do to keep from throwing up. "This is…this isn't a good idea, Erlking. I'm not… I don't know what you think I'm capable of, but it's not…that."

"In Eoghan's hands, you were capable of destroying mountains," he said. "I wonder what you're capable of in your own?"

And there he left me, disappearing into a swarm of black moths. My world tilted as I leaned onto a nearby tree, the ghost stories forgotten for this very real terror in my heart.

CHAPTER FIVE

AYLA

"Good night, Ayla."

I shouldn't have been daydreaming, but it was hard when the sound of my name on his lips sent chills down my spine. I'd told him I'd asked everyone to call me by my name in private. But he was the only one— and every time he spoke my name, the brief euphoria was immediately overcome by the reality of what could never be.

Still, a queen had to have some pleasures in life.

Especially since Lord Galliford was true to his word. The next morning, he was packed and preparing to leave. I met him in the courtyard, a passive look on my face as I prepared to play his game.

"Are you sure you can't stay?" I asked, as if him leaving was a mere curiosity to me.

"If you are unwilling to negotiate—"

"I don't think a negotiation is one side telling the other what they will accept," I replied with a steely gaze. I'd come up with that brilliant line while lying in bed the night before. "So yes, if *you* are willing to negotiate, I'm willing to listen. Otherwise…" I brightened into a smile. "Please give Her Majesty my best."

Galliford sniffed and turned his horse, galloping through the front gates with his traveling party. I watched him go, doubt creeping into my mind once more, but I brushed it aside. Nothing to be done about it now.

Bronwen was waiting for me in the entrance hall, her hands twisted with worry. "Is he gone?"

"Yes," I said. "What's wrong?"

She cleared her throat. "Lords Cormac and Pádraig, and Lady Róisín are waiting in your office."

I squeezed my eyes shut and blew air between my lips. The three richest and most powerful merchants out of Orapus had been hounding me to fix the border problem for weeks now. They wouldn't be happy when I told them what happened.

"I suppose I'll handle it," I whispered weakly. "Thank you."

Taking my time, I ascended the spiral staircase of the castle until I reached the level where my office and bedroom were. It was tempting to continue to my room, bury myself in my sheets, and call it a day. But that wasn't what a queen should do.

I stopped by the window, my heart skipping at the sight of soldiers trotting along the green. Ward was beside them, his body upright and strong as his legs pounded the ground. He was calling time to the soldiers, and every one of them listened without question. What was it like to be so beloved by one's subordinates? I hadn't a clue.

Too soon, they rounded the corner and were gone, and thus my excuse for dawdling was as well.

Squaring my shoulders, I turned from the window and crossed the hallway, putting my hand on the knob. As the door swung open, the merchants turned to give me a once-over. Cormac was a grain merchant with farms to the north and west of here. Róisín owned a fleet of ships that traveled between here and Konevell over the water. And Pádraig transported livestock along the border with Sudaemor. Each of them represented a huge section of Pennlan's economic power. All of them were furious with me before we even began.

"Where is Lord Galliford?" Pádraig asked, rising and looking behind me.

I turned my face away as I crossed the room to sit at my desk. "Unfortunately, he's left a little early."

"Did you manage to negotiate the removal of the blockade?" Róisín asked.

I sat down, unable to hide my burning cheeks any longer. "No."

They erupted in a chorus of complaints, Cormac even rising to his feet with fury etched on his face. I let them bellow and bark at me. At the end of the day, the blame for this could all be placed at Eoghan's feet—and on me for failing to fix it.

"We are losing money by the day," Róisín said. "We need somewhere to send our wares."

"I have a…plan," I said, slowly. "I do, I promise."

"And what is it?"

I tapped my fingertips on the desk. I hadn't planned on telling anyone about asking the Erlking for help, at least not until Cade got back to me. But if I didn't give them something, I feared they might uproot and move to another kingdom.

"I sent word to the Erlking," I said quietly. "I'm hopeful he will allow not just trade, but an easier path toward moving the goods accumulated in Orapus." I averted my gaze, moving papers on my desk. "They have magic, so they could scoop up all the crates and send them to the fae realm in the blink of an eye."

I chanced a look up at the merchants, and my heart sank as I saw no looks of joy. In fact, they looked even more disgruntled than before.

"I know you believe all is forgiven," Cormac began.

"I don't," I said, a little too quickly. "I don't. But it's an option. The gates in Críoch are open, after all. And if it shows Konevell and the others that we can do just fine without them, it might force their hand."

"I don't understand why they've become so recalcitrant all of a sudden," Padráig said. "And why Galliford would travel all this way to meet with you just to turn and leave?"

If I told them what he'd offered, they might pressure me to accept it. They wouldn't care how the borders were opened, as long as they could make money.

"I believe that they're testing me," I said, hoping Ward's counsel would be helpful. "They see me as a weak and ineffective queen, adrift since Eoghan disappeared. They believe that they can bully and intimidate me into doing whatever they want." I folded my hands on my desk. "I believe this is a short blip in the longer game of ruling a kingdom."

"And in the meantime—"

"I have sent word to the Erlking," I said, cutting him off with all the confidence I didn't feel. "I expect to hear back any day now with good news. And when I do, you will be the first to know." I smiled. "After all, fae gold is the same as the human kind, isn't it?"

They wore identical looks of disdain, and I could practically hear their mutual desires to pack up and leave the country as they rose.

"Just give me a few more weeks," I said, not caring that I sounded a little desperate. "I'll find a solution—a lucrative trading partner. Whether it's the fae, or…" I swallowed. "One of the other kingdoms. I promise, I won't let you down."

The first two walked out without another word, but Cormac stopped and lingered in the doorway. "Things were much better when Eoghan was in charge."

It was hard not to flinch. "You only think that because he was doing whatever he could to keep you from being suspicious of him."

"Then perhaps you should follow in his footsteps. Because what you're doing now clearly isn't working."

>—» >—» >—» >—»

"Am I a bad queen?"

I asked the question as soon as I walked into Captain Gabhann's office, without waiting for her to speak or even welcome me inside. My stalwart captain had been another of the very few allowed to maintain a relationship with me, and I felt she was the only adult left in Pennlan.

"You aren't a bad queen. You've just been given a…difficult situation." She beckoned me to sit, and I sighed into the chair, tilting my head backward.

"I think I should marry one of them," I replied, staring at the ceiling. "It seems to be the only solution."

"Is it?" She sat back in her chair. "Why not just turn that little stone on and show them what real power is? Scare them into submission?"

I was glad my gaze was already averted, so she wouldn't see my shame. I perhaps should've told the captain of my castle security that the greatest weapon the kingdom possessed wasn't working for its sovereign, but every time I came close to revealing the truth, guilt and shame stopped me.

"Not to add to your dismay…"

I turned to her, my heart dropping into my stomach. "You promised me you'd give me more time."

"And I have. Four extra months." She smiled, the lines of her face showing her age and exhaustion. "But the time is drawing near for you to pick a successor. I can't stay your captain forever—as much as you'd like me to be."

"Please," I said, leaning forward. "I need… I need you. I don't know what I'm doing."

"Well, first of all, queens don't beg like that," Gabhann said with a stern look. "And I'm not leaving *yet*, but within the next few months. I need you to decide on a successor so I can make sure they have a handle on things before I go."

I frowned and crossed my arms over my chest. Gabhann had spent weeks scouring the countryside for the best of the best, introducing me to captains of respective villages who would be primed to take over for her. But none of them had felt right.

"I need to see more options," I said.

"You can't delay this forever."

"I'm not delaying it, I'm just…" I leaned forward. "You're one of the three people I trust to keep me from making mistakes. I can't—"

"Who are the other two?" she asked.

"Cade, obviously," I said. "And I suppose... Ward has become something of a confidant."

"Do you trust his judgment?"

I nodded.

"Then why not make him your captain?"

I sat up. "Ward? Captain?" I frowned, considering the option. He'd been promoted to Gabhann's lieutenant after saving the castle and had taken to it like a fish to water. But to take over for Gabhann? Who would be the adult in the room?

Me. The thought was terrifying.

On the other hand... More time with Ward, more *alone* time was always welcome. And I did trust him more than anyone else, save Cade. I already knew he would go to the ends of the world for this kingdom. Perhaps he *was* the obvious choice.

"Think about it," she said.

"I just did," I said slowly. "I think it's a great idea—if you do."

"I think he could use some polish, of course. But the *most* important thing is that *you* trust him. The last thing you want is a captain you keep things from."

Like how I can't use the stone? I hadn't told Ward about that either. "I do trust him," I said softly. "I trust him with my life."

"I will start training him immediately," she said then smiled. "In fact, I'll have him provide you the status of the soldiers tomorrow in your office."

"Actually," I grinned as I rose, "I think I'd like to get out of the castle. He can accompany me on a ride, and we'll discuss what we need to there."

And despite my growing fear about the last pillar from my childhood leaving me for greener pastures, I was actually excited about the future.

Chapter Six

Ward

There was something invigorating about rising with the sun, running in the cool morning, watching the world come to life. I called the cadence every few minutes when the footfalls had fallen off-rhythm, but this morning, we were mostly in sync, so I could think.

"Besides that, I have you. Why would I need anything more than that?"

The words had come out so easily, and the surprise on her face told me she'd read between the gaping lines I'd left. I'd been trying to keep my flirting to a minimum, but it was damn near impossible when we were in the same room.

But that would have to stop. She wasn't doing it intentionally; she'd grown up alone, thanks to Eoghan's scheming, and took her friends where she could. But I wasn't sure I could *only* be her friend.

"Because if you were to want this power, you'd have to marry me."

It was easy to believe she was hinting at something. But while Ayla had a rebellious streak, she wasn't going to throw away one of the most important diplomatic tools she had in her arsenal. Not when the other four kingdoms were practically falling over themselves to get it.

As the castle came back into view, I made up my mind. Someone else would need to step in as Ayla's confidante. Perhaps Elodia. She seemed quick on the uptake and would be excellent company. She could study and learn all the intricate details of the different human kingdoms and keep the envoys entertained with her affable nature. Meanwhile, I could slink back to the barracks every night, and, in time, forget about

Ayla—and get out of the habit of saying her name.

As we came into the green, a figure was waiting at the door, his arms crossed. Platt.

"What's up his ass?" Elodia asked.

"Who knows?" I muttered as the soldiers came to a stop. I ignored him as I addressed the soldiers. "Good work this morning. I'll see all of you at ten sharp to do an initial sweep of the village before the festival begins. Dismissed."

They saluted in unison before dispersing. Rutley and Elodia hung behind, but I waved them off. No use delaying the inevitable.

Once the green was clear, I took a deep breath and turned to face Platt, who'd marched across the grass to stand behind me. He had been like me once: young, fit, and eager to prove himself. But after years of working under Captain Gabhann, he seemed to have let himself relax. His uniform was a little tighter than perhaps it once had been, his boots not as shiny. His hair was longer than was allowed, but no one except Gabhann could tell him otherwise.

"Morning, Lieutenant," I said with a curt nod. "How can I—"

"Do you think it's funny?"

I blinked. "I'm sorry… What?"

"You show up here, green as an apple, and just expect to receive special treatment because you happen to be screwing the queen?"

I took a step back. "Again… What the hell are you talking about? And I'm not *screwing* anyone—"

"You got lucky with that wizard," he said. "It's a good thing the queen saved your ass."

I was at a loss. Platt hated me on a good day, but this seemed more than the usual disdain. "I have no idea what you're talking about. Does this have to do with the festival or—"

"You'd better watch your back," Platt said, poking me in the chest. "The soldiers tolerate you now, but once they find out you've been tapped to be captain, they'll leave in droves. Then who will protect your precious queen?"

I could've sworn he'd said— "Tapped to be *what*?"

But Platt was too lost in his own mind, walking away and muttering to himself. I licked my lips, looking this way and that. He must've dreamed it. There was no way Captain Gabhann would step down, not so soon after the mess with Eoghan. And even if she was, she'd be crazy to pick me over Platt.

"What was that about?" Elodia asked, appearing with Rutley around the corner.

"I have absolutely no idea," I replied, running a hand over my short hair. "But I'm going to find out."

>->>->>->>->>

I walked down the dark hallway, rehearsing what I'd say to Captain Gabhann. She was brusque and no-nonsense, and working directly for her had given me a new appreciation of her longevity in the castle. Eoghan's betrayal had been personal for her, considering she was supposed to protect the sovereign, and she'd had no clue of his plan for Ayla. Which was why the talk of her resignation was troubling—and probably false.

I rapped on her door twice then came inside when beckoned. She was at her desk, a steaming cup of black tea by her side and a stack of papers in front of her. She wore small glasses on the bridge of her nose, and for the first time, I noticed the curls of gray mixed in with the light brown hair.

"Sit," she said. "I expect Platt's gotten hold of you."

"Y-yes, he has." I sat awkwardly in the chair. "But he's just... You aren't retiring, are you?"

"Did the soldiers have a good run this morning?"

"Yes, ma'am," I said, perching on the edge of the seat. "We took the long route this morning and still made good time. But—"

"They appreciate the ability to stretch their legs," she said. "I can't remember the last time Platt took his out for a run. I don't think he remembers how."

I hid a smile. "Some of his guards joined us this morning. I hope that's all right."

"It's more than all right," she said. "Ward, I'm sure you've heard the rumors that I'll be stepping down soon."

"You aren't leaving," I said with a firm shake of my head. "You can't possibly—"

She held up her hand. "I've served our queen, her father, and her father's parents. I've carried the Pennlan flag for most of my life, with gratitude. But my bones are old, and it's time I pick a successor." She smiled, the wrinkles on her face growing more pronounced, as if they were unused to it. "You've been an excellent lieutenant these past six months. Not only have you earned the trust of the soldiers who report to you, but you've become a trusted advisor to the queen herself."

It took all my training to keep my face passive. "Thank you, ma'am. But Platt—"

"Platt has never given me confidence. He lacks creativity, motivation, any of the qualities I'd look for in someone responsible for protecting Ayla."

Ayla. She said the queen's name as if she were her own daughter.

"When I looked in the mirror and asked myself who I'd want in charge if that bastard wizard should return... I think I'd pick the man who set out on a dangerous quest to retrieve a stone and didn't stop until it was back in the hands of the rightful owner."

I searched for an argument. "I'm young—"

"So is the queen. I believe you have her best interests at heart when you give her advice."

I could think of a thousand reasons I wasn't the right man for this job. But this...this was the sort of opportunity that didn't come along often. Gabhann went on to describe the salary increase, and my mind raced with possibilities. Once upon a time, when I'd taken this job, I'd hoped to save enough gold to travel to a faraway land, start my own life where no one knew me. That dream had slipped after the journey to retrieve the stone—and Ayla.

"You show up here, green as an apple, and just expect to receive special treatment because you happen to be screwing the queen?"

Platt's words sat uncomfortably in my gut. Did Gabhann know what her soldiers thought of me? Could she tell that my heart was at war with what was right and what I wanted?

She was droning on about the responsibilities, most of which I knew, and I had a feeling that even if she did know, she didn't think it was a problem. After all, I was a loyal soldier. I hadn't yet acted on my impulses, as much as I wanted to.

"I meet with the queen daily, or every other day, at least. She's very interested in the state of her royal guard, understanding any issues that she might be able to resolve, and knowing the dangers that we're keeping an eye on."

I didn't know what to say. My heart was clear—but my head wasn't so sure. Would it be possible to spend time with Ayla in close quarters and keep myself from falling for her?

"Because if you were to want this power, you'd have to marry me."

Damn her.

"Well?" Gabhann asked. "Are you up for the job?"

No. "Yes, ma'am. It would be my honor."

"Good. You'll take over those sessions, starting tomorrow."

"Tomorrow?" I blinked. "But the festival—"

"Platt has been given his orders. Her Majesty would like to go out riding, so it's a perfect opportunity for the two of you to discuss the important business of the day."

I had no choice but to say something. "Captain," I began slowly. "There are rumors—"

"I have heard them." She waved me off. "Talk is talk."

"I worry if we spend more time together… People might make assumptions. The last thing I want is for Her Majesty's marriage prospects to be dulled by any discussion of impropriety."

"Her Majesty is doing enough to dull her marriage prospects," Gabhann said with a wry snort. "But I wouldn't worry. She's made it abundantly clear that she wants to wait to be married. I don't think anyone will change her mind once it's set."

"I—"

"I trust that you understand your place in the world—and Her Majesty's."

Painfully so. "Of course."

"Then there's nothing to concern yourself with. You will do your job, and she will do hers. Eventually, the curiosity will die down when there's no fuel added to the fire."

"Platt—"

"In a few weeks, you'll have the power to dismiss him, if you see fit," she said. "But I would recommend you let him blow off whatever steam he has. He does have his uses, which is why I've kept him on as long as I have." She offered me another small smile. "But I think you understand how to use those around you for your benefit."

I didn't look too far into that statement, knowing I might find an observation bordering on an insult. So I nodded. "Thank you for this opportunity. "

She nodded in acknowledgement, so I rose, saluted, and walked out of her office.

Some part of me knew I should've been ecstatic. To have arrived and been promoted so quickly was impressive enough, but to take over the captain's job? The salary for a year might set me up nicely if I chose to leave. I could finally realize my dream of owning property, making a life for myself. All it required was for me to keep my emotions in check and go riding with a beautiful woman.

And yet, I found myself looking at the gray sky above and wishing for rain.

Chapter Seven

Cade

In the past six months, I'd learned more about magic than in my entire eighteen years previously. Clíodhna seemed to teach with the breeze, arriving at the small classroom with a new idea of what to share with me every morning, and rarely did it have anything to do with what we'd gone over the day before. The first few days, I'd thought it was because she'd forgotten, but it became apparent that she was trying to cram as much knowledge into my empty brain as she could in the shortest amount of time. After all, we didn't know when I'd be called back to Pennlan.

As usual, I arrived in the classroom early—my fae teacher wouldn't arrive until at least fifteen past—but someone else was already waiting.

"Riona?"

The young half-fae wore a look of apprehension, holding a small journal in her hand, as well as a quill. "Morning."

"Are you taking a lesson with me this morning?" I asked.

"I—"

Clíodhna appeared in a puff of snowflakes. "Well, don't just stand there. We have much to discuss this morning."

Riona shuffled to the table next to me and seemed eager to disappear. Unfortunately, her grandmother's focus was squarely on her.

"What has your grandfather taught you?" she asked. "Have you covered conjuring and spellcasting?"

Riona's pale cheeks reddened as she shook her head. From her performance during our journey to find the Pennlan stone, I'd known she was a little green. But that she hadn't even studied the basics of magic was concerning. No wonder she'd been so helpless.

"Potions? Transformations?" More headshaking. "Your grandfather didn't even instruct you in the art of magical sensing?"

"He did not." Riona's face was now the color of a tomato, and her grandmother softened, but only a little.

"Child, my anger isn't directed at you. It's at your overprotective grandfather. Teaching you basic theories wouldn't have attracted the wrong kind of attention."

"What do you mean?" I asked. "The wrong kind…? Do you mean Eoghan?"

"Partially," Clíodhna said with a tense smile as Riona's grip on her quill tightened. "Though as we all saw, the wizard didn't need her to know anything in order to wield her to destroy."

Riona's knuckles were white, and she said nothing.

"Then who—" I began, but Clíodhna had already moved on.

"Enough chatter. We have theories to learn. The Erlking has a very specific request for you, wizard. He wants to see if you can create one of those portals."

I blinked. "Portals? What portals?"

"The kind your master made to travel from Pennlan to the fae realm and back again," she said. "The Erlking believes it will solve your queen's problem."

I swallowed. I'd done it once, in the heat of the moment, but couldn't recall the process. "So…how do I do it?"

She tilted her head. "You're the wizard. Figure it out."

I blew air between my lips. This was the sometimes frustrating part about learning from Clíodhna. Her knowledge of the possible was vast, but how to get the magic in my veins to do it was another story. Many mornings, I found myself staring at my staff in confusion, wondering how to make it do the thing Clíodhna said it could.

But I would get no quarter from her today. She'd turned her focus to Riona, barking questions at her as to her magical abilities and demanding that the half-fae conjure various things.

With difficulty, I tuned them out and closed my eyes, tapping into the hum of magic in my veins. There was a great deal of logic in magical practice, and one merely had to tease out the *way* one wanted to conjure for it to work. My mind, however, kept drifting back to Ayla, and the possibility that I could see her again.

"I don't see any portals," Clíodhna called.

"Working on it," I muttered. *Focus.*

What I was looking for, I supposed, was the creation of a doorway. An opening from here to there that one could step through. That was what Eoghan basically did.

So I was here, obviously. The there part… Where would I want to go?

Not too far, just in case, so I decided to attempt a portal to my rooms.

Now that I had the here and the there sorted, the only thing left was to create the doorway.

I focused on the concept of a *door*, of physical separation between here and there, and my fingers twinged with magic, urging me to pick up my staff. Eoghan's portal had been a circle, so I drew one with the tip of my staff. Round and round, focusing on the here and the there and the doorway between them.

I cracked open an eye, heartened by the a golden circle of magic hanging in the air, but disappointed to see Riona and Clíodhna where my bedroom should've been.

"Hm."

"What are you thinking?" Clíodhna asked.

I explained, and she tutted. "Did you try opening the door?"

"Well…" No. I hadn't.

I closed my eyes again, walking the same thought path as before, except now, I added the focus of *opening* the door. Once more, my staff begged to be picked up, to draw a circle. So I obliged.

"Your room is a mess," Riona drawled.

I cracked open an eye and gasped. There was a window into my (yes, very messy) room hanging just in front of me. Clearly, Clíodhna and Riona could see it too from their angle. Riona's brows were up, as if she were surprised I'd accomplished what Clíodhna had set out for me. But the *sidheog* queen was beaming.

"Excellent work," she said. "You are dismissed for the morning. As for you…" She turned back to Riona. "We have a lot of work to do."

⇥⇥⇥⇥

I may have been dismissed, but I didn't go far. I kept practicing the portal magic to different parts of the castle—the library, the ash forest where I'd found my staff, even the training ring. I was still a little nervous to go somewhere too far to walk back from, but the more I conjured the portal, the more confident I felt.

Especially as I considered the implications. Should word of one of the stones come, it might be a matter of days or hours to retrieve it, instead of weeks or months.

Not only that…but if I could walk through a doorway to anywhere in the world, perhaps that meant I could return home to Pennlan. To Ayla. Not as if I had much time for anything else, but I could spare an evening here or there to speak with her, instead of sending letters. To actually hold her in my arms instead of hoping she wasn't in someone else's.

My stomach rumbled. The hour for lunch was growing near. Clíodhna would probably have me practicing my fighting skills instead of portal creation, so I needed my strength and focus.

Much like everything else in this world, dining in the fae realm was full of its own quirks. My breakfast appeared on a tray in the morning, and a small meal of bread and cheese arrived at night. But midday, all those in the castle gathered in a large room with one long table to eat. It was chaotic, with creatures buzzing around both on foot and by wing, and if one was too late, all the food would be gone.

It had taken me about two weeks to even find this place, and once here, another couple of days to understand that it was every thing for themselves. I was able to grab a drumstick of some cooked fowl, an apple, and a slice of warmed bread before I was pushed from the line.

"Watch it."

I looked down. I'd almost knocked Riona over. "Oh, hey. How'd it go?"

She rolled her eyes, elbowing her way to the dessert table and loading up with sweets and nothing else. Then she made a beeline for the very end of the table with few inhabitants. I followed, sneaking in to grab another drumstick, knowing she'd need her strength for her own afternoon bout with Aldrick.

"You didn't answer my question," I said, sitting down next to her. "How'd it go?"

"About as bad as you'd expect," she said before shoving a raspberry-filled pastry into her mouth. "Clíodhna wants me to use magic I don't… have." She swallowed. "Hopefully, she'll get bored with me and turn her attention back to her star pupil."

"I'm not…" I put the second drumstick on her plate as she tore into another icing-covered delicacy. "You need something substantial."

"It's my last meal," she said, pushing the drumstick away. "I'll eat what I want."

"Oh, come on, don't be morbid," I said. "It'll be fine."

The conversations around us muted, as if someone had stuffed cotton balls in my ears, and a very particular taste crept across my tongue. Having spent so long in the fae realm, I'd long stopped noticing the different magic that assaulted my senses, so it was jarring to feel it once more. But I knew this sensation, and based on the way all color had drained from Riona's face, my hunch was confirmed.

"Don't fill up on garbage," Aldrick said, behind me. "I don't want a sluggish pupil for our afternoon session."

She swallowed and nodded.

"And wipe your face," he snapped. "You look like a child."

"She *is* a child," I said, turning in my seat and taking my staff in my hands. "She's barely seventeen."

The fae stared down at me as if my very existence was offensive to him. He was a head taller than I was—a feat, considering I was taller than most humans I met. His white-blond hair lay in stark contrast to his rust-colored skin, and his gold eyes held no warmth. But all I could sense was the magic radiating off him. He was showing off, perhaps for my benefit.

But I wasn't the same wizard I'd been six months ago, and he wouldn't dare attack me openly, in front of all these fae. Not when he was already on such thin ice after what he'd done to us in the forest kingdom.

"I expect you in half an hour," Aldrick said, after a moment. "Don't be late."

The conversations around us reignited as he left us, and I rubbed my ears, trying to clear the magic from them. But Riona's expression stopped me. She looked on the verge of tears.

"I don't know how anyone expects me to stand against him," she said. "Even in training… He's more powerful than I could ever imagine."

"I don't think you'll let Aldrick kill you. You're far too stubborn for that."

"Fine, then he'll just break all my bones."

"Then you'll go to the infirmary. They'll heal you in moments."

"Still hurts to have bones broken."

"True." I tilted my head. "It's going to be fine. You know what to do. You've done it before."

She rose abruptly, avoiding my gaze. "I'll see you in there."

CHAPTER EIGHT

RIONA

I rubbed the back of my neck, as I considered skirting the edict the Erlking had passed down. Would the punishment be worse than whatever Aldrick had in store for me? I was confident he would be creative in his torture.

I dragged my feet as the clock ticked closer. My heart thudded somewhere in my stomach, which had not easily digested the raspberry tart. Against my will, my feet walked me into the open field behind the Erlking's castle. Magical lines designated each of the five training arenas. Clíodhna was waiting in one, floating in mid-air with her legs crossed beneath her.

My grandmother and I had never been close, as I'd grown up in the Erlking's castle, but she'd shown her affection from a distance. Although no one had told me I was Leandra's daughter, I'd somehow always known —and that it was imperative I tell no one. When I was old enough, Clíodhna would send letters and small gifts, though they were always unsigned. Two summers ago, the Erlking had even let me journey with one of my aunts to visit the *sidheog* castle, but even then, Clíodhna and I didn't spend hours talking with one another. This morning's lesson had perhaps been the longest I'd been in the same room with her, not counting my visit with Ward and Cade.

So it was surprising when I walked by her, and she called my name. She opened her eyes and placed her feet gently on the ground.

"Are you prepared for your training this afternoon?" she asked.

"No," I said. "I don't see how I could be."

She smiled. "You will run away from the Erlking's castle to journey through the wildlands, but Aldrick scares you?"

"I had help," I said with a grimace. "And Leandra told me to go. She wouldn't have done that if she didn't think I could handle it."

"And why is this any different?" Clíodhna asked. "The Erlking's opinion weighs less than your mother's?"

I didn't think my mother's spirit would happily send me to my death, but our conversation ended when Aldrick's moths fluttered into the ring, manifesting into the fae himself with a flourish. His scowl deepened when he noticed who I was speaking with.

"I wasn't aware there would be an audience," he said. "I hope you aren't planning to interfere. I have a direct—"

"Yes, yes," Clíodhna said. "An edict! Such magic required to compel you to do what you should be honored to do."

I winced as Aldrick's gaze darkened. "And why would I be honored?"

"I'm sure you'll figure it out," Clíodhna said as Cade walked through the surrounding hedges. "I must get to my pupil. Good luck to you both."

She evaporated into snowflakes and floated to the other side of the ring, meeting Cade, who wore a frown.

"Come along, worm," Aldrick said with a sneer. "We must get to your training. After all, it's such an *honor* for me to be spending my time teaching a half-fae."

He might as well have called me a piece of filth. I said nothing, girding myself. The insults would be the least of my concerns—

My thoughts abruptly ended as a flash of black lit up my awareness. I flew through the air, my chest stinging with pain, before landing hard on my shoulder. I barely had a chance to realize what had happened before it happened again—this time, sending me tumbling backward.

"Wait—" I cried, my voice strangled, but Aldrick wasn't going to let me have a breath.

It was all I could do to keep conscious, the onslaught of magic pummeling every inch of my body. My vision swam as I drifted in and out of the darkness before finally letting it envelop me completely.

As if carried by the current, my mind was swept back, back, back until I could no longer feel my body. But there were footsteps crunching on icy ground, cold against my cheeks. My lungs no longer ached from bruising, but from the chilly air that came from my lips.

I opened my eyes and found myself in a frozen garden, silent and serene. This place was familiar—I'd visited it in a dream. No, I'd been *visited* in a dream. This was where Leandra had come to me and told me to seek out Cade and Ward. This place between the living and the dead. Would she find me to impart some new wisdom?

I exhaled, finding myself at peace as the world beyond melted away. I could stay here as long as necessary, living in this imaginary place. Aldrick would tire of torturing an unconscious body, perhaps, and I could just exist in peace.

Riona…

The chill turned into an unwelcoming tremor across my body. The voice wasn't Leandra's, but that evil that haunted my dreams.

"No, no…" I whispered.

Not here. He hadn't invaded this place, too. It would be too horrible for words.

A shadowy figure walked through the open gate and I felt myself scream—but it wasn't just in my mind. In a flash, I was back in the training ring, the sensation of my body coming back to me in a rush of agony. Blood was in my mouth, between my fingers, dripping into my eyes.

But the magic had stopped its assault. There was someone in front of me, his staff alight with green.

"Enough," Cade barked.

"Stay out of this, wizard," Aldrick snapped back. "The Erlking wanted me to train her."

"This isn't training. This is you having fun," Cade replied. "Training would be you helping her. She has absolutely no idea how to fight. Zero."

I winced. *Don't rub it in.*

"Then she will learn, or she will die," Aldrick said.

"I hardly believe that's what the Erlking meant," Cade said. "And I'd be happy to ask him myself."

"Do you let this wizard fight your battles, too, worm?" Aldrick said. "It's no wonder Eoghan was so easily able to overpower you. Perhaps I should just kill you and save us all the trouble."

I worked my lips, but I was too ashamed to say a word. I wiped blood from my mouth where I'd bitten my tongue but couldn't feel the pain amongst all the other injuries. My ankle was throbbing and turning purple, and it hurt to breathe—perhaps a shattered rib.

"Heal yourself," Aldrick said. "And be better prepared tomorrow. I'm not going to waste my time with you if you aren't even going to put up a fight."

He disappeared, or so I assumed because I didn't hear him speak again. My eyes were starting to swell; if I didn't move quickly to the infirmary, I'd be unable to find my way there.

Cade put his hand on my shoulder and squeezed. "Let me heal—"

"No. I can handle it."

"Like you did in the wildlands?" There was a little smile in his voice. "C'mon, let me help."

"You've helped enough," I said, throwing his hand off me. "Do you understand that Aldrick is going to make things ten times worse for me now? The next time, you might not be there."

"I can't see how he could make things worse, considering…"

I licked my lips and turned away from him. "You just don't understand."

"I could help you, in the evenings," he said. "I've gotten pretty good at understanding fae magic, after fighting with it all this time. I could teach you a few—"

"I don't want to learn," I said, wiping my mouth again. "I'll talk to the Erlking. He'll send me back to the library and—"

"You're allowed to use your magic there, aren't you?" Cade narrowed his gaze. "You just don't want to."

"I'm done having this conversation," I said, limping away.

>→»→»→»→»

I reached the infirmary from sheer stubbornness, but as soon as my head hit the pillow, I lost consciousness. In my dreams, I felt the call of that secret place, that cold, frozen garden that had once been so comforting. But knowing who lay there kept me from venturing any closer.

I awoke some hours later when the room was dark and silent. My injuries itched with fresh healing, but soon they would disappear completely. My shame, however, wouldn't go away so quickly.

I became aware of a presence standing nearby and jumped as the snowflakes formed into my grandmother. It was hard to discern her expression in the dark, but I could only guess it was a mixture of disappointment and disgust.

"Why aren't you using magic?" she asked.

"I am," I said, adjusting myself on the bed. "Aldrick didn't—"

The bed dipped as she sat down and a moonbeam fell across her face. "Cade believes you were holding back intentionally, as do I. He says you told him you weren't permitted to use magic in the library, even to reshelve books." She narrowed her deep blue eyes. "Why?"

"If I could do everything magically, I'd have nothing to pass the time with," I said, though there wasn't much conviction behind it.

"You may have the ability to lie, but you aren't very good at it," Clíodhna said. "I watched your session with Aldrick. You didn't even put up a fight."

"I haven't been taught how to muster a single spell," I whispered, hoping that might suffice as an excuse. "It's not as if I spent my youth casting and conjuring or playing with the other fae children. Most of them avoided me at all costs."

Clíodhna seemed to see right through me. "Which is why your grandfather is expediting things, placing you in the most danger he can without actually risking your life. Any other fae would take it easy on you, thinking you were a lesser being, due to your father. He hopes to draw your instincts to the forefront."

My instincts. I was sure I had them, but they were in a constant battle with my internal disgust.

She clicked her tongue, impatiently. "I don't have all night. It was clear Eoghan—"

I couldn't help the wince that crossed my face or the way I turned my head away. It was as if she'd summoned him to the infirmary, hiding in the shadows and waiting to take my free will once again. Wanting me to hurt those I cared for. Taking the magic that had been untrained and untested and forcing it to do things…

"Ah…" She nodded softly. "So that's it."

"What's it?" Sweat had broken out behind my neck, and my voice had taken on a higher pitch. "There's nothing. He has nothing to do with this."

But the secret seemed to have slipped from my very tight grip, out in the open for everyone to hear and know. Clíodhna said nothing, as if waiting for me to finally come clean. But it was too hard, too much to form into words. There was just shame, disgust, misery.

"Your mother never spoke about…what happened," Clíodhna said, her voice growing sad. "She arrived in the *sidheog* lands a broken woman. I believe she stayed alive just for you, but once you were born…" She sighed. "No one told you how she died, did they?"

"She killed herself," I whispered.

"Not four weeks after you were born," Clíodhna said. "I feel like it was… She never spoke to me about her suffering. About how dark her days had become. Perhaps if she had, she might still be here." She tilted her head. "I don't want the same for you."

I shifted uncomfortably. "I don't want Aldrick to kill me, if that's what you're suggesting."

"Then what do you want?"

"I want..." To be rid of Eoghan's memory. To never be reminded of that loss of control, the fear that I might be forced to kill my beloved sister before I'd even gotten the chance to know her. Using magic—even the most basic of spells—was an ever-present reminder of the dangers that lurked in the shadows. "I want to return to the library and be punished through boredom."

"You are no longer being punished," Clíodhna said. "The Erlking meant what he said when he wanted you to take your place amongst his children. But in order to do that, you have to be able to stand against the strongest amongst them. That begins with defeating your mental demons first, and the rest will follow." She pressed a firm hand on my shoulder. "If it were anyone else, I wouldn't believe it possible."

She left me there, her confidence in my abilities ringing hollow in the cracks of my soul. And as I sat in the silence of the infirmary, still nursing my injuries, I realized I would rather let Aldrick beat me to a bloody pulp for the next month than touch the tainted magic in my veins.

CHAPTER NINE

AYLA

I bounced on my toes, hoping I didn't look as eager as I felt. I'd spent the night daydreaming about Ward, our ride, where I might take him, what we might discuss. Even just being alone with him, away from the castle, was exciting. We could talk about whatever we wanted without being overheard. Not that we were going to talk about anything other than business…

Footsteps drew my attention, and my face brightened. But Elodia and Rutley turned the corner, and my face fell before I could stop it.

"Expecting someone else?" Elodia asked, smirking. Then, when Rutley elbowed her roughly, she added, "Uh, Your Majesty."

"Perhaps," I said, turning back to my horse and tightening the saddle straps again to hide my embarrassment. "Good morning to the two of you."

"It's a pleasant day for riding," Rutley said, trying to cover for his friend's familiarity. "Isn't it, Your Majesty?"

"I was worried about rain, but it seems to have passed," I said, looking up at the blue sky. "Where are you two off to this morning?"

"Well, since our boss has been otherwise detained," Elodia said, that knowing smirk still teasing the corners of her lips, "we've been asked to keep an eye on the festival today."

"Oh, that's right," I said, tapping my fingers to my lips. "Perhaps we might venture into the village after our ride and see what the fuss is about."

"Have you never been?" Rutley asked.

"No." I glanced up at the blue sky. Cade and I had often talked about going, but Eoghan had forbidden us to leave the castle. He'd been concerned the fae would infiltrate the traveling bards and musicians and kill me where I stood. Or so he'd said.

I tightened the straps again, clearing the memory and accompanying anger from my mind. Eoghan was gone, so why did I continue to let him rule my life?

"What's your favorite thing to do?" I asked, plastering a smile onto my face.

"At the fair?" Rutley asked, rubbing his chin. "I'd tell you, but then your opinion of me might sour."

I couldn't help the smile. "There's not much that would shock me."

"He likes the ale," Elodia said with a snort.

"But never on the job," he said with his hands in the air. "And even drunk as a skunk, my sword is still good."

"If you can stand up straight."

"Stand up better than you," he grunted, rubbing his ear. "I've still got that scar from when you swore you could shoot an apple off my head." Sure enough, there was a small chunk missing from his left lobe.

"But did you die?"

I stifled a giggle as Rutley grunted. And very suddenly, I was overcome with sadness for my own best friend, far away in the fae realm. We certainly had our share of horror stories and near misses, especially as he was learning his magic.

But my musings were cut short as Ward turned the corner. He was desperately handsome today, even though his lips were pressed in a thin line. His eyes narrowed at the sight of Elodia and Rutley speaking with me, but whatever suspicions he had were kept to himself.

He approached me stoically and bowed. "Your Majesty."

I opened my mouth to remind him that we were on a first-name basis now but glanced at the other two soldiers. "Are you ready to ride today?"

"Would it be possible to meet in your office?" he said, his words stilted and forced.

"It would not." I hoisted myself into the saddle. "Now hurry up. We have lots to talk about."

>→ >→ >→ >→

There was nothing like the wind in my hair and the sound of hoofbeats. It had been ages since I'd ridden, and I was grateful for the space—and the company. Though it seemed the company wasn't grateful for me.

Ward's responses had come in one-word answers, his jaw set in a firm line. It was so unlike him, so very…cold. I'd thought today would be fun, full of our usual banter and joyous conversation.

My mind swirled with possible scenarios. The only thing that seemed to have changed was his promotion. Was that why he was so taciturn with me? Was he angry about it? Annoyed that he would have to spend more time with me?

Gabhann told me that he'd arrived at the castle an ambitious man, eager to rise in the ranks. Could it be now that he'd achieved what he'd set out to do, I was no longer interesting? Had all the flirting and conversation been a ruse?

I stared at my hands, clearing my throat to clear the panic. "The fair is in the village," I said, trying to sound conversational.

"Mm."

"I'd like to walk through it once we finish our discussion," I said. "If you'll—"

"I will find Elodia and Rutley to accompany you," he replied curtly. "I'm sure they'd be happy to."

My heart sank into my stomach as we broached the final hill between us and our destination. The pond was frequented by ducks and other waterfowl, and as a girl, I'd spent hours with Cade under the canopy. I'd been itching to bring Ward here for weeks, though now I was starting to regret it.

I slowed my horse to a stop and turned in my saddle, a little breathless from the ride. "This is my favorite place."

His dark eyes met mine, and to my immense relief, the ghost of a smile appeared on his lips. "I can see why. It's very peaceful here."

My confidence restored, I hopped off my horse and undid the saddlebag full of meat, bread, and hard cheese. Ward rushed forward to help, taking the bag so I could carry and unfold the blanket under the tree. He set up the food and handed me a canteen filled with water.

"Thank you," I said, taking a long sip. "It's hotter than I thought it would be."

"It's warm for fall," he said. "But it should get colder soon."

"Do you think we'll see snow?" I asked, handing the canteen back to him. "It happens so infrequently down here."

"Perhaps."

I opened my mouth to ask if he'd seen snow on his journey north in the fae realm, but I knew the answer to that question. Of course he had.

"Did you write that letter to Cade?"

I nodded. "He said he'd take my concerns to the Erlking, but I haven't gotten another letter since. Hopefully…" I licked my lips, unsure if I wanted the fae to come to my aid or not. "Well, hopefully one of the human kingdoms will stop trying to marry me and we can start some real negotiations."

Ward cracked a smile. "Surely, one of their options has caught your eye. They can't all be eight-year-old boys."

Some had, for sure. With Eoghan no longer dictating that only the oldest eligible bachelors could seek my hand, the parade of suitors had been more age appropriate. Some were quite handsome—the nephew of the king of Driwania was striking with prominent lips and cheekbones so sharp they could cut stone.

But when it came to marriage… "I just can't bring myself to accept any of their proposals."

"Why not?"

"Maybe I'm not quite ready to be married," I said, searching for an excuse. "After all, I've only been queen for six months—only been able to make my own decisions for that time, too. I want to stretch my wings, so to speak, before someone comes along to clip them."

He chuckled, a deep sound that softened my mood considerably. "Marriage doesn't have to mean clipped wings, Ayla. I would hope you'd find someone who'd help you fly higher."

I settled against the tree, staring out onto the plain. "That's the goal, but that's not always the case."

An uncomfortable silence drew out between us, at least for me. I kept thinking of what to say then second-guessing myself. Unhappiness settled in my chest, and tears worked their way up from somewhere deep inside. But I swallowed them, refusing to admit defeat just yet. I'd been fooled by Eoghan, but surely…surely not Ward, too?

"Are you…happy with your promotion?" I asked, sneaking a look at him.

"I'm honored."

He certainly didn't sound like it. "I hear a 'but'…"

He cracked a smile, and my heart flip-flopped. "There's no but. I'm honored to accept it."

I sighed and leaned against the tree. "Ward, if we're going to work together, we need to have a relationship built on trust. I can tell you're holding something back from me. You are free to be honest here." I tilted my head. "There's not another soul for miles. No one will hear what you say."

I'd intended my words to be comforting, but based on the way he began to fidget, they'd had the opposite effect. "That's the problem."

"Why?"

"Because…" He turned toward me, uncertainty in his gaze. "You don't think…we're getting too familiar?"

"What?" I sat up. "Familiar? In what way?"

He let out a long breath. "Ayla, you can't be… I'm not the only one who…" He shook his head. "Do you remember that walk we had in the garden?"

Every night. My cheeks warmed. "Yes, of course."

"It wasn't as private as we'd hoped, and our…friendship has been noticed by the guard," he said. "I've been accused of getting this position because of it."

"What…" The wheels turned in my head as I understood what he was saying. "That's preposterous. You earned this position when you came up with the plan to defeat Eoghan."

"*You* defeated him. I merely distracted him."

"Allowing me to defeat him," I said. "Ward, *Captain Gabhann* was the one who recommended you to this position, not me. Though I was overjoyed when she did."

"You shouldn't have been," he said. "There are other soldiers who've been here longer who would've made better captains. One brilliant event doesn't overshadow years of experience."

A little fear settled in my heart. "So you're declining the position?"

"No, I just…" He shook his head. "We have to be careful. You and I can never be together, so—"

My heart stopped in my chest. "You…" I swallowed as the warmth in my cheeks spread to my forehead, the back of my neck, down my chest… "You want us to be together?"

He was silent for a long time. "What I want or don't want isn't important. Your focus should be on the kingdom. I wouldn't want any potential suitors to get wind that your heart has settled on another." He paused. "If it has."

My heart was dancing in my chest. "But if I'm not planning to marry any time soon—"

"That's just it, Ayla," he said softly. "I don't think…if we took that next step…I'd be able to let you go to someone else."

Another period of quiet blossomed between us, punctuated by the wind rustling the leaves above our heads. I understood what he was saying, on some level, but all I could think of was this handsome man had said he wanted us to be together. What might it feel like to finally get that kiss I'd been denied all those months ago?

"Ward..." I whispered. "I—"

But his gaze had gone past me, and his brow had furrowed in concern. "Someone's coming."

I spun around, spotting the cloud of dust. Ward's hand went for his sword, but as the rider came over the hill, his uniform was familiar. Still, I'd been explicit that we weren't to be disturbed, so it had to be important.

"What is it?" Ward called as the rider slowed his horse.

"Your Majesty, Lieutenant," he said, out of breath. "Come quickly. There's...news on the stone."

"What news?" I said, breathlessly.

"You just..." He shook his head. "You'll have to see it to believe it."

Chapter Ten

Ward

The guard tried to tell me more about who had come and what news they'd brought on the stone, but every time he tried to speak, he seemed to almost *forget* what he was talking about. Then he would remember, only a little, and wave us on toward the castle.

We rode into the green, and I hopped off my horse, throwing the reins at the stableboy with a hasty apology. He, too, seemed to be unable to tell me what was waiting in the castle.

"Do you think it's Eoghan?" Ayla asked me as fear flashed across her face.

I didn't want to spook her, but it was certainly a possibility. I stepped forward and forced a confident smile onto my face. "If it is, we will handle him."

She glanced down at the stone hanging from her neck, as if she'd forgotten it was there. I let her go first as a show of support, but my hand gripped my hilt tightly as we hurried through the hallway. Every maid and guard we passed just pointed, unable to say what was waiting for us. My heartbeat was in my throat as we came into the great hall.

A creature stood there, a fae I'd never seen before—which was saying something, considering I'd spent weeks among them. His skin was even paler than Ayla's, a milky color that was almost transparent, matching his stark blond hair. His eyes were the fae gold, but so light they were nearly white, punctuated by a dark black pupil that seemed even larger than normal. When he smiled, long incisors appeared on either side, giving him a wild, feral look.

"Your Majesty," he said, his voice deep and velvety. "I'm Lynton. From the kingdom of Gwyllion."

I was speechless, staring openly and perhaps a little rudely. "W-welcome, Lynton," Ayla stammered before collecting herself. "You've brought news of the *seod croí*?"

He cracked another smile, one that wasn't all that friendly. "Indeed."

"I'm sorry," I said, glancing at Ayla. "I'm unfamiliar with the kingdom of Gwyllion. Where…exactly is it?"

"In the mountains where you sent your scouts," he said. "I wouldn't expect the humans to know the name. Our society has been hidden from the world for the past thousand years."

It was then that I realized what he was—and my pulse quickened with hope. "You're a troll," I said, after a moment.

"A…" Ayla turned to him then to me. "A troll?"

"The Erlking had told us he thought the trolls had taken a piece, but he wasn't even sure they still existed," I said. "Clearly, you do."

"As I said, we've been concealed from the rest of the world," he said stiffly. "And there are many enchantments that keep us that way."

"Fascinating," Ayla breathed.

But I cleared my throat. "You said you had news of the stone?"

"I do," he said, his voice even. "But it is for the queen's ears only."

"Ward is my captain," Ayla said. "Or will be soon. Whatever you have to say to me, you can say to him, too."

The troll made a face but nodded. "Then at least offer a weary traveler food and drink. The conversation may be long."

"Of course," I said with a nod. "Would wine suffice?"

"That would be lovely."

>→ >→ >→ >→

Bronwen moved quickly, and within minutes, Ayla, Lynton, and I were ensconced in her small library. Lynton sipped the wine slowly, making a face as he tasted it. Then he spoke again.

"Our king became aware of your scouts when they came to a border town. He keeps ears in the human villages in case of trouble, and when word reached him that the Pennlan stone had been returned to you—and that you'd been able to use it—he was eager to send his fastest rider to seek an audience with you."

I sipped my wine slowly, watching the troll with suspicion. The creature was unlike anything I'd encountered in the fae realm, and there was something about his story that didn't sit right with me.

Ayla was oblivious to my concerns, clearly itching to pepper the troll with questions. But she seemed to settle on platitudes. "How long was your journey?"

"Over a month. It was quite difficult," Lynton said as he sipped slowly. "The sun is harsh, you know, for those who never see it."

Another curiosity. "If the journey was so long and arduous, why not send a letter?" I asked.

"I was clear that this news was for the queen's ears only," he said.

"Can't you enchant a letter for the queen's eyes only?" I asked.

He smiled, looking me over. "Are you a study in the limits and nuances of troll magic, captain?"

"I have spent time in the fae realm, yes," I said.

His eyes flashed dangerously. "Then you know nothing of my kind."

"But aren't you…fae?" I asked, noting his pointed ears and golden eyes.

"There are different kinds, of course. We trolls have never been… We are of the same cloth as the *daoine maithe, sidheog,* even the forest fae. But they never felt that way about us. So when I say the fae, *clearly* I don't include our kind, because they never included us in their numbers."

"Makes sense," Ayla said, even though I was sure it didn't to her. I took another sip of my wine to keep my mouth occupied instead of responding.

"If my king deemed this message important enough to send a messenger, then it was so," he finished.

"And what is this message?" Ayla asked.

"First, a question," he said. "Namely, if you have a stone of your own, and it is functional, why are you seeking the one in the troll's care?

"Not seeking, per se," Ayla said. "There's a wizard named Eoghan —"

"We are familiar with Eoghan," he said. "The wizard who lived here for twenty years."

"Under false pretenses," Ayla added with a grimace. "He had a long-term plan to take the stone for himself—one that changed after the fae Leandra escaped his clutches."

Lynton tilted his head to the side; this was new information to him. "How would he take the stone? And what does the greater fae have to do with it?"

"Eoghan has a devious spell, one that can take control of a fae's mind and magic. His initial plan was to use Leandra, who had married my father and could use the stone, but she managed to break free of his control." She swallowed. "He then thought he might…manipulate and marry me, when I came of age."

"Surely, you were too smart to be fooled."

"He had us all fooled," I said with a look.

"We've banished Eoghan, but banishment isn't permanent." She licked her lips and thumbed the stone. "Especially since there are three more pieces out there. The last thing we want is for Eoghan to get his hands on that power. So we were seeking the other three pieces to ensure that…well, he *doesn't.*"

Lynton took another long sip of his wine, as if drawing the moment out. "The second part of my message is to relay an invitation for Her Majesty to visit Gwyllion. King Edric thought it would be better received if the request was delivered in person."

My eyebrows shot up, and Ayla's lips parted in surprise. "He wants me to...visit?"

Lynton nodded. "Your scouts told us of this wizard, and the king was similarly concerned. He believes an alliance between our kingdoms would be a show of force against him. Even if he were to find the other two—"

"It would be two against two," Ayla said with a nod. "I think that —"

"An alliance is fine," I said. "But the queen can't travel halfway across the continent. I'd be happy to make the journey for her."

"Does this...man speak for you?" Lynton asked.

"Absolutely not," Ayla said, glaring at me. "I'm perfectly capable of answering the invitation—and I'm going. After all, I'm the queen."

I cleared my throat, wondering how much we could argue in front of the troll. "It is precisely *because* you're the queen that I don't think you should go. It took him a whole month to travel here—"

"So?"

"Then it's a month to get there," I said patiently. "And a month to return. That's a long time to be away from Pennlan."

"I can rule from anywhere. This is an important visit," Ayla said, her green eyes boring into mine.

"Besides that," Lynton said with a dirty look at me. "King Edric specifically asked for the queen. After all, it's the Pennlan line that controls the stone. There are specifics that can only be negotiated between the owners of the respective pieces."

"Then how about the king travel here?" I asked, a little more heatedly than intended.

"Ward," Ayla said with a steely look as she rose. "I would be honored to accept your invitation."

"There is more."

"Of course," I scoffed.

"King Edric asked me to extend the invitation to your sister as well."

"My sister…" Ayla looked taken aback. "Why her?"

"King Edric would like to offer an olive branch to the Erlking and resume peaceful relations. Assuming, of course, we get to retain ownership over the stone."

That seemed in sharp contrast to the angry way Lynton had just been describing the fae, but perhaps his personal opinion was being overruled by his monarch.

"So why not invite the Erlking, or one of his other…other envoys?" Ayla asked.

"Because while King Edric is eager to reopen lines, he's not eager to invite a full-blooded fae into the kingdom until he can be sure of the current Erlking's intentions. The human blood in her veins makes her less of a…threat."

"She's not a threat at all," I said.

"I wouldn't expect a human to understand," Lynton replied with a sneer.

"I don't know if the Erlking will allow Riona to come," Ayla said after a moment.

Lynton started. "She's not here?"

"No, she's…" Ayla considered her words. I doubted she wanted to share the entire sordid history. "As I said, I don't know if the Erlking can spare her. But he may be able to send someone else."

He shook his head. "It must be the half-fae. Those are my orders from Edric himself."

"I'll see what I can do," Ayla said with a solemn nod.

"Are you sure this is wise?" I interjected. "Seems fishy that they want Riona to come. She's a kid. She can't speak for—"

"Ward," she said, glaring fire at me, "why don't you start preparations for my departure? I'll pen a letter to Cade to discuss Riona. Lynton, I'll have a room readied for you."

He seemed uncomfortable. "How long we can depart? King Edric is eager for my return."

"Cade and I have a special way to communicate with each other," she said. "Hopefully, I'll have my answer within the day."

>-» >-» >-» >-»

I followed her out of the room and waited until we were just out of earshot. "Ayla, you can't be serious."

"No, *you* can't be serious," she said, whirling on me with fire in her green eyes. "Speaking over me like that—"

"I'm sorry," I said, waving my hand. "But I just find this whole thing suspicious. He shows up out of nowhere for the first time in a thousand years and wants you *and* the stone to travel? And Riona?"

"What, exactly, would you have me do? Decline their offer?"

"*Yes*," I said. "You told me yourself that you're in a delicate dance with the other *human* kingdoms. You can't just up and leave for a few months to journey to the troll kingdom. Not to mention it's dangerous. As your captain—"

"You aren't captain yet," she said. "And maybe I'm second-guessing my blessing on that promotion if you're going to be like Eoghan and keep me locked up in this castle for the rest of my life."

The words echoed between us, and my heart dropped into my stomach. She'd spoken so surely, as if she had no doubts in her mind. But her words cut me deep.

"Is that what you think I'm doing?" I asked, my voice quiet.

She licked her lips, hesitantly, then lifted her chin. "I'm queen, Ward. And if I say I'm going then I'm going. I don't want to hear another word about it."

CHAPTER ELEVEN

CADE

I tossed and turned all night, anger coursing through my veins. I couldn't believe the Erlking would be so callous with his own flesh and blood. Aldrick intended to kill Riona—and if he'd explicitly been told not to, he'd clearly settled on beating the daylights out of her. Clíodhna had watched and hadn't interfered, but I couldn't. Not when it was so clearly a one-sided fight.

I supposed I could've seen why the Erlking might've wanted to keep Riona's magical tutelage to the basics. Aldrick, at least, seemed to find her very existence an affront to his sensibilities, but underneath, there was a current of jealousy. If Riona had been able to truly explore what she knew, she might not have made it to sixteen.

I arrived early at our small classroom and paced, hoping I might be able to talk with Riona before Clíodhna arrived. The minutes ticked past nine, and my fingers drummed loudly on the table. Finally, at twenty past, the scent of honey crossed my tongue, and I looked up expectantly.

Riona walked into the room gingerly, avoiding my gaze. The faint bruising around her face was nearly gone, but she was clearly still in pain.

"Riona—"

"Don't."

I sighed and sat down. "I can help you. We can practice—"

"I said *don't*," she barked, glaring at me furiously for a moment before returning to stare at the table. "I want to learn about theories or whatever Clíodhna has for us and just not think about yesterday."

"And what about this afternoon?" I asked. "Aldrick's going to do the same thing—"

"That's my problem."

There was something more, something I wasn't understanding. This seemed to be beyond just her lack of skill. She seemed bound and determined not to use magic in any way—and if she ended up dead, that was an outcome she was willing to accept.

But I wasn't.

"What can I do?" I asked, after a moment.

"Just stay out of it."

"Not an option," I said. Then, smiling, I added, "Ayla wouldn't forgive me if her little sister was hurt on my watch."

Finally, a small look. "I suppose she wouldn't."

"So let me help you. At least let me teach you basic defense spells."

The small crack in her door slammed shut. "No."

Any further discussion ended when Clíodhna appeared in a puff of white. She glanced at her granddaughter for a moment, but immediately launched into a discussion of magical theory and portals. My anger returned—no one seemed to care that Riona was clearly struggling with something—and simmered under my skin during the entire lesson. As we broke for lunch, I couldn't even recall what had been covered.

"Riona—"

But she was gone.

>⇥ >⇥ >⇥ >⇥

I shouldn't have skipped lunch, but I couldn't trust myself not to react if I ran into Aldrick. So I returned to my room, intent on taking back the stack of books and getting more for the upcoming evening, but when I walked through the door, I stopped short.

The small chest was glowing; a new letter from Ayla. But it wasn't just glowing gold—it was glowing red. Urgent.

My pulse quickened as I crossed the room, praying the news inside was about a stone and not about Eoghan.

Cade,

You won't believe it. A troll arrived from the mountains, bringing with him an invitation for me to meet with his king in the mountains. They have a piece of the seod croí and they want to form an alliance with me so we'll be better prepared in case Eoghan reappears. I need you to come with me. Please come home as quickly as possible.

All my love,

Ayla

P.S. - The troll also asked for Riona to accompany us as a representative of the Erlking. Something about her half-human blood being less of a threat. I don't know if the Erlking would let her go, but you might ask.

My heartbeat was in my throat as I read the letter three times. I wasn't sure which news to focus on. Trolls still existed, they had the stone, they wanted Ayla to travel to the mountains, and they wanted Riona to negotiate an alliance on behalf of the Erlking.

It was that last bit that gave me the most pause, though it was somewhat difficult to understand. But I wouldn't be able to make heads or tails of this by myself, so I pocketed the letter and hurried out of my room.

I followed the path Riona had shown me a few days ago to the Erlking's receiving room, two requests on my mind. The room was packed, and I even spotted a few fae creatures who'd been here the first time. But I didn't have to wait long.

"Wizard!" Birch beckoned me forward, earning me scowls and hisses from those around me.

I approached the throne. "I've got news from Pennlan. A…well, it seems the trolls have invited Ayla to visit."

The Erlking's brows rose almost to the crown atop his head. The previously buzzing room went silent—but not from the Erlking's charms. I felt every eye on the room on the back of my neck as I handed the

Erlking the letter. He scanned it with a frown.

"How much do you know about the trolls?" he said softly.

"Nothing, other than they were given a piece of the *seod croí*." I began to tick off my fingers. "One to the mountains, one to the sea—"

"Yes, yes, I'm familiar." He waved me off. "They are fae, of course, but more cousin to brownies and other fae in the wildlands than to the *daoine maithe*. They don't have the sort of magic that the greater fae do. Theirs is based in rock and stone, instead of aether. It's been theorized that's why they took a piece for themselves."

"Took?" I blinked. "Clíodhna told us it was given to them to hide."

He chuckled. "The story might have been sanitized over the years, but no. The only folk that were actually *given* a stone were the humans in Pennlan, and that was after the other pieces mysteriously disappeared. The trolls always considered themselves to be on par with the greater fae, though the realities of their magic proved otherwise. Erlkings of the past have theorized the trolls would show up once they unlocked the secrets of their piece."

"Do you think they have?"

He chuckled. "No. They don't have the skill."

"Maybe they're concerned Eoghan will come calling and are trying to reform alliances," I said.

"It certainly sounds that way."

"What about Riona?" I asked, a little hesitantly. "Can she come with us?"

It wasn't as if I thought she would be of great value to us, even though the trolls had requested her. I just couldn't stomach the thought of leaving her here alone. Aldrick would show her no mercy, and she wasn't going to get it from Clíodhna or the Erlking. At least if she was with us, she would have a small reprieve. And perhaps I could get to the bottom of what was really bothering her.

The Erlking looked conflicted. "She still has much to learn."

"I can continue her tutelage. I won't be as..." I cleared my throat.

"*Thorough* as Aldrick, perhaps. But I know enough now that I can teach her the basics."

He considered me for a long time, and I was sure he would deny my request. But to my surprise, he dipped his head. "Very well. I trust you'll keep a close eye on her."

"Of course." I smiled. "Thank you."

The back of my neck burned, confusing me for a minute. Then I realized—he'd issued an edict that I protect her. I was a little put off that he didn't trust my word, especially after all this time, but I couldn't blame him for wanting a little extra assurance.

"Now, wizard, show me what you've learned with Clíodhna." He rose and clapped his hands. "I hear you've been creating portals with ease. We should find Riona with Aldrick in the training arena. Why don't you take us there?"

Chapter Twelve

Riona

If I'd thought that Aldrick might've gotten bored beating me senseless the day before, that notion was dispelled the moment the clock struck one. Before I'd had a chance to say a word, a powerful blast of magic had me rolling across the training ring. Even if I'd had the will to fight, it wouldn't have mattered. Aldrick outmatched me in every sense of the word. I was nothing but a mouse to him; the cat would play until I had no bones left to break.

Magic swam beneath my consciousness, desperate to be used, to protect me from the pain. But I kept it tightly contained, knowing that with its release would come the disgust, the slimy feeling of knowing someone else's hands had been all over it. My words to Clíodhna about not wanting Aldrick to kill me came back, and the idea sounded more appealing now. After all, what good was a half-fae who refused to use her magic?

"Pathetic," Aldrick said, appearing before me in a swarm of moths. "Are you even going to attempt to fight? Or will you just lie there like a rag doll?"

If I could've formed words, I might've reminded him that he probably preferred me to be a rag doll. I stared at the blue sky above, going to the back of my mind, desperate to return to that secret place. But I remained stubbornly conscious as magic jettisoned my form backward along the gravel. I'd never become so acquainted with the ground before.

When I didn't respond, he continued his assault, magic pummeling me from head to toe. The world was starting to fade in and out, and the attack stopped just before I lost consciousness.

"You are a disgrace to your mother's memory," he said, standing over me. "A disgrace to the line of Erlkings. An abomination." He knelt closer, his perfect face almost a mockery of the pain he'd inflicted. "It's no wonder the wizard was able to use you so easily. A stronger fae might've fought him off. Might've used that pretty stone to destroy him instead of being used like a puppet. Instead of spilling the most closely guarded secrets of the Erlking."

Tears welled in my eyes, though it was hard to tell if it was from the pain or the words. I couldn't deny them, not really. I'd been able to keep from hurting Ayla, but I hadn't been able to stop myself from telling the wizard about the four stones. And now, months later, I was still tainted by his evil.

"You should've been drowned," he said. "There is no place for half-bloods in this realm. Not in the Erlking's court, and not in the human realm either. You have no purpose but to be a risk to us all should that wizard return."

It was hard to breathe now, between the feeling of someone else in my mind and the pain in my body. I just wanted it to stop. I wanted all of it to *stop*.

"Do us all a favor and just die," he said, standing and gathering more magic in his hand.

Because I had nothing left, I let go. Let go of my will, my mind, my fears, my desire to see my sister again. I fell backward, hearing the call of that frozen garden and knowing that I could keep walking and join my mother. But there was something else. Something stirred in my bones, released from the tight grip I had on it.

My fingertips warmed and as I weakly lifted my hands, they were *glowing*. It wasn't my magic, and yet it was. It was something familiar and unfamiliar.

"What—"

The power burst from my body in a beam of light, slamming into Aldrick with the force of a wave crashing against the shore in a furious storm. The brightness faded, and I realized I was sitting up, staring at my uncle's crumpled body in the corner. Silence reigned, except for the beat of my heart and the sound of air coming from my lips.

My body hummed with power. The magic was strange, foreign. Slimy. Him.

I shuddered and immediately regretted it, as my body was still broken. I gave my roiling stomach strict orders to stay where it was, as I didn't want to know what it felt like to throw up with a broken jaw.

But tingling spread from my fingertips to my toes, and a burning sensation washed over my face as my bruises healed. I looked around until I saw the source and I swallowed—hard. The Erlking and Cade were behind me, the Erlking's magic responsible for my quick healing.

"Impressive," he said with a smile before scowling at Aldrick. "Get up, boy. I have to speak with you."

My tormenter rose slowly, shaking his head and blinking. I must've done a number on him because he glowered something awful at me then the wizard.

"Did you intervene again?" he growled. "The Erlking—"

"I didn't do a thing," Cade said, almost proudly. "That was all Riona."

Aldrick's anger came back to me, and I shrank, wishing I could tell all of them it had been something else. Someone else. Someone who lived in my mind and still controlled me—even if it was just by fear alone. But if I did, the outcome might've been worse than keeping silent.

"I have come to let you know that your lessons with Riona will cease until her return," Birch said. "You are released until such time."

Aldrick snorted, rubbing the back of his neck. Mine burned with the same feeling. The look on his face had me wishing that I could stay and get his revenge out of the way now. Left to stew for a few weeks or months... I didn't want to think about it.

"You may go," Birch said.

Without another word, Aldrick disappeared into a flock of black moths.

"We're... We're leaving?" I repeated, after a moment. "We're going back to Pennlan?"

"The trolls came to visit Ayla," Cade said. "They want her to travel to their kingdom and forge an alliance. They've asked for you to come as well."

I worked my jaw, wondering if I'd been knocked unconscious and was dreaming. "Trolls? I thought they were a myth."

"Apparently not," Cade said, turning to the Erlking. "I need to return to my room to gather my things."

"Of course." Birch nodded. "We welcome you back at the conclusion of your journey to continue your training."

He bowed. "Thank you, Erlking."

And with that, Cade opened a portal to his room and stepped through, leaving me alone with the Erlking for the second time in a week.

"He has been given an edict to keep an eye on you," he said, after a long pause. "Though I don't think it's necessary, I wanted to ensure your safety, should you happen upon Eoghan."

I swallowed my fear. "Are you sure it's a good idea for me to leave? What if he..."

"Takes control of you again?" He nodded. "The stone is safe with your sister, and the added benefit of a wizard in your traveling party puts my mind at ease. Not to mention that little display of power you showed just now." He smiled. "I knew you would eventually get there."

I squirmed, that slimy feeling crawling up my arm. If only he knew that power wasn't mine... "Odd that the trolls have reappeared. Odder still they want *me* to come."

"Adversity makes for strange bedfellows," he said. "There have been six Erlkings since the fae have spoken with the trolls. They've taken great pains to keep themselves, and their prized possession, hidden. But it's clear something has spooked them into reappearing."

"But why ask for *me* specifically?" I asked.

"Apparently, your half-human blood has put their minds at ease."

"And you'd let me speak for you?" I continued, searching for the logic in all this. "What if I say or do something that…"

"What? Ruins the relationship?" He chuckled. "My dear, the trolls and fae haven't spoken in a millennium. I doubt there's anything you could do to make things worse."

I searched for an excuse—anything—to dissuade him.

"Unless the trolls have unlocked some magnificent secret to their piece of the *seod croí*," he said with a chuckle, "they aren't very dangerous. Their magic is best suited for turning desolate land into farms and the like. If they have something up their sleeves, I'm confident you will be able to handle it—as well as the wizard." He paused. "Unless you'd rather stay and continue your lessons with Aldrick?"

He was smiling, perhaps knowing that my one assault was an aberration. The memory left a bad taste in my mouth. If I was thrown into training with Aldrick again, I might use that magic. And that was something I hoped to avoid.

"No, I'm willing to go," I said. "I just…wanted to make sure you'd thought this through."

"I'm the Erlking, granddaughter. I don't make decisions without thinking them through."

⤐ ⤐ ⤐ ⤐

I was torn between elation that I was no longer Aldrick's plaything, dread that I was going to make a huge mistake, and excitement that I was going to see my sister again. Just as I was finishing up my packing, I felt a prickle on the back of my neck as if something powerful were approaching. In the middle of my room, a golden circle appeared, and Cade walked through, dressed in his traveling cloak with a bag slung over his shoulder.

"Ready?" he asked, as if it were no big deal for him to conjure magic like that.

"This portal magic…I don't like that you can just drop in on me," I said, stuffing another shirt deeper into my bag. "Seems like you should still knock."

He snorted. "Well, it's not as if I've practiced far distances yet."

"You figured it out." I ducked a smile. "What do you think about this troll? Trap or…?"

"Why would you think it's a trap?"

"Why wouldn't you?"

We stared at each other for a moment, expecting the other to break first.

But I was, as usual, more stubborn. He let out a sigh. "Well, in the first place, trolls are fae, right? They can't lie?"

"You've been here long enough to see how they can wheedle their way around it," I replied. "I suppose we'll just have to be specific when we speak to this troll. Make sure it's all…right." I pulled my bag over my shoulder. "We should get going if we want to make good time."

"Or I could just conjure a portal."

I blanched. "You said you haven't practiced far distances."

"No time like the present." He grinned. "Besides, I think we'll know fairly quickly if it doesn't work."

Cade turned away from me, clutching his staff in his hand and drawing a circle in front of him, a golden trail hanging in the air. He met the top of the circle and traced it again then a third time. I couldn't see his face, but his shoulders were tense.

The circle pulsed brighter, then the space between the golden lines shifted. A different world came into view, with stone floors, drafty air, the scent of fire and something else—something earthy—floating through to my bedroom. Cade turned to me, his smile wide.

"Well, that was easy," he said, offering his arm.

But I didn't take it. Recognition had dawned as I realized Cade had created a portal into…the basement of the castle. *His* study. Fear swelled in my chest. I took a step backward until Cade's hand touched my arm.

"Hey." His smile was sympathetic, understanding. "He's not here. Promise. You're safe with me."

I took a shaky breath, ashamed that my emotions had been so clear on my face. And with a calming breath, I nodded and walked through the portal with him.

CHAPTER THIRTEEN

AYLA

I thumbed the stone as I wandered the castle, my mind elsewhere. I was sure of my decision to leave, very sure—and yet…yet I worried. But that was the girl who'd listened to whatever Eoghan said without question. And back and forth I went, not wanting to show weakness, especially around Ward, but also…

"Your Majesty?"

I jumped, looking up into the steely eyes of the troll. It was still somewhat jarring to take him in, with his almost-translucent skin and pointed ears. My gaze lingered on the ears, reminding myself they were no longer a sign of danger or someone trying to kill me. He was a friend. A friend who also hated the fae who lived to the north of my kingdom. In some weird way, it almost made me like him more.

"Lynton," I said, after another long pause. "I trust you slept well."

He nodded, surveying me. "I did. Thank you for accommodating me on such short notice."

"Absolutely." I shifted from foot to foot. "Would you like to go for a ride today?"

"I believe it's best make haste back to Gwyllion," he said. "Our king is eager to meet with you, and the longer we wait, the more chance that wizard has of discovering our kingdom."

"Of course," I said. "As soon as my wizard returns, we will start our journey."

"Your…" He narrowed his gaze. "*Your* wizard? Different than the one who tried to steal the stone?"

"Y-yes," I said. "Cade is my friend. He protected the stone from Eoghan. He'll be a valuable asset to us."

"I don't believe he will be necessary," Lynton replied. "Unless you believe there is something nefarious with our offer? Or you believe you are in need of protection, even wielding the stone?"

I hesitated. "Cade knows more about magic than I do, and I'd be remiss if I didn't bring every expert at my disposal to our discussion."

He sniffed, and I silently celebrated my quick thinking. "Very well. How long until he arrives?"

"Not long, I hope. A week, perhaps less." Ward had mentioned he and Cade had been able to get here much faster when they'd come to rescue me. But I wasn't sure what tricks Cade had up his sleeve. "I know he'll come as quickly as possible."

"And the fae girl?" he asked, his tone somewhat impatient. "Will she be coming as well?"

"I don't know." Some part of me hoped the Erlking would see fit to keep her under lock and key. It wasn't as if I didn't want to see her…but I didn't.

Lynton's eyes grew larger as he stared at something over my shoulder. I turned, and my heart jumped into my throat.

Cade stood in the hallway, looking so much *older* than the last time I'd seen him. Taller, too, if that was even possible. His black hair was even longer than before, gathered in a ponytail at the back of his neck. His cheeks had become a little more defined beneath that deep rusty brown skin, and a little dark stubble peppered his cheeks. Cade had left a gangling boy, but he'd definitely returned a man more comfortable in his own skin.

His dark brown eyes lit up when he saw me. "Ayla!"

"You're here!" I stopped myself from running forward, remembering at the last minute that the troll was watching. "How did you manage this?"

"Been practicing some things," he said, finally noticing the creature behind me. "You're the troll, I presume?"

Lynton surveyed him with unreadable eyes until he nodded. "I am."

"Lynton," I replied, hoping Cade hadn't offended him. "This is Cade. He's the wizard who'll be accompanying us."

"I see." He tilted his head. "Your magic is…" His nostrils flared. "Interesting."

"And yours…" Cade chewed the inside of his lip. He'd told me once he could almost taste the fae's scent; I wondered what the troll smelled like.

"Um. Hi."

My happiness evaporated in an instant. Raven hair, green eyes, and a face so similar to my own it was jarring. Like Cade, she'd aged in the past six months, and no longer looked like the child who'd stood between me and Eoghan. When we locked eyes, I was transported back to those terrifying moments when my entire world was turned upside down, when the man I'd trusted like a father turned into a monster.

"The Erlking let you come," I managed after a too-long pause. "That's great."

She nodded, her gaze on the troll. "He would like to reopen the lines of communication. Since we have a common enemy."

"Indeed." Lynton smiled thinly. "Well, if we're all here, it seems we're ready to travel. In the morning, shall we depart?"

"Of course," I said. "But before we go, please join us for dinner tonight. One last meal before we set out."

He looked as if he would've rather declined but nodded. "Of course. Tonight, then."

I remained silent as he left us before turning to Cade, the tension leaving my shoulders as I drank him in. "You're a sight for sore eyes. Did you grow taller or something?"

"All that fae food did me well," he said, his grin spreading across his face. How could a person look so different and yet so familiar at the same time? "You look positively regal, Queen Ayla."

I rolled my eyes. "Hardly. It's the same old me, just with a heavier crown. Half the time I…" My words trailed off when I realized Riona was still standing there, her hands clasped behind her back. "Oh. You're still here."

"Yeah," she said with a nervous smile. "Thank you for inviting me."

"It wasn't…" I cleared my throat. "Sure. Glad to have you. If you'd like to run upstairs and find a servant named Bronwen, you can have her lead you to a room."

"I don't need to rest," she said. "Not really, I—"

"You should lie down," Cade said. "Especially after the afternoon you've had."

She looked ready to protest but nodded. I half-expected her to turn into those butterflies, but she slowly walked toward the door, casting me one final look before leaving Cade and me alone.

"Brr." Cade quirked a brow. "What's that about?"

"Hm?"

"Did Riona do something to get on your bad side?" he asked. "Because I've seen warmer welcomes to advancing armies."

"Oh, stop," I said, grabbing his arm and leading him out of the hallway and into my study. "It's fine. How in the world did you get here so quickly?"

"Portal spell," he said, proudly. "I just created a doorway between here and there and walked through."

"The fae seem to be teaching you a lot," I said with a grin.

"That one didn't come from the fae," he said, though his eyes lost a little of their luster. "But yes, they've been quite welcoming and helpful. It's been a wonderful six months." He paused, looking around the hall. "Feels strange to be back here. Especially without…"

"Yeah," I said, a little shiver passing through me. "I half-expect him to walk through the door any moment and chide me for distracting you…"

He looked at me for a moment then grabbed his staff. The tip glowed a brilliant gold, and a bottle and two glasses appeared on the table.

"Shall we?" He grinned, a little devilishly. "Sounds like you could use it."

I gestured to the bottles. "Pour away."

He served me, and I took a long sip, letting the alcohol soothe the tension in my shoulders as I watched the man my best friend had become. He was Cade, of course, but his use of magic was so much more natural than when he'd left here. Meanwhile, I still felt like the same old girl who'd let Eoghan nearly destroy her kingdom. Who was still looking for the old wizard to save her.

"So..." He glanced at the door. "That troll is something else, huh? What do we think about him? The Erlking said the last time the trolls were seen was when the *seod croí* was split."

"What does he say about them?" I asked, a little nervously.

"He was concerned that they've suddenly reappeared after all this time. But they both think Eoghan is a graver threat, and if we can ally ourselves with the trolls, then we'll have two stones to his...well, hopefully none."

"Hopefully." I smirked. "Take that, Ward. The Erlking agrees with me."

"What?" His smile widened. "What's Ward done?"

"Just... He doesn't think it's wise for me to leave. Thinks I'll be 'safer' here and that there's a trap waiting for us in the mountains." I huffed, carefully watching Cade's expression. "Silly, right?"

He seemed conflicted for just a moment then brightened. "Absolutely silly. You've got me, you've got the stone. If the trolls try *anything*, we'll handle them together."

My instinct was to clamp down, to keep my thoughts to myself, but I couldn't hide from Cade. Of all the people in this world, he was the one person I could be honest with.

"Can I tell you a secret?" I whispered.

"Of course." He leaned in. "Anything."

"Cade, the stone… It hasn't…" I swallowed. "I haven't been able to use it since Eoghan was… Since then. It hasn't so much as flickered in the last six months. I think I broke it."

He frowned, which didn't give me much confidence. "I'm sure you didn't break it. Maybe it just…hasn't been needed? It was a decorative piece for a few hundred years."

I worried at my bottom lip. "I don't know if I can trust that. Maybe Eoghan cursed it on his way out. But I'm afraid if he shows up again, I won't be able to do anything about it." I worked the stone in my hand. "*That's* why I'm so keen on leaving. Edric's a fellow stone-bearer. He might know something I don't."

"Why not ask the Erlking?" Cade asked.

I made a face before I could stop myself. "I don't want them knowing I can't use it."

"Why not?"

"Because…" I searched his face, looking for that dislike of fae that we'd once shared. But all I saw was confusion. "Do you really trust them?"

He laughed, as if I were speaking nonsense. "Considering I've been sleeping in the Erlking's castle, eating their food, being trained by them… Yes, of course I do." He patted my hand. "And you should, too."

My face warmed, and I snatched my hand away. "Well, perhaps when we get back, if the trolls don't have anything to offer, I can ask."

CHAPTER FOURTEEN

WARD

Wisely, I kept myself scarce after my argument with Ayla and focused on preparing a contingent of guards to come with us. I'd no idea what to expect in the mountains, or even how long we'd be on the road, so I told the group to pack light but be ready to protect the queen by any means necessary.

"And there's no talking her out of this?" Elodia asked. Of course, she and Rutley were included in my list of soldiers to come. I trusted them with my life, and if all else failed, they'd be on my side in the event of any future disagreements with Ayla.

"If there were, I wouldn't be here," I replied with a solemn sigh. "Dismissed."

As usual, Rutley and Elodia hung back. We stood in silence for a moment, the three of us perhaps thinking the exact same thing.

"So... I don't know about you," Elodia began, "but I've never climbed a mountain before."

"Never even seen one," Rutley grunted.

"Same," I said with a heavy sigh. "I hope this troll has some kind of magic up his sleeve to expedite this journey. Ayla's never left the castle. I can't imagine how difficult it'll be for her to travel across flat land, let alone..." I shook my head. "But she'll do it, stubbornly, I'm sure. So we just need to be ready for anything."

"I thought you said the troll was a guy?" Elodia said, looking over my shoulder.

"I did," I said, following her gaze.

My brows lifted as a smile grew on my lips. A figure with dark hair and pointed ears stood with her back to me.

"Riona?" I called.

"Ward?" She turned, taking a step toward me. She seemed to have lost some of the childlike roundness to her face. She still resembled Ayla, but not as much now—she looked, perhaps, more like her mother. But even though she was different, she still had that air about her of a kid trying way too hard.

"I was hoping you'd come," I said, closing the distance and enveloping her in a hug.

She returned it, squeezing me tightly before looking over my shoulder. "Who are you friends?"

"Riona, this is Rutley and Elodia," I said, gesturing to them. "Guys, this is—"

"I gathered," Rutley said, nodding toward her. "The ears gave you away."

"The face, too," Elodia said with a smirk as she held out her hand. "Pleased to make your acquaintance. Ward's told us all about you."

"He has?" She looked at me with a curious expression. "What did he say?"

I shifted. My description of our travels in the fae kingdom weren't that complimentary of her. But then again, she'd been clearly in over her head.

Luckily, I was able to find a new topic when I noticed faded yellow splotches on her face. "Are those bruises?"

She shrugged, avoiding my gaze. "The Erlking thought it was time I get out of the library and into the training ring. That, or he wanted to kill me, I'm not quite sure."

It was an attempt at a joke, but there was a note of seriousness in her voice. "It wasn't Cade—"

"No, of course not," she said with a soft smile. "He put Aldrick in charge of my tutelage."

I shifted, taking a minute to associate the name to the person. "Al... The one who wanted you dead? The fae who sent us through the *aos sí* to be ghost food?"

"Yep."

"Why would the Erlking ask *him* to train you?"

"No idea," she said, her gaze growing distant. "Or maybe it was part of my punishment. One can never tell with the Erlking."

I nodded, understanding dawning. "Well, that certainly explains why you're eager to go to the troll kingdom."

"I'm not eager," she said, though it was quiet. "But they did ask for me."

"What do you know about them?" I asked.

She gave us a quick history lesson about when the *seod croí* was split and the trolls absconded with their stone. She assured us that the Erlking just wanted it safe and had no interest in trying to bring it back to the fold.

"So if you were to go up against a troll, man to man," Rutley said. "Who would win?"

"I mean, that's tricky," she said, her face flushing a little.

"On average," I said, hoping to save her from explaining herself. Clearly, she hadn't made it very far in magical training.

"Obviously, no one's seen one for a while," she said. "But historically, they don't have as much magic as the greater fae would have. So if they've got an ulterior motive, Cade *should* be able to handle them."

"And you, too," Elodia added.

"Sure," Riona said, a little too quickly. "But that's probably why the Erlking let me go, too. They think I'm weak, he thinks they're weak, and neither of us can get into too much trouble."

"Let's hope that's true," I said with a little bit of a sigh.

I half-expected her to argue with me, but she didn't. "Ayla told me to find someone named Bronwen so I could get settled, but I haven't been able to find her. Do you think you could help?"

"Sure," I said, nodding to the others. "My guess is we'll be leaving in the morning, so make sure you're packed."

"You got it, boss."

>⇥ >⇥ >⇥ >⇥

I found Bronwen and got Riona settled in a room not too far from Ayla's. The half-fae girl was quieter than usual, a little more pensive, which I'd chalked up to her being uncomfortable around new people, so I stayed behind to catch up on what she'd been doing in the fae realm. It was about as riveting as my time had been, with a good chunk in the library and very recently being allowed to study under Clíodhna.

"I wrote Ayla letters," she said, almost hinting at something. "But I never got a response."

"Did they come in Cade's little magic box?" I asked.

She shook her head. "I didn't know they were communicating like that. I was sending them the regular way, I suppose." She picked at her nails. "I thought maybe she'd just not gotten them, but…"

"But?"

"She seemed pretty eager to get rid of me," she said, looking out the window at the sunset beyond. "Is she mad at me or something?"

"She hasn't said anything," I replied, but I couldn't help remembering the small flinch every time Riona was mentioned. "I'm sure the letters just got lost, that's all."

She nodded but looked like she didn't quite believe me. "I suppose."

There was a knock at the door, and Bronwen reappeared, her hands in her apron. "Pardon the interruption, Lieutenant, but Her Majesty would like both of you to join her for dinner this evening. The…er… other visitor from the troll kingdom will be in attendance as well."

"Thank you," I said, rising slowly. "Surprised Ayla asked me to come."

"Why?" Riona asked.

"I'm not in agreement that she should be going at all," I said, offering my arm to Riona. "But I've been overruled."

She didn't respond, a curious look on her face.

We arrived in the dining hall to the sounds of slightly slurred conversation. Ayla's cheeks were bright red, and there was a hint of redness in Cade's dark cheeks as well. They wore easy smiles as if they'd spend the afternoon having much more fun than Riona and me.

But as we walked into the room, Ayla's expression darkened, and Riona shrank beside me. I wanted to tell her the look was directed at me, but I didn't have time.

"Ward! Riona! 'Bout time you joined us." Cade bustled over to us, his movements slow and unsteady as he swept Riona into a hug and clapped me roughly on the back. He turned to the nearly-empty bottle of wine and tapped it with his staff. It glowed gold, and the red wine inside swirled and refilled. Then he tapped his wine glass and two more appeared beside it, already full, before walking over to us and shoved the glasses in our hands.

"Cheers to being reunited," he said, raising his glass. But he seemed the only one who wanted to be there, as the rest of us begrudgingly clinked our glasses together. Ayla wouldn't meet my gaze, Riona's was cast downward, and I couldn't help but notice how close Cade and Ayla stood.

I swallowed my jealousy, remembering there was no need as she wasn't ever going to be mine. "Cade, how was your time in the fae kingdom?"

Cade launched into a long discussion about his studies, and within seconds, I was lost. Ayla seemed enchanted by it all, her gaze bright with wonder. And Riona... Riona was watching her sister with a frown.

"Sounds like it's been fruitful," I said, after Cade's long monologue ended. "I'm glad to hear it. Maybe now you won't lose your stick."

"It's a staff, you rube," he said, but there was a smile in his voice. "And yes, it certainly helps that the staff was actually made for me versus stolen from somewhere else."

Ayla's gaze passed behind me and her smile grew a little strained. "Lynton, please come in. Would you like some wine?"

"I suppose." The troll walked into the room, his gaze firmly on Cade before turning to Riona with more curiosity. There was something there I didn't like, but I swallowed my thoughts. "I do hope we're still planning to leave in the morning, Your Majesty. The journey to the troll kingdom will be long."

"Yes, of course," Ayla said, though I could tell that little fact was slipping her mind the more she drank.

"It may not be, though," Cade said, perhaps a little more sober than Ayla. "I should be able to create a portal there. Bring us right to Edric's front door."

"Are you sure about that?" Riona asked. "Didn't you *just* learn how to do it?"

He waved her off. "I have the concept down."

Riona frowned, and I narrowed my gaze. Perhaps he wasn't as sober as I'd thought.

"Just tell me where it is," he said.

The troll smiled, his lips pulling over his teeth. "I'm afraid that's impossible. The location of the troll kingdom is a closely guarded secret. It's why we've managed to stay hidden from the…" His gaze raked over Riona. "Less desirable inhabitants of the continents. Those who would want to take the stone from us."

"The Erlking has no desire for the stone," Riona said. "I'm going in the spirit of peace. That's why you invited me to come, isn't it?"

"Of course." He brought the wine to his lips. "But the fact remains, you may be able to expedite the journey, but we will have to walk up the mountain on foot—at least five days."

Ayla brightened. "Oh, well, that's much better than a month. It should be lovely. Bronwen won't have to bring as many dresses for me"

I swallowed my comments along with a gulp of wine. Even one day climbing a mountain sounded torturous to me, and I spent half my day running around the kingdom.

The troll cleared his throat. "The mountains are a little dangerous, Your Majesty. It would be best if we kept our traveling party small so we don't attract creatures. I'd hoped it would be just..." He glanced at me. "Just the three of us. And perhaps the wizard."

"Absolutely not," I said, unable to contain myself. "If the sovereign is leaving, we will be bringing a contingent of soldiers. Especially, as you say, because the mountains are dangerous."

"I'm more than enough to protect her," Lynton replied. "But it's easier to do if there are fewer people to protect."

"The soldiers can handle themselves."

"I doubt they're prepared for the creatures in the mountain."

"Then it's a good thing I am," I replied with a steely glare. "I've trekked through the fae wildlands. I'm sure I can handle a few snow monsters."

"I don't see the harm in letting a couple soldiers come," Ayla said, flashing me a warning look. "Will they be ready in the morning?"

"Yes. As will everything else." I brought the wine to my lips again to stop myself from speaking further.

"Then it's settled. The five of us, plus a small cohort of soldiers, will leave through Cade's portal." Ayla smiled. "It'll be fun."

I glanced around the room, sensing that the only ones who thought so were a couple bottles deep.

Chapter Fifteen

Cade

I woke early, my head sloshing around like it was full of sand. I rolled onto my side, fumbling for my staff to conjure a glass of water. I downed it quickly, then refilled it and drank more. Perhaps having an entire bottle of wine with Ayla the day before a long journey hadn't been very smart.

The hour was early, but the troll had requested all of us join him before sunup. He seemed... Well, strange was an odd description, considering how many strange creatures I'd met in the Erlking's castle. But while there were aspects of him that were familiar—the golden eyes, the pointed ears—the rest of him was something to behold. We hadn't had much time to get to know one another, but we would become well acquainted on the...

I groaned, the events of the night before rushing back to me. We were leaving this morning to climb a mountain—assuming I would be able to make a portal from here to there.

The wine had definitely been speaking for me. I'd been able to create a portal from the fae realm to the castle because I knew the castle inside and out; it was home. Trying to create a portal to a wholly unknown part of the world? Should've kept my mouth shut.

But I pushed myself out of bed, my hand finding my staff without a second thought. I held it between my hands, remembering Clíodhna's words when I'd conjured my first portal.

"You're the wizard. Figure it out."

I gathered magic, drawing a circle in the air in front of me. Golden magic trailed behind, hanging in the air as I considered the distance between here and there. Round and round I drew, as my mind settled on a place I'd been to once—the very end of the fae realm where we'd retrieved the stone.

Before my eyes, the vault disappeared within the circle, fading into the dark nothingness we'd walked through to get to the Pennlan stone at the north end of the *sidheog* lands. A cold breeze ruffled my cloak as I pulled my staff back upright and closed the portal.

Okay, that was a faraway place, but one I'd been to before.

I turned to the map on the wall and picked a random spot in Driwania, a country to the south of us. Then I stared at it, unsure what to do next.

"You're up early," Riona said with a yawn behind me. "Considering the amount of wine you drank last night."

"I thought your room was upstairs," I said with a frown.

"Felt a little frigid up there," she said, absentmindedly looking at the door. "Anyway, you needed help getting to bed, so I stayed down here to make sure you were okay."

I would have to ask about that later, but for now, I had more pressing matters. "I think I promised everyone I'd make a portal to the troll kingdom."

"You did."

"I have no idea how to do that."

She snorted, sitting on the table. "I figured."

I turned, annoyed. "Any ideas? Or are you content to sit there and laugh at me?"

"You're the expert in portal creation," she said with a shrug. "How've you done it before?"

"Well, places I know are easy," I said. "I just think about where they are on a map and—"

"Then do that," she said, as if it were obvious. "Just a place you haven't been before." She walked to the map and put her finger on the small icon of the Pennlan castle. "You know you're here." She moved her hand until she had a point in the south. "Use that to orient yourself and go here."

"I'll give it a try." I shook my shoulders as I stared at the map, imprinting a clear picture of it in my mind before closing my eyes. I envisioned the small circle that represented Pennlan castle. Then I turned, noting the roads that we'd traveled north toward the fae kingdom. Then, I spun south, seeing the roads I'd taken once or twice. But they were clear enough, so I followed them.

The world sped up beneath my mental map. Squiggles and ink marks transformed into the towns, roads, and rivers that dotted the land. And as my magical self drew closer to the border with Driwania, towns and cities I'd never been to before appeared until the final destination was glowing like a beacon in my mind.

I held that in my mind and rotated my staff in the air, casting the portal spell.

"Oh, wow!"

I jumped, expecting to hear Riona, but instead, it was Ayla who was clapping enthusiastically for me.

"Cade!" She ran to my side, her eyes wide with excitement. "That's incredible!"

I warmed at her praise as I closed the portal, lest we invite someone in from Driwania. "What are you doing down here? Shouldn't you be upstairs getting ready?"

"Couldn't sleep," she said. "I…" Her gaze landed on Riona, and a flash of annoyance crossed her face. "Anyway. I thought I'd come make sure you had everything you needed."

I looked at my staff. "To be honest, I wanted to make sure I could do it. Would be a bit of a bad first impression to have promised the troll a portal I couldn't conjure."

"He'd probably leave you behind," Riona said, standing in the corner. "He doesn't seem to like either of us very much."

"He doesn't seem to like anyone," Ayla replied, turning away from her. "So do you really think you can get us close to the troll castle?"

"I can try," I said. "I feel more confident about our chances now that I was able to conjure that portal." I smiled as I twisted my staff in my hand. "You know, the Erlking asked me to learn portal magic to help you move your goods from the border. Maybe when we get back, we can start moving things from here to there."

"Does this mean you'll be back more often?" Ayla asked with a grin.

"Seems like it," Riona said, a hopeful look on her face. "The Erlking was eager to help you with your backlog of goods."

Again, a flash of annoyance flitted across Ayla's face as she forced a smile. "Well, we should get going then. I'm sure the others are ready."

>→ >→ >→ >→

When we reached the entry hall, a loud conversation was happening between Ward and the troll envoy. He'd gathered four of his soldiers and what appeared to be a large assortment of weapons and supplies. I thought it all useful, considering we were bringing Ayla along, but the troll had other plans.

"You bring what you can carry," Lynton snapped. "And we don't need soldiers."

"The wizard will handle this," Ward said. "And if our queen is coming, I say we do."

"It will take us longer to climb the mountain."

"We aren't climbing, or did you mishear what Cade said last night?" Ward said.

The troll released an impatient sigh. "It's as I said, that's impossible. There are too many spells and enchantments on the kingdom to allow a wizard to just magic himself inside." He shifted as his gaze landed on Ayla. "Two additional guards should suffice."

"Fine," Ward barked, looking at the four assembled. "Rutley, Elodia, you're coming. Bertram and Rengold, you stay here."

The two dismissed looked rather pleased to be staying behind, one of them yawning as they gathered their things and left the atrium. The other two soldiers, much closer in age with the rest of us, stood loyally beside Ward as they glared at the troll.

Finally, Ward noticed Riona and me. "Good. We're all here. Let's get going, Cade."

"Now?" I looked around.

"We've wasted enough time," Lynton said with a sneer. "We won't get much daylight on the mountain, and I'd like to move as quickly as possible."

I licked my lips and walked into the center of the room, feeling the gazes of everyone on my chest acutely. I drew a circle in the air with my staff, gold dripping from the tip, and only then remembered…I had no idea where we were going.

"Uh…" I looked at the troll. "Where are we going, exactly?"

His nostrils flared. "The base of the mountains."

"Which is…where?" I turned to him fully. "I need something to target."

"I don't know how to answer the question," he said with a sneer.

The trolls don't have magic like we do. I cleared my throat. "Perhaps a map might help."

I conjured a map from the vault, and the troll took a step back in surprise as it hung before him. He settled himself, dropping his hand from his chest, and examined the map.

"Here." He pointed. "This is as close as I believe we can get."

I felt every eye on the room on the back of my neck. I was confident in my magic, thanks to the earlier practice, but it was still a little unnerving to perform in front of an audience. My staff was a calming presence, easy in my hand and quick to call forth the magic in my veins.

As before, I used the Pennlan castle to orient myself on the map then headed east. Rivers and towns flew past me as large mountains loomed in the distance. I was able to pass some of them but couldn't go any farther than the base in the center of the range. I mentally landed in a frigid forest, sensing that this was as good as we were going to get.

With the place firmly in my mind, I drew a circle in the air, calling my magic to bridge the gap between here and there. Ayla's surprised gasp behind me told me what I already knew; I had created the portal.

"That's incredible," she whispered.

"That's…" Even Lynton was surprised, his golden eyes wide. Then he cleared his throat and returned to his usual borderline-annoyed gaze. "I suppose we should get going. The sun will be up soon." He walked to the portal then hesitated. "Does it… Is there anything…"

"You can just walk through," Riona said, breezing by him and stepping through to the other side. She turned and gestured to the air. "Easy."

He glared at her then straightened and stepped his long legs through. He seemed nervous, glancing around and sniffing the air. "This will do."

"It cut a whole month off our trip, but yeah, 'it'll do,'" Ward grumbled, looking at his soldiers. "Let's go."

They followed him through the portal, and I moved to do the same, except I realized we were missing one person from our traveling party. Ayla stood somewhat frozen, her face even paler than usual. Her breath was coming in short bursts as she stared, transfixed, at the portal.

"What is it?" I asked.

"It's…" She turned to me, fear in her eyes. "I'm really doing this, aren't I?"

"If you want," I said, gently. "You could stay."

"No, I have to go…" She screwed up her face and picked up the small traveling pack by her feet, sliding it over her shoulders. "I have to do this. I *need* to do this."

I watched her, knowing it was better for her to talk it out than to try to help her.

"Ayla?" Ward reappeared in the visage of the portal. "Are you all right?"

"Fine," she said, losing her fear almost immediately. "Let's go."

And without another word, she stepped through the portal and into the world beyond—and I followed suit, closing our doorway to Pennlan.

CHAPTER SIXTEEN

RIONA

There was new magic here. The air sat uncomfortably on my skin, the taste in my mouth unfamiliar and bitter. Dead leaves crunched under my boots, the trees above our heads bare against the gray sky above. The sun was rising, perhaps, but it would be a while until we saw it in this valley.

Lynton made no conversation as he began walking through the pathless forest. Rutley and Elodia followed then me. But Ward hung back, keeping close to Cade and Ayla.

Ayla… I buried my hurt. She hadn't said more than two words to me. It was a far cry from when I'd first arrived in the kingdom, when we'd spent a few days getting to know one another. Had something changed? Had I unknowingly offended her?

I pushed those thoughts to the back of my mind. If, as the troll said, the path was dangerous, I would have to keep my wits about me.

"Hold on," Ward said as Lynton turned to walk. "Where, exactly, are we going?"

"The troll kingdom, obviously."

"Aren't we there?" Ward asked.

Lynton released an impatient breath. "Gwyllion exists beneath the mountain and there is only one entrance at the peak. As I said, it will take five days to get there. There are human villages along the way, and if we make good time, we should be able to sleep in an inn every night."

"Human…?" I whispered.

"I'm confused," Ward said. "How can there be humans on the mountain if it's troll country?"

"I would expect they migrated here," Lynton drawled. "Built themselves houses, brought livestock."

"You know what I meant," Ward growled.

Ayla cleared her throat. "What I think Ward is trying to say," she said with a look at him, "is that we were under the impression trolls haven't been seen in centuries. If there are humans here, wouldn't they know about the trolls that live beneath them?"

"No. They don't know of the trolls."

We shared a confused look.

"The longer we stand here, the more daylight we burn through, and there's precious little as it is," Lynton said. "I suggest we get moving so we can reach the first village before nightfall. It's too dangerous to be on the mountain at night—both in terms of the temperature and the creatures who come out when the sun goes down."

As if that were the last word on the subject, the troll turned and walked through the trees.

"I suppose we should follow him," Ayla said, hiking her pack higher and walking past us, then Cade, and the two soldiers. Ward and I remained still, Ward watching the troll's retreating back with suspicion. Then, finally, he began to walk, and I did, too.

>→ >→ >→ >→

The morning brightened, though the sun didn't cast much warmth. Our party started fairly close together, but as the terrain grew rockier and the inclines steeper, distance grew between Lynton at the front, Ward and me, the two soldiers, and, taking up the rear, Ayla and Cade.

Every so often, Ward would glance behind him, but for the most part, his suspicious gaze was on the troll. Finally, I could take the silence no longer and spoke.

"Like old times, hm?" I said.

He jumped, almost as if he hadn't known I was there then smiled, though it was forced. "Yeah. Any secrets you're withholding from us this time?"

"None that I can think of."

"Good. There's enough subterfuge without you adding to it," he said, glancing behind him. Ayla and Cade had fallen back behind the two soldiers now. "I don't know what this troll was thinking."

"Hm?"

"If his plan was to bring *just* you and Ayla, and this is the path, then…" He shook his head. "There's no way she could've done this by herself. It's too difficult."

"Don't let her hear you say that," I said with a small smile.

"I'm getting tired of all these half-truths," Rutley said, coming to stand next to Ward. "Seems like we shouldn't go any farther until we get a straight answer out of him."

"I believe him when he says the mountains are dangerous," Elodia replied, gripping the bow slung around her shoulders.

"We have a fae and a wizard, what can they do?" Rutley said.

"A lot," Ward said, looking behind me to where Ayla and Cade were climbing over a rock. "Let's keep moving."

The two soldiers kept close to us this time. They seemed to be loyal to Ward—then again, they'd have to be to go on this quest with him. But it was more than that; it was how they seemed to defer to him, to follow his every move.

"Is this anything like your journey through the fae realm?" Elodia asked me.

"It wasn't as steep," I replied lightly.

Ward snorted and actually cracked a smile, the first I'd seen from him all day. Then he paused, turning and furrowing his brow. "Where's Ayla?"

The four of us stopped, and my pulse sped as we waited. Ward took three steps forward before the top of Cade's head appeared, followed by the rest of him. He reached down and pulled Ayla up over a particularly large stone. Her pale cheeks were red with exertion and it was clear she was already exhausted. I glanced at the sky; barely midday.

"Let's stop to rest," Ward said.

"We shouldn't stop until nightfall," the troll said, giving him a dirty look.

Ward's brows rose. "Well, that's clearly not going to happen." He jutted his thumb at Ayla, who was still making her way to the rest of the group. "She can't keep up this pace."

"She will have to."

Ward narrowed his gaze, and I put a hand on his arm to keep him from advancing on the troll. "In case you forgot, troll, we are *human*," he said. "Humans from a very flat land."

The troll's nostrils flared. "Fine. You may rest for five minutes. Then we must continue."

"Why have we stopped?" Ayla's breath was labored and there was a light sheen of sweat on her forehead. "What's wrong?"

"Nothing's wrong," Ward said. "But we need to rest for a bit."

"Rest?" She cleared her throat, her cheeks growing redder. "I don't need to rest. I can keep going."

"Ayla," Cade said, coming to stand beside her. "Ward's right. This is just the first morning. If you wear yourself out too quickly, the rest of it will be much harder. Better to take a moment to keep up your stamina."

She pursed her lips at Ward. "I'm not delicate, Ward. I can handle this."

"Rutley's the one who's tired," he said, nodding to the other soldier.

He blanched before Elodia elbowed him roughly. Then he nodded. "Right. Super tired. These legs are old."

I bit my lip to stifle a giggle.

"Well, perhaps your *lieutenant* should've prepared you better," Ayla said, glaring at Ward. "But if you must rest, I suppose I will as well. Cade, come sit with me."

The wizard offered Ward an apologetic smile and followed his queen, settling on a rock next to her.

"Brr," Elodia said. "I take it things haven't improved?"

"I have no idea what you're talking about," Ward said, a little sadly. "I'm going to see if there are any streams around here where we can refill our canteens."

He turned and walked away, leaving me with the two soldiers. Elodia watched him with pity in her gaze, but Rutley seemed oblivious as he reached into his pouch and tore off a piece of dried meat.

"You want?" he offered to me.

I shook my head, glancing around at the flora. Nothing looked familiar, but I didn't know why I'd thought it would. I was hundreds of miles from the fae kingdom. The only person who knew anything about this place was the annoyed-looking troll standing with his arms crossed on the trail ahead.

"Something tells me he'll get us moving at five minutes exactly," Rutley said with a sigh as he sat down on a nearby rock. "This is going to be a long journey."

"You said it," Elodia replied, looking at me. "So, fae girl—"

"Riona," I said softly.

"Riona, right." She put her hands on her hips. "What kind of magic can *you* do? We've seen it from the wizard, but nothing from you, yet."

"I'm saving it," I said, hoping that sounded convincing. The conversation piqued the troll's interest as well, as his golden eyes seemed to be pointed at me.

"For what?" Elodia asked.

"The right moment," I said, sweat breaking out on the back of my neck. My tongue tingled, the first sign that I was skirting too close to a lie.

"Which is when, exactly? You can't conjure us a carriage to crawl up the mountain?"

"I don't think such a thing would work," I said. The tingling ceased.

"Have you rested enough?" the troll asked. "We still have much ground to cover."

Ayla groaned, and Cade stood. "This is madness. I'm sure I can create a portal to the troll entrance. There's no need to climb—"

"Then by all means, wizard, please conjure us a portal," Lynton said, crossing his arms over his chest. "The entrance is at the top of the mountain."

Cade opened and closed his mouth, shifting on his feet. He took his staff in his hand, drawing a circle in the air as he'd done before. Round and round, but no other side appeared as it had before. Cade's brow furrowed, and he lowered his staff as he wriggled his ears as if to clear them.

"What's wrong?" Ayla asked.

"I can't focus," Cade said, staring at his staff. "I don't—"

"I suspect the wizard is coming into contact with the protective magic on the mountain," Lynton said. "It's designed to keep magical beings such as the fae and other…creatures away from our front gates. That includes restricting the use of your magic."

Cade looked at me, and my heart seized. "Can you use magic, Riona?"

At once, every eye was on me. I opened and closed my mouth, the magic in my veins humming with the chance to be used. But there was something else, something darker and disgusting, that prompted me to say:

"No. I can't use magic at all."

It was the boldest lie I'd told in some time. The words burned like hell on my tongue, a reminder that my mother's blood was forbidden to speak such untruths. But my father's blood, thankfully, just made it hurt and didn't strangle me.

And yet, as the words left my lips, a feeling of relief came over me. There would be no risk that I would be goaded into tapping into this evil power if no one expected me to, no risk that the monster living in my veins could reappear and take control. Everyone would be safe.

The troll stared at me as if he could see right through me then shrugged. "It's as I said, wizard. We will have to walk."

Chapter Seventeen

Ayla

As much as I'd protested the rest, I'd needed it. I'd expected the trip to be difficult, but I suppose my definition of difficult was a bit skewed. I'd never been so tired, sore, or cold in my life—and we'd only been climbing for a couple of hours at most. My feet were most likely bleeding from the blisters that had already formed, and the backs of my legs were tight and painful. Just when I'd thought we'd reached the top of one hill, more would appear. And we still had the rest of this day and four more to go.

The day inched on. My body ached, my fingers were numb from the cold, and every step was like walking on knives. It was hard to remember why I was torturing myself when I was in the thick of it. With a growl, I told myself to get it together. This was my mess to clean up. I hadn't killed Eoghan when I'd had the chance. The sooner I met with Edric and got answers, the better.

Ward and his two soldiers walked in near silence, but every so often, he'd cast a glance in my direction. When he did, I would straighten my back, increase my pace, and glare at him as if daring him to say something. He would then turn away and keep walking.

"Thirsty?" Cade offered me his canteen, the one Ward had refilled when we'd stopped.

I debated taking it, but my throat was parched. "Thanks."

He pointed his staff at me and concentrated.

"What are you doing?" I asked.

"Trying to refill it," he said. "Did I do it?"

I peered inside the canteen, but I already knew the weight hadn't changed. "No."

"Damn." He ran a worried hand through his hair. "I don't understand how this is possible," he murmured to himself. "What kind of magic prevents magic?"

"Could this be their stone?" I asked.

"Perhaps." He sighed. "I guess we'll have to rely on Ward to find streams."

I frowned, glancing at the gaggle of knights at the front of the group. I took another sip of the canteen, but it was no longer refreshing, the cold liquid burning my chapped lips. The sweat under my shirt was cold, too, and I rubbed my numb hands together to thaw them. Warmth spread across my fingertips, as if I were dipping them in tepid water. I looked up at Cade, who was concentrating.

"Did that help?"

"Yes, actually," I said with a soft smile.

"Thank goodness it's not all gone," he said. "At least that should last you a little while."

I didn't have the heart to tell him the warmth had already faded. "You shouldn't be using your limited magic on me."

"Why not?"

"It's not fair," I replied. "You wouldn't be casting warming spells on the others, would you?"

"I would," he said. "I'll probably end up doing it by tomorrow. They're such lightweights, especially Ward."

I rolled my eyes at the weak attempt at humor. "I don't need everyone pretending they're not doing things for my sake."

He surveyed me closely. "Why does it bother you?"

"Because…" I glanced at Riona, who was chatting affably with the two soldiers. I wasn't sure I felt jealous, but I certainly felt…something. "Because it does. I don't need special treatment."

"You're the queen. Out of all of us, you absolutely *should* get special treatment."

I flexed my hands, trying to coax warmth back into them. "Cade, I can't complain or get special treatment or else…"

"Or else what?"

"Or else he'll be right," I admitted through gritted teeth.

"Oh?" He tilted his head. "You two seem…at odds. So that's new?"

My gaze darted to the back of Ward's head. "I suppose it is."

"Were you two…" He seemed to consider his words. "Together?"

"Together? Like…" Heat flooded my cheeks, remembering the moment out on the green, when he'd looked at me like he wanted to kiss me. It seemed like ages ago. "No. Not really. I guess I'd thought we might…but I don't know anymore."

"Why?"

I sighed and lowered my voice so it wouldn't carry. "Because he hasn't even been officially promoted to captain, and it's gone to his head," I said. "He was telling me I couldn't go on this quest, talking over me, acting like…" I chewed my lip. "Acting like he was trying to control me while telling me 'what's best' for me. Like…" I motioned helplessly in the air.

Cade nodded, as if he understood. "Ayla, I think Ward was just worried about his sovereign leaving the safety of the castle. To be honest, he's…not the only one."

I narrowed my gaze at him. "What was I supposed to do? Not go? Let Eoghan—"

"No, I think you did the right thing," he said, holding his hands up in surrender. "But I don't think Ward is…" Again, he considered his words. "I think he *does* have your best interests at heart. He's loyal to Pennlan, and his job is keeping you safe. He made that clear to me six months ago. I don't think he's had that big of a change of heart."

I slumped a little. "So you're saying I overreacted?"

"I'm saying…" He shrugged as Ward turned again, watching us

with something unreadable on his face. Whatever unspoken thing passed between them seemed to change Cade's mind. "No. He's being overbearing. You can be mad at him if you want."

I smiled. "Thanks." I took his hand in mine. "Have I mentioned just how glad I am—"

"Yes, you have." He squeezed. "I'm glad I'm here too."

⸻

If I'd thought my body might get used to the pain, I was (literally) sorely mistaken. Ward insisted we rest every few hours, and while the break was welcome, getting back up to continue was harder each time. I almost would've rather go on without stopping.

I could find solace in the fact that nearly everyone else looked as miserable as I was. Even Ward, who regularly jogged around the castle, was starting to slow down. The only one who seemed unbothered was Lynton, who would stop and sigh exasperatedly as he waited for the straggling group to catch up.

"If he wants us to move faster," Rutley said, coming up beside Cade and me, "he should use some of that troll magic and help us along." I stifled a giggle, and he broke into a smile. "Yer Majesty."

"Only four more days of this," Elodia whined. "Say, wizard, you still having trouble with your magic?"

"Yep."

"Great."

The sun was moving overhead, and as morning turned to afternoon and afternoon began to dim, exhaustion settled in the back of my mind. It was getting difficult to see when the troll announced he'd found the village he'd been seeking. As I crested the hill, my lips parted in surprise. It was a cozy-looking town with thatched roofs and chimneys with swirling smoke. My hands were numb, and I was eager to warm them in front of a fireplace.

"There is an inn," he said, descending into the village.

I winced as my aching feed protested. "Hopefully, there's room for all of us."

"If not, Cade can sleep in the stables this time," Ward said with a smirk.

Cade glowered at him, and Riona ducked her head to hide a smile.

"Captain," Elodia said. "If this is a human village, like he says, we should probably keep Her Majesty's identity a secret."

"Why?" I said with a frown.

"That's a good idea," Ward said. "The last thing we need is to invite trouble."

I opened my mouth to complain, but Cade cut me off.

"I have to agree with him," Cade said. "Especially with my magic acting up."

I sighed. "Fine. Let's just get down there before my fingers fall off."

We descended into the village, and I wished I had the energy to really take it in, but all I wanted was to get indoors again. There was little activity on the streets, but the few people still out and about gawked at the strange creature leading the traveling party.

And yet…as soon as they turned away from him, their confusion melted away and they went back to whatever they were doing before.

The first time it happened, I chalked it up to trolls being common occurrences. But then a small child tugged at his mother's shoulder and pointed at the troll. But after he'd passed, the boy's finger dropped and his eyes glazed over. Then, he turned and began talking about something else. It was eerily similar to what I'd seen from my own soldiers back in Pennlan. Had Lynton cast this magic on every human he'd come into contact with?

But I seemed the only one who noticed the oddity, as the rest of the group was keen on reaching the small inn at the end of the road. Once I stepped through the threshold, heat spread across my face, and I realized just how cold I'd been. Ward walked up to the innkeeper to negotiate rooms for the night while the rest of us cozied up next to the roaring hearth.

I sank into the threadbare couch, releasing a sigh. "It feels good to sit."

Cade joined me on the couch, glancing behind him. "Did you notice the villagers when we walked in?"

"It was as if they forgot the troll existed after he walked by," I said. "How do you think he did that?'

"I know nothing of the trolls and their magic," he replied as he surveyed his staff, "but I sure wish I had mine back."

"It'll come back," I said, hoping I sounded enthusiastic as I rested my head on his shoulder and yawned. "I'm sure of it."

Chapter Eighteen

Ward

There was no one at the front desk, and the adjacent dining room was similarly empty. The clock on the wall showed a later hour than I'd thought. My confidence in us not only finding a hot meal, but even beds, was dwindling. Cade might have to have his magical breakthrough quicker than when we'd walked through the fae realm. I'd watched him struggle all afternoon to cast the most basic spell, and it didn't make me feel any better about bringing Ayla. The whole point of him coming was so that he'd be an extra layer of protection for her. Now he was just…

Ayla laid her head on his shoulder and closed her eyes, a smile on her face.

With a growl, I turned away. No use torturing myself.

I marched up to the clerk's desk, slamming my hand down on the bell and hoping someone heard me. I waited another few minutes then hit it again. Then again.

"That bell did nothing to hurt you," Elodia said, coming up beside me. "Don't take your frustrations out on it."

"I'm not." I smacked it again so hard that it flew across the counter to the floor. Elodia raised one eyebrow at me, and I grunted. "It's been a long day."

"Sure." She turned and leaned against the counter. "And it doesn't piss you off that Ayla refuses to look at you and is cuddling up with the wizard."

"It doesn't." I shifted my weight. "She can cuddle with whomever she wants."

"Mm."

The curtains behind the desk rustled and a short man with rust-colored skin and white hair appeared. He bent down slowly to pick up his bell and brush the dirt off it.

"Sorry, I was already in bed," he grunted, giving me a cold look. "What can I do for you?"

"Beds." Elodia elbowed me, so I cleared my throat. "I mean, we need beds for our group. Seven of us. And dinner, if you have it."

"I have three rooms," he said. "And dinner is whatever's left of the stew, but I can't promise much. How many bowls?"

I turned behind me to count. "Seven."

"I see only six of you."

I blinked, furrowing my brow at him. "I'm sorry?"

He sighed, a little annoyed. "Three gold for six bowls and three rooms."

"Seven," I insisted, turning to count. Ayla, Cade, Riona, Rutley, the troll, Elodia, and myself. "There are seven of us."

"I count three women, three men, including yourself." He shrugged, his tone growing harsher. "Am I supposed to see another one?"

"I do not require food," Lynton said, appearing beside me.

I turned to the innkeeper, looking for his response, and to my surprise, he looked stricken, like he was having some sort of episode.

The troll swiped the key off the counter and walked up the stairs. As soon as he was gone, the innkeeper softened.

"So..." He stared at the keys, confused. "Suppose I only have two rooms available then. Six bowls?"

My jaw fell open as I looked between the innkeeper and Lynton. "You didn't see that troll just now..."

The innkeeper chuckled. "You must've heard too many fairy tales. There's no such thing as trolls—haven't been seen around these parts in over a thousand years." He handed me the bowls. "If you ask me, you should eat and get some rest before you continue. Seems the mountain air has made you a little loopy."

He disappeared after that, and I just stared at the space he'd left, replaying the scene in my mind. He'd seen Lynton, had looked right at him. Then…just *forgotten* him. Just like the soldier back in Pennlan.

"You saw that too, right?" Elodia asked, beside me.

"I mean, I think I did," I said, picking up the keys and bowls. "Some strange magic floating around this mountain."

"You said it."

I brought the bounty back to the group, who perked up. Even Ayla opened her sleepy eyes and didn't have contempt in them, for once.

"We have two rooms," I announced. "So that means we'll be doubling up. Riona, you, Elodia, and Ayla—"

"I'll room with Cade," Ayla said, standing up quickly and snatching the key out of my hand. "Come on, Cade."

I worked my jaw and watched her disappear up the stairs, Cade offering me an apologetic smile as he followed behind her. That left…

"One room for the four of us," Rutley said with a grimace. "I guess we can cuddle."

"You can cuddle with yourself," Elodia said. "The fae girl can fix things, can't she?"

"I can't use magic either, remember?" she said with a grimace.

I released a groan. "Let's just see what we have to work with, then we'll panic."

⇥ ⇥ ⇥ ⇥

The room was minuscule, with one small bed crammed in the corner. Even if we all slept on the floor, I didn't know if there was space for three of us to stretch out. I glanced at the ceiling, annoyance rising and falling like the tide. Three magical creatures in the group and none of them were any use.

"So who gets the bed?" Elodia asked, grimly.

"We can take turns," Rutley said. "One hour each. I'm sure the troll will have us up early anyway."

There weren't any arguments, so we ventured back downstairs, gathered the bowls, and walked into the small dining area off the main entrance. The stew was only lukewarm, and nearly gone, so we shared what was left. Then we settled around the table and ate in silence.

I stared into the murky depths, biting back my frustration. It was, perhaps, too late to turn around, and I doubted Ayla would be amenable to such a thing. So the only thing to do was try to sleep and soldier on.

Footsteps down the stairwell drew my attention. Cade had come down alone, but I hadn't expected Ayla to make an appearance anyway. His useless staff clicked on the wooden floor as he joined us at the table.

"How is she?" I asked, not meeting his gaze.

"Exhausted. But she won't let you know that," he said.

"And how's…" I gestured to his staff. "That whole magic thing going?"

"I don't understand it at all," he said. "The magic is there, I can feel it. But every time I try to cast, it's like…" He made a noise like rushing water and gestured around his head. "I can't focus."

"What does that matter?" Rutley asked.

"No focus, no magic," he said with an apologetic smile. "I couldn't even conjure a bowl to the room. So here I am."

I made a noise. "There's nothing left. We took the last of it."

"What meager amounts there were," Elodia grumbled.

"You didn't save any for us?" Cade asked, annoyance in his voice.

"I thought you could, you know, magic more," I said, a little guiltily.

"I can try…" He pointed his staff at my half-empty bowl and stared at it intently. His nose twitched, and he jerked as if something were buzzing around his face. But although his staff glowed softly, nothing happened. "Damn it all."

"Well, that sucks," Rutley said. "What are we supposed to do if we encounter something that wants to eat us out here?"

"Use your sword, you dolt," Elodia said. "You still know how to do that, don't you?"

He grunted and returned to his stew.

"I'll keep trying, but...I don't know," Cade said, almost defeated. "I've gotten used to having it at my fingertips." He caught my gaze, a little mirth in his eyes. "What is it about these trips and me losing magic?"

"I don't know, but it really makes things harder," I said. "Considering the four of us get to share one bed."

He made something of a strangled noise. "There's only one in our room, too."

My pulse spiked, and I gripped the wooden bowl harder. "Make sure you..." I stuffed down visions of what he and Ayla might do with one bed. "The troll will probably want us up early. I wouldn't stay up too late."

"I'm not planning on it, but sleeping on the floor..." He made a sound as he looked back toward the stairwell. "And now I have to tell Ayla there's no dinner for her."

With a sigh, I thrust my half-eaten bowl into his hands. "Here, I'm done."

"Are you—"

"She's the one who needs to keep up her strength." I grunted, my stomach protesting. "So make sure she eats all of it."

He rose slowly, nodding. "I'll keep working at it. Maybe it's like the fae realm, and I just need to get used to whatever magic is in this land."

"No." Riona's voice was quiet from the other end of the table. I'd almost forgotten she was there. "The reason you couldn't use it in the fae realm was because that staff wasn't made for you. Your new staff doesn't have that same problem." She lifted her gaze to stare at him. "There's something else happening. Something..." She licked her lips. "Something else keeping it from you."

Cade rubbed his chin thoughtfully. "What is it like when you try to cast?"

"I just can't," she said with a glare.

"Are you—"

"If I could," she snapped, "I wouldn't be sleeping on the floor tonight." She rose and handed me her bowl. "You can have mine. I'm going to take the first shift of sleep. Wake me in an hour or two."

The group remained silent as she ascended the stairs. Elodia was the first to speak. "Why do I get the feeling everyone's pissed at everyone else on this trip?"

I sighed, the back of my head aching. "I'll go talk to her."

⸙ ⸙ ⸙ ⸙

I knocked softly on the door and cracked it open. Riona was a dark blob on the small bed. She'd cast the blankets and pillows on the floor, presumably for us to share, though it wouldn't do much against the cold.

I sat down next to the bed, leaning up against the wooden frame and waited.

"Yes?"

"You okay?"

"Fine." She flipped away from me.

I kept silent, rubbing my hands together and waiting.

"Ward, go to bed."

"I'm just sitting here."

"You're..." She sat up, annoyance clear on her face, even in the dark. "Just stop. Nothing's wrong, other than..." She huffed. "Ayla hates me."

"Ayla doesn't hate you, she just..." I shook my head. "I don't even know what to tell you. She's angry with me, so I don't have any advice."

"Why is she mad at you?"

"Because I had the audacity to care about her," I said, more under my breath than to Riona. "It's probably better that she's mad at me than the alternative."

"Meaning?"

I didn't really feel like elaborating. "Hopefully Cade can reason with her," I said, after a long pause. "They're clearly back to being best friends." I stared at the floor, a chill skittering down my spine. "Though it would be really nice if he could use his magic. I don't like our chances on this journey without a little magical help."

"I think if he could use it, he would," Riona said, very quietly. "He's not about to let Ayla suffer needlessly."

I noted she didn't include herself in that statement, but I didn't want to pry. Riona had always kept her secrets, and usually for good reason. Her heart was always true, though.

"I'm sure everything will be better once we reach the troll kingdom," I said, lying down on the floor and covering myself with the threadbare sheet. "If we don't kill each other before then."

She snorted. "Sleep well, Ward. I missed you."

"Likewise."

Chapter Nineteen

Cade

I walked into the room, but it was dark. Ayla had taken the bed, curled up in a ball and already asleep, so the stew would have to wait. I left it on the bedside table; she would need to eat in the morning before we set off.

I knelt on the bare floor, holding my staff aloft and waving it, intent on breaking through this…whatever was preventing me from doing the simplest spells. As the magic stirred in my bones, a loud rushing echoed between my ears, like I was standing under a waterfall. The sound was deafening, and no matter how much I focused, breathed, bore down, and dug deep, commanding the magic remained firmly out of my grasp.

I released my hold on it, and the sound stopped immediately, replaced by the soft snores coming from the bed. I exhaled and sat on the floor, a chill permeating every inch of me. For a moment, I considered crawling into bed with Ayla, just for warmth, then dismissed it.

I held my staff to my chest. As before, the hum grew louder.

I furrowed my brow. *Concentrate.*

Warmth tickled the bottom of my feet, and I held onto that feeling, using it to concentrate more—to push more. The warmth became a heat that spread up my ankles, soothing the pain. But before it could go farther, that damn interference became deafening, and I lost it again.

Closing my eyes again, I gripped my staff, focusing on how the wood felt in my hand. The hum grew louder, but I dug my nail into my other palm. I took several deep breaths, focusing on the way my staff rose and fell with each one. Magic slipped from me, gliding along the floor and circled Ayla's feet, climbing her calves to her knees—

"C-Cade?" Ayla stirred. "What are you…?"

"Does it feel any better?" I asked.

"Y…yeah, actually, it does." She sat up, rubbing her face. "I meant to wait for you, but I…guess I fell asleep."

"There's stew on the table," I said, sitting up. Again, I dug my nail into my palm, focusing on the bowl as I cast a warming spell on it. Within seconds, it bubbled.

"I could kiss you," Ayla whispered, grabbing the bowl and bringing it to herself. She ate in silence, slurping the food in a very loud, unqueenlike way. But I was just happy I could do something for her.

"It's not much," I said, a little forlornly.

"It's everything," she said, putting down the empty bowl and staring at me in the dark. I thought she might go back to sleep, but instead she drew a sharp breath then another—she was crying.

"Ayla?" I was on my feet in an instant, the ghost of pain in my heels, and I rushed over to sit next to her. "What is it?"

"Nothing."

"Clearly, it's something." I rested my hand on the small of her back. "What's wrong?"

"I just…" She wiped her face hastily. "I just need to cry for a moment, so I don't tomorrow in front of everyone else."

I half-smiled. "What's that mean?"

"I'm not going to show any of them that I'm miserable. Especially *Ward*."

"We're *all* miserable," I said with a small laugh as I pulled her close to me, happiness washing away my exhaustion and misery. Ayla was stubborn to a fault and refused to show weakness to anyone—except me. I was her safe place, even after being separated for six months. My greatest fear was that she would forget me, that she'd be Ward's and I'd be forever relegated to being her friend. Sitting here, holding her like this

—even freezing, sore, and a little hungry—I was happier than I'd been in months.

A soft snore came from her, and I chuckled. With care, I laid her on the bed and covered her with the blanket. She rolled onto her side, murmuring something, then she was still. I leaned over and kissed her temple.

"Good night, Ayla."

>⇥ >⇥ >⇥ >⇥

The next morning came far too quickly, and by the looks of things, nobody had gotten a good night's sleep, save the troll. He was back to marching up the rocky path with aplomb, while the rest of us were still getting our legs underneath us.

"I would kill for a coffee," Rutley whined. "Either of you magic users got it back yet? Want to rustle me a cup?"

I wished I could, but even the thought of conjuring was met with that deafening sound that had plagued me. Riona didn't even respond, the bags under her eyes more pronounced than the night before.

The sky overhead was an ominous gray, and I said a silent prayer that the weather would hold off until we reached our next destination. Ayla's lips were already a pale pink, and with my lack of magic, I wasn't sure I could cast anything to keep her warm.

But she was determined to keep herself from seeming tired. She was surer of her feet now, needing less help from me to climb over the rocks that marked our path. The moment of weakness the night before seemed to have rejuvenated her.

Midday, we crested another large hill, and my heart dropped to my stomach. The mountain was split in two with a precipitous drop between. A small, rickety wooden bridge connected the two sides, and I had a horrible feeling we'd have to cross it.

"What…is that…" Ward said.

"A bridge," Lynton said, not breaking his pace.

"If you can call it that," Elodia muttered, looking at Ward. "Is it safe?"

"I guess we'll find out," Ward muttered.

The six of us watched the troll as he held onto the rope on either side, walking gingerly across the old wood. It didn't bode well that even this seasoned traveler was taking his time, testing each piece of wood before putting his weight on it.

"There has to be another way around," Rutley said, craning his neck. "Maybe we could go down and up—"

I peered over the side, finding a steep cliff that ended in a white-capped river speeding down the mountain. There didn't look to be any easy way down, across, or back up.

"C'mon," Ayla said, lifting her chin. "If Lynton says it's safe—"

She walked toward the bridge with all the confidence I was sure she didn't feel, standing in front of the first step and waiting a moment. She placed one booted foot on the step, and it held.

"See?" She cast a relieved look over her shoulder.

I moved to go next, but Ward held up his hand.

"You stay here, in case we need a magical assist," he said, watching Ayla inch across the bridge.

"I can't—"

"If Ayla goes tumbling, I *assume* you'll figure yourself out and save her," he replied with gritted teeth. "Seeing as you're a wizard."

I swallowed, nodding. Perhaps the presence of my very best friend dying would snap me out of whatever issues I was having.

Ward straightened his shoulders and walked toward the bridge. He took several steps, and the bridge swung dangerously. Ayla released a cry of surprise as she hung onto the sides, freezing in place. I pointed my staff at the bridge, but the noise was so loud I winced and grabbed my head.

"Cade?" Riona said.

I shook my head, gritting my teeth through the pain between my ears, but I couldn't seem to focus. All I could do was watch as the bridge slowly stopped swinging, leaving Ayla and Ward suspended over a raging river below.

"You okay?" Ward called to Ayla.

"I-I think so," she replied, chancing a look over her shoulder. "What do I do?"

"Keep going," he said, tightening his hold on the rope bridge. "I'll stay here until you're across."

Ayla turned, fear on her face as she nodded. But she slid her foot across the next one, then the next, hanging onto the rope for dear life. After an eternity, her feet landed on solid ground and we released a collective sigh of relief.

Ward slowly tested his feet, taking an even longer time than Ayla. When he reached the other side, she looked relieved, saying something to him that I couldn't hear.

"Who's next?" I asked, looking behind. "Riona?"

"I'll go last," she said.

"I'm the heaviest," Rutley said with a sigh. "I'll go last. That way if it breaks, at least we'll all be across."

"It won't break," Elodia said, but she gave him a nervous look as she prepared to cross. She was lighter than Ward, so she was able to move faster and got to safety quickly.

"You next," Riona said.

"You next," I replied, pushing her forward.

She was the smallest of us, and lightly walked across without much trouble. I glanced at Rutley, and he gestured for me to go. With a heavy breath, I set one foot on the bridge, realizing just how rickety it really was. The wind whipped across the ravine, and I had to slump a little to hold onto the rope with one hand. My staff was glued to my other hand, testing the weight of the bridge before I did. It shouldn't fall out of my hand as my old staff had, but I didn't want to test that theory.

I didn't breathe until my staff landed on hard rock and the rest of me followed. I pressed my hand to my chest as Ayla came up beside me, relief clear in her eyes. But it was short-lived as we turned to watch the last, and heaviest, among us take his turn.

Rutley took his first step and gave us a thumbs-up. The bridge swayed more than with any of us, buckling under his weight. He moved gingerly, testing the wood. The tension in my chest eased slowly as he made it the first quarter, then half, then—

A loud crack echoed over the ravine as his foot went through the bridge. Ayla released a scream, covering her mouth, and Ward called Rutley's name. For a brief, terrifying moment, half of Rutley's body dangled over the raging river, his grip on the rope the only thing keeping him from falling.

"Cade, do something!" Ayla cried.

I stepped forward, but as soon as I tried to cast, the sound was back, so loud that I hissed in pain, grabbing my head. "I...I can't..."

"What do you mean, you can't?" Ward said, panic in his voice. "Cade, he's going to fall—"

But before our eyes, Rutley grunted and pulled himself up back onto the bridge. He walked quicker than before, but still cautiously. Then with a heave, he landed in a pile on the other side, panting.

"Don't scare us like that," Ward said, holding his hand out to help Rutley stand.

Rutley waved it away, placing his hand on his chest. "I'll try not to, but no promises." Ayla laughed as he sat up and got to his feet slowly. "Thanks, wizard."

I frowned. "For what?"

"Pushing me back up," he said. "You...did, didn't you?"

I shook my head. "I don't think so. My magic is still..." In fact, I was sure I hadn't.

"I dunno, maybe the troll did something," he said. "Because I don't know how I got myself back up."

"We're stronger than we think when our lives are in danger," Riona said, standing a ways up the path. "And our guide is leaving us, so we'd better get moving."

CHAPTER TWENTY

RIONA

I kept my ears open, making sure no one suspected I'd helped Rutley on the bridge. The consensus as the day wore on seemed to be that Cade had powered through his mental block. Even he seemed convinced of it.

I kept replaying the scene in my mind, drowning in silent guilt and disgust at myself. Whatever block plagued Cade didn't bother me. Quite the opposite, in fact. There seemed to be something in the air that called to the power within me. Not the magic I was born with, but the other, more deadly power *he* had somehow tapped into. The magic that manifested not as butterflies but raw energy.

The longer I spent on this mountain, the wider the separation between the two kinds of magic became, until they felt like distinct beings living inside my body. It was the raw magic that had saved Rutley, breaking free from the tight grip I held on it to push him back up to safety.

This magic, though, was tainted. Wrong. Sullied by *his* fingerprints. Using it, even unbidden, made me want to hurl myself over the edge of the cliff.

My inner angst went unnoticed. The rest of the group seemed to have bonded over the near-death experience, and I was grateful Rutley had captured their attention. He walked between Cade and Ayla, regaling them with tales of his exploits in the southern town where he grew up. Elodia and Ward were behind them, Ward wearing a soft smile and

Elodia, who'd come from the same town, offering her rebuttal to Rutley's stories.

Lynton showed no outward signs that he was listening or cared that one of us had nearly fallen into the ravine. If Rutley had perished, the troll undoubtably wouldn't have blinked an eye. He was single-minded in his task, and that was to bring myself and Ayla to the troll kingdom. The other travelers be damned.

I watched him with curiosity whenever we rested for a few minutes. Did he suspect I was hiding the truth? He was impossible to read.

I lengthened the distance between myself and the troll so I could remain closer to the group to overhear their conversation. The excitement from the morning had waned, and there was silence, save the sounds of labored breathing from the uphill climb. This stretch of land was steep, and even I was finding it difficult to stretch over the large rocks lining our path.

"Hurry up," Lynton barked as the distance between him and the tail end of the group grew.

"What did you expect?" I asked, breaking my silence as I came up beside him. "Ayla is a queen. She's not meant for travel like this."

"I expected you would help your sister," he said, leveling his gaze at me.

I swallowed. "I'm having trouble with magic, same as Cade."

He arched one pale eyebrow. "Are you?"

"Shouldn't I be?" I replied, daring him to spill his secrets. "If you have some information to share, by all means, please share it."

But he merely lifted a shoulder and said nothing.

I cursed him silently, annoyed he hadn't taken my bait.

The group was impervious to the troll's complaints. Ayla, in particular, looked like she was going to cry. As annoyed as I was at her, my heart broke at the thought of her being in pain.

The raw magic skittered in my bones, promising that if I just let it out, it could solve all the problems. Heal Ayla, cast a warming spell over the group. Maybe even conjure one of those portals to cut our trip significantly.

But that voice was laced with poison, sounding too much like *him* for me to trust it.

"Hurry up," Lynton barked again.

"We need to slow down," Ward called. "We can't keep this pace up."

"We cannot afford to," Lynton said. "We're behind as it is. At this rate, it'll be well past dark when we reach the village."

"We'll get there when we get there," Elodia said. "There's no use pushing us faster. We'll double up on rooms again, if that's the case."

"It's not the lack of lodging that concerns me," he said, finally stopping to stare down at all of us. "There are creatures in the mountain that hunt at night. A group as loud as this…" He pursed his lips for a moment. "It would be best if we were inside the village when night falls."

>⟶ >⟶ >⟶ >⟶

But night came too quickly, and even though the warmth from the sun was meager, it was sorely missed when the light disappeared. In the dark, Cade's muttered frustrations were punctuated by the sound of creatures rustling from their daytime lairs. Ward and Rutley kept ready hands on their swords, and Elodia kept her arrow nocked. Ayla's hand was firmly planted in Cade's, her other one grasping her cloak tighter around herself.

Every so often, her and Cade's faces would flicker to life in a spark of gold light, but it would go out as soon as it appeared, Cade would release another growl of frustration, and the cycle would renew again.

"Quit messing with that," Lynton said from somewhere in the distance. "You'll attract more trouble."

"We'll break our necks first," came the annoyed response from Rutley.

"Your necks will be the least of your worries."

His footfalls stopped ahead of me, the shadowy figure going stick-straight. My breath came in small, visible puffs as I waited and listened for whatever had tipped him off. The rest of the party felt the change in energy, stopping where they stood and looking around.

"What do you—"

"Ssh," Ward barked, quieting Ayla.

"Don't shush—"

"Ssh," Cade said, as the tip of his staff lit up again, illuminating her wide, frightened eyes.

After a tense few moments, Lynton finally shifted. "Nothing. Let's —"

I saw movement out of the corner of my eye and cried a warning as it descended on Elodia. She turned quickly, releasing the arrow, but it sailed by the creature into the dark sky. Ward rushed forward, disappearing into shadow as he wrestled the darkness from her.

"Look out!"

Ayla's scream came from behind, and I spun around as two more shadows descended from the trees. Cade's staff flickered gold, illuminating furry beasts—wolves the size of small horses. The light was a little more consistent now, glinting off the sharp, white teeth and long snouts as they inched closer to the pair.

Magic hummed beneath my skin, begging to be let free, to flood the night with the energy that had been building for days. But I could hear his voice, his laugh, the feel of his hands on my magic, forcing me to move, to hurt, to *kill*...

My stomach came to my throat, and it became hard to breathe. I took a step back, pressing my hand to my chest and shaking my head to clear the fear. But the danger before us was nothing compared to the monster in my head.

Panic reasoned with sanity in my mind. Ward and the others were trained soldiers, they could fight off some monsters. Cade would figure it out. The troll might even lift a finger. They didn't need me to step in. They didn't need me at all.

Something landed hard against my back, and I fell forward, the air pushed from my lungs. A drop of drool splattered on my neck as claws dug into the ground around me. The creature pulled its paw, wrenching me onto my stomach as its nails ripped my shoulder. In the darkness, golden eyes stared down at me, teeth sharp as knives growing closer and closer as it moved in for the kill.

Now's the time, Riona.

The magic broke free from within me, knocking the creature off me and slamming it into something hard. It released a pathetic whimper of pain, and the shadow didn't move. I turned, my heartbeat throbbing in my chest as I searched the darkness for the others. I shuddered, the pain fading as my skin knitted itself back together until it was nothing but a faint memory.

I sucked in a breath, the sounds of the struggle coming back to me again. With a clearer head, the magic was back under my control, stuffed back inside the box it had escaped from. But it had tasted freedom, and it wasn't content to stay put. It wanted to help.

In my mind's eye, tendrils of magic escaped from my body, helping to guide Ward's sword, Elodia's arrow, Rutley's fists. And it found Cade's staff, twirling up it with an intimacy that felt enticing and wrong at the same time, breaking through the spell keeping him unfocused and helping him tap into the river of power in his veins.

Suddenly, the space was bathed in golden light. Cade's face was a mask of pain and his grip on his staff was vise-like. But the brightness seemed to scare off the wolves, who backed away and ran for the safety of darkness. Three were dead—including the one I'd faced off with.

"Are they gone?" Ayla asked, her fingers white on Cade's cloak.

"I think so," Ward said, wiping his bloody sword on the ground. "Are you all right, Ayla?"

She nodded, but her pale face told a different story.

"Riona. Where's—" Ward spun, stopping when his gaze landed on me. Relief shone there then a little confusion as he spotted the wolf behind me. "Did you… Did you kill that one?"

"No," I said, shaking my head as my tongue burned. "It was dark. I don't know who did. But thanks—it was about to eat me, I think."

"And that is why I wanted to get to the village," Lynton said, breaking through the silence. He stood far away from us, clearly above the fray. He didn't appear to have a hair out of place.

"Sorry that we're human," Ward growled at him, his sword still dripping with blood. "Cade, keep that light on. If we're going to get eaten, I'd like to see it coming."

But the light disappeared, followed by the usual curse. "Let me try again."

This time, the magic beneath my skin wouldn't stay put, racing from my fingertips to Cade's staff and illuminating it with a bright gold.

"There." He smiled, seemingly sure it was his magic doing the work. "At least I have that."

"Good," Ward said with a firm nod. "Keep your eyes open, and let's get the hell off this path as quickly as we can."

Chapter Twenty-One

Ayla

I'd tasted fear before. When Riona had been under Eoghan's control, and he'd told her to kill me, I'd thought my life was over. I'd been weaponless, powerless, weak. Just as I'd been when the wolves attacked—as I'd been all day. I'd never been so grateful that Ward had insisted on coming, though my pride wasn't ready to admit that to him yet. But the watery tea rippled in my trembling hands, and I fought back tears for the second night in a row. Ward was speaking with the innkeeper in hushed tones, though every so often, he would turn to look at me with concern in his eyes. I'd quickly hide behind the mug, hoping he didn't see just how affected I was.

We arrived in the village perhaps half an hour after the wolf attack. Ward negotiated lodging for the night. Elodia and Rutley sat next to the fire, bandaging their wounds and commiserating over their pain. But as deep as the gashes had looked in the dark, they weren't that bad now. At least, not life-threatening.

"Maybe the teeth just looked longer," Elodia said, wincing as Rutley sewed up the bloody rip. "Because I was pretty sure it about tore my arm off."

Rutley finished with Elodia then sat so she could mend the wound in his leg. I couldn't help but marvel at him. He'd almost died *twice* today, both times saved by a flash of Cade's magic that had broken through whatever curse lay on this mountain. And yet, he seemed unbothered, like it was another day in the life. What I wouldn't give to be so nonchalant about danger and almost-certain death.

I tore my gaze away. Cade stood in the corner, gripping his staff and furrowing his brow as he muttered to himself. He was staring intently at Elodia and Rutley, perhaps attempting to cast a healing spell on them. But there was nothing from his staff, not even a faint glow. He cursed softly, rubbing his head and concentrating again.

"Well, there are a few more rooms than last night," Ward said, walking over with a handful of keys. "We—"

Lynton swiped a key from his hand and disappeared up the stairs without a word.

"Have three rooms this time," Ward finished, without missing a beat. "Ayla, I assume you—"

"Want to room with Cade," I said, though there wasn't much heat in it.

"Right. So Elodia, Riona, you get this one. Rutley and me in the other." He looked exhausted, a little defeated. "Try to get some rest."

"Boss, there's something weird going on," Rutley said, glancing up the stairs where Lynton had gone. "The wizard's magic showing up and disappearing? What's that about?"

"Maybe the troll decided to cut us a break," Ward said, sinking into the chair across from us. "Release Cade from whatever spell he's under so we weren't wolf food."

"Troll magic doesn't work like that," Cade said. "The Erlking said it isn't like fae magic. It's based in rock and ore, not aether."

"Except we have no clue what their magic is capable of now," Riona piped up from the corner. "I think it's very plausible that Lynton decided it was better for Cade to have his magic."

"And yours?" Ward asked. "Any improvements?"

"None," she said, stiffly walking over and taking the key from him. "I was as helpless as the rest of you."

"We weren't helpless," Rutley muttered.

"You know what I mean," she said, catching my gaze for a moment.

There was something there…something that made me feel she wasn't telling the whole truth. But it was gone in a flash. "Look, I'm sure all the mysteries will be solved as soon as we get to Gwyllion. The sooner we sleep, the sooner we get there."

>→ >→ >→ >→

I felt like I'd barely laid my head on the pillow before there was a rude rapping at the door. The rest of the group was similarly groggy, Cade glaring daggers at the troll, who seemed impervious to the annoyance. He merely led us out into another freezing dark morning and on our way.

The path had grown much more treacherous overnight, with a thin layer of ice covering everything. We had to move even slower, being surer of our footing before applying weight. Lynton only seemed to notice when he'd have to stop at the top of a large hill and wait for the rest of us to follow.

We had fallen into something of a pattern, with Riona following close behind Lynton, Ward, Elodia, and Rutley in the middle, and Cade and me in the rear. Ward and his soldiers were in deep conversation, Ward's hand resting on the hilt of his sword most of the morning. When we stopped to rest, I found out what they'd been talking about.

Ward walked up to me, a grim look on his face. I tilted my chin up to him, expecting a fight. Instead, he pulled a small knife from beneath his cloak and handed it to me, hilt-first.

"What's this?" I asked.

"No one on this trip should be without a weapon," he said, his gaze darting to me as if expecting me to strike him.

"I have a weapon," I said, my voice quiet. "The stone."

His lip twitched. "It didn't seem to help last night."

It was almost a dare, a question of why I hadn't used it to help save us. I snatched the knife out of his hand and pulled it from its sheath. "I don't know how to use it."

"Pointy end goes into the other person," he said, his face serious.

"I know that," I said with a scowl.

"It would make me sleep better at night if you had it," he replied. "Especially once we get into the troll kingdom."

I rolled my eyes. "They aren't our enemy."

"We don't know who or what is waiting for us there," he said. "And we still have two more days on the mountain. I just…"

"He's right," Cade said beside me. "Until I figure out how to use magic again, you need all the help you can get."

I closed my fingers around the hilt.

"So…" Ward cleared his throat and looked furtively at Cade. "Any better?"

"If you're asking if I figured out why I suddenly had a moment of clarity, the answer is no," Cade said. "And if you're asking if I've had one since, the answer is also no."

Ward motioned toward his two soldiers. "Rutley and Elodia are practically healed. Not even a scratch on them. And considering… Well, it wasn't a paper cut. Humans don't heal that fast."

Cade furrowed his brow, looking at his staff. "I mean, I don't *think* it's me."

"Can't you smell the magic?" Ward asked. "Like you did in the fae realm?"

"I can, but it didn't… I guess I was too busy trying to fight for our lives to remember," he said with something of a defeated sigh. "Sorry. Next time, I'll try to remember to take a long sniff."

"Has anyone thought of just asking Lynton if he released the curse?" I asked mildly. "He is part of our traveling group, after all."

"Be my guest," Ward said. "Since you're on such friendly terms with him."

I rose and adjusted my cloak over my clothes, giving him a haughty look. "Fine. I will."

I crossed the small clearing to where Lynton was seated on a large boulder, staring off into the distance, smoking a pipe that gave off purple smoke. He looked up at me with those golden eyes, his face unreadable.

"Are we ready to continue?" he asked.

"N-no," I said, clearing my throat. "I just wondered if you had an explanation for yesterday's…events."

"Which ones would those be?"

"The wolves, in particular," I said, my pulse quickening. "And Cade regaining the use of his magic."

The troll took a long drag of his pipe. "What sort of explanation are you looking for?"

"The kind where you tell me if you happened to release him from whatever curse is on him for a moment," I said. "And if you did, can you release him again?"

Again, he inhaled deeply, his thin cheeks puffing as he took his time. The silence dragged out between us, but I held my tongue, feeling that if I spoke again, I would lose some sort of upper hand I wasn't even sure I had.

"No." Smoke billowed out of his lips as he spoke. "What you have referred to as a curse on your wizard is merely the result of him not being invited, and the magic of the mountain doing its best to deter him from continuing." He put down his pipe. "In my experience, most magical users would be too nervous at the thought of losing their magic to continue. But your wizard is…stubborn."

"He doesn't need his magic in order to be useful," I said, though that wasn't wholly true. "And you didn't answer my question."

"Which is?"

I cleared my throat. "Why did he suddenly regain the ability to use magic last night? And how can he get it back permanently?"

"I have no clue," he said. "Perhaps he managed to briefly overpower the troll magic, which should be impossible, considering the source of it. Or maybe *someone else* helped him along."

"Someone—" I began, but Riona piped up behind me.

"What do you mean, the source of it?" she asked, coming to stand a distance from me. "What is the source of the magic on this mountain?"

He surveyed her for a long time, and I was sure he was going to ignore her question entirely. "Our piece of the *seod croí*, of course."

I blinked. "What does that mean?"

"If you and your party would continue, I will tell you," he said. "Because the day is getting away from us."

We packed our things quickly and set off. This time, I was right behind Lynton. I waited at least ten minutes before prompting him again.

"At the time the *seod croí* was split, trolls did not possess the sort of magic that would allow us to do much more than mine for treasures in the earth," he said, his voice soft. "In taking our piece, we hoped we might unlock its powers and imbue our race with something a bit more…" He turned his head to look beyond me, at Riona. "Like our cousins."

"Did you succeed?"

He cleared his throat. "I'm not well-versed on this subject. But there is some magic afoot in the mountain."

"So…" Ward said from right behind me. "Those weren't regular wolves last night, were they?"

He shook his head. "No, and there are many more creatures like it around, hence my desire to get to the next town quickly."

"Is that why no one remembers who you are?" Elodia asked. "Because of this magic on the mountain?"

"We have taken great pains to hide ourselves from those who would take the stone."

Ward scoffed. "So if the wolves have turned into magical beasts, why not the humans?"

"They have been allowed to settle here. Their presence benefits us."

"And the wolves don't?" Ward pressed. "What else is on this mountain?"

"I hope you never find out," he said. "The walk is about to get much more dangerous, so I suggest you save your breath."

Chapter Twenty-Two

Ward

The more I heard from the troll, the less I believed him. Perhaps I just had a sixth sense for treachery among magical creatures, but something was off. And unlike when I had the same feeling about Riona, I didn't sense that this troll had our best interests at heart.

This was the third full day, and if the troll was to be believed, we would reach the entrance to Gwyllion tomorrow. It was hard to believe, but I would've rather stayed on the mountain, even with the frigid temperatures. Once we crossed the threshold into troll country, we would be in enemy territory, and I liked my chances better in the elements.

As predicted, our journey became rockier and more difficult—especially as a light dusting of snow fell, causing us to slip and slide across an increasingly narrow path. Since Cade could do nothing to keep our cloaks dry, we had to endure the wetness seeping down to our skin. I kept a close watch on Ayla, though she rebuffed any questions from Elodia on how she was doing.

What started out as a thin layer accumulated, and my boots began sinking into the snow as we climbed. My hands were numb, and my toes frozen in my wet socks. Ayla's cheeks were bright red, her lips a little pale as her teeth chattered.

"How much longer until the next village?" I asked the troll.

"We should reach it before nightfall," he said without turning.

"We'll freeze to death before then."

"Just keep walking," Rutley said, blowing into his hands. "Just keep walking."

The wind had picked up, and gentle snowfall was now inching toward blizzard. We wouldn't last long in those conditions, but I couldn't see an alternative. The path had grown quite narrow now as we circled the mountain, and there wasn't much keeping the wind from buffeting us.

"Keep your eyes peeled for a cave," I told Elodia and Rutley. "We have to stop sometime."

I dropped back to walk closer to Ayla, whose gaze was steadfastly on the ground. Cade walked between her and the edge, blocking some of the blowing snow, but it wasn't helping that much.

"Now might be a good time to have that magical breakthrough," I said, my voice carrying over the wind.

"I'm starting to doubt the theory that it was the troll who got me past it," he said, his teeth chattering.

"Then who could it have been?" I asked, rubbing my hands together. "And can they hurry it up and give us some heat?"

He shrugged, staring ahead with a shake of his head. "Maybe we'll find shelter soon." He turned to Ayla. "How are you doing?"

"Fine," she said through clenched teeth.

But she was far from fine. Her face was bright red, and her hands were turning white as they gripped her wet cloak around her. She wasn't going to last much longer in these conditions, especially as they continued to worsen.

I shrugged off my cloak and handed it to her. "Here. You need this more than I do."

"No, I don't," she said, fire in her eyes as she rebuffed me. "I'm fine."

"Ayla—"

"Don't coddle me," she snapped.

"I'm not *coddling* you," I snapped back, the cold and my exhaustion finally breaking through my temper. "I'm trying to make sure you don't die out here."

"I won't die."

"Won't you?" I grabbed her hands, pulling them in front of her eyes to look at them. "You're getting frostbite." I began to pull my gloves off when she stuffed her hands into her cloak.

"Am not."

"Ayla," Cade began, but I shot him a dirty look.

"Can you give us a minute?" I barked. "Just one."

He seemed like he'd rather have stayed, but he kept pressing on.

"What?" Ayla snapped, moving from leg to leg. "Make it quick."

"Look, I don't know what I've done to make you mad, or if you still think I'm trying to control you like Eoghan did. But we are too far into this mess to turn around, so the only thing that matters is that I get you to the troll kingdom in one piece. So all I ask is that you just *cooperate* a little more so I can do that to the best of my ability."

She softened for just a moment, and I thought I might've gotten through to her. But a distant rumbling drew my attention upward. It sounded almost like thunder.

"What's that?" Ayla asked, squinting into the wind.

There was a cry from the group ahead that sounded like Lynton. Cold slipped down my stomach as the sound became louder, like something rushing toward us. I yanked Ayla forward to find the rest of the group, but the ground had started shaking, making the already difficult walk even more so.

"Ward, slow down—"

"No time!" I called, pulling her to me and throwing her over my shoulder.

I ran toward the group as the rumbling grew to a roar. I didn't know why—they were as exposed as we were. Luckily, the wind seemed to be at my back, pushing me to run faster.

Lynton was kneeling on the path, snow covering the hood of his cloak and matching the white of his hair. As we came within a few feet of him, the ground shimmered, like it was made of liquid. It splashed to one side then the other, like wine being swirled in a glass, until it crashed over our heads and met the other side—solidifying immediately into a rock tunnel.

"Wha—"

A deafening boom echoed through the tunnel, and I winced as my ears rang. The spot where Ayla and I'd been standing was now a wall of moving white snow. I watched it, mesmerized, my arm tight around my queen as I waited for the chaos to end.

"Put me down," Ayla said, elbowing me in the back of the head.

I gently placed her on the ground, making sure to keep a hand on her arm in case I needed to move her again. Her breath came in short puffs as she stared over my shoulder.

"What happened?" she whispered, her hand falling on top of mine.

"Avalanche," Lynton said. "We will give the snow time to settle before continuing."

"That's…all you have to say?" Elodia asked, gesturing to the tunnel. "After you just created this…this thing? What was that anyway?"

"Troll magic," Cade replied, his eyes wide as he touched the wall. "It was magnificent."

"Why is this the first we're seeing of it?" Rutley asked, a scowl on his face. "You could've made a better bridge a few days ago, eh?"

"Or made the mountain easier to climb?" Elodia asked.

"Or—"

"I use magic when it's necessary," Lynton replied, as if that were an answer. "Until now, it hasn't been necessary."

I could've begged to differ, considering how many times we'd collectively been in danger. Even if he could've used his magic to carry Ayla, it might've made this journey easier. I opened my mouth to add to the chorus, but Ayla tugged my hand and shook her head.

"Leave it be. He did just save our lives," she said, looking behind her at the wall of snow. "And hopefully, he's our way out of here."

>–» >–» >–» >–»

The minutes wore on, and I kept having to remind myself that despite his not lifting a finger to help until now, it didn't appear Lynton wanted us dead. But he didn't seem in any great hurry to get us out of the tunnel either. He was content to sit on the ground cross-legged, leaning up against the wall.

"What's he waiting for?" Riona asked, coming up next to me.

"No clue," I replied. "Are you okay?"

She nodded, glancing over to where Ayla and Cade were sitting. "That was a close call though. Why were you two so far from the group?"

"Trying to get your sister to listen to reason," I replied.

"How'd that work?"

I honestly wasn't sure.

Lynton drew everyone's attention as he rose to his feet. "The sun has set. We will sleep here tonight and continue to Gwyllion in the morning."

"Sleep…here?" Ayla blanched. "In this cave?"

"We'll freeze to death," Cade said. "And starve."

"You will survive the night," Lynton replied, walking to the wall of the cave. He put his hands on the rock, and it rippled again. A spot on the ceiling swirled, as if it were water going down a drain, except it was swirling upward. A little snow fell through the open hole, but a rush of fresh air came into the cave.

He kept his hands on the side of the cave, closing his eyes as he concentrated. Magic throbbed in the veins of the rock as it sped from his fingertips.

Cade took a step forward. "What are you—"

"Hush. I need to concentrate."

I crossed my arms over my chest, growing more irked by the moment by this new display of magic, but withholding judgment until I saw what the outcome was.

Directly beneath the hole in the ceiling, four pieces of firewood appeared, as if birthed by the floor itself. Ayla squeaked with surprise, and

Cade was on his feet in an instant.

"You can summon things?" he bellowed.

"Certain things," he said. "I'm unable to make a fire. I assume one of you can handle that."

Elodia was the first to move, pulling her flint from her pocket and casting the troll a dirty look as she set to work on it. "I need kindling, too. Not just logs. Haven't you ever made a fire before?"

"It's been a long time." He put his hands on the wall again and sent the magic in search of it.

"So…why can't he bring us dinner, too?" I muttered as small twigs appeared beneath the four logs. The rest of the group seemed to have the same thought, watching the troll with wary, hungry eyes. Everyone except Ayla, who was bound and determined to keep a positive attitude.

Riona exhaled softly as Elodia got the fire going, and within minutes, it was a nice size. The annoyance at the troll was gone, in favor of relief as the group crowded the fire to warm their frozen fingers and toes. I kept to the side, letting the others get their fill, as I watched the troll. He'd retreated to the back of the cave, wrapped his cloak around himself, and closed his eyes.

"Nobody has any other magical tricks up their sleeve, do they?" Rutley asked, glancing around. "Your Majesty?"

Ayla jumped, as if the question were accusatory. "What do you mean by that?"

"Nothing," he said, averting his gaze. "Just trying to make light of the situation."

"O-oh." She wore a weak smile. "Very funny."

But it didn't escape my notice that she clutched the stone around her neck. Curious.

One-by-one, the group peeled away from the fire to find a soft place to sleep for the night until it was just Cade and Ayla. He yawned and asked if she was ready, and she shook her head, holding her fingers to the fire. He caught my gaze and nodded.

"You'll take first shift?" he said with a small smirk.

I snorted, remembering the nights when we had to watch each other in the fae realm. "Sure. Get some sleep."

"Don't stay up too late," Cade said to Ayla.

She didn't meet my gaze as I sat down next to her, finally breathing in the warmth of the fire. It felt much warmer than it should've, but that was probably because I'd been freezing my butt off for five days. I rubbed my numb hands together and blew into them.

"Are you all right?" Ayla asked softly.

"Me? Never better." I shifted. "You?"

She didn't respond right away. "You… You saved my life today."

"It's my job." I'd almost forgotten about throwing her over my shoulder. "Besides that, I'm sure the troll's magic would've reached you. After all, you're the most important person on this trip." I snorted. "The rest of us? Not so sure."

She pulled the stone from beneath her dress. "Am I just a job to you?"

I released a breath, warmth creeping up my toes from the fire. "You know that's not true."

"Do I?" She rubbed her hands together. "It seems like…ever since you got this promotion—"

"I haven't gotten it yet."

"Well, since you were *told* about it…" She finally met my gaze. "You've been different. Overbearing. Demanding. Overprotective."

"I haven't changed a thing," I said. "This is who I am when my monarch is in constant danger. An anxious mess who's apparently a glutton for punishment." I turned to her, seeing a little hurt on her face, and I found myself reaching for her hand and squeezing it. "It's because I care so much about you that I'm so cautious."

She looked at me, her already large eyes going wider. "You care about me?"

"Of course I do. I didn't take nearly the same amount of caution with Cade," I said with a smile. "You can ask him how I treated him during the first leg of our trip."

She returned the squeeze. "I may just do that. Tomorrow, though."

"Get some rest," I said, a little sad when she released my hand. "Tomorrow, we reach the troll kingdom. We should be ready for anything."

Chapter Twenty-Three

Cade

I drifted in and out of sleep, waking when Ayla settled beside me then falling back into dreamless slumber. Every so often, I'd rouse to check on Ward and the fire, both still burning bright. Finally, I woke up enough to realize that those four logs had been burning an *awfully* long time—more than they should have. Something magical was going on.

I sat up and found the troll on the other side of the cave, leaning against the wall. He at least looked to be asleep, with his mouth slightly parted and a drop of drool falling out of it. The rest of the group was similarly sound asleep, including Riona.

"How long have those logs been burning?" I asked Ward.

He shrugged. "Longer than I would've thought. What do you think?"

Another look at the troll. Still asleep. "I'm out of my depth. I've never seen magic like what the troll cast to make this cave." I tilted my head upward. "Clíodhna says I can do pretty much anything, but I doubt I would've been able to turn rock into liquid like he did."

Ward rubbed his face. "Would've been nice if he'd helped at literally *any* point in this trip. It's clear he was holding out on us."

"Maybe," I said. "Maybe not. The Erlking told me that the trolls were…well, they weren't ever anything to be concerned with. Lesser fae, basically. Dangerous when provoked, but against the *daoine maithe* and *sidheog* and the like, they couldn't hold a candle. Perhaps gathering kindling is as much as they can do." I ran my hand along the ground, feeling the grooves of the stone that the magic had traveled through. "I'm not sure how he managed to pull wood through the rock, though."

"I'm sure he'll *absolutely* be willing to chat with you about it tomorrow," Ward said with a yawn. "If you're up, I'm going to hit the hay."

"Sure," I said, a little distractedly.

Ward lay back where he sat and was out in moments, but I kept watching the troll, waiting for him to wake up and cast more magic. It was the first time I'd seen him so vulnerable, which was odd in and of itself. He'd been nothing but cagey, and it was growing harder to justify his behavior the longer we spent with him. But at the end of the day, he had saved us, and managed to get a fire to keep us all warm. So perhaps everything would be answered in due time.

I poked the log with the end of my staff then realized…the logs weren't actually on fire. The flames were sitting *on top* of them, like there was glass between the two. I leaned in closer, sensing the warmth, bringing my hands close to the flame to make sure it was real. It was. But it wasn't burning a thing.

Again, I looked at the troll, but he could've cast a long-lasting spell. After all, I didn't know much about troll magic. Anything was possible.

I turned to the other side, searching for the figure of the only other magical user in the group. From where I'd been before, I couldn't see her clearly, but now I could. And based on the tension in her shoulders, she was awake. I picked up my staff and used it in the only way I could, to poke her in the back of the calf.

She jumped and turned, her eyes wide with concern as she stared at me. "What?"

"Come here."

"Why?"

I glared at her. "Come. Here."

She scowled and got to her feet, walking over and sitting down. "We don't actually need to sit here and watch the fire, by the way. You can go to sleep."

"I'm aware," I said, keeping my voice low so no one could hear us. "Because *you're* the one keeping it lit, aren't you?"

"The troll's doing it."

But for the first time, I noticed the way her tongue moved around her mouth after she spoke. Like it was uncomfortable. Like something tasted bitter in her mouth. A lie.

"You can't fool me," I said. "You have your magic, don't you?"

I expected her to lie again, so I could confirm that little quirk in her mouth. But instead, she just sank lower and sighed heavily. "Don't tell anyone. Especially Ayla."

"Why in the world would you lie about something like this?" I asked. "And why wouldn't you help?"

"It's…" She shook her head. "It's hard to explain." She went still, staring at the fire as I waited for more, but it seemed I'd have to drag it out of her.

"You've been acting strange since before we left the fae realm," I said. "You wouldn't lift a finger to fight Aldrick."

"It wouldn't have mattered if I did."

"Clearly, it did," I said. "As you blew him into next week."

She winced. "I don't know… I don't know how I did that."

"You got out of your own head," I said, sitting back on my hands. "That's my problem, usually."

She grew quiet again, rubbing her hands together with a distant look—the exact one Ayla wore when she was trying to hide something from me. They were too much alike for their own good.

"Riona."

"What?"

I elbowed her gently. "I'm not your enemy."

"It's not that." Again, she grew still, but this time it appeared she was trying to come up with the right words. "I don't know if you'd understand."

"I bet I could."

"I don't know if *anyone* could understand."

"I'm sure I could try," I said, nudging her. "C'mon."

"Since…since six months ago," she began quietly, "my magic hasn't really…felt like my own."

I blinked. "What does that mean?"

"Ever since…" She swallowed, and based on the haunted look in her eye, I could fill in the blanks. "Using magic feels like…feels like *he's* still in my head." She took a shaky breath. "And since we've been on this mountain, *that* part of me has grown stronger. Like something's pulling it to the forefront. Like it's not really in my control." She finally met my gaze. "I'm afraid, if I give in like it wants me to, if I let it just…do whatever it wants…then he'll…" She couldn't finish.

"Riona." I didn't know what to say. "It's not possible for Eoghan to still have control over you. The spell was broken. He's been banished to who knows where. You're safe from him."

"Are you sure?" She lifted her gaze to meet mine. "Are you *absolutely sure* this voice in my head isn't him?"

"We're sitting in a cave the troll made from liquid rock," I said with a small chuckle. "What I know about magic could…"

"What you know of magic could fill a piece of paper."

Eoghan had cast that aspersion so cruelly, as if he hadn't been the one to teach me. But in hindsight, every lesson, every spell, every moment had been in pursuit of sending me on that quest to retrieve the stone. And he hadn't even been sure I would've been more successful than any of Pennlan's soldiers who'd died trying to retrieve it—he just didn't want to risk his own neck. So why not find a young wizard from a nation far away, drag him away from everything he knew, and mold him into exactly what he needed?

I glanced at her. Perhaps it wasn't out of the realm of possibility that Eoghan was in her brain. But more likely she was just reeling from a trauma that hadn't yet healed.

"I can't... I can't let it out, not until I know for sure. I need..." She licked her lips. "The last thing I want is to make things worse. To be under his control...to hurt Ayla, or you, or Ward, or anyone on this trip. So until I'm sure what this is...I'm going to pretend like I'm struggling the same as you. That way no one asks me to do anything, and I just keep my head down until we reach the troll kingdom."

"But you have let it out, haven't you?" I asked. "You saved Rutley." I paused, furrowing my brow. "And you healed their wounds. You're the one who put magic in my staff to light our way, right?"

"Yes. But... It wasn't me."

I still didn't quite understand what she was talking about. I'd never heard of anyone having two sets of magic within them. But she seemed convinced of it.

"You wanted to help, though, didn't you?"

She shook her head, clutching her stomach like she was going to vomit. "The thing is...it's come out. All day today... Keeping us warm and on the path." She nodded to my feet. "Your feet from blistering. Frostbite from setting in. I've been *bargaining* with it all day. It wants to do more, but I won't let it." She gestured to the fire. "Like this..."

In an instant, the fire disappeared. Then she heaved a breath, and it came back, warming my skin with even more gusto than before.

"It's hard to explain," she said, wrapping her arms around her knees. "But it's almost like...like a wild animal that got out of my grasp. And it took everything I had to pull it back into its cage again."

This was beyond my scope of knowledge, and yet, I felt compelled to help her. It wasn't just the Erlking's edict to keep her safe, either. There was something about the way she watched the fire, about the way she seemed on the edge of collapsing into her own fears. We'd never really spoken about what had happened when Eoghan had taken her mind and her power. If it had been me, if he'd forced me to do the things he'd made her do...perhaps I'd also have a hard time trusting myself to use magic.

"I won't tell anyone," I said. "Especially Ayla. But when you feel like you hear these voices, I want you to talk to me, okay? We can figure out what's going on."

Her gaze finally broke from the fire to meet mine, and there was relief there. "So you don't think I'm crazy?"

"The point is, you aren't alone anymore. You know that, right? You have me. And Ayla."

Riona snorted as she rolled her eyes. "She'd have to speak to me first."

"What's that mean?"

"Oh, come on," Riona said, nodding to where Ayla was sleeping against the wall. "You can't tell me you haven't noticed her avoiding me."

"She's not…" I cleared my throat. "She's under pressure."

Riona wore a look of doubt. "Maybe. I'm not the best judge of character right now, anyway. Too busy trying to keep my mind from splintering into a million pieces."

"You should talk with her. At least try. You might find you're going through the same thing."

"I doubt it." She hopped to her feet. "I'm going to try to get some sleep. Hopefully…hopefully, tomorrow we reach the troll kingdom, and all will be well."

Chapter Twenty-Four

Riona

I barely got any sleep, waking up every few minutes to make sure the fire was still going, and that the evil beast of magic was still in its cage. And when I was awake, I worried that I might've been too hasty talking with Cade about my magical struggles. He and Ayla were close—what would she say when she found out I'd been lying?

But perhaps he could be trusted. He seemed sincere when he told me he'd keep my secret. And we had become friends in the fae realm. My only friend, in fact.

Too soon, the troll was awake and loudly announced it was time to continue our journey. As the group grumbled and groaned their way to waking, Lynton walked to the edge of the cave, where the snow had begun melting from the heat of my fire. He knelt and pressed his hands on the ground, causing that predictable ripple. Only this time, it splashed up, creating a step, then another, until it formed a staircase. A gust of frosty, fresh air barreled through the cave, reminding us just how warm the fire had been.

Ayla was first, wrapping her cloak tighter around herself, followed by Ward, then his two soldiers, and finally it was just Cade and myself. I fidgeted under his stare, waiting for him to leave.

"Riona—"

"Not a word," I said, brushing past him. "You promised."

I expected the staircase to end at the top of the cave, above the cascaded snow that had buried us. But it kept going, winding up the mountain. The end was nowhere in sight. As the sun peeked out from behind the clouds, it fell hot on the back of our necks, the glare giving me a headache.

Lynton, of course, showed no signs of exhaustion, though he had donned a protective bonnet over his head and hair.

"My ass," Rutley cried, rubbing his hindquarters with a sigh. "I don't think I'm meant for this."

"It's still as flat as ever," Elodia remarked, walking by him, but stopping to grab his hand and help him up the next step.

"Nobody wants to hear about your ass, Rutley," Ward grunted. But he rubbed his own, wincing and continuing his climb. "Say, Cade—"

"Nope," he replied with a sigh.

I held my breath, waiting for him to give my secret away, but he didn't. He was keeping his word—for the moment, at least.

"Just keep climbing," Lynton said. "We are nearly there."

"He's been saying that for days," Ayla grumbled—the first sour note from her the entire trip.

But he was right, and eventually, he disappeared over a ridge at the top. I wasn't sure what I was expecting, but as we crested the last few steps…my brow furrowed and uncertainty shot through me.

There was nothing. No door, no village, no city. Just a large landing and another section of the mountain rising even higher into the blue sky above. Beside me, Ayla let out a whimper of misery, and Ward and the two soldiers looked angrier by the moment.

"Well?" Elodia barked. "Where the hell is it?"

Lynton didn't reply, walking up to the large, smooth rock face and pressing his hands to it. A breeze of earthy scent wafted by my nose, much as it had when he'd created the rock tunnel to save us from the avalanche. The rock face rippled, as if it were water, then folded back on itself like a curtain, revealing a large, dark cave.

"Great. More traveling," Ward said. "Still don't see a damn city."

"Patience, please." Lynton was already inside the cave. "And come along."

"Is it safe?" Ayla asked, clinging to Cade's arm. "Do you think the rock will topple onto us?"

"I doubt he dragged us all the way here to kill us," Rutley said, adjusting his bag on his shoulder. But he looked apprehensive just the same. "C'mon."

Together, almost as a unit, we inched across the open plain and into the darkness of the cave. The temperature stayed the same—frigid—but at least the wind was gone. My eyes took a moment to adjust to the darkness, and when I could finally see my hands in front of my face, I noticed the ground beneath our feet. We were walking on a downslope now, but to where?

"What is that?" Ward called, pointing to something in the distance.

"A much faster ride to the bottom of the mountain," Lynton said, standing next to what appeared to be three carts on a track. "Please, get in."

"Absolutely not," Ward said. "That looks like a death trap."

"You are, of course, welcome to walk, but the incline is quite steep," he said. "And it might take you a few days to get there."

"Hang on," Elodia said, holding up her hand. "If we're going right back down the mountain, what was the point of climbing the damn thing?"

Lynton sighed. "Because, as I said, this is the only entrance. There is no way to walk through the mountain from the bottom."

"You just wanted to make it as difficult as possible?" Ward said, his tone dripping with sarcasm.

"Precisely."

Ayla shared a look with Cade then climbed into the closest cart. "Well, no time like the present. At least it'll be nice to sit."

I crammed into a cart with Elodia, Ward, and Rutley, pressed into a corner as we stared nervously at the tunnel in front of us. There didn't seem to be any harnesses or straps to keep us in place. Lynton climbed into the first cart and leaned down to touch the rock. His magic rippled through the ground and opened a hole where the tracks seemed to terminate. And with a push, we tilted forward and down.

The cold air whipped my hair backward, and only my death grip on Ward's arm kept me from flying out of the cart. Over the sound of whistling wind, someone was screaming, and I had no clue if it was me or any of the other terrified travelers.

The magic in my bones throbbed as it desperately tried to break free, but I managed to keep a tight grip on it, even as panic flooded my body. Whatever had been calling it the past four days was growing stronger, almost deafening. I feared what would happen when we reached the city. And what we might find.

A dim light became visible in the distance, growing steadily brighter as the angle of descent lessened and we slowed. There seemed to be an archway up ahead that we were headed straight to.

By magic or design, the cart slowed until it came to an easy stop just on the other side of the arch. A collective gasp left the traveling party as we all craned our necks to take in the view.

The city sat in a cavern that looked nearly the size of the mountain itself. Houses, shops, even a large castle were all made from the same grayish rock that had been underfoot. The streets, too, were stone—as were sculptures of trees and other flora. Perhaps an attempt to remind the city of what life was like in the sun.

Because there was barely any sun to speak of. Dim light shone in from small holes in the cavern ceiling, assisted by large hanging mirrors. Lamps filled with tiny blue flames adorned every house and dotted the streets.

"That was…" Ayla's hair was a mess, her face pale as she slowly unclenched her hands from Cade's arm.

The wizard looked as if he'd lost his lunch, his legs wobbly underneath him. Even unflappable Ward looked unnerved by the journey.

"Come," Lynton said, in his usual way. "King Edric is waiting."

The town was condensed, for lack of a better word. The houses sat right next to one another, one long row after another. They were made of every color of stone, some with two stories and some with more, with roofs that were somehow made of stone as well. The street we walked on was narrow, but it wasn't as if there was a lot of traffic. In fact, the only troll we could see was Lynton.

"How many trolls live here?" Ayla asked.

"A few thousand," Lynton replied. "All that's left of our race."

"Well, where are they?" Ward asked. "You'd think we'd see a couple out and about, at least."

Lynton didn't respond but simply hastened his steps, almost as if he were eager to be rid of us and our questions. He took a hard left, revealing a wider road that led to a castle built into the side of the cave. I counted at least twenty spires, each of different sizes and shapes. Even the Erlking's castle wasn't so big.

I snuck a glance at the others, wondering what was going through their minds—especially Ayla's. She seemed almost like she was forcing herself to remain neutral when she wanted to react. Part of me wanted to reach out to her, to remind her that both of us had been invited to this strange place, to ask her what she wanted me to do. But I kept quiet.

"That's some waterfall," Elodia said.

I hadn't even noticed the sound until she'd pointed it out, a low roar that echoed in the space. Water poured out of a hole at the very top of the cave, cascading down into a large pool a stone's throw from the castle. There was something…mesmerizing about it. Something that tasted like home.

The front door of the castle was open without a single soldier guarding it. The front hall was lined with those same blue-light lamps that flickered and danced in their glass cages.

"Is this magic?" Cade asked, walking up to one.

"No, it's gas," Lynton said.

Ward frowned. "Gas?"

Whatever Lynton wanted to say, he thought better of it. "The king is waiting."

There was a fountain in the center of the courtyard with a sculpture of a troll holding something aloft. He was riding what appeared to be a griffin, and water was pouring out of the animal's mouth. I drew closer to the well. Something was…familiar about it. Like the waterfall, it drew me closer to it, as if there was a song—

"Riona?" Ward called.

I stopped, realizing I'd left the group and was standing in front of the fountain. "Sorry. Coming."

But as I turned away, that damned magic in my bones throbbed, like something in the water was calling to it. A shiver rattled my body as I hurried to follow them inside the castle.

CHAPTER TWENTY-FIVE

AYLA

I barely noticed the strangeness of this place, too focused on the task that lay ahead of me. All Lady Enid's decorum lessons came flooding back. Queens don't bow. Head up. Feet planted. I was Edric's equal in every way. So why did I feel like I was woefully out of my depth?

A calloused hand slid into mine, squeezed, then let go. Ward. Somehow, the gesture took the edge off my nerves.

Lynton led us into a large throne room, and there sat...well, not what I was expecting. King Edric had the same translucent skin as Lynton, and the pointed ears of the fae, but his hair was brown instead of white, falling on his forehead. His eyes, a piercing gold, immediately found mine, mesmerizing me. If one could look past the throbbing veins under his skin, one might even call him handsome.

Before the king could speak, Lynton bowed at the hip. "I have completed what you asked of me. The queen and her...traveling companions have been brought to Gwyllion."

"Very good," Edric replied with a nod. "You may go, Lynton."

He didn't need to be told twice. Before our eyes, the troll melted into the rock and was gone.

Edric shook his head, as if expecting such behavior before turning to me with a warm smile on his face. "Queen Ayla of Pennlan, I presume?"

"Y-yes." I caught myself, took a breath, and remembered I was supposed to be projecting confidence. "Yes, Your Majesty. I'm Ayla of

Pennlan. It is wonderful to finally meet you."

He took my hand and kissed it gently. His lips were impossibly soft, his skin warm. When he looked up into my eyes, the tension between my shoulders loosened. He looked almost human.

Ward's loud throat clearing brought me back to myself, and I quickly removed my hand from the king's.

"I was so happy to receive your invitation," I said.

"I only wish it wasn't under such dire circumstances," he said, his gaze moving beyond me. "I'll have you know, Princess Riona of the fae realm, that you're the first non-troll fae to set foot in this city."

I waited for her to respond, and when she didn't, I turned. She looked like prey caught in a hunter's snare. I motioned for Cade to nudge her, and he poked her gently with the back of his staff.

"Oh, right. Um." She twisted her hands. "Thank you?"

Cade snorted, but I just huffed silently as I tried to redirect Edric's attention before he thought us all idiots. "And the rest of my traveling party. Ward, Elodia, Rutley, and Cade."

Edric's gaze turned to Cade, and his brow furrowed. "A wizard?"

"He's nothing like Eoghan," I said, perhaps a little too quickly. "He and I were both equally betrayed by him."

"And he can't use his magic," Ward added dryly.

The tension hadn't left Edric's face. "I see."

"Lynton said it was because I wasn't invited," Cade said, inching forward. "Perhaps now that you've met me, you might…invite me? Or release me from whatever curse you've laid upon me."

"Unfortunately, wizards don't have the best history on this continent," Edric said. "You'll forgive me if I remain a little skeptical. Besides…" He brightened. "There's no need for you to wield magic in here. You are welcome guests, and anything Her Majesty might need will be provided."

Cade frowned, but I couldn't really argue with Edric—at least not yet.

"We understand and appreciate you letting us come," I said.

"Indeed," Edric said. "We have lots to discuss. Perhaps over dinner? I confess I wasn't expecting…so many of you, but we can make room quickly." He offered his arm. "Shall we?"

"Wait a minute," Ward said, holding up his hand. "We've traveled all this way for one thing. Where is your piece of the stone?"

"I assume you traveled to *discuss* the stone, not to take it." His voice was even, but there was a tone of warning in it—especially as his gaze flickered to Riona.

"Of course we're here to discuss it," I said quickly. "But…it would be nice to see it." I licked my lips as I thumbed its sibling around my neck. "It would help my good captain sleep better tonight, at least."

Edric turned from us, walking back to his throne. He placed his hands on either side of the seat, and a faint rumbling echoed from across the room. When he turned, he opened his palm to reveal a small, brown gem.

I put my hand around my stone, wishing it would do *something* to show it was still functional. I foolishly hoped being so near to its brethren would bring it back to life, but it remained dormant under my fingers. But, thankfully, so did Edric's.

"Are we waiting for something?" Rutley asked.

"A demonstration—" Ward began but I turned, giving him a look that could kill.

"It's clearly the stone," I snapped. "We don't need *any* demonstrations. Not now, anyway." I turned to Edric, forcing a bright smile onto my face. "Now, let's see about that dinner."

>→ >→ >→ >→

"This is…delightful."

It was difficult to find anything more complimentary to say about the meal the trolls served us. Everything was bland, saltless, or overripe, to the point where I wondered if their trolls had taste buds.

But it was important to keep up appearances, so I forced a smile with every bite. The dining room was intimate, with the seven of us just barely fitting around the rectangular table. Edric sat at the head, and he had insisted Riona and I sit to his left and right, respectively. Cade was next to me, Ward to Riona, and the other two rounded out the end of the table. Everything in this room was made of stone, unsurprisingly, even down to the goblets from which we drank our wine and the forks we used to spear the overcooked meat.

"It's amazing to me how easily humans can lie," Edric said, a kind smile on his face. "Trolls, like the fae, are unable to. Isn't that right, Princess Riona?"

"It's just Riona," she said, her words barely a mumble. "I'm not… I'm not really a princess."

"You are the daughter of the Pennlan king, aren't you?" Edric asked.

She gaped like a fish, and I felt compelled to step in.

"She wasn't raised in Pennlan," I said. "In fact, I didn't know about her until six months ago."

"Interesting," he said. "I confess, I was most eager to meet you. To find out where the fae ended and the human began."

"Um. Thank you?"

I wished she was close enough to kick. She could at least *try* to act regal. I gave Ward a look, but he was too busy glaring at Edric to notice me. My kingdom for a group who knew how to behave at the dinner table.

"Trolls and fae have a long history," Edric continued. "Are you familiar?"

"Kind of," Riona said. "My grandfather wasn't even sure you still existed until Lynton showed up."

I squirmed, the familiar tone of her voice was like nails on my skin. "And we were so grateful you did."

But Edric seemed keen to talk to Riona. "And your grandfather is the Erlking, isn't he?"

Riona nodded, and I waited for her to speak, the silence deafening.

When she didn't, Cade blessedly chimed in. "He was most eager to restart conversations."

"And how do you know this, wizard?" Edric asked.

"I've been training with the fae these past six months, after Eoghan's... Well, you know." He twirled his fork. "In both practical magic and theory. I was hoping I could learn from you as well." He cracked an affable smile. "I've always been eager to know all I can about magic. Wherever it comes from."

Edric wiped his mouth with the napkin. "Surely, Lynton told you all about the limitations of troll magic."

"He wasn't exactly chatty," Cade said.

"Nor did he lift a finger to make the queen's journey easier," Ward replied.

"But..." Edric looked at Riona. "Surely, you were able to help your sister."

Riona licked her lips, but Cade stepped in. "She has the same issue as me."

"Interesting," Edric said, surveying her. "In any case, as limited as our magic is, Lynton still should've done everything to make your journey less difficult. He's a fairly literal man, so perhaps he thought his job only extended to getting you here, not ensuring your comfort."

"Are all of you like that?" Ward asked. "Literal?"

"Most fae creatures are," he said with a small smile. "Considering we are unable to lie. But Lynton is, perhaps, more than most. There are a very small number of trolls who can leave the safety of the mountain, and none I trust as much as Lynton to get the job done. His only failing is his...personality."

I didn't mean for the giggle to escape my lips, but it didn't seem to bother the king all that much.

"What we saw of his magic was impressive," Cade said. "And what we saw in the throne room, of course. But Lynton was able to summon kindling through the rocks. Is that... I suppose we were wondering, why not send *us* through the rock?"

"Because you would die," he said. "Troll magic must use rock as a conduit, and though it's quite interconnective, it requires us to break items down to their most basic level to fit through the cracks and veins of the stones. Trolls, of course, being made of the magic, can assemble and disassemble themselves with ease. But anything else..." He lifted a shoulder.

"Fascinating," Cade said. "I'd love to see more."

"There's not much more to see, I'm afraid. It's why we were considered a *lesser* fae by the *daoine maithe*." He turned to Riona again. "Is that still a term used in your world, Princess Riona?"

Again, Riona jumped at being addressed. "Yes, but it's not meant to be...derogatory."

"It never is, is it?" Edric said with a smile.

"Is that why you stole the *seod croí*?" Ward asked.

"Ward," I barked, glancing at Edric and hoping he hadn't been offended.

"No, it's a valid point," Edric said. "Before the great war, the trolls lived amongst the fae. We inhabited the land north of the *daoine maithe* and south of the *sidheog*."

"The wildlands?" Ward asked.

"Is that what they call it now?" Edric said with a sad chuckle. "It used to be troll country."

"There's not much there now," Cade said. "Mostly because the *aos sí* is keeping the lesser...er...the creatures there from crossing into the *daoine maithe* lands."

Edric sat back and surveyed us. "How much do you all know about the creation of the *seod croí*?"

"All I know is the wizard Laughlan created it," Cade said. "Along with a fae."

"Aoibheann. They were lovers, you know," Edric said. "They created the *seod croí* in some unholy union between them, so they say. It was the most powerful object in existence, intended to calm the constant wars that had plagued the continent for hundreds of years. And for a while, it did."

"Until it didn't," Ward drawled.

"What happened?" I asked.

Edric nodded. "The accounts vary. Some say that the *seod croí* poisoned Laughlan's mind. Others believe it was the power itself, and the ability to bring entire countries to their knees, that drove him mad. But however it happened, he wielded it in such a way that required… correction.

"Naturally, no one race—not the fae, nor the trolls, nor the creatures of the sea, or the humans—could defeat him alone. The only one who had any chance of getting to him was Aoibheann, and although her lover had turned into someone no one recognized, she was still uneasy about fighting him. But when he massacred an entire village of humans who'd dared defy his edicts, there was no other choice.

"They met him on the fields of the *aos sí*, and the casualties were immense. After a long battle, Laughlan was defeated, and the stone taken into their possession and split into four pieces." He cracked a wry smile. "I'm sure you know the rest."

"Do you know what happened to the other two pieces?" I asked, hopeful.

"No. But if I had to guess…" He shrugged. "The *fuath*, river fae, were at the battle. Perhaps they, too, got…" Another smile. "Sticky fingers."

"And what about the aether?" Cade said.

Edric looked confused. "Aether?"

"*One to the humans in Pennlan, one to the mountains, one to the sea, and one to be buried in the aether*," he recited. "That's what we were told."

Edric tapped his finger on his chin. "I have no idea. The aether is all around us. Perhaps the fae managed to destroy their piece so the whole stone could never be used again."

I exhaled. "That would be lovely if they did."

"In any case, in this room, we have one half of the stone," Edric said. "And that is more than any creature's had in a thousand years." He leaned across the table and took my hand again. "I hope that we can form an alliance that will be mutually beneficial for our countries."

"That's my hope as well," I replied, resisting the urge to remove my hand, especially as I felt Ward's gaze on me.

I had a feeling we would have some words once the dinner was over. But for now, whatever this Edric wanted, I would oblige. At least until we had some agreements on paper.

Chapter Twenty-Six

Ward

I didn't like King Edric one bit. Not the way he leered at Ayla, nor the way he seemed focused on Riona for some reason. She was uncomfortable with his attention, and it seemed she would've rather melted into the floor than spend another moment with him.

Not to mention…it hadn't escaped my notice that our only way out was a cart pushed by magic—and we were severely lacking in that department. We were effectively trapped in this place, especially if Edric decided he didn't like us all that much. Ayla was doing her best to keep him placated, but there was something…something that kept me from fully trusting the words that came out of his mouth. From the looks on the others' faces, I was alone in that sentiment.

When dinner was over, Edric escorted us out of the dining room, telling Ayla about how the castle and cave were formed.

"When the trolls arrived at the mountain," he said, "it was solid rock. It took several months to figure out exactly how to hollow out the inside so it didn't collapse on itself." He took in a breath. "And it's held fast these past thousand years from the magic of the troll king."

"Amazing," Cade said with a smile. "So it passes down the generations?"

"My father died when I was young," he said. "I've been keeping it aloft a long time. Should I die, it would collapse."

"Let's hope that doesn't happen any time soon," Ayla said as we came to the bottom of a staircase.

Edric turned to her and kissed her hand. "This is where we part for the evening. I hope you can join me for breakfast, and we can begin the important work you've arrived here to do."

"Of course," Ayla said. "I would love that."

"And Princess Riona, too," Edric said, catching her with his gaze again. "After all, we're here to discuss alliances. Wouldn't be prudent without the Erlking's envoy."

Ayla's mask slipped, and a flash of annoyance appeared before she hid it once more. Riona mumbled something and nodded but didn't seem like she really wanted to spend *any* time alone with either of them. I couldn't blame her.

"Well, I bid all of you a good night."

And with that, Edric melted into the floor and disappeared. We stood in shock for a moment before another pair of silver threads flowed through the ground, manifesting into two translucent-skinned attendants who said nothing but beckoned us to follow them. They were the third and fourth trolls we'd seen in a city supposedly full of them.

"What time is it?" I asked, jogging up to walk side by side with them.

"We don't keep time here," she replied. "But it is time for bed."

It was still mid-afternoon when we'd climbed into the cart, and I didn't feel remotely like sleeping. "So how does night and day work here? The lights don't seem to change all that much."

"We go to bed when we go to bed and wake up when we wake up."

"But what about—"

"Ward," Ayla snapped. "Quit pestering them."

They didn't look pestered to me, but I didn't want to risk Ayla's anger again, not when we were finally getting back to a tepid friendship.

After climbing a spiral staircase that reminded me of the hundreds of stairs we climbed earlier in the day, we reached a landing that looked too wide for the tower we were in, almost like the three doors had been crammed in as an afterthought. The attendants opened the first door, revealing a grand room with a four-poster bed, sitting area, and what appeared to be a private bath with running water.

"Fancy," I muttered.

"This is for Princess Riona," the attendant said, her lips barely moving as she spoke.

She walked to the other door, revealing an even grander room larger than the first, with a sitting area, private bath, and four-poster bed. This one had a window that overlooked the waterfall that had been a constant background noise since we'd arrived.

"This is for Her Majesty," she said.

"Breathtaking," Ayla said with a small sigh.

The attendant opened the middle door, and an audible breath came from all four of us. It was…it was a room. With two bunk beds crammed into a small space.

"You couldn't have made room in Ayla or Riona's?" Rutley muttered behind me.

"This will be fine," Ayla said with a bright smile. "We appreciate your hospitality."

The attendants nodded then melted into the floor as if they were made of molten rock. Their silver threads ran along the veins in the stone floor until they disappeared down the stairwell.

"That…" Cade shook his head. "Wow."

"Are we alone?" Ayla asked.

"As alone as we're going to be," I said, peering around.

"Good." She put her hands on her hips. "We need to talk."

"Ayla, you—" I began, but Ayla held up her hand. Her gaze was fixed on Riona, who wilted under her glare.

"I don't know what kind of formal tutelage you had in the fae realm, but you clearly need to brush up on your etiquette," Ayla said.

"I'm…sorry?" Riona blinked, taking a step back. "What do you mean?"

"When you are addressed by a king, or anyone, for that matter, you need to speak clearly." Ayla crossed her arms over her chest. "Sit up, look him in the eye, talk with conviction. You muttering and mumbling the way you did was embarrassing."

"Ayla—" Cade started, but Ayla held up her other hand.

"You are here representing not just your country but Pennlan, or so the troll king believes." She tilted her chin upward. "And so you should behave as if you're an ambassador."

"I will," Riona said, her cheeks turning pink. "Sorry I embarrassed you."

She walked stiffly to her bedroom, slamming the door shut behind her. The sound echoed in the stairwell as the remaining four stared at Ayla with shock.

"That was a bit harsh, don't you think?" Cade said.

"You're supposed to be teaching her, aren't you?" Ayla snapped. "Since neither of you can do magic, might as well teach her how to be a lady. I won't have her acting that way tomorrow."

Cade's brows rose to his forehead. "She's not—"

"Clearly, the trolls believe her to be of importance," Ayla continued. "Now can I count on you to teach her or do I have to do it myself?"

Slowly, he nodded.

"As for you." She whirled on me. "It's clear that everything is fine. There's no need for you to be demanding things of our very generous host. *Especially* acting like he's hiding the stone from us or doing something he's not supposed to. He's welcomed all of us into his home and given us a place to stay. If we want to protect Pennlan from Eoghan, we need his alliance."

"And what kind of alliance are you anticipating?" I asked. "Because it seemed to me he had only one kind in mind."

"Oh." She waved me off impatiently. "Don't be jealous."

"Of what?" Cade said, stepping forward. "I have to say, I agree with Ward."

"That's a first," I muttered under my breath.

"We just need to figure out what Edric is after," Cade said, his voice gentle, like he was taming a wild animal. "And make sure he doesn't—"

"Doesn't what?" Ayla asked, her voice cold. "Take advantage of poor, innocent Ayla, who can't tell when someone's flirting with her?" She looked between us both. "Well? Do you really think so little of me?"

I didn't know what to say, and by the look of Cade, neither did he.

"I *know* he was being overly friendly," she said. "But I'm willing to put up with it considering *I don't see an exit in this place. Do you?*"

I opened and closed my mouth, shocked that she and I were thinking the same thing.

"It's clear Edric controls who comes and goes, and until Cade gets his magic back, it behooves all of us to stay on his good side," she said. "Or am I the only one who knows anything about diplomacy?"

"Fine," I replied. "We'll play nicely. Until he gives us a reason otherwise."

"Thank you." She turned on her heel, walking toward her bedroom door.

Cade started after her, and she glared at him over her shoulder.

"Where do you think you're going?" she asked. "I don't need an escort."

With that, she slammed the door as loudly as Riona had.

Cade stared at the space she'd left, his mouth slightly agape.

I clapped him on the shoulder and squeezed. "C'mon. It's not so terrible on Ayla's bad side. We even have separate beds now!"

⤞ ⤞ ⤞ ⤞

Rutley and Elodia had already claimed the top bunks when we walked inside, but that didn't bother me much. Their boots and gear were propped against the wall, but there wasn't much space for it, let alone four people wandering around. After I deposited my things next to theirs, I crawled into the bottom bunk, finding the mattress lumpy and uncomfortable.

"D'ya reckon they made the mattresses out of stone, too?" Elodia asked, the bed squeaking above me as she adjusted herself.

"Better than the wooden floor. At least we have blankets," came Rutley's response.

The semi-decent accommodations didn't fool me one bit. "In the morning, I want the two of you to patrol the castle," I said. "Find out everything you can about the layout, strengths, weaknesses—number of soldiers."

"I didn't see one on the way in," Rutley said.

"Me neither," Elodia said. "Which was…strange. Though I suppose if the entire kingdom exists in a magical fortress that can only be accessed by climbing a mountain, maybe that's defense in and of itself."

"We can't be too careful," I said. "And see about finding another way out."

"You got it, boss," Elodia said with a loud yawn. "But tomorrow."

"Tomorrow." Rutley shifted in his bed. "Hope there's better breakfast. That was the worst meal I've ever had."

I smiled. "At least there was food. When we were in the fae realm, we went a few days without eating a thing. Didn't we, Cade?"

He didn't respond, and I half-expected he'd be asleep. But after a moment, he released a deep sigh as he rose, put on his boots, and walked out the door.

"What's up his butt?" Elodia asked.

"Not the queen," Rutley replied with a snort.

"Easy," I said, glad I was able to hide a smile.

"Oh, come on, he's been blowing smoke up her dress since we left Pennlan," Elodia said. "I know it drives you crazy."

It did, but I wasn't about to tell them that. So I reached over to the one lamp in the room and turned it off.

"Good night."

CHAPTER TWENTY-SEVEN

CADE

Ayla's door was closed, and I thought better of knocking, even though I wanted to. Instead, I quietly padded down the spiral staircase, lit by those strange lamps with the blue flame. I stopped to inspect one of them, noticing a small pipe coming from the bottom where the flame was lit.

I kept walking, almost hoping I'd run into a soldier who'd send me back to bed. That Edric had no guards posted—no soldiers wandering around, not even a sentry—concerned me. It gave more credence to Ayla's theory that we were at his mercy to come and go.

The hall was decorated with paintings of landscapes and sculptures of trees. I stopped at one. The sparse, unwieldy trees and rolling hills looked an awful lot like the fae realm. I realized with a start that it must've been what the wildlands looked like when the trolls lived there. The rest seemed to paint a picture of the world outside the mountain, a world Edric had never seen.

When I passed a window, I peered up toward the cavern wall, finding the small holes that seemed to let in a little light. I'd never given the sun a passing glance before, but now I found myself missing it dearly. How sad it must've been to grow up without knowing the warmth of a summer day. Was the *seod croí* worth it?

I looked out at the city below. It appeared almost like a glittering jewel box, each building colored with brilliant reds, greens, even oranges and yellows. A couple deep purples. The waterfall was to my left, spewing out water in an unrelenting torrent. The water fell into a basin then cut through the city, flowing toward the castle where it created a moat of sorts.

I spent too long staring at the waterfall before peeling myself away, walking with my hand dragging against the rock and getting a faint taste of earth if I concentrated hard. In the fae realm, even the air seemed alive, vibrating with magic and movement. There was certainly magic here, but it seemed much more contained, living in the veins of the stone walls versus flying around uninhibited. As much as Edric talked about it not being as powerful, they'd managed to create this magnificent cavern and kept it together these past thousand years. I'd never seen rock move in such a way—not that Eoghan and I'd spent time manipulating anything other than raw power.

I glanced at my staff, trying to cast and once again hearing the rush of water. *That* spell, along with the memory spell, seemed…too powerful for how Edric described the troll's abilities. Was their piece of the *seod croí* fueling that magic? I wanted to see more, to understand it the way I'd begun to understand the other fae. Though Edric saw me as a threat, I felt more an eager student in front of a brand-new book.

But my hopes were mostly dashed; it seemed there wasn't another soul in the castle. I meandered down the long hallways, trying to keep up with the lefts and rights I took, but losing the thread eventually.

Finally, I heard footsteps and soft voices in a room just beyond the dark hallway where I was walking. I kept toward the sound, finding a trio of silver-haired servants cleaning—but it was the oddest cleaning I'd seen in my life. One was next to a statue, pressing her hands against the rock face. It melted into water in her hands then reformed into an entirely different statue. She did the same to the other two, transforming them from two bushes to statues of what I assumed were trolls of some importance. Two other servants were cleaning the floors, but instead of a mop and bucket, they merely had their hands on the floor, magic flowing through the rock as it shifted from emerald to ruby—and growing shiny as they worked.

I inhaled, finally getting a good whiff of that earthy scent I was now sure was troll magic. Like the fae, trolls seemed to have a slightly different scent from person to person. Riona had the most unique of the fae, hers sweet, like honeyed mead, where the others were more bitter and bold, like wine. I wondered what uniqueness I could get from the trolls, once I had full use of my magic back.

"Excuse me," I said, stepping inside.

The servants stopped dead, turning to me with wide, fearful eyes. Before I could say anything, they melted into the floor as Lynton has done. Under my feet, three threads of silver wove through the veins in the rock. I followed them, marveling at how they seemed to dive and skip in the dark threads of the stone. Was this how trolls traveled, like the fae manifested into butterflies?

"Wait," I called, hoping they could hear me in their stone-forms. "Please, I just want to talk!"

They doubled their speed, and I had to break into a run, nearly missing them as they wove around corners and dashed into the walls. But their movement was just visible in the scant light, so I kept up my pursuit.

"I promise, I'm not going to hurt you!" I panted. "I just wanted to ask about your magic."

But I turned a corner and found myself standing in a garden, the servants gone. I walked out slowly. It wasn't a *real* garden made of plants —the flora was comprised of emeralds. Each leaf on the bush had been intricately carved, right down to the veining and texture. I touched one of them, expecting a velvet leaf but instead finding cold rock.

I strolled through the garden until I reached the end, expecting a gate or some kind of fence keeping the city from the royals. But it was open, a path winding down into the city below.

"Trouble sleeping?"

Edric stood behind me, his face a mask of kindness, but there was something else behind his gaze. Something I didn't like.

"I just thought I'd stretch my legs," I replied, lowering my hand. "I hope that's all right."

He didn't respond, coming to stand beside me. "And harass the staff?"

"Harass…" I cleared my throat. "I just wanted to talk with them. Ask them about their magic. I find it fascinating, you know." I glanced at him. "They were…real trolls, right? They seemed—"

"Of course they're real trolls," he said with a chuckle. "This isn't the fae realm where we enslave lesser creatures for our own benefit."

"The fae don't enslave lesser creatures," I said, slowly. "At least, not that I saw while I was there."

"And you saw a lot?"

"I was there for six months in the Erlking's castle." I lifted a shoulder. "I saw a lot."

He pressed his lips into a thin line. "Things were much different when the trolls lived amongst them. But perhaps enough time has passed that the current Erlking has softened his approach."

I twisted my staff. "I can't speak to his approach, but I did see him pass an edict that brownies should be treated better in the castle. If that gives you any indication." I paused, recalling the burning feel on the back of my neck. "Do the Erlking's edicts affect you, too?"

"When we left the fae realm, our connection to the Erlking was severed," he said, though he rubbed the back of his neck—curious that he knew how to do that. "We are our own people. We hope to remain that way, even with reopening the lines of communication." He glanced at me. "I'm encouraged that the Erlking honored our request to send the halfling instead of one of his minions. Though we could have done without the…additions."

"Ward insisted—"

"Not them." He turned to me. "Queen Ayla seems to attract wizards, doesn't she? Is it the power of the stone that draws you, or something else?"

I chuckled. "You clearly have the wrong picture of me."

"Do I? Was it not your master who ensnared the fae girl?"

"Yes, but—"

"Then how can we expect any different from you?" Edric said, though it didn't sound like he was asking. More like stating a fact.

"Eoghan found me in the southern islands. Brought me to Pennlan. Raised me alongside Ayla. Neither of us knew anything about his greater plans. And..." I didn't really want to offer up this fact, but I hoped it would ease his mind. "I think he trained me to seek out the Pennlan stone for him. He made it clear that he half-expected me to perish on the journey."

Edric didn't seem moved. "But you didn't."

"I didn't," I said. "But it was close. Birch had charmed it so only Leandra's daughter could retrieve it. A fact we didn't know until Ward almost drowned trying to get it out of the lake."

Edric watched me closely. "I see."

"I'm loyal to Ayla," I said, pressing my hand to my chest to show my sincerity.

"Yes, that much is clear." He tilted his head. "What *exactly* is your relationship with the queen?"

"Ayla and I—"

"Are lovers?"

My stomach did a flip-flop. "Not exactly. Just very close. We were raised together."

"By Eoghan."

"Yes," I said. "Which is why I say both of us were betrayed by him. Whatever you've heard about him... I'm the opposite."

"My opinion of wizards was formed long before I even heard of your former master, and it hasn't much improved," he said. "The rest of the citizenry here feels similarly, unfortunately. I fear that you walking amongst them would cause undue fear." He tapped his foot on the ground, and the open gate in front of me melted together into a solid wall. "Therefore, I must ask that you remain inside the castle walls. And perhaps..." He cleared his throat. "In your room unless you have an escort."

"But—"

The ground rippled beneath my feet, crawling up to encase my calves with stone. I jerked at them, nearly toppling backward, but they were solid. Edric said nothing but flicked his hand, and the stone pulled me backward, rushing me back through the garden, through the hall, up the stairs, before depositing me unceremoniously on the floor of our dark room and slamming the door behind me.

"What the—" Ward's voice echoed in the dark. "What happened?"

"Edric," I said, wincing as I rubbed my sore rear. "Sent me back to my room."

"What'd you do?"

"We were having a nice chat in the gardens," I replied, standing slowly. "And he told me I wasn't allowed out and about without an escort. Because I'm a wizard." I blew air between my lips. "Which seems awfully rude to me. He doesn't even know me."

"You should definitely go back and give him a piece of your mind," Elodia said, sounding half-asleep. "Instead of keeping us all awake."

I glared into the darkness and popped myself back onto my feet, crossing the room. But when I tried the doorknob, it wouldn't turn. "Uh. I think we're locked in here."

The mattress squeaked, and Ward's footsteps clomped past me. The door knob jiggled under his hand then, to my annoyance, the door opened, sending a beam of light into the room.

"Well, that's... It was locked," I said.

"Seems like it's fine now," he said, glaring at me as he walked back to his bed. "Go to sleep, Cade."

The door shut, and the room went dark again. I pursed my lips in annoyance then reached for the door—it was yet again locked.

So it was just me. Perfect.

Chapter Twenty-Eight

Riona

Princess.

I'd never considered myself royalty. Fae didn't operate in those terms, at least not the way humans did. The fae who lived in the castle were given the same kind of room, invited to dine in the great hall with everyone else. No one really got special treatment, at least not like this. It felt like I was interloping on Ayla's realm, and she absolutely did not welcome me.

The room Edric had prepared for me was surely something to behold. The bed was soft with thick blankets to keep the cavern chill off me. They'd laid out a silk nightgown and fluffy robe, and there was a roaring fire in the hearth with a tea kettle and a cup of what smelled like lavender on the mantel. It was certainly a room *fit* for a princess.

I just wished I felt like one.

I lay in bed, replaying the dinner and the way Ayla had berated me over and over again. I hadn't wanted to embarrass her, nor had I thought anything I'd done was worthy of it. But I'd also never been…well, *seen* like that. My entire life I'd been treated like an afterthought, someone to be stepped over. I was never really given anything other than a room and a nanny to teach me to speak, read, and write. My natural inclination was to blend into the wall—not just because I had nothing of value but also for self-preservation. I'd been led to believe I was at a disadvantage because of my human father. That I wouldn't ever stand a chance against a fae who challenged me.

Lies.

I twitched as that voice whispered in my ear and rolled onto one side. I wanted to sleep—five days of hard climbing up a mountain had caught up with me—but there were too many thoughts in my mind.

I kicked the blanket off and walked to the mantel, picking up the cup of tea and inhaling it. It was surprisingly still hot, even though it had been sitting for at least two hours. More troll magic, perhaps. I brought the cup to my lips and took a hesitant sip, finding it just as lackluster and watered down as the food at dinner had been. But it warmed me from head to toe and distracted me from distressing thoughts.

With cup in hand, I canvassed the room. A writing desk full of paper and ink—not that I'd be writing to anyone—sat in one corner. In the other, a wardrobe full of dresses that were at least a foot too long. They must've anticipated I'd be more like the fae in that regard.

I could fix it. Let me fix it.

I went stick-straight, the voice coming through my mind like it was right next to me. I turned, looking for anyone else but knowing I was alone. Just me and this voice in my mind.

I took another sip of the tea, and the hissing in my ear became louder. I put the cup down on the desk and walked to the other side of the room, where a stone door led into another room—a bathroom. There was communal bathing in the fae realm, so having my own private place was strange. Especially one so beautiful.

Movement caught my eye, and I turned to stare at my reflection in the mirror. I did look a sight, with matted hair stuffed into a braid, dirt on my face and cheeks, and leaves sticking to my tunic. No wonder Ayla was embarrassed by me. I walked to the tap and turned it on, listening to the sound of rushing water instead of the voice in my head.

But as soon as I put my hands under the tap, the voices came back with a vengeance, hissing and laughing in my ear. And when I stepped away, my palms were *glowing*.

I raced from the bathroom, breathing heavily and refusing to look at my hands until the tingling in them ceased. Then, nervously, I glanced down.

Back to normal.

I exhaled, running a hand through my hair as I considered what that might've been. I debated crossing the room to ask Cade, even just to make sure someone else saw what I was seeing. But I was afraid of what other questions that might bring up. He already knew more than I was comfortable with.

But after the tongue-lashing from Ayla, I probably needed to at least wipe myself down so I didn't look like a hellion. So, using as little water as I could, I scrubbed my face until it was pink and plucked the flora from my clothes. My hair would have to wait; I hadn't brought a comb. It usually wasn't necessary.

But as I stared at my reflection, wishing it was more...*regal*... I realized that my version of necessary wasn't going to cut it this time. If only I knew how to get there from where I was.

⋺⋺ ⋺⋺ ⋺⋺ ⋺⋺

When I woke, a servant was stoking the fire. When she noticed me stirring, she melted into the floor. I sat up and watched as a silver thread flowed through the floor and out the double doors. I supposed trolls didn't like walking when they could do...that.

The servant had also left a fresh cup and a kettle, as well as a handwritten note inviting me to breakfast. I turned the letter over, seeing no mention of Ayla, but assuming she'd be there, too. I didn't want to meet with him alone.

I dressed in my traveling clothes and started climbing the spiral staircase. I passed several landings with doorways until I heard voices in the room at the top. There were neither walls nor a ceiling, just a stone railing that lined the edges to keep any wayward people from flying down. Sunlight streamed in from the small openings at the top of the cavern, reflecting off the mirrors to brighten the city below. It was a gorgeous vista, with every color of rooftop twinkling like dim stars.

"Do you like it?"

I jumped, and if the stone railing hadn't been there, I might've toppled over the edge. Edric was standing right behind me, his breath warm on my ear. I had no space to inch away, frozen like a helpless creature in a hunter's snare. Ayla had beat me there and was watching with a frown.

"I do," I stammered, after a moment. "It's very pretty."

"How does it compare to the fae realm?" he asked.

"It's fine," I replied, sliding across the railing as gracefully as I could to get away from him. "Why do you ask?"

"I'd just like your perspective, that's all," he said, his smile genuine. "As a person who's seen both."

"It's different, of course," I replied. "The fae realm is pretty big." I hoped I wasn't insulting him. "It took us weeks to walk from one end to the other."

"And why were you walking?" he asked. "In search of the Pennlan stone? Where was it hidden?"

I supposed it didn't matter now, but I couldn't help but feel like I was sharing a secret. "The *sidheog* lands. At the very northern edge of the realm."

"So you have seen the breadth of the lands," Edric said, offering me a seat at the table. "And yet you think my humble little fiefdom compares well."

"It does." It didn't, of course, and my tongue burned as I spoke, but it was better to be nice than to insult him.

"And fae can't lie," Edric said with a grin to Ayla. "So we know it's the truth."

There was something about the way he spoke, that perhaps he *knew* I wasn't telling the truth…but once he sat down, his attention returned to my sister, and I was able to catch my breath. The meal was once again bland—cream-filled pastries that needed more sugar, some sad-looking fruit, and a sweet wine that had come from a bad year. But I watched

Ayla eat without complaint and knew I needed to emulate her as well as I could.

"So you send your folk out into the world," Ayla said. "Under this magical spell that makes all creatures forget them."

"Indeed," Edric said. "Of course, they still have to return up the mountain with their wares, so often half of what we barter for is ruined on the journey."

"Why not just make another door?" Ayla said, gesturing to the city. "Somewhere level with the city? Why make your people climb the mountain then take that…" She paused, perhaps collecting her thoughts. "That lovely cart ride."

Edric smiled. "When we came here, we were so scared the fae would invade and take away this blessing, the source of our power, that we took all precautions to keep ourselves hidden. If that meant making the entrance difficult for visitors and locals alike…well, then that's what it took."

"Clearly, you have alternate ways of keeping evildoers in check," Ayla replied, with an almost too-sweet smile. "Which reminds me… would it be possible to release Cade from the bind? I promise you he's not a danger to you or to anyone in this town."

Edric's face slid a little. "I was considering it, to be sure, until I found him wandering the castle last night."

"You…did?" Ayla frowned. "Where?"

"In the gardens. He was trying to get information out of the servants," Edric said. "He promises it was all innocent, and perhaps I might be inclined to believe him. But I just…" He sighed again, looking off into the distance. "We've spent so long keeping our people safe from creatures like him. I can't risk being wrong."

Ayla licked her lips, leaning forward. "I trust Cade with my life."

"And can you be sure that the wizard Eoghan isn't pulling his strings?" Edric asked.

He was looking at Ayla, but his words cut me to my core. My cup fell from my hand, spilling tea everywhere. I jumped up quickly, my face hot and my gaze anywhere but on the king's.

"I'm so sorry," I stammered.

"It's no problem—" Edric began, but it was too hard to breathe. I had to leave. It would've been impossible to hide my reaction should Edric cast that same accusation at me.

"I need to go lie down," I said, backing up. "I'm sorry. Please forgive me. It must be the altitude or the height getting to me."

"Of course," Edric said, coming to his feet. "Let me—"

"No," I said, firmly. "No, please, stay with the queen. I'm fine."

And with that, I turned and ran as fast as I could back to my room.

Chapter Twenty-Nine

Ayla

"Well, that was something."

I couldn't believe Riona had been so rude. Her tea was still splattered across the table, dripping over the side. There were no servants to speak of, so Edric and I did our best to mop up the mess. My face burned, and my heart pounded as I fumbled through apologies.

"Please, think nothing of it," Edric said with a wave of his hand. "Lynton is my only cousin."

"Your…cousin?" I sat back down in my chair. "I didn't realize—"

"It's not something he likes to announce," he said. "It's hard being the only family of the king—harder still to be his little cousin's errand boy." He smiled. "Beneath his begrudging respect is, I hope, affection. I'm sure the same could be said for your sister."

Half. "I'm sure," I said, hoping we could get off the subject. "Though I have to say, I'm pleased we have some time alone. We have a lot to discuss—especially about our stones."

He was wearing his around his neck today, on a chain similar to mine. "Indeed. When I heard you had used yours, well…I was overjoyed. We'd almost thought that the fae had deceived you and given you a false one."

I half-laughed. "I doubt Leandra would've stolen it if it were."

"But she didn't steal it for power," Edric said with a curious tilt of his head. "She took it to protect it from Eoghan, isn't that right?"

"Yes, of course." I cleared my throat. "In any case, I'm so interested to learn how you've managed to harness your power to help your people. So far mine is..." I licked my lips, wondering how much I could share, even in confidence. "Well. It's been in my possession for only six months, so I'm sure there's much to learn."

"You know more about it than I do," he said. "You've wielded it."

We were getting dangerously close to a confession I wasn't sure I wanted to make just yet. "Yes, but beyond just wielding it. There's immense power inside this thing. I just wish I knew more about it so I could...use it better. What is wielding yours like?"

"Unfortunately, when the *seod croí* was split, each piece took on a different aspect of its magic. The power that lies in my stone is different from the power in yours. So we can compare our power all day long, but I doubt we'd find much similarities."

I smiled weakly. "That's...a shame."

"Oh, there's still more to be gained from an alliance." He added a couple of strawberries to my plate, one of which was molding slightly. "Tell me, what are things like in Pennlan? In the human realm? I'm jealous Lynton got to travel so far from home and see it."

I doubted Lynton was the kind of person who would stop to smell the roses. "It's beautiful. The sun, in particular." My gaze darted up to the ceiling above. "I don't suppose you've ever seen it, have you?"

"We try to stay below ground as much as we can," he said, sitting back. "Thin skin, as I'm sure you've noticed."

I nodded, trying not to stare at the pulsing veins on his wrist as it moved across the table. "Do you think you'll stay under here forever?" I asked. "Or is it your hope that by opening talks with the fae, you might be able to leave?"

"Oh." He sighed. "One can only dream of the possibilities. But I suppose I'd have to have your sister sit at the table with me for more than five minutes to have that conversation."

And we were back to Riona. I twisted my napkin in my lap. "She's certainly...in need of guidance."

He helped himself to some more of the wilted strawberries. "You know, I can't help but feel we're kindred spirits, Ayla—Can I call you Ayla?"

"Of course, Edric," I said. "I prefer it, honestly. I've never been comfortable with the noble title. Not as princess, nor as…queen." I shifted. "I suppose that's because I never really held a position of power growing up."

"See? Kindred spirits." He flashed me another handsome smile. "My father died unexpectedly, and the weight of the crown fell heavy on my shoulders. Every soul in this place… It's all we have left of our people. If I mess that up, if I make the wrong choice…" He sighed. "I just wish I had a map to know how to do it all."

I turned to him, a smile on my face. "Exactly how I feel."

"Yours, I'm sure, is compounded by the betrayal of that wizard." He poured more tea into my cup. "He raised you, didn't he? After the murder of your father which…" He stopped. "He caused, right?"

That old anxiety bubbled to the surface. "Yes. It was all such a… horrible time. Finding out everything in such short order… Eoghan's betrayal, Riona's existence. That everything I'd known in my life was a lie…" I forced myself to stop talking for a moment. "My apologies. I didn't mean to go on like that."

Edric reached across the table to take my hand. "As you said, everything said here at this table is in confidence. You can be honest with me."

Could I? His smile was kind, but there was something holding me back from revealing *everything*. "I suppose the hardest part is just knowing who I can trust. Even…myself at times. It makes ruling a country quite…difficult."

"Surely you can trust your own people?" he said. "That captain of your security seems most interested in your well-being."

I half-smiled. "He takes his job very seriously. I don't think he's forgiven himself for leaving me alone with Eoghan while he went in search of the Pennlan stone."

"Then let's not make him suffer needlessly," Edric said. "I was thinking of taking you on a tour of the city today. He is welcome to come, as are his two soldiers."

I brightened. "Oh, a tour would be lovely!"

"Your appearance yesterday caused quite a stir. I thought it might be best to show the townsfolk that you aren't invaders."

"Of course," I said. "And Cade as well, right?"

Edric sighed heavily. "Ayla, as much as you trust him, I can't. And even if I did, his presence might cause panic." He tilted his head. "You have to understand that the only wizard my people know is the one who created the *seod croí* and nearly destroyed our entire race. Seeing a man wielding a staff…"

"I suppose Cade will understand," I said. "If we can find him a library, at least, he can busy himself in there."

"That I have," he said with a smile. "We also might find your sister and see if she wants to come."

"I think we should leave Riona to settle," I said, almost too quickly. "Maybe she can join Cade in the library. I know the Erlking was eager for her to continue her tutelage."

"A fae and a wizard together…" He chuckled. "*That's* never caused a problem before."

⤐ ⤐ ⤐ ⤐

With Edric by my side, we walked down the spiral staircase to the landing with the three doors, and Edric rapped on the center door. There was a ruckus on the other side, and the door swung open in a hurry. I half-expected the group inside to still be asleep, perhaps caught lazing about, but they were all dressed and ready for a fight.

"Good—" I began.

"About time you showed up to let us out of here," Cade growled, taking me aback with the ferocity. "Keeping me locked in here all night was really cute."

"For your own protection, and my servants'," Edric said gently, though there was a note of warning in it. "But you must've had everything you needed. I ensured breakfast was delivered."

"And it was delicious," Ward said, standing. Although he was a terrible liar, I did appreciate the gesture. "Thank you for your hospitality."

"Of course."

"His Majesty would like to take me on a tour of the town," I said, hoping to calm all the tempers involved. "Are you three ready to go?"

"Absolutely," Elodia said, popping upright, even though she wasn't wearing pants.

Rutley, whose shirt wasn't buttoned, also came to his feet. "Always."

"Give us five minutes," Ward said with a little shake of his head. "To get decent."

"Three?" Cade said with a frown. "So I am locked in here."

"It would be best if you stayed in the castle, for your own protection," Edric said.

"Please, Cade?" I placed my hand on his arm and gave him a pleading look. "For me?"

He let out a noise, but the fight disappeared from his face. "Fine. What should I do in the meantime?"

"Edric has a glorious library," I said. "Maybe you could find Riona and take her there? Perhaps…*have a talk* with her?"

"Why?" Ward said. "What happened? Where is she?"

"She's fine," I said, hoping it quelled the conversation. "Please, Cade? Maybe you could find the library and spend some time in there?"

Again, he sighed. "For you, Ayla. Anything."

"Then it's settled," Edric said, offering his arm to me again. "Shall we?"

Chapter Thirty

Ward

I kept my face passive, grateful Edric was at least allowing us to accompany our queen. I believed Cade when he said he hadn't been able to leave the night before, more than the troll's explanation of why. But until I could speak with Ayla in private, I would play the part of silent, dutiful soldier.

That was, until we came to the front of the castle, and my hand flew to my sword. Creatures resembling giant, eyeless rodents were hooked up to an open-air carriage. They scratched and sniffed the ground but stayed in place.

"What…are those?" I asked with a grimace.

"They were once humble moles, but after a few centuries of trollish magic in their veins, they've grown to this size," Edric said, continuing to walk Ayla closer to them. "They're naive to the mountain, specifically the underground. But we've domesticated them for various tasks, such as escorting our esteemed guests through the town."

Ayla glanced at me over her shoulder. "I'm sure they're perfectly…" They snorted loudly, spraying spit across the floor. "Lovely."

"They don't happen to be able to move at super-fast speeds, do they?" I asked, queuing up behind him. The horses that had carried us across the *sidheog* lands had done so in mere hours instead of weeks.

"Like the *donn cúailnge*?" Edric asked with a smile. "You seem to know plenty of the creatures in the fae realm."

"I spent several weeks *walking* through the fae realm," I replied. "I saw a lot of…different things there."

That earned a snort from the troll king. "I assure you, even if they were able to travel like the *donn cúailnge*, there's nowhere for them to go in here. It will be a nice, leisurely walk."

Ayla climbed into the carriage and Rutley, Elodia, and I queued up behind. Edric took the reins, snapping them to goad the creatures forward. The wheels turned slowly, causing enough of a noise that I could fall back in line with the other two and have a semi-private conversation.

"I don't believe him for a second," Rutley said.

"The only one who does seems to be Ayla," I said.

"She doesn't," Elodia said. "She's just trying to stay on his good side. You heard her yesterday."

I wasn't so sure of that. Ayla wasn't a great actress—her honesty was one of the things I liked most about her—and she seemed comfortable next to the troll.

"What do you think happened to Riona?" Elodia asked. "We should've checked on her before we left."

"Cade can handle it," I said. "They're friends now. Probably something with her magic, I'm sure."

"Or maybe she's freaked out after spending time with Ayla," Rutley muttered. Then, when Elodia elbowed him, he shrugged. "What? She's been a real—"

"*Be* that as it may," I interjected. "She's still our queen, and I'm still your superior. So be respectful."

"Yes, sir." Rutley mock-saluted me. "But also, as the troll pointed out last night, Riona is *technically* our princess."

"To think," Elodia said a little thoughtfully, "if something were to happen to Ayla, Riona would be our queen. A *fae* in charge of Pennlan."

"Nothing's going to happen to Ayla, so let's knock off that conversation," I replied with a huff as the carriage got a little farther away. "And hurry up, they're losing us."

The walk from the castle into the main village was impossibly short, but as soon as we rolled into the main square just beyond the gates, we were met with a growing crowd. The whole village, it seemed, had turned out today. They, at least, didn't mind the giant mole-looking creatures, too curious about the band of humans. Ayla smiled and waved at them with all the grace a queen should have, and Elodia, Rutley, and I kept close to the back of the carriage.

I kept my eyes peeled for problems, though I felt the only troll I needed to worry about was in the carriage with Ayla. Those in the crowd seemed docile, coming in all different sizes, shapes, and hair colors, sharing only the pointed ears and translucent skin among them. There was a hum of conversation, but excitement was clear on everyone's faces.

"Do you notice anything strange?" Elodia said, her hands resting by her side. "See anyone younger than eighteen?"

I frowned, scanning the crowd. "Or older than forty."

"I'm sure they're around somewhere," Rutley said, his gaze dancing around the crowd looking for it. "Somewhere."

"Maybe they had a plague that wiped them out?" Rutley said.

I craned my neck. "Edric might've mentioned it."

"Her Majesty will be with us for a few days, perhaps longer," Edric said, addressing the crowd. "As will her companions. I hope you will treat them with respect."

A chorus of mumblings and nodding of heads came from the crowd, as if they were all of one mind. Then they dispersed, walking back inside their businesses and homes—almost as if something compelled them to do it.

"Did you—" Elodia began, but I waved her off.

"I did," I replied. "Keep your eyes open."

Edric led Ayla into a shop, his hand on the small of her back. I was right behind them, suddenly hit with the scent of bread. There were hanging baskets in the window, but they were all empty. And on the shelves behind the baker were flattened loaves.

"Good morning, Your Highness," the shopkeeper said to Edric.

"I'm humbled to have you in my store."

"What do you have for us today?" Edric asked, as if he were a commoner himself.

"Not much, I'm afraid," the keep replied, reaching behind the counter and bringing up a basket of bread. "It's been a few weeks since we've had a delivery of wheat here. The last attempt seemed to have disappeared on the mountain."

"I'll put Lynton on it," Edric said. "Especially now that we have guests. We need to have the best for them."

As they left, Ayla pulled Edric aside. "What did he mean, disappeared on the mountain?"

"It's a hard journey, as you well know," Edric said. "Even harder with the sorts of things we need to feed our people. This time of year, the snow is high, so we have to prioritize what we carry. Wheat, unfortunately, isn't high on the list. It's something of a delicacy."

"We would've been happy to carry more," Ayla said, looking at me as if I'd agree with her.

"I carried enough," Rutley muttered behind me.

"It's not something you need to concern yourselves with," Edric said.

The king seemed keen on showing Ayla the best parts of his town, but they were all…lacking in splendor. The only thing worth mentioning was the woodworking shop, where an expert craftsman was building furniture from wood off the mountain. He offered to make Ayla a chair, and she politely declined, telling him we'd have no way of carrying it.

"Especially since…well, you won't give Cade his magic back," she said, almost a dare to the king.

He flashed her a too-familiar smile. "Then perhaps we'll have to find you something small enough to carry."

His idea, it turned out, was to visit a jeweler, a middle-aged troll with a kind face and long blond hair. I was a bit confused why the trolls —who seemed to manipulate and manage rock with ease—would need something like a jeweler, but when we walked into the shop, there was an artistry about the items he'd made.

"Absolutely beautiful," Ayla whispered, looking at a bangle intricately molded from solid gold.

"Thank you," the jeweler said with a bow. "Would you like to try it on?"

"Oh, I couldn't—"

"Yes, you can," Edric said, taking the bangle and putting it on her wrist. But it slid right down to her elbow—too large.

"Oh, goodness. Let me take that into the back and fix it," the jeweler said, rushing forward.

"I'll join you," Edric replied, a frown on his face.

With them gone, I took the opportunity to sidle up to Ayla, now that Edric was out of earshot. "If he comes out with a diamond ring, I'm going to have some questions."

"Don't start," she muttered. "I thought you were giving him the benefit of the doubt?"

"I'm here, aren't I?" I asked, leaning on the counter. "And I'm behaving myself."

She cast me a look then glanced back behind the curtain. "At least someone is. I swear, Riona was as skittish as a rabbit this morning at breakfast. Barely said a word until she spilled her tea everywhere and ran from the table like the king had personally offended her."

"Maybe not the king," I said with a bit of a wince.

"What does that mean?"

"You were pretty harsh to her last night," I replied.

She opened and closed her mouth, pink appearing at the top of her cheeks. "Well…!"

"Well, what?" I said, chancing a look at her. "She's a kid, Ayla."

"She's seventeen."

"A young seventeen, then," I said. "And your sister."

"Half." Ayla turned to me. "Half-sister."

I narrowed my gaze. "Still half your blood. You should treat her like it."

"I don't even know where to begin with her," she said. "It's almost like starting from scratch. Basic etiquette, manners, how to walk, even." She pinched the bridge of her nose. "Goodness, I sound like Lady Enid, don't I?"

"You do," I said, nudging her. One of Ayla's first acts as queen was to fire her abrasive tutor. "So maybe do the opposite of what she did."

I expected more fight, but Ayla just shook her head. "I can't afford to have her screw this up. It's not just the stones and Eoghan. I need this alliance or Pennlan's is going to be in a great deal of trouble."

"I get that," I said. "But as someone who spent his life as a burden to my older brother, maybe try helping her instead of yelling, you know? All she wants is your approval. Don't make her beg for it. She's the only family you have left. It'd be a shame for you to push her away."

"I don't know if I..." she whispered then seemed to think better of it. "It's complicated."

"If you ask me," I said, as Edric's voice became louder behind the curtain, "you two just need to have a talk and be honest with one another. You're too busy trying to keep your feelings bottled up that it's making you both crazy."

"I don't know if I should be *honest*..."

"Lay your cards on the table," I said, as Edric walked out with two boxes in hand. "Then figure out what kind of relationship you want with each other."

"I hope I'm not too forward," Edric said. "But I thought you might appreciate having something to showcase your status."

He handed the top box to Ayla, and she gently opened it, revealing a precious tiara covered in glittering blue gems. It was more ostentatious than the crowns she wore back in Pennlan, even the one she'd worn on her coronation. She pulled it from the box, the sparkles glittering in her eyes, and licked her lips nervously.

"It's…it's beautiful," she said. "But I can't—"

"Please remember what we can do with pebbles," he said. "I promise you, it was no great feat to create this. But I hope it will help you find your footing." He tilted his head. "I know it would help me."

She let him carefully lay the crown atop her head, and I couldn't deny it made her look more like herself. She even stood straighter, the weight of the crown helping keep her posture.

"Magnificent," Edric said.

"And the other?" I prompted.

"Ah, well." He opened the box, revealing another, less ornate tiara covered in green emeralds. "For your sister."

Her upper lip twitched, and I nudged her gently. She took a breath then forced a smile.

"I will see to it that she wears it well."

Chapter Thirty-One

Cade

I'd watched the entourage leave from Ayla's large window. I didn't like how close Edric was sitting to Ayla, didn't like that Ward was going, and most of all, I didn't like that I was the odd man out. It wasn't even being left behind while they explored the village. It was this confounded hold on my magic. Cautious, I could understand. But Ayla's word should've counted for enough to release me.

Once the carriage had disappeared past the front gates, I sighed and turned away, walking toward the door and opening it with a little trepidation. I touched my toe to the outside, waiting for the floor to push me back, but it didn't. One small victory, then.

I crossed the landing to the door on the other side and stood there, waiting. Then, I raised my knuckle and rapped.

"Riona? Are you in there?"

No answer.

With care, I turned the knob and cracked open the door, just in case she was indecent. But she was standing next to the window, staring out into the distance. She turned her head toward me an inch to acknowledge me then went right back to the window.

"Are you all right? Ayla said—"

"What? That I'm an embarrassment? That she'd rather I hadn't come?" Riona shook her head. "That makes two of us."

"She was harsh last night, but that's not who she is," I said, closing the door behind me. "She told me you were acting strange this morning at breakfast. What happened?"

She exhaled loudly. "Edric said… He asked if Eoghan was pulling your puppet strings."

I frowned. "Why would he say that?"

"But the *way* he said it," Riona said, ignoring my question. "It's like… It's like he *knew*."

"Knew what?"

She pursed her lips, roughly sloughing off my hands. "The thing I told you, remember? About *voices*."

"O-oh." I shook my head. "Riona, I'm sure that's not what he was insinuating. If anything, *I'm* the one who should be insulted. He was talking about me, after all."

"I shouldn't have come." She wrapped her arms tightly around her midsection. "I'm a liability. I don't know what the Erlking was thinking, sending me."

"You were invited."

"But still. Why not push back?" She released herself. "Why just send me along?"

"Because he trusts you," I replied.

"And I didn't tell him about this power," she replied. "Not that it was this…"

"This what?"

"Loud." She turned to me again, fear in her eyes. "All last night, there were whispers in my mind. Like a drum." She chewed her lip again. "I've been thinking. What if…what if Eoghan's plan is to wait until Ayla and Edric combine their stones into one then compel me to take the stone for him?"

"That's ludicrous," I said. "For many reasons, the top of which is that Ayla and Edric aren't thinking of combining their stones. At least…" I frowned. "Not to my knowledge. Did they discuss it at breakfast?"

"They're only thinking of combining one thing," Riona muttered. "I left in a hurry. I don't know. I have nothing to offer, and it doesn't seem Edric even wants to talk with me about an alliance with the fae."

"Maybe because you keep leaving before the conversation can happen," I replied. "I think you just need to relax. No one here is out to get you, and I'm sure whatever magic you're feeling is just a reaction to the trolls. First time in a new place, you know? I'm sure if I had access to my power, I'd be feeling the same way." I gripped my staff, wishing it would light up in that familiar way it did.

"Still nothing?" she asked.

I shook my head. "Ayla promised she'd put in a good word for me, but considering I was left behind this morning while they wandered the town together..."

"I'm sorry."

"I don't mind that as much as..." I dug deep for magic and found nothing. "I miss it, you know? I'd gotten used to being in total control of this extension of me. Now it's...well, it's like someone hacked off my right arm."

"I've never been comfortable using magic," she whispered. "It wasn't exactly encouraged by my nanny growing up, and I wasn't given the same tutelage as the other fae. What I managed was learned to keep myself safe in the Erlking's castle."

"Maybe this power inside you is something even greater than you think? Maybe *that's* what the Erlking saw in you when he put you and Aldrick together." I watched her face carefully. "You're Birch's kin. He's not going to send you to slaughter. He doesn't strike me as that malevolent."

She chewed her lip and remained silent.

"The bigger question is how long do you think we have until Edric suspects you're not being wholly truthful?"

"I don't know. Part of me thinks he does already."

"Why don't you just come clean?"

"Are you kidding? Ayla would murder me," she said. "She wouldn't understand."

"She would, I bet you," I responded. "You need to give her more credit."

"She already hates me."

"She doesn't hate you." Riona quirked a brow, and I cleared my throat. "She's just under a lot of pressure, that's all."

"And I shouldn't add to it by letting her know I could've magicked us all up the mountain." She rubbed her hands together and stared off into nothing. "Not that I could have, without you know...potentially releasing an evil wizard on us all."

I could've tried harder to convince her she was talking nonsense, but somehow I guessed that wouldn't work. So I pushed myself off the bed and grabbed my staff. "Let's take a walk. Get out of this room and clear your head. I hear there's a library that might be interesting. Then maybe we can figure out how to broach this subject with Ayla."

><del>)-»>-»>-»>-»</del>

I wanted to help Riona, but I also had an ulterior motive in mind. With her on my arm, I might be less likely to run afoul of Edric. He seemed keen on upholding appearances in front of Ayla, and my assumption was that the same was true for Riona.

My experiment seemed to work as we walked leisurely down the long, empty hallways. I told her about the servants I'd seen the night before, then being locked in my room for asking them innocent questions.

"Nobody around now to ask, I suppose," she said with a small shiver. "It feels desolate here."

"Not at all like the Erlking's castle, eh?" I nodded to the paintings on the wall of the landscapes. "These paintings don't move."

"How boring." She cracked the first smile I'd seen from her in days. "Makes me a little homesick, I guess."

"At least there's not a free-for-all with dinner," I said then, glancing around to make sure there was no one around, I added, "but I do miss the food."

Her eyes widened, and she leaned in. "Right? Everything last night was—"

"Hang on a second." I straightened, catching a whiff of something earthy. There was no one in the hallway on either side of us, but instinctively, I looked down at the stone floor. Like water rushing through a valley, small multicolored threads of liquid traveled through the veins of the stone. I gripped my staff, the deafening sound already growing in my mind as I reached for magic.

I took a step back as the liquid pooled in place on the floor, spurting up like a fountain until it formed an old troll with pale, translucent skin, pointed ears, and long, silky white hair.

"What the..." Riona gasped beside me.

"Greetings." His voice was wizened, as if it hadn't been used in years. "I assume by your look and staff that you are Princess Riona of the fae realm and the wizard Cade?"

I worked my jaw as Riona stayed quiet beside me. "Y-yes. That's us. Who are you?"

He pressed his hand to his chest and bowed slightly. "I'm Avram, His Majesty's scholar. I give aid and guidance to our king in different areas of science and history." He tilted his head, golden eyes shifting to Riona. "And I have been waiting for you, Princess Riona."

"I'm not..." Riona started, holding up her hands. "I mean... I'm not the one who... I'm not all that interesting."

"On the contrary." Another step closer. "You're a fascinating anomaly, Princess Riona."

I resisted the urge to roll my eyes, but Riona took hold of my arm. "In what way?"

"A child of a human and a fae," he said. "It's rare for species to mix like that."

Riona's grip tightened, and I cleared my throat. "It happens, on occasion. But Riona considers herself more fae than human."

The man's eyes glittered as he surveyed her intensely. "I'd love it if you'd visit my study," he said. "There's much we can talk about."

"A study?" I lit up. He was creepy, but I was eager to get my hands on troll literature. "Like a library? Do you have books? Any I can read?"

He turned to me, looking me up and down.

I felt the same disdain that Edric cast in my direction, and my heart sank a little. "I promise, I'm not here to harm anyone," I said, hoping it sounded sincere. "Your king's binding spell on me is working, so there's no need to worry." I lifted my staff and pointed it at the wall, furrowing my brow. I was able to muster a single spark, but that was it. "See?"

"I'm afraid I am too busy to entertain," Avram said. "However, if *Her Highness* would like to visit—"

"I'll visit. With Cade," Riona said, giving me a knowing look. "But not today. Tomorrow, perhaps."

Avram bowed. "I'll be seeing you, Princess."

"What's that supposed to mean?" Riona asked, glaring at him.

"At dinner tonight," he replied. "King Edric has invited me to dine with you." Another bow. "I look forward to continuing our conversation."

And with that, he melted into the floor and disappeared.

"Ugh, another dinner?" Riona looked at the ceiling. "Can I skip? Say I'm sick?"

"Somehow, I don't feel like that'll fly," I said, watching the space the scholar had left with curiosity. "That guy was—"

"Creepy." Riona wrapped her arm around mine as if she'd fall into the floor if she let go. "C'mon, let's head back to my room. I've had enough exploring for one day."

Chapter Thirty-Two

Riona

I wasn't sure what it was about Avram that set me on edge, but *something* told me he wasn't to be trusted. He stared at me like I was a rare gemstone, some prize that he was keen on winning. I didn't want to be alone with him—and considering the trolls could travel through stone, I wasn't sure one of them wasn't lurking just beneath my feet.

Fortunately, when Cade and I returned to my room, there was already someone waiting there. Two someones, in fact.

"There you are," Ayla said, barely looking at me as she bustled around the room. She was sporting a brand-new crown on her head and had pulled out every dress in my wardrobe and laid them on the unmade bed. Ward watched the two of us curiously but said nothing.

"What's going on?" I asked.

"We have a few hours before dinner," Ayla said, straightening. "I thought it would be best if we had a little time to discuss your etiquette. You know, things to say, to not say, how to speak—"

"I know how to speak," I said, hanging back close to Cade.

"Do you?" Ayla asked.

Ward cleared his throat loudly and shook his head, and Ayla, to my surprise, softened. "What I mean to say is… It was clear from last night that you might need some help. This diplomacy thing might be new to you, as I understand you weren't required to attend such things in the fae realm."

"It's not really a thing in the fae realm," I replied. But her new tone relaxed me a little. "I guess I need some help."

"Sit. We have a lot to cover," Ayla commanded as she pointed to the small dressing station.

With my shoulders slouched, I took two steps before she told me to stop.

"Stand up straight," she said. "Don't stomp around like an oaf. You're a princess—"

"I'm not, though."

Ward made another sound as Ayla opened her mouth. She hissed at him before looking at me. "Riona, you…you are *technically* the princess of Pennlan. You may not have grown up there, and you may not know our customs, but as far as Edric is concerned, you are as royal as I am. So the first lesson of the day is to stop telling people you aren't who you are."

It was the first time she'd acknowledged my place, and yet—she'd still stopped short of claiming me as her sister.

I continued walking, mindful of my posture and the loudness of my steps, and took a seat. I'd expected her to roughly undo the plait in my hair, but she was gentle as she untangled the mess and took a comb to my locks.

"How was your tour?" Cade asked.

"Curious," Ward said.

"*Lovely*," Ayla replied with a look in the mirror. "The people were welcoming, kind, and overjoyed to meet us."

"Probably because you didn't have a wizard with you," Cade said with a frown.

"Well, maybe," Ayla said with a half-smile. "But they seem so very eager to please Edric. He is a beloved ruler, it seems."

"Probably because they don't know any differently," Ward replied. "After all, every one of them was born under the mountain, like their parents and grandparents and so on. They have no idea of any other life."

"Well…" Ayla cleared her throat. "That's true."

"I did notice something strange, though," Ward said. "Did you see any kids? Babies? Old people?"

"They're probably…around," Ayla said, busying herself with my hair.

"We saw an old person today," I said, wincing as it felt like a fistful of hair got yanked out of my head. "A creepy scholar."

"Riona, you can't—"

"Creepy is an apt description," Cade said. "He wanted Riona to come to his study to talk."

"Well, that's a good thing, isn't it?" Ayla said. "That's what you're here for, right?"

I winced again. "I would've thought that conversation would happen with Edric."

"You'd have to speak with him first," Ayla replied, the comb digging into my scalp a little harshly.

"Ow," I said, though the comb wasn't what hurt me.

"Sorry," she muttered.

"You'll get to see for yourself how weird he is," Cade said. He'd migrated over to sit on the other side of the bed from Ward. "He's invited to dinner tonight."

"Good. It'll be a chance for Riona to give everyone a better impression," Ayla said. She was able to run the comb the length of my hair now, and there was something quite soothing about it. I leaned back in the chair, but the combing abruptly stopped.

"That'll do for now," Ayla said. "We need to wash it, but I'm not sure we'll have time with all we need to cover."

"What do we need to cover?" I asked, turning in the seat.

"A lot."

⇥ ⇥ ⇥ ⇥

A lot was an understatement. Ayla schooled me in everything from how to sit, crossing my legs just so, to how to enunciate certain words. I was a quick study, as I'd always been, and though I found the entire exercise dull, it was an effective distraction from the constant pull of that other magic in my mind.

As the day wore on, Ayla tired of scholarship and moved on to the dresses.

"Where'd these come from?" I asked.

"They were in your wardrobe," she replied, picking up a pretty green dress. "This one matches your eyes. And your new tiara."

"What tiara?" I asked.

"Ward?" Ayla said. "Ward. Wake up."

Cade kicked him from across the bed, and he woke up with a snort. "Wha?"

"Where did you put the other box?" Ayla asked.

He pointed to the writing desk, where there was a small box. Ayla crossed the room to retrieve it, bringing it back to where I was seated and placing it on the table. Inside was a small tiara similar to hers, except green. I stared at it, knowing it was for me, but not quite believing it. I'd never been given anything so fine before, never even *seen* something so pretty.

"Are you sure?" I asked, catching Ayla's gaze in the mirror.

"You are a princess." She placed the tiara on my head. "Might as well look the part."

Looking was one thing, feeling it another. My steps were careful and small as I balanced the ornate object on my head as we left for dinner. Ayla seemed more used to hers, walking with confidence down the stairs. She'd chosen Cade as her escort, and he seemed happy to be back next to her.

"Can you walk any faster?" Ward grumbled, looking up at me as I carefully took each step.

"You can go on without me," I said, holding onto the railing. "I don't need an escort."

"Her Majesty insisted."

I chanced a look at him. He was wearing an amused smile, one that made him look a little more familiar.

"Did she?" I asked, reaching the step where he stood. "She seems to have decided I'm not worth ignoring."

"We had a talk," Ward said, gently taking my arm. "That thing won't break if it falls, by the way."

"I might." I let out a breath. "I'm not ready for another one of these dinners."

"Just pay attention, watch Ayla, and speak as little as possible," Ward said. "That's what I do, anyway."

>-» >-» >-» >-»

With Ward's arm through mine, I felt a little more confident walking into the dining room, though that sentiment was tested when I saw the old scholar from earlier. He seemed preternaturally focused on me, his golden eyes finding mine within seconds. I swallowed, remembering what Ayla had said about appearances, and held tight to Ward as we ventured further into the room.

Edric wore a black tunic, and his brown hair was tied back. He'd already found Ayla, engaging her in conversation the way I was sure Avram wanted to engage with me. Cade, poor guy, was trying to get a word in edgewise, but it was clear the king only had eyes for one person.

A meek-looking servant handed me a drink without looking me in the eye and did the same to Ward. He took a long sip of his without breathing then released a sigh.

"I needed that."

"Liquid courage?" I muttered, my lips on the rim of the glass.

We were beckoned to sit down shortly thereafter, and as much as I wanted to put distance between myself and Avram, he took the seat to my left.

"You look quite beautiful this evening," the old man said, cracking a smile.

I felt Ayla's gaze on me and swallowed the grimace of disgust. "Thank you."

"We appreciate the gifts, Edric," Ayla said, pointedly looking up.

"Tiaras," Ward muttered under his breath.

"O-oh!" Another forced grin. "Thank you. It's the finest thing I've ever owned."

"I'm sure that's not true," Avram said. "The Erlking must dote on his grandchild."

I thought about responding in truth, about telling him that the Erlking hadn't acknowledged me for the first sixteen years of my life. But something told me Ayla would frown on that dinner conversation.

"He did," I said, my tongue burning as I spoke. No wonder the fae didn't spend much time on platitudes and political niceties.

"Avram, what is your role in the castle?" Ayla asked, blessedly turning the conversation away from me.

"I'm His Majesty's expert in many different areas. Most notably, I have dedicated my life to understanding the intricacies of the *seod croí*." He smiled, wrinkling his face. "It is the most interesting of objects."

"What have you discovered?" Ayla asked.

"Ah, well, I'm afraid that's not to be shared," Avram said, looking at Cade. "Mixed company and all."

The wizard made an indignant noise, and I felt the need to stick up for him, since nobody else was. "Cade doesn't have his magic. What harm could there be in sharing information with him?"

"Plenty."

"Oh, Avram," Edric said with an affable smile. "The wizard is merely curious. We can share a little with him, can't we? He is, after all, a student of magic. Isn't that what you told me?"

"Very well," Avram said. "Earth magic—that is, the kind of magic trolls are born with—is unique. Connective. A troll could spread magic across oceans using the threads in the seafloor bed. It's possible for us to touch every single person on this continent and beyond."

"Just touch," Edric said with what I assumed was supposed to be a reassuring smile to me. "Or else we'd be on the throne of your grandfather."

"Edric mentioned that you're able to break matter down to its most basic level," Cade said. "And have it travel through the rock."

"Yes, but that is just a party trick," Avram said. "Our real magic lies in the art of memories."

"Like making people forget you exist?" Ward asked. "We saw a demonstration of that on the journey here."

"Yes, that is quite a *useful* trick when one is trying to keep their people's location a secret," Avram said. "But no, in this case, I'm talking about the ability to pull memory from the earth. Unlock the past."

"What do you mean?" Cade asked. "Unlock the past?"

"Perhaps instead of telling them, we could show them," Edric said. "A demonstration of our most sacred magic."

"If the king insists," Avram replied with a sigh. "Follow me to my study."

Chapter Thirty-Three

Ayla

Having only a rudimentary understanding of magic, I was out of my depth. But from the look on Cade's face, he was as confused as I was. We didn't have time to confer, as every footstep echoed in the stone hallway. Avram led us into what he'd coined his study, a large room filled with books. Next to me, Cade was practically salivating. But we didn't stop there, walking down a long passageway. It was gloomy and damp, and the lights on the wall did little to illuminate things.

We entered an empty, circular room with a single lamp hanging above our heads. Ward, keeping close to me, made a sound, and I couldn't deny the whole place was unnerving.

"Where are we?" I asked.

"This is our most treasured room," Avram said. "The place where we can call upon the memories stored in the earth to show us the past."

He walked to what at first appeared to be a solid wall, but when he put his hands to it, the rock melted away, revealing a shelf of different stones. They were unimpressive, appearing to be common rocks that could be found on any landscape across the continent. But Avram plucked one from the shelf, cradling it as if it were more precious than gold.

The elder troll placed it on the ground, and it absorbed into the floor. The lamp disappeared into darkness, and I instinctively grabbed the closest hand. The calluses on the palms told me it was Ward's. His fingers closed around mine, and some of my fear abated.

Light blossomed back into the room. The ceiling was now bathed in vivid color, almost like looking through a window into a field.

"This is…" I swallowed. "What is this?"

"As I said, the earth holds memories—much better than the air or the water," Avram said, his voice full of wonder. "The rock I placed in the floor was taken from a moment in time when the course of history changed."

"The *aos sí*," Cade murmured. "I saw… I mean, I was given a vision of this place. Of this battle." He swallowed, and his brown eyes shimmered in the light. "Is that what we're about to see?"

Avram frowned. "I'm not sure *how* a wizard… But never mind." He shook his shoulders, and his breathy voice resumed. "A thousand years ago, when the *seod croí* was whole, the species of this land gathered in the *aos sí* to take a stand against the wizard Laughlan."

Footsteps, thousands of them, thundered through the room—an army. They were split into factions, each with different armor. The fae were the most recognizable, with their tall stature and pointed ears. But Pennlan's colors were represented, and a surge of pride came over me as they walked shoulder to shoulder with the fae. A third faction was comprised of creatures I'd never seen before, a cross between man and fish with webbing around their faces. And finally the trolls, with their bodies covered in armor and what appeared to be sun hats.

Just as I got a good look at the army, the picture zoomed through the crowd until it landed on five creatures leading the march. A female fae with ebony skin, her hair coiffed in locks down her back. A male fae who shared some of her features but had lighter skin—the Erlking, based on the crown he wore. A troll who very closely resembled Edric stood next to them, his hand resting on a rather impressive axe. Next to him, a pale, female fish creature who wore a tiara of pearls and had thick lips. And finally…

I wasn't sure what it was about my ancestor that looked familiar. The king of Pennlan. My something-great grandfather. Unlike Edric, who seemed to share much of his ancestor's features, this king looked nothing like me, at least at first. But there was something in the shape of his nose that called to me. He couldn't have been older than twenty.

"He's so young," I whispered.

"Laughlan killed his father," Edric said, and I jumped, almost forgetting he was nearby. "That's why the Pennlan people came our aid when none of the other human kingdoms did."

So we were *very* much alike, then. "What are they waiting for?"

"That."

A black cloud billowed in the distance, drawing closer to the armies. A restless shiver rippled across the crowd as they knew, perhaps, this was a losing battle. Even though I knew the outcome, there was something devastatingly ominous about the impending darkness.

"Is that…a man?" Ward asked, fear evident in his voice.

My heart dropped into my stomach. Even though this was a memory, the *evil* that emanated from that thing was palpable. As it drew closer to the quintet of leaders, including my ancestor, I held my breath.

"You shouldn't have come, mo anam cara."

The female fae gripped her sword tighter, staring into the darkness. It was then that I remembered what Clíodhna had told me, about who'd made the stone.

"That's Aoibheann," Riona said.

Edric nodded. "Fearsome fae warrior, half-sister to the Erlking. Lover to Laughlan."

Aoibheann stepped forward, her hand resting on the spear on her back. "Give me the stone, *mo anam cara*. It's corrupted you."

A breathy chuckle echoed from the darkness. "You'd like that, wouldn't you? For me to give up the stone so you can destroy me." The darkness faded around him, leaving a wizard holding a staff. He was handsome, with black hair pulled back into a ponytail, and pale skin dappled with the remnants of a beard. But his eyes…there was something wrong with them. They were pitch black.

At the sight of him, Aoibheann showed her first bit of weakness, the grip on her staff loosening for just a moment. Laughlan seemed to be waiting for that and unleashed a torrent of dark magic that covered the entire picture.

"What happened?" I said. "Where did it go?"

"The actual battle is too horrible to show you," Avram said with a sad shake of his head. "Nearly every soul you saw standing there didn't make it to the end."

I exhaled, thinking about the sheer numbers I'd seen there. So much death. "But what happened?"

"The battle was fought," he said. "And won. But only just."

The picture brightened once more, and my stomach came to my throat. Piles of dead bodies littered the once-green field. The fish creature lady who'd stood next to my ancestor was dead, her head five feet from her body. My ancestor was missing an arm, but he seemed to have been tended to by magic, because the stump was no longer dripping. The others…

The wizard hadn't brought an army; he'd *made* one. He stood in the center of the field, black magic swirling around him like a vortex. As it cracked lightning to the ground, black beasts appeared with razor-sharp teeth, giant wolves the size of horses. They ran forward, snapping and biting at whatever they could reach. There was no fighting them. Swords and spears went right through them, but their teeth were deadly, tearing into flesh with a sickening sound as they moved on to the next victim.

"Laughlan! This isn't who you are," Aoibheann cried, blood dripping down a nasty gash in her face. She gripped her arm that hung by her side as she limped toward the wizard in the center of the chaos.

One of the shadow creatures bounded toward her, and she used a column of black crows to disintegrate it, gritting her teeth from the pain. She fell to one knee, crying out—but not from her wounds.

"*Mo anam cara*," she whispered through her tears. "Please, come back to me. Don't make me… Don't make me do this."

Her crows bombarded him, heading straight for his heart. They tore through him momentarily, but he healed himself within seconds, his staff glowing bright with a grayish color.

"You can't—"

The words died in his throat as the multicolored stone fell from his neck, cord sliced by a simple knife, and into the hands of the Pennlan king. He stared into the wizard's eyes, frozen for a moment in fear, as if he knew he'd just angered the most powerful creature in history.

Before the wizard could speak, he was blasted backward by a cannon of water—from where, I had no idea; there wasn't a body of water around. And before he could recover from that… The final blow came from his lover, who used her fae magic to drive a stake through his heart.

The picture faded, as did the sounds of battle, and I came back to myself, my body, my feet on the ground. I cast a quick look around the room at the others, and was relieved to find them with the same shock and horror I felt on their faces. Cade was staring at his hands, his brow furrowed in concentration. Riona looked shell-shocked. Even Ward, unflappable in most situations, was pale as he finally tore his gaze away.

"That was…" I began quietly.

"Now do you understand why we don't trust your kind, wizard?" Edric said softly, his gaze landing on Cade. "It's truly nothing personal."

He weakly nodded. "I'm nothing like Laughlan, though."

"Laughlan started off with the best of intentions," Edric replied.

"We understand," I said. "And our apologies for not…for pushing the issue. Cade doesn't need his magic, not until we're back in Pennlan."

He swallowed but didn't argue.

"What other memories are stored here?" Cade asked, looking at the shelf.

"Troll history," Avram said. "Nothing of interest to a wizard."

"When we left our lands," Edric said, by way of explanation, "we had to bring with us our most sacred history. The other stones tell tales of kings and legends even older than the *seod croí*."

Cade made a sound of disagreement, but I cleared my throat. "Thank you, Avram, for showing us this. It's much different to simply be told about the power of the *seod croí*. Seeing the destruction it could wreak should Eoghan get his hands on all four pieces..." I closed my hand around the necklace. "Our alliance becomes more important than ever."

"Indeed." Edric nodded. "Now, I believe that's enough excitement for one day. Why don't I escort you to your rooms, and we can continue our talks tomorrow?"

Chapter Thirty-Four

Ward

"Wow."

Cade spoke for all of us as we settled into our bunk beds and turned off the light. I wasn't sure if it was the vision that made me uneasy, or imagining what Eoghan would be like if he managed to find all the stones. He'd been terrifying enough even without a stone at his disposal. When he'd had Riona under his control, he'd destroyed a mountain with her power. But she'd been able to fight him, at least a little, and he'd never realized the whole of what he could do.

If he managed to get his hands on one of the other pieces... I shivered.

A pair of soft snores echoed from above and beside me. Clearly, Rutley and Elodia weren't too concerned by it. But they hadn't faced Eoghan, either. To them, it was a pretty lightshow.

I wondered what was going through Cade's mind. "You up?" I asked.

"How can anyone sleep after seeing that?" came the response.

"The blissfully ignorant." I sat up, throwing my legs over the side of the bed as I turned up the lamp a little. Cade was also sitting up, staring at his staff with wide eyes.

"Really puts those revenants in the *aos sí* into perspective," I said.

"Puts everything into perspective," he said. "I've been asking myself *why*. Why would Eoghan spend all this time and energy waiting around for Ayla to be of age? Why was this stone so important to him? But..."

He licked his lips. "That power Laughlan had was…" He shivered. "Too much for one person to hold."

I watched him for a moment, somewhat glad I had no concept of magic.

"Well, we've got half of it," I said, rubbing my hands together. "And the other half…"

"I don't want to think about him having half of it," Cade said, his gaze finally meeting mine. "We have to stop him before he gets there. We have to."

"We will."

There was a soft knock at the door, and I shared a concerned look with him as I crossed the room. I cracked open the door and relaxed.

"Riona." I opened the door wider. "What's up?"

"Couldn't sleep," she said. "Not in that room alone. Not after…"

"Same," Cade said, rising and rubbing his hands together.

The three of us stood in the dim light and stared at each other, none of us wanting to speak first. Luckily, Elodia did it for us.

"If you three are going to be up and chit-chatting, go somewhere else." She flipped over. "Some of us are trying to sleep."

⤛⤜ ⤛⤜ ⤛⤜ ⤛⤜

We moved to Riona's room, which was still something of a mess from Ayla pulling all her dresses from the wardrobe. Riona had made space on one side of the bed, but it didn't look like she'd spent much time sleeping.

I sat at the small table, Cade took the other chair, and Riona sat on the edge of the bed. The tiara she'd been wearing was on the bed on top of the dress, as if she wasn't quite sure where it should go. We sat for a moment, each of us locked in our own thoughts.

Before any of us could speak, there was another rapping at the door, and yet again, I was the one to answer. Ayla stood there, wearing a robe over her nightgown and her auburn hair free around her face. Her face was pale, and her stance guarded.

"Elodia said you were over here," she said softly.

"Couldn't sleep?" I asked, leaning against the door.

"I don't see how they can," Ayla said, glancing at the next door over. "There was…so much death. So many people. And for what?" She shook her head. "I can't even fathom…"

"Come on in," I said, opening the door wider. "I think we're all up for the night."

"I don't want to intrude," she said.

"Intrude on what?" I replied, glancing behind me. "Come on."

With Cade's help, we cleared the dresses off the bed, and the four of us sat on the corners. Ayla sat close to Cade, and Riona seemed far away from everyone. But there didn't seem to be much animosity between us —for once.

Ayla broke the silence first. "I just can't get it out of my head."

"Me neither," Cade said. "I was just telling Ward, seeing what the stone can really do, it kind of makes sense why Eoghan did what he did." Both Ayla and Riona glared daggers at him and he coughed. "I meant… That kind of power is seductive. So I can see why he'd be drawn to it."

"This is just one-fourth of the power," Ayla said, looking at the stone. "And it's…. It's so much."

"No wonder the earth kept the memory of the battle," Cade said, looking at his staff next to the bed. "If only I'd known, I might've been able to grab a pebble. Might have another memory."

"You passed through *aos sí*, right?" Ayla asked.

Riona shivered. "Let's not talk about it."

"Why? What happened?"

"Riona, the revenants can't get you here," I said with a small smile as I nudged her. "They're on the other side of the continent."

She made a face.

"When we reached the edge of the *daoine maithe* lands," Cade began, "we had two options: go through the forest realm or venture through the *aos sí*. Riona had a very clear opinion about which we should do."

"Clearly, not walk through the graveyard of monsters who wanted to eat me," she said.

"That's not…" Ayla laughed nervously. "That's not true. Is it?"

Riona lifted a shoulder.

"We opted for the forest kingdom, but the Erlking had placed a barrier spell around it that only Riona could pass through," Cade continued. "Aldrick showed up and very clearly told us if we stayed in the forest kingdom, we'd run afoul of the Erlking."

"And to think," I replied, sitting back and smirking at Riona, "if we'd listened, we might not have been in such dire straits. Maybe the Erlking would've welcomed us into his castle."

"The Erlking only tolerated you because Eoghan represented a greater threat," Riona said, a little snootily. "If we'd been caught before we'd taken the stone, you two would have been…well…" She shrugged. "I don't know. But it wouldn't have been good."

"Finish the story," Ayla said, reaching across to poke Cade.

"So we journey back to the *aos sí* and, of course, night falls. So we're walking through this creepy ancient graveyard in the dark, and we start to hear this unnatural scream. The mounds start moving and this…creature comes bursting out of the ground."

Again, Riona shivered, and I patted her leg comfortingly. "They can't get you here."

"You say that…"

"What did it look like?" Ayla asked, her gaze fixed on Cade.

"Like a fae creature, except decayed," he said, gesturing to his head. "Missing chunks of skin. Long, stringy hair."

"Okay, enough," Riona said.

"If you don't want to hear, you can go to your room," Ayla snapped.

"This is *my room*," Riona shot back with more than a little fire.

I had to snort, getting both their attention. "What?" Ayla said.

"What's so funny?"

"Just…" I rubbed my mouth, trying to wipe the amusement from it. "You two, fighting over your room. Sound kind of like sisters."

Riona's gaze shot to Ayla's face, which had grown a little pink. "If you're eager to see the revenants, I'd be happy to drop you off at the northern border," Riona replied. "And you can go see for yourself."

"Do you think they were fae?" Cade said, staring off into the distance. "Or something else? Maybe they were trolls."

"Whatever they are, they almost killed us," Riona said. "So let's not speak of them again."

Ayla played with the corner of the blanket. "I used to wish I'd gone with you. But after climbing the mountain…" She tilted her head. "This might be my last adventure."

"I'd like that," I replied with a casual smile. "You're much easier to protect when you stay within the walls of the castle."

She caught my gaze, and I half-expected her to chastise me. But she just lifted a shoulder in a half-shrug.

"We need to look for the other two pieces," Cade said, bringing the conversation back to the topic at hand. "If Eoghan gets his hands on them…"

"Edric said we should look for the *fuath*," Ayla replied.

"There are a few in the fae realm," Riona said. "But they're usually found near waters and oceans."

"Maybe there's a group of them who split off and headed somewhere," I said. "Especially if they stole a piece of the stone like the trolls did."

"What about the aether?" I asked. "Where do we even begin with that one?"

No one seemed to have an answer to that question.

Ayla looked timidly at Riona. "The Erlking doesn't… I mean, you don't think he knows where it is, do you?"

"I honestly don't know," she said. "It's not as if we're great friends, and he tells me everything."

"But you knew where the Pennlan stone was," Ayla said.

Riona's face flushed, and she looked at her hands, saying nothing.

"I bet he knows," Ayla said, more to herself than anyone else. "He has to know. I bet he knows where they all are and didn't want to tell us because he was afraid Eoghan would…" She sighed. "I don't know."

I watched Riona's face closely to see if she'd reveal anything. But she'd retreated into her own mind, staring off into the distance.

"What other memories do you think the trolls have on that shelf?" Cade asked.

"You heard them," Riona said, playing with the quilt. "Troll legends and such."

"It would've been nice if they had a memory from when the Pennlan stone was given to the king," Ayla said, lifting the stone. "And the parameters that were set on it."

"Sounds like the trolls were long gone by that point," I said. "And were probably the *reason* for the parameters on the stone."

"I just wish he'd tell me more," Ayla said, toying with the stone around her neck. "I hate being the only one who has any experience with this thing."

"You aren't," I said with a little laugh, nodding to Riona. "What was it like when you had the stone?"

Riona looked up, shocked. "What?"

"When you wielded the *seod croí*," I repeated. "What was it like?"

Her face had gone pale. "I don't understand the question. Are you saying what was it like…when… When I wasn't in control?"

"No, of course not." Ayla cleared her throat. "But when the stone was in your hand, when you used it. What was that like?"

"I'm sure I don't remember," Riona said through clenched teeth. "Considering my body and mind weren't my own."

Ayla seemed oblivious to Riona's growing discomfort. "I heard… voices when I had it. Right before I banished Eoghan. Did you hear anything of the sort?"

"There was only one voice in my mind," Riona said, her face now bright red as her eyes flashed with danger. "And I was trying my damndest to keep it from making me kill you."

Ayla finally looked up at Riona's face, and I felt the need to intervene, if only for my queen's safety. "It's late," I announced. "We should all go get some sleep."

"But—"

Cade took Ayla's hand. "Come," he said. "Let's get you settled back in bed."

He practically dragged her from the room as she sputtered in confusion and apology. Then it was just Riona and me.

"Riona—"

"You said it was late. I'm tired." She grabbed the corners of her blanket and threw them over her head, curling into a ball.

"You can talk to me about it," I said gently. "If you want."

"I don't want. Go to bed."

Chapter Thirty-Five

Cade

"What's gotten into her?" Ayla huffed as I closed her bedroom door behind us. "I was just asking a question…"

"She's understandably sensitive about Eoghan," I said. "And the *aos sí*…well, let's just say it wasn't her finest hour."

Ayla turned to me, one eyebrow raised. "What do you mean?"

"I mean…" I laughed a little, the memory funny and not at all terrifying in hindsight. "She curled into a ball and we had to save our own butts. Not that she had much to offer at the time, magic-wise. That's when we realized we might not have been following a dangerous creature…rather a kid who'd run away from home."

Ayla sat on the bed, pulling the covers over her legs. "She still gives me that feeling. Like she's constantly in over her head and just trying to keep from drowning."

"Yeah, that's kind of how it is with her," I replied, sitting next to her and leaning against the headboard. "But she won't admit to it—ever. Stubborn as…" I chuckled. "Well, you."

She sighed, shaking her head. "I don't like that. I don't like…being compared to her."

"Why not?"

"It's hard to explain." She yawned. "I guess it's late." She cast me a furtive look. "Maybe… Could you stay in here tonight?" she asked, looking up at me with those beautiful eyes. "I'm not sure I can sleep alone after watching that memory."

My heart swelled, and I pulled the blanket over me. She nestled up next to me and sighed happily. "Do you remember when we used to do this when we were kids?"

"The one time, you mean? Before Eoghan punished me for a month."

She opened her eyes, staring off into the distance. "He did everything in his power to make me dependent on him alone, didn't he? And now that I'm without him…"

"You're doing great," I said, rubbing her back gently. "Promise."

She looked at me, and my breath caught in my throat as I wet my lips expectantly. She moved toward me, and I thought I might burst…

…until her lips met my cheek.

"Night." She nestled under the covers.

My breath came in short puffs, my heart still racing as I watched the back of her head. After my body caught up with my ears, I cleared my throat.

"N-Night." I turned away from her, laying on my back as I covered my eyes to steady my breathing. A soft snore came from beside me, warming me again. As carefully as I could, I rolled back over to press a kiss to her cheek, wishing it was her pink lips. But instead, I scooted to my side of the bed, closed my eyes, and looked for her in my dreams.

⇥ ⇥ ⇥ ⇥

Unfortunately, my dreams had other plans. All night long, I was plagued by visions of Eoghan wielding all four pieces, raining terror across Pennlan and the lands beyond. When I awoke after a particularly vivid dream, Ayla was stroking my head, a smile on her face.

"You were crying out," she said. "Are you all right?"

"Yeah." I sat up. "What time is it?"

"Morning," she said. "I think. They brought me a tray of tea." She snorted. "I don't think they expected to see you here."

I wished that something scandalous *had* happened. "I'll just get some at breakfast."

She hopped out of bed, already dressed, and based on the wetness of her hair, she'd had a bath.

"How long have you been up?" I asked, sitting upright and stretching.

"I didn't sleep much last night," she said. "Kept waking up. Thinking about Eoghan. Replaying everything he ever said to me in the context of what I know now." She looked up. "Worrying about how I'm going to manage this alliance with Edric."

"One thing at a time," I said. "You're going to talk with him again today, aren't you?"

She nodded. "Alone. It's probably time to get down to business." She chewed her nail. "I don't even know what to say. I've never felt so lost." She put her hand down. "Damn Eoghan. Damn him for making me feel this way."

"You know what to do," I said. "You've always had a good instinct for ruling. Even when we were children. You just need to trust yourself to do the right thing."

She smiled weakly. "Have I mentioned how grateful I am that you're here?"

We walked arm in arm up the spiral staircase until we heard voices. The three soldiers had beaten us to breakfast, and Ward actually seemed to be in a congenial mood until he saw me. Then his eyes were like ice, glaring at me as if I'd taken his favorite thing.

Which… I might have.

"Good morning," Edric said, beaming at us. "I trust you slept well, Ayla."

"I did, absolutely." She released my arm, and I felt a little cold as she crossed the patio to greet Edric properly.

Ward took a stiff drink and clenched his jaw as Edric kissed her hand. "Did you have a good night?" he asked as I came up beside him.

"Slept like a baby," I said, hoping it would calm him down a little. "You?"

"Wondering where you went." His dark eyes bored into mine. "Where's Riona?"

I frowned, counting those assembled and not seeing her in our number. "No idea. Coming, I'm sure."

We started breakfast, and there remained an empty seat between Elodia and Rutley. Ward's gaze darted to it and the stairwell, and I had to admit, mine did as well. Riona had been upset the night before and was perhaps having a morning to herself to regain her sensibilities. I hoped.

"What would you like to see today, Ayla?" Edric asked.

"I was actually hoping we could sit down and start discussions on our alliance," Ayla said, catching my gaze. "Get some thoughts on paper, hammer out some details on how and when we'll use our stones, should the worst happen."

He smiled, but there was something behind it I couldn't read. "I'd love to have that discussion." He turned to the rest of us. "And as for the rest? I'm sure I can arrange another tour."

His gaze flicked to me, and I could already predict what he was going to say. "Don't worry," I said, holding my hands up. "I'll stay in the castle. Perhaps I can pick Avram's brain for more information about the memory stones."

"Avram is quite detained today," Edric said.

"Detained? How so?" Ward asked. "I thought he wanted to speak with Riona?"

"The scholars, they're always so busy," Edric said.

It didn't escape my notice that he hadn't answered the question directly.

>→ >→ >→ >→

For the second day in a row, I watched my traveling party gather and leave without me. Ayla and Edric took a left at the bottom of the stairs, already starting their discussions. She seemed much more confident, but perhaps that was just a facade.

Ward, Elodia, and Rutley gave some vague description of what they were going to do, but I saw them head toward the front gate, and something about entries and exits in the town.

As for me, I headed straight to the three-door landing and rapped on Riona's door. "Riona? Are you up?"

When there wasn't an answer, I cracked open the door and walked in. The lights were still off, but the fire was roaring. There was a steaming cup on the mantel. And Riona was curled under the blankets still.

"Riona?" I tiptoed into the room and pulled back the blankets. She was in her nightgown, which made her already pale skin even more so. "Riona?"

She blinked, moving slowly as she moaned. "W… Cade?"

"You must've been up late," I said, sitting on the edge of the bed.

"I don't think so," she replied. "I have a splitting headache."

I frowned, pressing my hand to her forehead. It was clammy and cold. "You don't feel feverish. Maybe you just need a glass of water and some fresh air."

"Hard to come by the latter in this place," she said, sliding her legs out from under the blankets. It was then that I noticed a small mark on her arm. It looked like a bite or bruise.

"What's that?"

"What's…" Her attention followed my gaze and she c. "No idea. Maybe I knocked it on something. Did someone slip me some wine last night? I'm so…" She shook herself. "Out of it."

"You missed breakfast," I said, feeling a little bad I hadn't brought her anything. "But I'm sure if you called loud enough, someone would bring you something."

"No, I'm fine," she said, slowly coming to her feet. "Where is everyone?"

"Ayla is off to discuss politics," I said with a heavy sigh. "Ward and the others…who knows? I've been told to stay inside the castle."

"What about me?" Riona asked.

"Since you weren't at breakfast, you weren't given an option," I said. "Much like me. We're stuck in the castle together, I believe. Perhaps we could find the famed library Edric mentioned and peruse through the books. Or find a kitchen to feed you."

She cracked a smile as she grabbed a new dress from the pile on the floor and walked into the bathroom. "I just hope we don't run into that Avram again."

"Supposedly, he's 'very detained,'" I said, mimicking Edric's low voice. "Whatever that means."

"I wonder what it is about me that's so interesting to Avram?" Riona called through the closed door. "I thought he wasn't ever going to look away from me last night."

"It's probably just that you're fae," I said. "He's never seen someone like you before. I'm sure it's fascinating."

"What about you? I'm sure he hasn't seen many wizards." She reappeared wearing the dress and braiding her hair. "Except that horrible one..."

"Yeah, exactly." I rose. "Shall we?"

"Since we have nothing else to do, sure." She took a step and swayed a little. "Kitchen first. Then library."

Chapter Thirty-Six

Riona

I was grateful for Cade's presence—and the steadiness of his arm. I must've been in a very deep sleep because I could barely even remember the night before. My dreams had been plagued by that secret place, that cold, dead garden where I heard voices. It seemed I would sink in and out of that world, coming out just to fall back in. I was sure I'd have slept for another day had Cade not woken me up.

It was clear from the wizard's eagerness he wanted an escort. I'd found it strange that Edric was so antagonistic toward Cade. But after seeing the memory stone, and what Laughlan had done, it wasn't so hard to understand. I'd been distrusting of Cade myself. Though once I'd gotten to know him, and saw just how uninformed he was, I'd realized he wasn't much of a threat.

We did find the kitchen, and I was actually grateful for the pitiful pastries and wilted fruit. By the time we left for the library, I felt more like myself and was in a much better mood.

"Well, it's not the Erlking's," Cade said with a smile as we walked inside the library. "But it'll do."

"As long as I don't have to reshelve anything," I said, walking to the stacks. It really was a pale comparison, but it truly was unfair to liken anything to what centuries of Erlkings had been able to amass. Not only that, but every book was illegible, as they all seemed to be written in some language lost to time. "Can you read…trollish, I suppose you'd call this?"

He pulled a book from the shelf and flipped it open, frowning. "Damn. No." Then his eyes lit up. "If only there was someone here who could use magic and translate—"

"No." I shook my head. "Don't even go there. I'm still…"

"Still?" He sighed, closing the book. "Riona, Eoghan's not going to jump out of your brain if you use something simple like a translation spell."

My face warmed. "Even if I *could*, I don't… I don't know how I'd do it."

"Well, the Erlking did ask me to continue your training. I can't show you anything, but we can work on your magical theory."

I shook my head. "I don't want to use magic, Cade. What if—"

"Trust me. Eoghan isn't here." He looked deep into my eyes, and something in my heart loosened. "And if he was, I'd fight him off."

A laugh bubbled up from my lips, and he released my shoulders. "You would, would you?"

"Of course," he replied. "Not saying I'd win, but…"

"Funny." I stared at my hands. Having him here made me feel safe. "Maybe we could practice. As long as you don't tell anyone. I don't want Edric finding out I lied." I swallowed. "Or Ayla, for that matter."

"You have my word." He handed me the book. "Now, when you're translating, you have to look beyond the words. Imagine the quill that scribbled them. Use your magic to lift the intent."

"Lift the…" I could almost picture what he was saying. I stared at the book, focusing on the quill strokes, hearing the sound of point against paper in my mind. I imagined an old-looking troll wearing a tattered robe, poring over the blank pages as he wrote from his own memory. What was he writing?

"Plants…" I muttered, the word coming from somewhere deep in my soul. The letters had been foreign, unfamiliar, but before my eyes, the quill strokes rearranged, forming something I could read. Something in the common tongue.

"Well, that's disappointing."

I looked up at Cade, frowning. "Did I not do it?"

"No, you did," he said, closing the book and putting it back. "But it's a discussion of how to garden in rock soil. Not all that helpful." He grabbed my hand. "Come on, let's see what else we can find."

>—» >—» >—» >—»

It was distracting, to say the least. The more I practiced, the quicker I became at the translation spell until it took just a few seconds of thinking. Cade assured me that the spell would wear off within a few hours and the text would revert to the trollish. So we plowed through book after book until we'd assembled quite a pile of translated books on the table.

Still, most of what we found was like the first, treatises on gardening, pottery, furniture-making, how best to build a house on a slope. But within the mundane, a picture of troll life before the *seod croi* emerged. Edric had said they'd lived in the wildlands, and based on the few pages I read, the land hadn't changed much. Desolate, rocky, cold with some lesser fae in the mix to cause problems to wayward travelers.

Lesser fae. Was it really so bad to use that term to describe creatures like brownies and sprites? It seemed an apt term—they weren't civilized like the *daoine maithe* or the *sidheog*, or so I'd thought. But maybe if I sat down and spoke with one of them, they might feel as the trolls did.

"It doesn't seem the current Erlking treats them poorly," Cade said. "But maybe in the past, it was a different story."

"Perhaps." I put the book back as Cade handed me another to translate. "What are you looking for, exactly?"

"I don't know," he said with a sigh. "Perhaps just something to pass the time. I'd hoped I could be more helpful, but it seems I would've been better served staying in the fae realm."

That makes two of us. "Ayla's glad to have you. She's barely let you out of her sight."

He smiled, the sort of smitten look he got when we'd talk about

Ayla. I used to find it endearing, but now…now, I couldn't quite understand what Cade—or Ward—saw in her.

"I don't know if I should go back to the fae realm when we go home," he said. "It seems like it might be better for me to stay in Pennlan."

"I'd miss you," I admitted softly. "It was nice to have a friend for once."

He turned to me, concern on his face. "You had friends, I'm sure…"

I shrugged. "My nanny kept me in my room most of the time. We had meals and lessons in there. On the rare occasion I got out for a stroll…" I could still hear the taunts. "I thought it wildly unfair for most of my childhood until…well, I realized why the Erlking had decreed it. Then I was grateful for the solitude."

He stared at me as if seeing me for the first time, and I squirmed under his pity.

"Oh, come on. You saw how they treat me," I said, my face warming. "This can't come as a surprise to you. If it weren't for my parentage, I would've been drowned as a baby, most likely."

He scoffed. "They don't drown children, Riona. That's barbaric."

"It used to be common practice."

I about jumped out of my skin as the creepy, wizened voice echoed across the room. Avram was alone, wearing his best robes. I hadn't even heard him come in, though I was sure he'd used his magic to sneak up on us.

"I apologize for eavesdropping," he said with a bow. "Your Highness."

I forced a smile. "No apology needed."

"I heard voices and I came to investigate. I can see you've been…" He made a face as he saw the stack of books on the table. "Busy."

"We'll put them back," Cade said, hastily. "I was just hoping to learn more about your people."

"I'm surprised you've been able to understand these texts," Avram said, walking to the table and opening the first page. "These are written in old trollish. Was such a language taught in your studies, wizard?"

The question was directed at Cade, but the old troll's eyes were on me. I opened my mouth, my heart thudding as I looked at Cade for a save.

"I've managed to translate them," he said, and I envied him the ease with which he could lie. "Some magic has gotten through, I suppose."

"I will have to ask the king to improve our charms, then," Avram said, with a frown. "It is dangerous to have any wizard magic in this mountain."

"He's not dangerous," I said.

"Neither was Laughlan when he started out," Avram said. "He and Aoibheann created the *seod croí* to help the continent, bring people together. Create a magic so powerful that no one would dare stand against it." He put his hands inside his robes. "Did you know what life was like before?"

Cade and I both shook our heads.

"War. What I showed you in the memory stone was nothing compared to the bloodshed that happened on a regular basis on the continent. Fae, human, even the *fuath* were in constant battle with one another." He picked up one of the books on the table and opened it. "Laughlan thought that if he created something so powerful, everyone would be too scared to fight. In the end, it poisoned his mind, and instead of deterring war, he created more."

I shivered. I didn't doubt that in Eoghan's hands, the outcome would be so much worse.

"But that's neither here nor there," Avram continued, his face brightening as if he hadn't just terrified the both of us. "I suppose translation magic is allowed, if it occupies the mind."

"If it would be easier, I'd love to have a moment to talk with you," Cade said. "Learn more about trollish magic and what's possible."

"Strange to see a wizard curious about magic other than his own. You have enough to be getting on with, don't you? Laughlan once said he could spend his life testing the limits of his own power and never come to the end of it."

Cade let out a sad chuckle. "Unfortunately, the only other wizard I've known betrayed and nearly killed me. So I'll take magical tutelage where I can find it."

"It would be a waste of both our time to teach you." He turned to me as Cade's face fell. "That being said, Your Highness, I would be eager to have some of *your* time to discuss the latest with the fae. King Edric has asked me to help him devise a strategy for dealing with our…former neighbors. I'd like to know how the current Erlking thinks."

"Cade is much more familiar with the Erlking than I am," I said as my tongue itched. "As you just heard, I spent most of my childhood with a nanny. Cade has had…" My tongue burned. "*Lots* of time with the Erlking. He knows him inside and out. If you want to devise a strategy, Cade is where you start."

I snuck a glance at the wizard, who wore a mixture of confusion and happiness. However, the troll simply made a face. "Some other time, perhaps."

Before either of us could respond, the troll disappeared into the floor and zoomed away.

"That was…" He turned his head to me. "For someone who can't lie, you're pretty good at it."

"It wasn't a complete lie," I said, running my tongue against the roof of my mouth. "Besides that, I don't like the way everyone's treating you like a pariah. You're here to help. They should let you."

"Don't worry about me," he said, waving me off. "I've got thick skin."

"No, but…" I shifted. "I know what it's like to be the odd man out. To feel like I don't belong somewhere. If I can keep you from feeling that way, too…"

He smiled at me. "You're a good friend, Riona."

Friend. More of the tension in my stomach relaxed. "So are you, Cade."

Chapter Thirty-Seven

Ayla

It was hard to keep my heart from pounding in my chest as I followed Edric into his expansive room with a large, round table. For all the build-up and effort to get here, we were finally going to do the one thing I'd hoped to accomplish. And here I was, terrified.

Perhaps it was because I'd never negotiated so boldly with another sovereign. All my interactions with other kingdoms had been through envoys and representatives. Like Lord Galliford, who'd come bearing the only bartering chips his queen had allowed. I just hoped Edric didn't offer up any children for me to marry.

"You look like I'm about to eat you," he said, staring at me from across his desk.

I cursed myself for looking weak. "Sorry. I shouldn't wear my emotions so plainly."

"But that's what's so refreshing about you," Edric said. "You're so… human. You can lie, you have real emotions, you love in one moment and yell in the other."

My cheeks warmed. "Who am I yelling at?"

"The servants mentioned you had some words with your sister the first night."

Hal— I stopped myself. "We're working through our relationship."

"Lynton and I certainly have our…disagreements," he said with a chuckle. "Family can be tough."

"I suppose we should get back to the topic at hand," I said, after a too-long pause. "Namely, Eoghan, and how we'll handle him if he should make his return—especially if he has the other two pieces of the *seod croí*."

"I don't know about you, but I'll probably cower."

"Edric."

He waved me off. "I know you're worried, but you needn't be. You have everything you need to defeat him—and you've done it before." He tilted his head to the side. "Haven't you?"

It took everything in me not to reach for the stone. "I wouldn't call banishment a *win,* but…"

"Then we'll trust that your banishment spell was effective and that the fae hid the other two pieces well." He sat back. "What else were you hoping? To take the stone with you? Combine them?"

"No, I just…" I couldn't help but grab the stone and twist it. "I suppose I was curious if they worked together. If being near one another would…enhance their existing capabilities."

"Would you be willing to part with your stone?" Edric asked then, to my worried look, added, "Just for the afternoon, of course. To let Avram look closer at it."

Everything in me told me to say no, but I needed answers. "I think I'd be more comfortable if I stayed with it. Or…more likely, Cade. He's my expert in magic."

"Avram doesn't like to be watched." He smiled. "The stone only reacts under your hand anyway, right? In Avram's hands, it'll be a pretty jewel."

But my gut was clear. "Cade goes."

"Very well." He clasped his hands. "I will warn you not to expect much. I fear there was something irreparably severed when the *seod croí* was separated. The pieces may never work together again."

"Then let's hope for our sake that's true," I said.

"For everyone's sake." He tapped his fingers on the table. "There was something else I wanted to discuss with you. I don't know if you've noticed, but our food and drink leave a little to be desired."

It took everything in me to remain passive. "I suppose I hadn't noticed."

"There's that beautiful ability to lie," he said with a genuine smile. "Once upon a time, Pennlan was the premier trading partner to the fae realm, including to us lowly trolls. I would like to reopen those lines of trade, if you'd be willing to discuss that with me."

A smile blossomed on my face. "Absolutely. We were…" I stopped, considering how much of our kingdom's woes I wanted to share. "We can start sending shipments as soon as we get back to Pennlan. We have… something of a backlog. Having a place for them to go would solve many problems."

"While I'm sure your goods are wonderful, and we will take them, I was thinking more…magical items. Goods from the fae realm." He paused. "You did open the border, didn't you?"

I hesitated, gripping my skirt. Trading with the fae had been put on hold the moment the troll showed up. "I can't speak for the fae. Only Pennlan."

He chuckled. "I suppose we really shouldn't be having this conversation without your sister. Considering she's the Erlking's chosen representative."

I forced another smile. "I believe we can make do without her. As I said, Pennlan has quite a backlog of perishable goods—wheat and some late summer crops. More than enough to get along with."

He tutted, and I felt like a child. "Ayla, I understand your impatience with the princess. I confess, it's a little disheartening to see her act so…" He sighed. "But as you said, you can't speak for the fae. We asked Riona to come, and so *she* is the one who needs to represent her kind. We can't have this conversation without her."

I forced a smile onto my face. "Very well."

>↠>↠>↠

I walked the length of the castle alone, and I was grateful for the chance to hide the dark cloud circling over my head. Of course, I was grateful Edric had proposed a trade agreement, but that it depended on Riona's participation… I should've expected this, I supposed, but I was still annoyed. But I was perpetually annoyed wherever she was concerned.

My footsteps echoed on the spiral staircase until I reached the three-door landing. I should have gone to Riona's door, but instead I found myself in front of the other door, hoping I'd find Ward or Cade there. I rapped on the door and waited, listening to the footsteps on the other side.

"Ayla." Cade opened the door wider. "How was your discussion with Edric?"

"Frustrating," I said, walking into the room. "He wants Riona in the room before we make any decisions regarding trade between nations."

"Why?"

"Because she's here on behalf of the Erlking," I said, a little impatiently. "And he would like to trade with the fae using Pennlan as a conduit."

"I see," Cade said. "Well, let's go get Riona. She's next door—"

"No." I sank onto an empty bed. "I just… How sure are we that *she* can speak for the fae? It's not as if she's displayed any great knowledge of diplomacy."

"The Erlking sent her."

"She was *requested*," I said. "There's a difference."

He sat down across from me. "Then put off trade discussions until the Erlking sends someone you feel is better suited."

"We can't put it off," I said, almost a whisper. "We have to make an agreement. Before we leave here. We have to—"

"Ayla, what's so important about getting a trade agreement with the trolls?" Cade asked. "We don't really need it. Pennlan has great relationships with the other kingdoms."

"No, we don't." I couldn't meet his gaze. "We have nothing."

"Surely, that's not…" He took a breath, perhaps reading the

expression on my face. "Why didn't you tell me?"

"I didn't want to put it in writing," I said. "But... Eoghan left us in a bad position. We're highly in debt, and the only thing the kingdoms want as payment is..." I dangled the stone. "This or sending you to live at one of the other kingdoms. And I wasn't going to do that."

"I would have gone," he said softly.

"Before Lynton arrived, I'd been entertaining the last envoy who would meet with me. But the only thing he wanted to discuss was a marriage with their eight-year-old prince."

"That's why you asked the Erlking for help," Cade said slowly.

"I didn't want to," I said. "Ward thought it was a better option than whoring myself out."

"Well, of course it's a better option. The fae are eager to rebuild the alliances," he said. "And the Erlking was...confused why it took you so long to respond to his messages."

I exhaled slowly. "Because I still don't trust the fae."

"Ayla."

"You don't go believing one thing your entire life then just believe something else," I replied hotly. "And I'm not the only one. The merchants... Even Lord Galliford thought the fae had bewitched me. Nobody believes Eoghan was...as evil as he is." I licked my lips. "I don't believe it half the time, either."

"But the trolls are *technically* fae—"

"Not fae like..." I blew air between my lips. "They seem as much in fear of the Erlking as I am. So the enemy of my enemy is my friend."

"Except they aren't your enemy." Cade narrowed his gaze. "Is that why...why you've been so mean to Riona?"

It was less a question, more of a statement. I didn't like the accusatory tone, either. "I'm not being mean. I'm just frustrated. She's supposed to be..."

Supposed to be what, I hadn't a clue. Not here, for starters. Back in the fae realm where I could pretend she didn't exist.

"If you ask me, I think it's time the two of you sat down and had a real discussion about…well, everything," Cade said.

"That's what Ward said," I replied. "Told me to have it out with her. Lay all my cards on the table."

"It's good advice. She's your sister—"

"Half," I whispered.

"You have to stop doing that," Cade said. "Sure, she's your half-sister, but she's still your *sister*. The sooner you start saying it, the sooner you'll accept it." He stood and crossed the small room to sit next to me. "I promise you, she's dying to get to know you better. She's so much like you, it's uncanny."

I didn't respond, the notion that this stranger was anything like me rubbing me the wrong way. "Edric will only discuss trade if she's in the room, so I suppose… I suppose we should…*talk*. Figure out what we want from him, and what she's willing to…or I suppose, what she's *able* to agree to."

"There you go," Cade said. "Riona will agree to whatever you ask of her, I'm sure of it."

Whether that agreement would hold up with the Erlking was another matter.

"You have to give her a chance," he said, a little softer. "She's risked so much for you. She ran away without a shred of magical knowledge and guided us through the wildlands. Saved our lives at least three times. All because she wanted to get the stone back *to you*. So you could protect yourself from Eoghan." He tilted his head. "Doesn't that at least earn her a little less shortness from you?"

It should have. But there was something deep within me that wanted nothing more than to erase her from my memory. "There's more." I slipped the stone from around my neck and already missed it. "Avram would like to take a closer look at it, and I hoped you might escort the stone for me."

"Of course." He took it from me gently. "Anything to be of use. I feel like all I've been doing is sitting around and being told what *not* to do."

"I'm sorry," I said. "I've been trying to convince him that you're not a threat. But I guess…" I shivered, thinking about the vision of Laughlan. "I guess when all you know of wizards is what they saw in that memory stone…"

"Shame there isn't more about the *seod croí*," Cade said, eyeing the stone. "But maybe Avram will be able to find something we haven't noticed about our stone."

"I trust that you'll keep a close eye on it," I said. "And make sure it's returned to me safely."

"I'll defend it with my life," he said, mock saluting and sounding a little too much like Ward for my liking. "Your Majesty."

Chapter Thirty-Eight

Ward

With Ayla and Edric busy discussing the futures of their kingdoms, I took my chances at the front gate of the castle. I still didn't know how much Edric controlled the city, and I wanted to look around without him peering over my shoulder.

"Gonna be a short trip if he's got some kind of magic on the castle keeping us inside," Rutley said.

"Well, never know 'til you try," Elodia added.

I walked up to the open gate and waited a moment. Then I took one step beyond the castle gate and held my breath.

"You haven't been turned into a statue, if that's what you're expecting," Rutley said with a chuckle.

"Then what are you two waiting for?" I snapped. "Let's go."

I kept looking over my shoulder, expecting Edric to show up and march us back into the castle, but we ventured all the way into the city without incident.

"Where to now, boss?" Elodia asked.

"Walk the perimeter," I said. "Look for tunnels or anything that might lead us out of here in a pinch. And maybe see how that cart works."

They saluted and split up, and I headed straight into the town center, taking in every shop and business. It seemed to be a thriving little city, though everything perishable seemed even closer to rotten than what we'd been served at the castle.

I found myself curious enough about the butcher shop to go inside. At least, it said it was a butcher shop. There wasn't much meat hanging in the window.

"Good morning," I said. "I think."

"What can I do for you?" he asked, beaming at me.

I hesitated, waiting for him to mention that I was human, and when he didn't, I shrugged it off. "I was just…passing through town and wondered where all the children are."

"Oh, they're around," he said. "What can I do for you?"

I tapped my fingers on the counter. "Where do you keep your livestock?"

"Oh. Around." He beamed again. "What can I do for you?"

I stared at him, curious. "Where do you keep your livestock?"

"Around." Another flash of a grin. "What can I do for you?"

I sat back on my heels, surveying him closely. It was almost like… he was forgetting what he'd said to me a few moments before.

I turned away then looked back at him. "Where did this livestock come from?"

"My farm. It's…" He blinked, looking confused for a moment. Then that blank smile came back to his face. "Good morning! What can I do for you?"

"Nothing," I said, stepping away from him. "Thank you for your time."

I walked a few blocks, watching the people closely. For the first time I noticed that as soon as I was out of eyeshot, they would have a spasm then seemingly do something else. It was very similar to what the humans on the mountain did when they saw Lynton.

But why would Edric need to cast that same spell on his own people?

I retraced the path we'd walked the day before until I found the jeweler's shop. We'd spent almost an hour in there the day before, and he'd seemed to remember more than a five-minute conversation. So maybe—*maybe*—he was exempt for some reason and might be able to tell me something.

I pushed open the door and held my breath as he looked up at me.

"Well, I'll be." He smiled. "A human! In troll country?"

I inwardly groaned. This didn't bode well.

"I was in here yesterday," I said, approaching him slowly. "Do you remember me?"

"No. Yesterday I was in the mines gathering gems," he said, wiping down his table with a cloth. "Then I…" He blinked as if he were on the cusp of remembering something. "Then I…"

I leaned in, waiting.

He looked at me, smiled and whistled. "Wow! A human! In troll country!"

"Damn it," I muttered. "So you're just as helpful, huh?"

"I'm sure I don't know what you mean." He beamed, much like the butcher. "What can I do for you?"

"Remember me, for one," I said. "And tell me why everyone seems to have a serious memory problem in this place."

I turned to leave when his voice stopped me.

"The humans…they helped us. I remember."

I spun around, hopeful. "They did?"

"They…" He pinched the bridge of his nose. "They were… They came to our aid… They marched with us."

"Marched when?" I asked.

"When we…" His face slackened then brightened. "Wow! A human! In troll country!"

>→ >→ >→ >→

I left the jeweler but didn't have anywhere to go. The villagers passed me by, had some kind of reaction, then their faces slid back to whatever expression they'd had before, forgetting I ever existed. They seemed happy, but was that because they were actually happy or because Edric had them under a spell?

And what was the jeweler talking about? Humans coming to their aid? If I hadn't known better, I would've thought he was talking about the battle of the *aos sí*, but that was over a thousand years ago.

Still, the question remained: why would Edric need to keep everyone in this town under a memory spell? Was it just for our benefit, only because the humans were visiting? Or was this an ongoing thing? And if so, what was he waiting for?

"Boss!"

I jumped, too lost in my own thoughts to hear my own name. Elodia came jogging up, waving me down.

"Sorry," she said. "Thought you might've been suckered in like these poor souls, too."

I nodded. "What did you find on the perimeter?"

"Nothing," she said. "I can't even find where that cart dropped us off. It all seems to have…" She gestured to the air. "Disappeared."

"Of course it did," I said, more to myself than her. "So there's no way out of here unless Edric lets us out."

"Do you think he won't?"

"I think it's dangerous to leave that decision up to one person—especially when we don't know his true intentions," I said.

"Well, Rutley's doing another loop, just in case there's something we missed."

We passed another group of trolls who stopped to stare at us for a moment before their memories were erased. I watched them go, noticing they, like everyone else, seemed young, fit, healthy. "Any sign of kids or old people?"

"Nope." She turned to watch the group continue. "Why would Edric need to put his own people under this forgetful spell?"

"Maybe so they don't know they've been stuck under a mountain their entire lives?" I offered, taking a shot in the dark. But it sounded plausible. "I doubt he'll tell us. Probably come up with some 'reasonable' excuse for everything."

"Or blame it on Lynton," she said.

"Speaking of," I turned to her. "Haven't seen much of our guide, have we? He dropped us off on the front step and disappeared. Wonder what that's about."

"Probably got tired of our nonsense," Elodia said with a snort. "Between Ayla's frosty reception, Riona's nervous tics, and Cade trying and failing to use his magic, we were probably an obnoxious bunch to travel with."

I couldn't argue with her there. "C'mon, let's go find Rutley and head back to the castle. I doubt there's much else we'll find out from these people."

We found Rutley walking a slow path along the edge of the cave. He reported nothing new from what Elodia had already told me. We were effectively trapped.

"No wonder he doesn't want Cade or Riona to have their magic," Rutley said.

"Yeah, Riona could blow a hole in the top of the mountain," I said, glancing up. "At least, she could under Eoghan's control."

"Seems strange, considering how…" Elodia trailed off. "Never mind. I like the kid. I shouldn't speak poorly of her."

"Then I will," Rutley grunted. "She's squirrelly. I think she's hiding something, too."

"Riona's always hiding something," I said. "But usually it's because she has a good reason."

"Is it?"

"I mean, sometimes."

Loud footsteps echoed in the street, and almost too late, I saw Lynton turn the corner. He wore a tunic and dark pants, his hair clean and swept behind his ears. He walked with intensity, ignoring the waves of greeting from the citizens who passed. They, at least, didn't forget who he was.

"Where's he going?" Elodia muttered. "And why does he look like he's about to murder someone?"

"I don't know," I said. "But I want to find out. If anyone in this place has answers, it's him."

"Do you think he'll tell you any?" Rutley asked.

"Well, no." I cracked a smile. "But whoever he's meeting with might spill something. Either way, I want to know where he's going."

⋗⋙ ⋗⋙ ⋗⋙ ⋗⋙

We kept a healthy distance, but Lynton seemed lost in thought and unaware that anyone was following him. He did seem to have a purpose in mind, though, as he walked into a small square with a fountain. The three of us found a hiding spot near enough that we could listen, and we crouched and waited with him.

After several minutes, Edric materialized from the ground, looking quite bored to be there.

"What is it you couldn't wait to tell me?" he drawled.

"It's been three days," Lynton growled. "What's your plan?"

"I have one. You just have to be patient."

"I've been patient," he said, walking forward. "I brought those humans here at great personal risk because *you promised*—"

"And your loyalty will be rewarded," Edric said. "Avram has what he needed, but he requires a little more time to put it into practice."

"How can we be sure it'll even work?" Lynton grumbled. "You've bet a lot on this."

"And it's my price to pay if it fails."

"That's the thing." Lynton turned around. "It's *not* your price to pay. It's mine. It's everybody who's been stuck here. You gave away the one thing we needed to keep them alive, and for what—"

"For something better." He smiled. "Don't worry. Everything's under control. Soon, we'll be able to leave this place and reclaim our lands." He tilted his head to look at the waterfall in the distance. "In the meantime, there's enough magic in the water to keep everyone placated."

"Placated." He snorted. "Is that what you're calling it?"

"You were one of the placated until I woke you up," Edric said, warning in his voice. "So I suggest you keep your tone to yourself unless you'd rather forget about your daughter again."

Lynton flinched and looked away.

"That's what I thought." He patted his cousin on the shoulder. "You'll just have to trust me. Not that you have any other choice. But I do have your best interests at heart. Now, if you'll excuse me, I have to go back to playing nice with the queen and her sister."

He disappeared into the ground, and Lynton took a few breaths, staring at the space he'd left. Then with a feral growl, the troll turned and marched away.

"That was…" Elodia breathed behind me. "What was that?"

"I knew that king was up to something," I said with a shake of my head. "What he's up to, I still don't know. But it's *something*."

"We need to tell the queen," Rutley said.

I almost agreed with him, but something held me back. Ayla had some blinders on where the trolls were concerned. She would dismiss what I told her—or worse—unless I had definitive proof.

"Let's get back to the castle," I said. "Not a word to Ayla or anyone else, for that matter. Not until we know what we're dealing with."

"What about Lynton?" Elodia asked. "Should we follow him?"

"Edric will notice something's wrong if we don't show up for dinner," I said. "But we know he's around here somewhere. We'll just have to find him again tomorrow."

Chapter Thirty-Nine

Cade

The Pennlan stone was foreign against my skin. Even though I didn't have access to my magic, I could feel something *living* inside it. Power, yes, but more than that. But every time I came close to putting it into words, that damn troll charm would roar to life, and I'd forget what I was trying to say.

It was probably for the best. I didn't want to get into the habit of holding it or sensing its power. It had driven two wizards absolutely bonkers, and I didn't want to make it three.

Still, I could honestly say my curiosity was driven by my thirst for knowledge. Perhaps with this peace offering, Avram might be a little less defensive with me and share more about troll magic.

I reached the observatory and rapped on the door.

"Ah. His Majesty said you'd be coming," Avram said, opening the door wider. "Very well, hand it over."

"That wasn't the agreement," I said, closing my hand around the stone. "Ayla asked me to chaperone."

"I assure you it will be quite safe."

"And I assure you that *I* am quite safe, too. So there should be no problem letting me observe your experiments."

He stared at me, huffed, then opened the door. "Take care not to touch anything."

The room was cramped with very little space to move. Large tables covered in interconnected glass tubes, cauldrons over blue flames, and other scientific minutiae had been shoved against all four walls. Bookshelves had been hung above them, with several of the old tomes sitting amongst the vials. I had so many questions, I didn't know which to ask first.

"The stone, please." Avram held out a pewter bowl. "You will let me have it to experiment on, won't you?"

"Yes, of course."

I put the stone in the bowl, and he snatched it back as if I'd change my mind.

"What sort of experiments are you going to run?"

"I wouldn't expect—"

"Indulge me," I said, leaning over to peer at a glass tube filled with a thick, red potion. "What's this?"

"Don't touch that. It's a very sensitive potion, and I'm not sure you'd like the result."

I stepped backward, unsure if that meant it was explosive or poisonous or something else.

"I'm using magic to understand the properties of the stone," he said as I walked up beside him. "Ours has a unique signature, of course. But the jagged pieces are in need of something."

"The other pieces?" I offered.

"Most likely, yes. But maybe something else." He put his hand on the table, and the troll's stone appeared. He put Ayla's next to it and turned it around until the jagged edges fit together. But nothing else happened.

"It's that something else we're looking for."

"Do you have any theories?" I asked.

"Unfortunately, those that split it aren't around to tell us anything," Avram said. "It could be that all four pieces need to be together in order for the connection to be reestablished."

I reached for the two stones, and the troll slapped my hand.

"Your queen may be willing to let you hold hers, but we are not willing to let you see ours," he said with a fiery look.

"I understand why you don't trust me, but I wish you would try."

He surveyed me. "You are…not from this continent, are you?"

"No. I'm not quite sure where I'm from," I replied. "Why?"

"You have a unique magical signature," he said. "It's unlike any other I've felt before."

"Probably because I'm a wizard," I said with a grin. "I'm probably the first one you've seen in person."

He didn't respond.

"I know… Well, I know that we have a pretty bad reputation between Eoghan and Laughlan. But I'm not like either of them."

"Mm." He turned away from me. "I'm going to continue working. If you must stay, I ask that you remain quiet and let me work in peace."

>→ >→ >→ >→

Avram didn't share what he was doing, but it didn't look to be much. If he was casting spells, there was no sign of them. Once or twice, I broke the silence and asked him, but it was met with a sneer. After a few hours, he finally turned to me and deposited the stone in my hand.

"I will need more time with it," he said, giving me a look. "If your queen feels safe enough to leave it with me—"

"I'm sure she'll feel safe enough to do that when you feel safe enough to share with me," I said, a little irked from being in this cramped room all day. "But in the meantime, where the stone goes, so do I."

I left the room, knowing I'd made no friends but not really caring. Avram was more than just reticent, he was downright rude. And I didn't really feel like trying to be nice when he didn't give me the same courtesy.

"…keep this to ourselves…"

I furrowed my brow, hearing Ward's voice in the hallway around the corner. I quieted my steps, finding him walking with his two soldiers. They seemed to have just come in from the front door of the castle. Had they been out in the city?

"Any orders for this afternoon?" Elodia asked.

"Get cleaned up," he said. "We'll make an appearance at dinner tonight. Tomorrow, I want to—" He looked up, seeing me. "Cade. Good. We need to talk."

"Where have you three been?" I asked, stepping out from my hiding spot and joining them. "I hope it wasn't disobeying Edric's orders to stay in the castle."

"You're the only one who was explicitly told that," Elodia said with a knowing look.

I couldn't disagree, but somehow, I felt Edric wouldn't be too happy. "Where did you go? And why?"

"Elodia, Rutley," Ward said. "Dismissed. I'll be up in a second."

They saluted and continued on their walk, Rutley throwing a look behind him to where I stood. Ward waited until they were out of earshot then motioned for me to follow him. He didn't say a word until we exited the castle into a sculpture garden.

"Don't want to be overheard," he said. "Though somehow I feel there's nowhere in this place that we'd be safe from that."

I crossed my arms over my chest. "What's wrong?"

"I wanted to get out into the city because I felt something was off yesterday," Ward said. "Plus, I wanted to find an exit, should we need one."

"Did you find one?"

"No. But that's the least of our problems." He leaned in. "Cade, *everyone* in this place is under a memory spell. The same one Lynton used on the humans in the mountain villages."

I stared at him, confused. "What makes you say that?"

He told me about the conversations he'd had, and how the trolls would seem to forget him after about a minute or so. I listened with a little skepticism, knowing that Ward had been looking for trouble since we'd arrived.

"Maybe the butcher has a memory problem," I said.

"The jeweler, though. We'd spent hours in his shop," Ward said.

"And he had no memory of it. He said…he said he remembers the humans coming to their aid. But when would that have happened?" He ran a worried hand over his hair. "What do you think?"

"I have…no clue. But I'm sure there's a reasonable explanation."

"Reasonable for whom?" He turned to me. "Cade, for just *one* second, try to pull your head out of Ayla's butt and use it. You've been denied the use of your magic. Riona's been denied the use of her magic."

I tried not to look guilty at that second statement, but Ward probably wouldn't have noticed anyway. He seemed to be on a rampage.

"Not only that, but we just saw Lynton and Edric get into it. Lynton was talking about some plan of Edric's, and Edric told him to be patient." He took a breath and stared at me. "Well?"

I sighed, torn between needing to be on Ayla's side and what my eyes were telling me. "Fine. It's suspicious. Avram was being very cagey just now. He has all these experiments in his observatory and refused to tell me anything about them."

"Good to know he's not to be trusted either." He smiled, clapping me on the shoulder. "So let's tell Ayla. Together."

"Unfortunately," I pushed his arm off me, "Ayla won't listen even if we tell her together."

"She will if you—"

"No." I shook my head. "Listen, this is bigger than just the Pennlan stone. Ayla's trying to cement trading alliances with the fae and the trolls since the humans aren't trading with Pennlan anymore." I couldn't help but continue, "Surely, she's told you about that."

"She has, but if the trolls trap us here or erase our memories or whatever they're planning, it won't matter *who* we trade with."

"I don't think that's what they're after," I said. "But Ayla's desperate. So we need to give the trolls the benefit of the doubt until we *know* for sure that there's something to be worried about. As much as I hate to say it, those trolls out there…what Edric does with them is of no concern to us. The only thing *we* need to worry about is getting Ayla that alliance she's after…and not doing anything that could potentially hamper it." I leaned in closer. "Including leaving the castle unaccompanied by Edric or any other troll."

"No need to leave the castle anymore," he said. "I had Rutley and Elodia do a loop of the city. We're sealed in here. There's no way out unless *Edric* says so."

"So you want to make him angry by snooping?" I asked with a quirked brow.

"Not snooping," Ward said with a sniff. "Just assessing the situation. I'd rather risk the troll king's ire than be caught flat-footed. At least we know we're trapped now and can plan accordingly."

"Edric seems nice enough," I began slowly.

"I don't believe a word out of his mouth," the soldier replied. "And neither should you." He stared out onto the city like a caged animal. "But I still think we need to tell Ayla about the people out there. Let her make her own decision about it."

"Ayla's got enough on her plate right now," I said. "Give her a few days to get this trade agreement with Edric before you bring all your concerns to her."

Ward ran his tongue along his teeth, annoyed. "There are four other human kingdoms, plus the fae. She doesn't need to beg anyone for a seat at the table. But fine. She can do whatever she wants. She's the queen."

CHAPTER FORTY

RIONA

I expected to be called for dinner, but when the servant came, she told me the king had been detained and would be unable to join us.

"The queen's asked you to join her in her quarters."

I steeled myself for another lecture, another round of pointing out every flaw I had, but when I walked into the room, she actually smiled at me. It wasn't totally genuine, but it seemed an attempt at one.

"You sent for me?" I asked, staying close to the door in case I needed to run.

"I thought we could have a meal together," she said. "Just the two of us."

I narrowed my gaze suspiciously. "Why?"

She straightened her shoulders, and the fake smile disappeared. "Because Edric wants you to join us for our trade negotiations, and..." She licked her lips as if she had a bad taste in her mouth. "Well, I want to talk about what the Erlking's allowed you to agree to and align that with what's in Pennlan's best interests."

I opened and closed my mouth, no idea what she was talking about. "Um. Whatever Pennlan needs, of course, we'll agree to."

"You can't..." She took a breath. "Riona, it's not your place to just say okay to *everything*."

"I don't really understand what you're asking me, then."

"Surely, the Erlking told you what you could and couldn't do. Advice, something to offer, approval to seek certain things." She tilted her head at me.

I shrugged. "He said I couldn't make our relationship worse."

Her eyes bugged out of her head. "That's it? He sent you halfway across the continent without *any* guidance?"

I shook my head.

"This is hopeless," Ayla whispered, sitting back. "I don't know why I thought this would work."

"Now wait a minute." I walked farther into the room. "What's so important about a trade agreement? We came here to discuss an alliance of the stones, didn't we?"

"In part," she said, picking up her fork and pushing a sad vegetable off her plate. "I don't know if you'd understand."

"Try me." I sat down.

She waited a moment. "Pennlan has an economy, but it relies on other kingdoms' goods to make up for what we lack. We have a number of fields for wheat, but we don't have ore and such for metalworks, for example. So if we want metal, we have to trade our wheat with the other kingdom for it."

I nodded. "Makes sense."

"But the problem is that these other countries have their *own* wheat, so there's not as much demand for ours," she continued. "Which is why we have to have *good* relationships with the other kingdoms so that they'll encourage their merchants to buy ours so we can keep things moving."

Again, I nodded.

"Now…" She licked her lips, a distasteful look on her face. "When I ascended the throne, I realized that we'd been *taking* much more than we were giving and we had a huge deficit."

"Why?"

"Eoghan promised them things," she said, and it was hard not to flinch at the easy way she spoke that monster's name. "Namely, Cade or myself. But neither of those things are available, and so the kingdoms have decided to slow trading with us. Many of our goods are sitting on the border, unused and decaying. So I need to find someone who'll take those goods. That's why I was hoping to get an agreement with the trolls. But they won't make any agreement without you present because they want to trade with the fae, too." She paused. "And my fear is that you may agree to something the Erlking doesn't want you to, thus making our entire agreement invalid."

"If the Erlking didn't trust me to make decisions, he shouldn't have sent me," I said. "He knew what this was. And...I think you can trust me, too."

She met my gaze, a storm of emotions hiding inside there.

"You can trust me," I said, reaching across the table to take her hand. She jumped, as if I were going to attack her, then settled.

"I suppose it's better to ask for forgiveness," she said, after a moment.

"That's my philosophy."

We sat in silence for a moment before Ayla spoke again. "Wine?"

"No, that stuff is..." I paused, wondering if this was a test of my etiquette. "No, thank you."

"It's garbage," Ayla said, pushing it away. "You don't have to pretend."

I sat up straight. "Really?"

"When the people here taste the Pennlan varietals, they won't know what to do." She chuckled. "They aren't as good as some of the others, but comparatively, they're delicious."

"Good. It's hard to know what to say when Edric asks me how the food is."

"What does it feel like when you...." She glanced from side to side as if making sure no one could overhear us. "*Lie?*"

"It's not pleasant," I said. "For a full-blooded fae, if they try to lie, their throats close up. For me, depending on the severity of the lie, it's either a tickle or..." I made a gagging sound.

She leaned in. "What's the worst lie you've ever told?"

"Well, I suppose the *biggest* was when someone asked if I knew who my parents were," I said slowly. "And lying to Ward and Cade when we were looking for the Pennlan stone…that was pretty tough. But more because I had to keep up a story than because of discomfort."

She smiled. "Ward tells me they were pretty put out with your half-truths."

"They didn't believe me even when I *told* the truth," I said, a wry smile coming to my mouth. "Cade, especially."

"Nice to see he's come so far, hm?" Ayla said. "I honestly couldn't believe he'd so eagerly leave Pennlan to study with the fae, considering…" She trailed off, her cheeks growing rosy again. "A-anyway."

But it was my turn to be curious. "How many marriage proposals have you gotten?"

"More than I care to count," she said with a sigh. "I wouldn't mind if it wasn't so transparently about getting the stone. If someone were interested in just…me…"

"Ward's interested," I said.

Her face reddened again. "Yes, but that brings with it its own set of complications."

"Like?"

"Well, he's not from another kingdom, so there's no political alliance to be had with him. And…" She became interested in her glass.

"And what?"

"And he's been kind of a jerk lately."

"How so?"

"He didn't want me to come, for one. And he's been suspicious of Edric."

"Probably because he's jealous," I said. "He and Cade butted heads the whole journey through the fae realm because they both wanted to impress you."

Her face flushed. "We didn't really talk much about that. Your trip. Why you decided to help them."

I hesitated for a moment, unsure if I wanted to share. But she seemed receptive. "Leandra told me to."

Her head snapped up. "She's—"

"No." I swallowed. "When I was younger, she visited me from time to time in a dream. I don't remember anything specific, except this feeling of..." I smiled. "Completeness." I cleared my throat and looked at my hands. "No one ever told me who I was or who my parents were, but I always knew it was my mother who came to me."

"But your grandfather surely acknowledged your relationship," Ayla began. "Or your grandmother?"

"It was safer for me if they both ignored me completely," I said. "Safer that everyone ignored me."

"Have you seen Leandra again?"

I twisted my hands on the fabric of my shirt. I'd visited that place, but it wasn't Leandra that haunted me there. "No. Not for a while."

"I'm sure that's because you're well taken care of," Ayla replied. "And no longer in need of her guidance."

I wished I could say that was the case, but I didn't argue with her.

"I don't..." Ayla inhaled quietly. "I don't remember her. Sometimes I thought I dreamed about her, but she wasn't very friendly in those dreams. I think they were just my poisoned imagination." She paused. "But on occasion, I'll have a vision of a raven-haired woman who had a pretty smile and held me to her bosom."

"She loved you," I said, a little dreamily.

"I wonder if my mother ever came to visit me in my dreams," she said softly. "Or if it's just a fae thing."

"I've never seen..." I swallowed, unsure what to call him. "Bresel. Just Leandra."

"I see."

More silence descended between us.

"I should probably go," I said. "Big day. Need to get some rest."

"Yes, me too." She looked at her hands. "You should probably take a bath tonight."

"Why do you say that?" I asked, trying to look normal.

"You've had the same smudge of dirt on your neck since we arrived," she said. "Might be time to hop in. Especially since we'll be in close quarters with Edric tomorrow."

I hadn't gone near the bathtub since the first night, when my hands had glowed. It seemed every time I got near water, the voices in my head grew louder.

But I didn't want to share that with Ayla, and she might ask questions if I showed up tomorrow with that dirt. So I forced a smile onto my face.

"I'll make sure to scrub harder," I said.

>» >» >» >»

I stared down the bathtub as if it were Aldrick, taunting me from across the training arena. It shouldn't have been so scary. Perhaps I'd even dreamed my glowing hands. We'd just arrived; I'd been tired. It was plausible. Yet I stood frozen in place, wishing I'd had the courage to ask Ayla or even Cade to be in here with me. A fearsome warrior I was.

I finally unstuck my feet and walked to the mirror, staring at my reflection. I didn't look anything like the princess they wanted me to be. I was just…an imposter.

But Ayla needed me to at least pretend to be something I wasn't. Besides that, the sooner we got this trade agreement out of the way, the sooner I could go home.

Home.

Then again, that wasn't appealing either. Aldrick would be waiting with a spell in hand, and the Erlking would just expect me to use magic to get out of it. At least here, I could pretend I was struggling.

Who are you kidding? You are struggling.

There really were no good options for me. So with a deep breath, I reached for the tap and twisted it on, the magic deep in my bones stirring to life. I put my hands under the tap and reveled in the warmth that rushed over them. It was soothing.

I cracked open an eye to check and exhaled. No glowing. Just normal water for a normal half-fae ball of anxiety.

There was another tap, and I turned it slowly, as a stream of something sweet and soapy mixed with the bathwater. Perhaps more troll magic, because it immediately relaxed the tension in my shoulders. I stepped into the bath, all my fears gone. My feet relaxed immediately, as did the rest of me as I sank deeper into the sweet-smelling liquid. I ducked my head under, blowing air out as calmness covered me head to toe.

I sat up, leaning back into the cushion they'd been so nice to leave for me, and for the first time in ages, I forgot what I was so worried about. I closed my eyes, letting myself fall deeper into relaxation, deeper into calm, deeper into…

My feet crunched the snow as a frigid breeze whipped against my cheeks. This silent garden was calm, and for once, so was I. Everything was dead and frozen, but also peaceful. I was at ease for the first time since leaving the fae realm. Inhaling, I filled my lungs with cool air and as I exhaled, my breath puffed up around my face. This place, this place was sacred and peaceful. No matter where I was in the world, I could always come here.

Riona.

I froze, looking around. The voice was garbled, familiar and yet not. As if it were coming from somewhere far away. There was a figure in the darkness, coming ever closer to me. My ethereal form was drawn to it, but I dug in my heels as best I could. Something was wrong about this place—about that voice.

But I was like a sinking stone, unable to break free of the prison that had once been a sanctuary. My body was like lead. It was a little hard to breathe, but with effort, I drew air into my lungs.

I sat up and immediately regretted it. My head felt like it was about to split open, my body felt like a sack of sand. Even thinking was hard, so I lay back down on the pillow and curled into a ball.

Pillow. I was in bed.

When did I get in bed? The last thing I remembered was falling asleep… In the tub.

Shame crawled up my spine. Not only was I in bed, but someone had *dressed* me in my nightgown. I shivered, my stomach coming to my throat at the invasion of my privacy. But I couldn't figure out why…why I'd fallen asleep.

I gathered my strength and crawled out of bed, keeping my eyes half-closed as I stumbled to the bathroom. It was clean—no sign of my bath the night before. My clothes, even, had been removed from the floor where I'd left them. Servants, most likely.

I turned to the bathtub to turn on that sweet-smelling tap when I realized it was gone. Maybe I'd imagined it. Maybe I'd had the wine I was sure I'd declined. Maybe…

Maybe I needed to find Cade.

CHAPTER FORTY-ONE

AYLA

I tapped my fingers against the stone table, feeling the minutes tick by. "I really don't know what could be keeping Riona."

Edric smiled and poured more tea into my cup. "I'm afraid it's me. Perhaps my troll nature is too much for her—"

"No, absolutely not," I said with a nervous smile. Even if it was, she should have… No, I would give her the benefit of the doubt.

"It very well could be," he said. "Trolls and fae, our history goes back generations."

"She came all this way," I said. "She wouldn't have if she were scared of you."

"Then perhaps she came as a spy for the Erlking."

My pulse quickened. "I can assure you that isn't the case. The Erlking…" I licked my lips, helpless. "If she was a spy, she wouldn't be avoiding you like this."

"How so?"

"Well, she would want to keep from garnering unwanted attention," I said, hoping my hasty thought would end somewhere good. "She would be getting close to you. Learning what she could."

"I suppose you're right," he said. "Apologies. Old habits die hard I guess."

"Riona is…"

I couldn't even find a charitable phrase. I'd thought we'd had a nice chat the night before, and she seemed to understand the importance of this conversation. I didn't dare suggest we continue without her.

"How did it go yesterday with Avram?" I asked, hoping to find something else to talk about until she showed up.

"He says he needs more time with the stone," Edric said. "He was…a little unnerved by the wizard watching him."

"I wanted Avram to get to know Cade a little more," I said. "And perhaps then, they might be able to share knowledge."

"Avram is more cautious than most, even with me," Edric said. "I think it might be a bridge too far to ask him to befriend a wizard—even a nice one."

At least he'd called Cade nice. "I was hoping someone like Avram would be able to…"

"Able to what?" Edric asked.

"Use it," I whispered, almost a confession.

Edric let out a little chuckle. "But the fae enchanted it so—"

"I know," I replied, letting the stone drop as I decided it was time to tell Edric the truth. "Can I… If I tell you something, will you keep it in confidence?"

"Of course."

I exhaled. "When I first touched the stone, when Eoghan…" I cleared my throat. "It came to life immediately. I heard voices. I saw… I saw a vision. And it was like breathing to use it. But ever since then…" I exhaled. "It hasn't even flickered."

"So…" He watched me intently. "You only used it the once?"

I nodded. "And I prayed that you or Avram or *someone* might be able to show me what to do. The fae have no clue, or at least no clue that they're willing to share. Cade doesn't know either." I turned it over again. "Maybe I was hoping by being near one of its brethren, it would…I don't know, spark a little, at least?"

He sat back, watching me, and I couldn't stop babbling.

"Now, I feel like I'm just waiting for Eoghan to come back and… And I won't be able to protect my kingdom if he does." I shivered. "I feel helpless."

"You aren't helpless," he said. "You have the fae—"

"I don't trust them," I said before I could stop myself. I covered my mouth as my face turned red. "I'm so sorry. I shouldn't have said that."

He was silent for a moment then pulled my hands from my face. "You and I are kindred spirits," he said with a knowing smile. "Sovereign to sovereign, this conversation stays between us."

"But I just told you Riona could be trusted."

"Well, I can agree with both sentiments," he said, cracking a smile. "Tricky creatures, the fae. They say they can't lie, but they'll twist the truth until you aren't sure which way is up."

"Riona—"

"Is only half. There's a reason we asked for her specifically."

Some of the tension in my chest loosened. "Still, I feel it's in my best interests to speak well of them, considering we're trying to open trade with them." I smiled thinly. "And you've been hiding in the mountain in fear of them."

He waved me off. "You don't have to like someone to trade with them. You just have to have something they want, and that tends to keep them in line." He paused, thoughtfully. "But it seems to me there's no reason for us to keep hiding. The current Erlking appears to have no interest in our stone. I think it's time for the trolls to rejoin the rest of the world."

I smiled. "On that, we definitely agree. A thousand years is long enough."

He sat back. "Now if I tell *you* something, will you promise you won't be angry with me?"

"Of course." I leaned forward.

"We haven't been *completely* honest with you," he said with a mischievous smile. "But only because I was afraid of what you'd say when I told you we'd already started construction on another doorway—this one at the foot of the mountain."

"I'd say..." I allowed myself to look a little put out. "Why not let us in that one? Why make us walk up the mountain?"

"We'd expected that your journey would take weeks—months, perhaps, not mere days. So we aren't quite finished with it yet." He lifted his tea to his lips. "But we've made significant progress. I'd like to share it with you and the rest of your party. This afternoon."

I smiled. This was a promising sign. "We would be honored to tour it with you."

"Then it's settled."

I tapped my fingers on the table. "You started construction on the doorway before you even knew what I'd come to offer you—before you had assurances that the fae wouldn't be after your stone?"

"What can I say?" He winked. "I'm tired of eating moldy vegetables."

>—→ >—→ >—→ >—→

As elated as I was that Edric still wanted to move forward, I couldn't help but focus on what I hadn't gotten—namely an actual trade agreement in writing. The doorway was a good start, a show that the trolls, at least, wanted to step into the future with us. But without anything set in stone, I was as empty-handed as the day I'd arrived.

The longer I stewed, the angrier I became at Riona. We'd opened up to one another. She'd promised she would help—agree to whatever I proposed. I supposed I'd believed that meant she would also *show up*. But I hadn't been explicit. Fae trickery.

I was so blinded by my thoughts that I nearly ran into the solid mass of a person.

"Whoa, whoa," Ward said, catching me by the arm. "You look ready to kill someone. What's wrong?"

"Riona is what's wrong," I said. "She *skipped* our important trade discussion. The nerve of her."

"She wouldn't have unless—"

I tossed his arm off me. "No Don't make excuses for her. It's very simple. She was supposed to be there and she wasn't—"

"Breathe," he said, taking my shoulders again. "Riona wouldn't do anything to hurt you."

"Wouldn't she?" I ran my tongue over my teeth. "She's fae."

"Ayla."

"What?" I glared at him then softened. "Ward, I need this agreement. She promised me she would be there. Now it's another day, and…"

"Why don't we go find her?" he said. "I'm sure there's a reasonable explanation for everything."

>→ >→ >→ >→

It took some time to locate her, as she seemed to be scouring the castle for something. I ignored the look of confusion and concern on her face; the only thing she should've been thinking about was our meeting with Edric.

"Where were you?" I snapped.

"I…uh…" Her face grew red as her eyes widened. "Oh, no. Ayla… Tell me I didn't miss it."

I crossed my arms over my chest, grateful at least she looked repentant. "You did. I had to cover for you. Again. But Edric's growing tired of you dodging him."

"I'm so sorry, I…" She looked lost, like she wasn't sure where she was. "I'm trying to…"

"Trying to *what*?" I couldn't help my temper. "Ruin this entire trip?"

My temper flared, and I might've flown across the room if not for Ward's calming hand on my shoulder.

"That's twice now," he said. "Is everything all right, Riona? You don't look well."

"I…" She gaped like a fish, looking bewildered and unsure of herself. "I don't know. I thought… I thought there might be…"

"Riona, Edric was offended you didn't show. He thinks you're trying to trick us." I shook my head. "Did anything I say to you last night make sense?"

"Of course it did," she said. "It was an accident." She glanced at the bathroom again. "I think."

"What does that mean?" I barked, taking a step toward her. "You meant to skip our meeting? You don't want to help Pennlan like you claimed?"

She stared at the floor and said nothing.

"Obviously, Riona didn't mean to hurt you or mess anything up," Ward said. "But she's here now. Why don't you two go find Edric and—"

"Edric's invited us to tour the new doorway out of the mountain," I said. "So the discussion will have to wait until tomorrow."

"Doorway? Where?" Ward asked with a frown.

"He said it's been under construction for a while in advance of our visit." I looked at Riona pointedly. "He was so optimistic about his chances of reopening things that he started it early. I can only hope the fae make good on their promises to remain peaceful."

"They will," Riona said. "They haven't told me otherwise."

I felt another snarky remark bubble up inside me, but there was a soft knock on the door. A servant was waiting.

"Sorry to interrupt, Your Majesty. King Edric has asked me to fetch you."

"So soon?" It hadn't been ten minutes since I'd left him. "We'll be down in a moment."

She bowed and closed the door behind her, and I turned back to Riona.

"Edric's already growing suspicious of you. You need to be on your best behavior and at least *try* to appear interested in what's going on around you."

"I will," she said. "But I need to talk with Cade before—"

"There's no time," I said. "Now put on a smile, straighten your shoulders, and for goodness' sake, don't mumble when he talks with you.

You have one more chance to make this right."

Chapter Forty-Two

Ward

Ayla marched down the stairs with conviction, followed by Riona and me. I didn't dare try to talk with Riona in private, as our conversation would echo down the stairs. But something was definitely wrong. I just had to wait until we were alone to broach the subject.

We reached the front hall, meeting Elodia, Rutley, and Cade there, but before we could speak, Edric arrived wearing the biggest smile I'd seen from him yet. Something about his happiness made me uneasy—especially since, if I listened to Ayla, their previous meeting had been a disaster.

"As I was telling your queen," Edric said, "I haven't been completely honest with you."

Elodia caught my eye, and it was hard to keep my face passive.

"When I sent Lynton to retrieve you," he said, "we'd also started work on a new road, one that wouldn't require travelers to hike for days up the mountain. We're nearing completion, and I would love to show you how far we've come."

"We're excited to see it," Ayla said, speaking for everyone. "Shall we?"

Edric took her arm and led the way, followed by Avram. Cade, perhaps elated that he was finally being allowed to go somewhere, left Riona and hurried behind Ayla. Elodia and Rutley followed them, and I took the opportunity to sidle up beside Riona.

We walked in silence, and I kept my ears open for the wisps of conversation from those ahead of me. But it was mostly Ayla gushing over Edric, perhaps trying to smooth things over. I noted he didn't attempt to speak to Riona—he barely even acknowledged her presence. But that just made it easier for me to get her alone.

Without trying, we ended up at the very back of the group, and when there was enough distance between us and Elodia and Rutley, I loudly cleared my throat. "So. What's going on with you?"

Riona didn't answer, her gaze somewhere far away as she worried at the bottom of her lip.

I gently elbowed her to get her attention. "I'm talking to you."

She sighed. "You wouldn't believe me if I told you."

"Try me."

She chewed her lip, nodding to the front. "I really wanted to talk with Cade before I told anyone else, just to make sure I wasn't...crazy."

That caught my attention. "What makes you say that?"

"Well..." She took a breath. "Since we've gotten here, I've been hearing...*voices*. They started on the mountain, but they've gotten worse since we arrived. Especially when I touch water." She glanced at me. "Think I'm crazy yet?"

"You know I never do." Did I understand it? No. But that was beside the point. "So that's why you've been acting so jumpy."

"Cade thinks it's because of the troll magic, but I don't know. It feels... It feels like..." She quieted, drawing into her own mind.

"You can tell me," I said.

"Please don't tell Ayla or anyone else," she whispered. "And don't arrest me."

I snorted. "Not a chance."

"It feels like Eoghan's still in my head. And my fear is that he's waiting for the two pieces of the *seod croí* to combine before he takes me over again." She shivered.

I watched her, knowing nothing about magic, but feeling like Eoghan hadn't left anything inside her mind except an unhealed scar. "So why'd you miss your meeting?"

"Well." She seemed heartened that I hadn't reacted to the news about the wizard. "At Ayla's suggestion, I decided to take a bath. I drew the water, the voices…" She furrowed her brow. "No. I drew the water, then there was this second tap with soap. It was very… Well, it smelled strongly. So I got in the bath, and I didn't hear the voices. But then…" She looked at me. "I guess I fell asleep."

"So you fell asleep in the bathtub?" I quirked a brow, waiting for more.

"But that's the thing. I don't remember… I woke up in my bed. In my nightgown." She chewed her lip. "And when I went back to check, that tap, it was gone. And I don't know if I dreamed it or if I'm just going crazy or…" She took a halting breath. "But that's the second time I've fallen into a deep sleep here. The first time, I woke up with a bruise on my arm I can't explain."

Something was suspicious, and it wasn't her story. "I believe you," I said. "Ayla…"

"Ayla's so angry with me," she said. "I didn't mean for any of this to happen, but I feel like something…something or someone is out to get me here."

"I don't disagree. We went into the town…" Something snapped in my memory. "Edric said there was magic in the water. Enough to keep the people 'placated' for a while."

"What?" Riona stopped walking for a moment. "Troll magic?"

"He didn't specify," I said. "But I wonder if that's what's going on. Maybe you're being affected by this spell." I paused. "Maybe it's on purpose, too."

"For what reason?"

My gaze drifted to the front of the group, where Avram and Edric flanked Ayla. "No clue. But if you want, I can have Rutley or Elodia bunk with you tonight."

"Good idea." She smiled at me. "And thanks for believing me."

"After all the crazy stuff we've been through, I'd be wrong not to," I said, nudging her.

Edric and Avram had reached the edge of the cave wall, and there wasn't a doorway to be found. But I'd come to realize that didn't mean much in these parts, especially as Edric pressed his hands to the stone. It rippled and fell away, as most doors did in this realm, revealing a large, dark cave. Something about it sent chills up my spine, perhaps because there wasn't an end in sight.

"It's magnificent," Ayla said, a little fear in her voice.

"Come, come!" Edric said, offering Ayla his arm. She graciously took it, though she cast a nervous look back to the rest of the group as if to make sure we were coming. We followed behind, the dark cave almost sucking the light from the city behind us. It took a minute for my eyes to adjust, even with the blue flame lamps lining the walls.

"You've been working on this for how long?" Ayla asked.

"A few weeks, since Lynton left for your kingdom," Edric said. "It's difficult work to tunnel under a mountain. There is much to contend with—the weight of the stone, the shape of the cave, that sort of thing. It's only for the most intellectual of trolls to attempt."

I stared at the back of his head. "I don't see your crew," I said, choosing my words carefully as I moved closer to Ayla. "Are they deep in the mountain?"

Avram glanced over his shoulder, disdain on his lips. "We did not want to conduct work while Her Majesty was in the tunnel. It could be dangerous. As with the cave, it takes a lot of magical concentration to keep the tunnel from collapsing from the weight of the rock. Any small adjustment could cause a catastrophe."

"I do appreciate that," Ayla said, her pace slowing until she was side by side with me. "I'm not a big fan of tight spaces." Her fingertips brushed mine before she took my hand. Her palms were wet, and the tightness of her grip told me she was absolutely petrified.

"Why wait so long to start the tunnel?" I said, giving her hand a comforting squeeze. "Why not wait until it was complete to send for us?"

"You'll recall, Captain, that we hadn't anticipated your return so quickly," Edric said. "Your wizard hastened things, so we had to take you the normal route."

"Ah, well. Let's just blame Cade," Ayla said, the fear starting to seep into her voice. "He's a good sport about that."

"Indeed," came his voice from far back in the cave.

I stopped, realizing I could see no one else.

"What's wrong?" Ayla said.

"Waiting for the rest of the group," I said.

"Keep up, please." Edric was also out of sight. "We don't want anyone getting lost."

I tightened my hold on Ayla's hand and felt her pulse quicken. "We'll be fine," I whispered to her.

"I know. I just…" She exhaled. "I feel like the roof is going to fall on us."

"It would be the first time." Edric appeared in the lighted halo ahead of us. "Now come, I'd love to show you what we've found."

She straightened her shoulders and started walking, but her pulse was still throbbing. "Coming!"

But as we stepped into the light ourselves, Edric disappeared into the dark. We kept walking, but I noticed that his footsteps had stopped echoing. The hair rose on the back of my neck as I looked for the rest of the crew.

"Elodia?" I called. "Cade? Rutley? Riona?"

My voice echoed, and there was no answer.

"Ward," Ayla whispered as a deep sound reverberated in the mountain. She grabbed my arm with her other hand and pressed herself to me as a pebble fell on my head.

I spun around, yanking her as I sprinted back the way we'd come. But I only got two steps before I ran into a solid wall. I turned the other way, finding another wall. And another. It seemed everywhere we turned, there was a solid piece of rock.

"Ward!" Ayla cried.

I turned again and found the open pathway forward. With Ayla's hand firmly in mine, I dashed toward the exit, all the while, cursing that damned troll king. There was a deafening crack overhead, and I pushed Ayla out of the way as something heavy knocked me to the ground, pinning my leg. I cried out as my bones shattered under the weight.

Ayla's hand gripped mine and her fingers brushed my face. "Ward —"

"Go!" I cried as tears leaked from my eyes, my head swimming from the pain.

Her other hand cupped my cheek. "I'm not—"

"You're the queen," I stammered as tremors shook my body. "Just go. Leave me here. You have to survive."

"This stupid thing," Ayla whispered. "*Work*!"

I realized she was yelling at her necklace. And it might've been the pain, but I thought I saw it flicker to life just as she dropped it back to her chest.

"I'm sorry." She was crying. "I don't know why it's acting up. Maybe I broke it."

"You…" I exhaled through my teeth. "You didn't. You're the only one who can use it. Maybe you just need—" Agony shot through my body, and I couldn't help the howl of pain that came from my lips. "Go without me. Please. Before it's too late."

She left my side, and my heart sank a little. I never thought I'd die in a cave-in.

"Ayla, I—"

"Is that a butterfly?"

I cracked open an eye and thought the pain was making me hallucinate—a vibrant purple butterfly was flittering through the darkness of the cavern. But then my mind caught up with me.

"Riona!" I called, my voice hoarse. "Over here!"

A swarm of butterflies appeared, removing the stone from my leg then encircling my chest, my arms, my legs, and lifting me off the ground. Behind me, they did the same to Ayla. As they carried us through the tunnel, I realized they were keeping the mountain from wholly collapsing in on itself.

The light from the city was almost blinding, and I squeezed my eyes shut as I was gently laid on the ground. My head was still swimming from the pain, but I heard voices—Ayla, Cade, Riona.

"Okay, Riona, you can do this." Cade's voice was calm. "Heal the bone."

"What if I—"

"You won't hurt him."

The pain lessened to a dull roar, and I sighed, relaxing onto the ground. My skin prickled and itched, like a scab healing over, and before long, feeling came back into my toes. I cracked open one eye and chanced a look at my busted leg. My pant leg was tattered and covered in blood, but…my leg was fully healed.

"Good job," Cade said, clapping Riona on the shoulder. "I told you."

With the pain gone, my mind came back to full strength, and I realized there were a pair of voices I hadn't heard.

"I…" I sat up quickly. "Elodia, Rutley—"

"Here, boss." Elodia knelt to the side of me.

Rutley the other side. "You look a mess."

I lay back on the ground, exhaling. "That was…" Again, my brain snapped into place as I turned to look at Cade and Riona. "You have your magic."

"I…" Riona swallowed as her pale face turned the color of a tomato.

I sat up. "You have magic. You've had it all this time, haven't you?"

Her blush deepened. Even as she sputtered her denials, the truth was evident on her face.

"This isn't the place to have this conversation," Cade said, casting a look around. "We need to get back and—"

"I think it's the right time. What other secrets have you been hiding from us?" Ayla asked as Edric came running up the hill.

"Oh, thank goodness you're all safe!" he cried.

"Yeah, thank goodness," I muttered.

"Going in there wasn't..." He sighed. "I perhaps put the cart before the horse. I was just so eager to show you what we'd done." He looked actually concerned, surprising for him. "Avram told me the mines weren't safe yet. We hadn't quite gotten them sturdy. But I thought he was being overly cautious, and so..." He sighed. "I'm so very sorry."

I looked at Ayla, expecting her to lose her cool, but she plastered a smile on her face. "Edric, all is forgiven, of course. We're just glad everyone is safe." She looked down at me. "Especially Ward. I don't know what I'd do without him."

Elodia and Rutley helped me to stand, my leg still a little weak, even though it was pain-free. "Yeah, just a lucky break that—"

"That we were able to get out," Cade said, with a meaningful look to me. "Why don't we get back to the castle, and we can discuss everything?"

Chapter Forty-Three

Cade

I couldn't stop replaying the cave collapse in my mind. Somehow, Riona and I had become separated from everyone else. As the cave groaned and crumbled, Riona managed to conjure a net of butterflies to keep the rocks from falling on top of us. She hadn't even asked for my help; it was her survival instinct. We ran toward the exit, coming across Rutley and Elodia along the way, and the four of us got to safety as quickly as we could.

"Where's Ayla?" Elodia had asked. "And Ward?"

My heart had dropped into my stomach when I realized they weren't amongst us. "Riona—"

"On it."

She hadn't even hesitated, sending a flurry of butterflies back into the cave. Moments crept by, agonizingly slow, as I gripped my staff and demanded my worthless magic do something. But as the interference had become deafening to the point of splitting my head, there was movement from the cave. Ward and Ayla came floating out, carried by butterflies.

I was so happy to see them, I didn't even care that Ayla was fawning over Ward. But I could see the fury boiling on Ayla's face. She managed to bury it when Edric arrived, but I could tell we were all in for it once we reached the castle.

Ayla led the way with Edric once more, graciously accepting all his apologies and acting like it wasn't a big deal that we'd all almost just died. Ward, limping along on his own two legs, watched them with an accusatory sort of stare. Riona hung toward the back, giving me a chance to talk with her.

"Do you think Edric knows what I did?" she asked.

"Probably."

"Why hasn't he said anything?"

"No clue."

Edric continued to offer his apologies, and I listened carefully to his words, searching for duplicity of any kind. But it all seemed contrite, and I could find no hidden guilt. As much control as the trolls had over the stone, I found it hard to believe the cave collapse had been an accident.

The five of us gathered in Ayla's room while the queen finished her conversation with Edric on the landing. Ward sat on the bed with his leg propped up on a pillow, though Riona's healing should've done the trick. Elodia and Rutley were on either side of him, watching him like a pair of mother hens over their chickens. I stood in the corner, still shaken by the events of the day. And Riona... Riona looked like she was about to jump out the window.

Ayla walked inside, her dress sporting a large stain on the side of it where Ward had bled on her. She closed the door behind her and took three steps into the room, holding her hands at her side.

"How long have you had your magic, Riona?" she asked. "And why did you lie about it?"

"It's complicated," I started, but Ayla's furious gaze stopped me.

"I asked Riona."

"I've had it all along," she whispered. "I didn't want to use it, so I let you believe I was struggling."

"Why didn't you want to use it?"

"Because..." She opened and closed her mouth, looking to me for help.

"She didn't feel it was right," I said, after a moment of tense silence, hoping my relationship with Ayla would smooth things over. "It doesn't matter why."

"I think it does," Ayla snapped. "What else has she been lying about?"

"Nothing!" Riona said. "I swear—"

"And what good is your word?"

"I'd say it's enough," Ward said, stepping forward. "Riona just—"

"Stay out of this," Ayla barked.

His brows shot upward.

"And *you* need to get off your high horse," Elodia snarled. "Ward's done nothing except try to please you this whole trip. He even let you leave—"

Ayla stomped petulantly. "I'm the *queen*. Nobody *lets* me leave anywhere—"

"Yeah, they do. Because queens aren't supposed to travel to dangerous lands," Rutley barked. "Because they could end up crushed under a mountain. Or at the bottom of a ravine."

"And if the *fae* who insisted she come along would do something about that, maybe I wouldn't have been in danger!" Ayla cried, pointing at Riona, who wilted into herself.

"Okay, everyone needs to take a breath," I said, holding up my hands. "Ayla—"

"I didn't *insist* I come along, by the way," Riona said, folding her arms across her chest. "I was invited. And maybe if you were nicer to me, I might've wanted to use magic to help you."

"Riona, that's not—" I began, but my voice was drowned out as the two sisters squared off with each other.

"Nicer? I've spent hours trying to help you!" Ayla said.

Riona scoffed. "You've been *nagging* me. Don't do this. Sit up. Don't wear that."

"And a lot of good it did you," Ayla said. "I asked you to do *one* thing. *One* thing to help me. And you couldn't even manage that."

"I'm *sorry*, but there's something wrong with this place," Riona replied. "And if you weren't too busy trying to avoid me or make me into something I'm not, you might've seen that."

"I *need* the trolls—"

"You have the fae!" Riona replied.

"And who can trust them?" Ayla barked back. "Sneaky, backstabbing monsters who want nothing more than to twist the truth to get their way."

Riona let out a breath. "And that's it, isn't it? You still hate the fae, don't you? You probably don't even see me as your sister!"

"*Because you aren't.*"

The words echoed in the room for a moment.

"I'm sorry?" Riona said slowly. "I'm *not* your sister? Then what am I?"

Ayla's nostrils flared. "You're just a reminder of the worst day of my life."

Riona released a small squeak as her eyes widened. I felt compelled to step in, but Ward held up his hand to silence me. This was between them.

"You…" Ayla began. "When I look at you, all I see is that moment when Eoghan revealed himself to be everything he wasn't. Before you showed up, everything was…everything was fine. And when you're not around, I can pretend that everything is *still* fine. But you…"

Riona's skin had paled considerably as every word seemed to strike her deep in her most vulnerable parts.

"I spent my entire life hating your kind with everything I had," Ayla continued, clearly needing to get this out. "I believed with my whole heart that your mother *killed* my father in cold blood—and wanted me dead, too."

"But she didn't." Riona's words came out a whisper.

"It doesn't matter. I can't erase a lifetime of feeling one way just because my father and your mother…" Ayla crossed her arms over her chest. "I just can't."

"Well." Riona swallowed as a tear fell down her cheek. "I suppose that's it, then." She started toward the door.

"Where are you going?" Ayla asked.

"Since it's clear you don't want me here," Riona said, "I'm going home."

"But you—"

"I don't have to do a damn thing," she barked. "I'll have someone else negotiate with the troll king. After all, you said I don't have the ability to speak for the rest of the fae realm. So I'm pretty much useless here. Might as well be useless in a place I'm wanted."

She walked to the door and slammed it behind her.

Nobody moved for a full minute. Finally, Ward rolled off the bed and let out a small wince of pain as he landed on his leg. But after a moment, he took a step forward then another. Then kept walking until he strolled out the door. Elodia and Rutley soon followed, both giving Ayla a very frosty look as they exited the room.

"So? Are you going to leave, too?" she asked.

"Never," I said. "But—"

She burst into tears, covering her face with her hands as her whole body shook with sobs. I crossed the room in three steps and gathered her in my arms. She only came up to my chest, but I held her tight to me.

"I was so scared," she whispered. "I thought I was going to die in that cave."

"I know."

"Why didn't you tell me Riona had her magic?" Ayla asked, looking up at me. "Why would you lie to me?"

"I didn't know until we were nearly here," I said. "She…made me promise."

"So? Cade, you're *mine*." She took a step back. "Not hers."

A little warmth spread over my chest at the firmness with which she'd called me *hers*. "She's my friend, Ayla. And ever since Eoghan… She's struggled."

Ayla glared at me. "We *all* have."

"She remembers everything he made her do," I said. "And she still thinks he's inside her brain."

Ayla turned to me, a little fear in her eyes. "He's…not, is he?"

"No. At least, I don't think so."

"That's not comforting." She looked at her hands.

"That's why she didn't want to use her magic. She was afraid if she did, he would take over her mind again. She's been terrified to even do simple spells." I looked at the door. "She wouldn't even use magic to defend herself against Aldrick." I paused, licking my lips. "You didn't mean that, did you? About her being a reminder… That's not how you feel, right?"

"I don't know how I feel." Ayla crossed the room to sit on the bed. "Seeing her…it brings me back to the reality that Eoghan betrayed me—betrayed all of us. And it just makes me *so angry* I can't even see straight."

"But that's not Riona's fault," I said.

"No, it's not," she whispered. "But she's a good scapegoat."

More tears fell down her cheeks and I sat next to her, pulling her back into my arms. She nestled into my neck, her tears dripping into my shirt.

She tilted her head up to look at me, tears in her lashes. "I'm so glad you're here. I don't know what I'd do if I didn't have you."

My heart skipped a beat. Her lips were so close to mine, red and swollen from crying. Her breath tickled my skin. Closing my eyes, I leaned in…

"What are you doing?" she said, backing up.

"I'm…" I licked my lips then tried again.

"Cade, I…" She stood up roughly, leaving me cold. "I don't…" She bunched up her face as she turned away from me. "Don't make me do this right now. Please. I beg of you."

"Five minutes ago, you said I was *yours*," I said, coming to my feet. "What did you mean by that if not—"

"I meant you're my best friend," she said, her voice full of tears. "I don't... You're the only thing I have left of my childhood."

I couldn't believe what I was hearing. "Ayla, I lo—"

"*Stop.*" She spun back. "Don't say it. Please don't say it."

Anger surged in me as I took a step forward. "I love you, damn it."

There it was. The sentiment had tumbled from my lips before I could stop it, but... I didn't want to stop it. Our lives had become so treacherous, and if I didn't tell her now, I might never get a chance to.

"I love you, Ayla," I repeated, taking her cheeks in my hands. "You've always been my everything. The only thing left of my childhood. I've wanted to tell you for years, but I never had the courage to say it."

She covered my hands with hers and pulled them from her cheeks. "And I love you. But as a friend. As my brother. Not as..." She stepped away, wiping her cheeks. Then, without another word, she left me standing in her room and in the wreckage of my broken heart.

CHAPTER FORTY-FOUR

RIONA

"I can't erase a lifetime of feeling one way just because you showed up."

I didn't want to cry, especially as Ward, Elodia, and Rutley followed me into my room. But I couldn't help the tears that flowed freely down my face. I knew Ayla had been distant, but I'd chalked it up to…I wasn't even sure. But surely not that my very *existence* caused her such misery. That was…

"She was out of line," Ward said, his arms folded across his chest. "Completely."

Rutley nodded, his cheeks ruddy with anger. "You said it."

"Riona just saved her life." Elodia balled her fists and paced in the room. "Not even a thank you. Just more of the same. Ayla's a real—"

"Elodia."

"Boss, she's being a real bitch right now," Elodia finished. "You can't deny it. She's been completely unreasonable this entire trip—toward you *and* Riona. It's unacceptable."

"You should go back in there and give her a piece of your mind." Rutley nodded. "Just lay into her the way she laid into Riona."

"Don't," I said, and the three of them jumped as if they'd forgotten I was there. "If she doesn't want me around, I won't be. Solve that problem for everybody."

"What are you going to do?" Elodia asked.

"I told you. I'm going home," I said, wiping my cheeks. "I'm not spending another minute trapped in this cave with her. I'm going to demand Edric let me out."

"Do you think he'll let you?" Ward asked. "He did just try to murder us."

"Accidentally," Elodia added.

Rutley snorted. "If you believe him. I don't. He's been holding up this mountain for however long he's been on the throne, and *suddenly*, he can't keep control of it? Coincidentally while we're all inside the cavern?"

"I believe you, except I don't know why he would invite us here just to crush us," Ward said. "Why put on an act for us? Why host us, take Ayla around the town? Pretend like all is well just to crush us?"

"Maybe he didn't expect Riona to step in and save the day," Elodia said.

Half an hour ago, I'd wanted to know why the cave had collapsed. Now, I found I didn't care. The drama in this cave could stay here. I wanted to see blue sky and feel the sun on my face and to forget I even had a sister.

"Edric can let me out, or I'll let myself out," I said.

Ward smirked. "That's the Riona I know. Show him who's boss."

Even his praise fell flat on my mood. I hated that Ayla had somehow managed to taint my friendship with Ward, too. "It was nice meeting all of you. Take care."

"I'll walk with you," Ward said. "C'mon."

I honestly wanted to be alone, but Ward's presence wasn't offensive. I didn't even look at Ayla's door as we walked out of mine. If my existence caused her angst, I wouldn't give another thought to hers.

"So, what will you do?" Ward asked. "Just go back to the fae realm?"

I honestly didn't know. Aldrick would be waiting, and the Erlking would have questions about why I'd left without making agreements. I doubted "I had a fight with my half-sister who hates me" would cut it as an excuse. But it might. Stranger things had happened.

Still, without Cade's portal magic, I'd be walking at least a month.

That would give me enough time to figure out what I wanted to do with myself. Maybe I'd just avoid going back to the fae realm entirely. Disappear into the aether like the stone had.

"Are you going to talk me out of this or something?" I asked. "Tell me that Ayla's really a nice person and I should give her another chance?"

He snorted. "Why would I lie to you?"

I turned to him. "Because you're in love with her. Aren't you?"

"Maybe I was." He paused. "I don't know anymore. She's not the person I thought she was. I don't even know if I can remain her captain."

I slowed my gait. "Just because of what she said to me?"

"Why not?"

"I don't know…" I crossed my arms over my chest. "I feel like…"

"You're my friend, Riona. And you've been nothing but helpful to Ayla. More than helpful. You've sacrificed so much for her. Leaving the castle, helping us through the fae land." He looked at me. "Getting the stone from that lake."

"Should've just left it there," I said. "Would've been far less trouble."

"True. But we didn't know that." He shrugged. "All I'm saying is that a little appreciation isn't hard to muster. And that she can't even do that…"

"You know, I used to dream about what it would be like for the two of us," I said. "Once she found out, of course. I thought we'd have… I don't know. Long talks. Picnics. She'd brush my hair." I looked at my hands. "I had some twin cousins around my age who used to share clothes. I always wanted that for us, too."

"I'm sorry. I know how it is to have a sibling who doesn't live up to your expectations," Ward said, nudging me. "We may not be related by blood, but I'll always have your back, Riona. Promise."

"And I, you." I nudged him back.

We walked in comfortable silence, and I was almost sad when Edric's office came into view. Ward wouldn't be able to accompany me inside, as much as I wanted him to. This was a conversation Edric and I needed to have alone. I wasn't sure what cards he was going to lay on the table, but he'd surely put more of them out without Ward lurking about.

Still, that probably meant goodbye. And I wasn't sure the next time I would see him.

"Ward, thank you," I said, turning to him. "For being a good friend to me."

"Of course, but…" He glanced at the door. "You don't want me in there with you?"

I shook my head. "I can handle this. I finally feel…"

I felt in control of myself for the first time in months. Perhaps it was the way I'd deftly healed Ward's leg, or perhaps I was just so angry with Ayla that I no longer worried about keeping Eoghan at bay to protect her. It was honestly a relief.

Ward pulled me in for a hug. "Don't you dare leave without saying goodbye."

I squeezed him. "I won't. I promise."

>-» >-» >-» >-»

Edric was waiting for me, and for all my bluster moments before, being alone with him felt like… I didn't know. But every instinct I had told me I needed to make this quick and get on the road. Or at least away from him. Perhaps I'd been too hasty in sending Ward away.

"Please, have a seat," Edric said. "I'm glad you finally feel comfortable enough to speak with me."

"I'm not sure comfortable is the right word," I replied, keeping myself as close to the door as possible. "I've come to let you know that I'm leaving. It was a mistake for me to come in the first place. Another fae with more…" I weakly waved my hand. "More knowledge would've been a better option."

"But Riona, we wanted you," Edric said, a curious smile on his face. "Before you leave, please, have a seat. One drink."

"I don't—

"It would be rude. Your sister wouldn't be too happy."

She wasn't happy whatever I did, it seemed, but the ploy worked to unstick my feet from the ground. "Very well. One drink."

I sat stiffly on the chair and watched as Edric poured a small glass of wine then had one for himself. He brought his to his lips and drank; I did the same, but only a little. It had a strange taste.

"So," he began. "I suppose I should apologize for what happened in the cave."

"Probably not a good idea to use it until it's complete," I said.

"It's a good thing you were able to save everyone."

My gaze shot to him, but there was no denying it. "Yes."

"I suppose I could ask what changed, but I think the more important question is…" He leaned his chin onto his hands and watched me intently. "How is a fae able to lie?"

I was leaving; it didn't matter now. "My father's blood. At least, that's what I believe. I've never…never really asked anyone."

"Not as if there's anyone *to* ask. Most halflings were drowned at birth, their parents jailed for crimes against the Erlking."

I shifted. "It's been a long time since that sort of thing happened."

"You'd be surprised at the things that endure over the years," Edric said. "That's the problem with being in two worlds, you never quite belong in either."

I took another nervous sip of my wine, wondering how long I needed to sit there before it would be considered polite to excuse myself.

"The trolls felt that way, believe it or not. We should've been as revered as the *daoine maithe* and *sidheog*. Even the forest fae had a seat at the table. But we…we were considered less than vermin. Condemned to live with the wild, uncivilized creatures. Forced to toil away in barren lands to make food." He twirled his wine glass in his hand.

"You talk as if *you* were slighted by the Erlking himself," I said. "Which, my grandfather isn't…" I couldn't quite think of the phrase I wanted. "He isn't like that. He's nice."

"Nice, hm?" Edric tilted his head. "What else is there to know about him?"

"He's..." I was having trouble thinking clearly. Perhaps the wine was a little more potent than I'd thought. "He is... He's Birch. Fair." Was that the word I wanted? "A little too trusting. He shouldn't have sent me. As I said." I shook my head gently, but even that made the world swim in front of my eyes. "I'm nobody."

"On the contrary, you are very important. You're the only one we really wanted."

I looked up quickly but regretted it as my head lolled from side to side.

"What..." My tongue was like lead. "What's happening?"

"I should test out this lying thing for myself," he said, looking at his wine. His movements were stilted, or maybe my perception of them was.

"I can't..." The cup dropped from my hand, and I slumped forward.

"You are exactly where you need to be," he whispered.

Everything went black.

CHAPTER FORTY-FIVE

AYLA

It was quite lonely, showing oneself to the world. I sat in my room, waiting for someone to come for me but not expecting anyone to. Cade was probably still reeling. I couldn't help the way I felt about him—I wasn't going to lie to him. I prayed that, in time, he might realize that his love for me was platonic as well. Or that he would get so angry with me that his feelings would change. It seemed to be the case with Ward, so perhaps I could get lucky twice.

And Riona…

I thought a lot about what I'd said to her—but more importantly, *why* I couldn't seem to swallow the idea that Riona was my sister, and why, every time I tried, it would come back up in hateful thoughts and words. But at the end of the day, there was no excuse for the things I'd said to her. She had no more to do with Eoghan's betrayal than I did. And to blame her for something she was an equal victim in was monstrous. It was no wonder all my friends had taken her side. I probably would have as well.

More than once, I thought about walking out the door, finding Riona and apologizing. But I was a coward, afraid of what truths she'd throw in *my* face. I was scared I'd run into Ward, or Cade, or anyone else. And I was even more scared I *wouldn't*.

Finally, a knock on the door—an invitation to dinner. By then, I'd made up my mind. I would apologize to Riona with no excuses, no explanations. Just an apology and a promise that I would do…I would do better. Whether she would give me the chance was unclear. But at least… at least I'd be able to look at myself in the mirror again.

When I arrived at the dining hall, I received a frosty reception—but at least they were there. Ward didn't look at me. Neither did Cade. I didn't try to engage either of them, nor Elodia and Rutley. They would get my apologies after Riona and either accept them or not.

I kept my eye on the door. Surely, she would want to eat before she left. But Edric arrived without her and beckoned us to sit down with him.

"I would like to take this opportunity to apologize again," he said. "I never meant for any of you to get hurt. I'm so grateful you're all okay."

I nodded. "I am, as well. Thanks to Riona."

"Where is our princess?" Edric asked. "I'd sent for her."

"I left her with you," Ward said with a suspicious glare.

"We had a good talk. But she told me she would be here for dinner before she left on her journey." He took a long sip of wine. "Strange."

"Perhaps she didn't feel like talking with anyone," Elodia said, her gaze on Rutley but her tone obvious.

"Perhaps." I picked up my drink. "I'll be sure to check on her after dinner."

I felt every glare directed at me. The air grew thick with unsaid words, and Edric cleared his throat loudly.

"I can't help but feel like I owe you more than an apology," Edric said. "I'm sure you're very angry with me."

I shifted. Nobody corrected him.

"And you have every right to be. It was foolish to send you into that cavern without testing it thoroughly. And foolish for me to think I could keep all of you safe. When the mountain began collapsing, I wanted to go back for you." He took a sip of his wine. "But Avram insisted I get to safety first. We were…in the process of gathering more help to look for you." Another sip. "But alas."

"I don't blame you," I said with a generous smile. "Accidents happen."

"They do, indeed. And I'm grateful for your generous spirit." He leaned his elbow on the table. "I can't help but wonder, though. How did you all escape?"

"Well, when we got separated," I began, "Ward and I..."

I tried to catch his gaze, but his stormy eyes were focused on the table. Whatever flicker we'd ignited as we thought we were going to perish had surely been extinguished.

"Ward's leg was caught," I said after a moment. "Then I..."

I would never forget the sight of that lone purple butterfly, followed by the swarm that had brought us to safety. The way she'd healed Ward's leg so there wasn't even a scratch.

"She's been terrified to even do simple spells. She wouldn't even use magic to defend herself against Aldrick."

And yet, she'd overcome that fear to save me. To save us. And I'd repaid her kindness by refusing to acknowledge our sisterhood.

"Ayla?" Edric prompted.

I glanced at the door, something urging me to leave. To find Riona. To apologize until she understood how deeply I regretted what I'd done. But to leave dinner would be rude.

Perhaps, though, it was time to take a leaf out of her book.

"You know," I said with an apologetic smile. "On second thought, I think the excitement of the day has exhausted me. I need to go lie down. Can we continue our discussion tomorrow?"

"Absolutely." He nodded. "Shall I walk you to your room?"

"Not necessary," I said. "But please, continue your meal without me."

⇻ ⇻ ⇻ ⇻

I doubted the group would have a lively conversation without me, but I kept walking. I needed to put eyes on Riona, to see that she was still here.

But as I continued toward the landing, I heard footsteps. Ward had followed me.

"I don't need an audience for this," I said, continuing my walk.

"Tough."

I tripped a little. Ward had never been so abrupt with me. I supposed I deserved it.

I kept walking in silence, waiting for the explosion from him. But perhaps he was just biding his time, allowing me to suffer in the anticipation of what was to come.

My pulse quickened as I took the final few steps. I had no idea what I was going to say to her—other than the obvious—or if she'd even listen. I certainly wouldn't.

Ward was right behind me as I approached her door. I almost asked again if I could have some privacy but thought better of it.

I knocked on the door. "Riona?"

I listened for sounds of movement, crying, anything. But nothing.

"I don't think she's going to answer," Ward said.

I tried not to bristle. "I know I made a mistake. I'm going to make amends for it." I tapped again when the door didn't open. "Riona? It's… Ayla. I need… I would like to speak with you about what I said earlier." I waited, listening for the sound of movement. "To apologize." Still nothing, so I knocked again. "Please let me apologize and I'll… You won't have to speak with me again."

I waited another few moments then turned to Ward.

"Can you try?" I asked, staring at the ground.

He crossed the landing and knocked. "Riona, let us in please."

Still, nothing. Ward furrowed his brow and turned the doorknob, finding it unlocked. He pushed open the heavy door and walked inside.

"Riona?"

The bed was made, the clothes put away. Riona's traveling pack was gone, as was her cloak. The room was empty.

"Hello?" I called, checking the bathroom and even the wardrobe. My heart sank. "She's gone. Where could she have gone?"

"She told you," Ward said, coming out of the bathroom. "She was going home."

"Edric said she wouldn't go until the morning," I said.

"I don't trust him to tell the truth," Ward replied. "She told me she wouldn't leave without saying goodbye."

Well, as far as I know, only one of them can lie. I thought better of it. "She's got to be somewhere around here. There's no way for her to get out."

"She said she'd let herself out if Edric refused." Ward picked up his stuffed pack. "I'll keep an eye out for any gaping holes."

I started. "Are you going to bring her back?"

"Nope."

I followed him out the door. "So…you're just leaving?"

"Consider this my official resignation."

I shouldn't have been surprised, but it still hurt.

"Elodia and Rutley will see to it that you get back home safely. As will, I'm sure, Cade."

I winced, but his back was to me. "Not so sure about that last one."

"Why?"

I could've lied, but I just didn't feel like it. "He…told me he loved me. Tried to kiss me."

Ward turned, only a little. "And?"

"He's one of the most important people in the world to me. But…" I sighed. "No, I don't love him. Not the way he wants me to."

"How…did he take it?"

"About how you'd expect."

"He'll get over it eventually."

It was hard not to hear the indictment in his words. I rubbed my hands together. "I'll have Elodia check on him, I suppose."

Ward shrugged on his pack and didn't respond.

"When you find her," I began softly, "please tell her I'm sorry."

"Are you?"

I nodded as a tear fell down my cheek. "I shouldn't have taken my pain out on her. And if she can ever forgive me, I'd like to try again."

"I don't know if she will." He walked to the door. "But I will deliver the message."

"And Ward?"

He stopped.

"I'm sorry I'm not the person you thought I was." My words came out a whisper. "Please be careful out there."

The only answer was the slamming door.

CHAPTER FORTY-SIX

WARD

There was a part of me, the part that sounded like Captain Gabhann, that wanted to stay. That reminded me of my duty to my kingdom, my title, and my people. But that part had grown quiet over the past few hours, even as Ayla had shown remorse for her coldhearted ways.

But Riona was part of my kingdom—she was *technically* my princess as Ayla was my queen. And there was something funny about the way Edric was sucking down his wine. It looked too much like Riona when she attempted to hide her lies.

Cade was waiting at the bottom of the landing, staring off into space with his arms over his chest. He seemed not to notice my presence until I called his name. Then his despondent look turned into a glare.

"Have a good chat with Ayla?" he asked.

"Riona's missing," I said.

"What?" He started walking beside me. "Edric said—"

"Edric's a liar."

"He's not supposed to be."

"Well, neither is Riona, and we see how that works," I replied. "I'm headed out to find her. I hope."

"I'll come with you."

"You should stay," I said. "Ayla needs someone to help her get down the mountain."

He glowered at nothing. "She needs a warm body."

"She needs her best friend," I said. "Just because..." I didn't know if I was the one he wanted to hear this from. "Just because she doesn't love you like that, doesn't mean—"

"Save it." He turned to me, a scowl on his face. "I know it's because she picked you instead."

I held up my hands. "I tendered my resignation. I'm leaving to find Riona. This has nothing to do with me."

He watched me warily and rubbed the back of his neck. "I don't know if I can stay, either. I don't like the idea of Riona out there on her own. The Erlking did make me promise to look after her. If anything should happen to her...he might not be too pleased."

I nodded. "I'm going to start out in the city—see if I find anywhere she might've escaped. If not, she may be hiding somewhere in the castle. Don't you have the ability to smell her or something?"

"It's been dull as of late, but somewhat," he replied.

I held out my hand. "If I'm not back by tomorrow morning, that means I've found a way out. Send Rutley or Elodia out to look for the exit then get Ayla to safety. If she resists..." I smirked. "Throw her over your shoulder and drag her out if you have to."

"I'll leave that to the soldiers," Cade said weakly as he took my hand. "But good luck. I hope you find her before I do."

"Me, too."

⤞ ⤞ ⤞ ⤞

It didn't take me long to walk a complete loop around the city and at least to my eyes, there weren't any new doors in or out. Even the mine where we'd almost died earlier that day had been closed off. That meant Riona was in either the castle or this city. I just hoped Cade was able to sneak around better than he had the first night.

There weren't many places to go, but the one place I'd almost gotten a straight answer out of someone was the jeweler. I didn't have a lot of confidence in my chances when I walked into his shop, and he greeted me with the same surprised expression he had the last time I'd been in here.

"Have you seen a young half-fae kid walking around here?" I asked.

"Fae?" He frowned. "The fae are after us. That's why we're stuck here in the mountain."

I leaned in closer. "That was a thousand years ago. They aren't after you anymore."

"They want our stone. Prince Edric said it was ours. Our right after losing so many during the battle. But it's not..." His eyes went slack. "It's not..." He blinked. "A human! In our city! What a surprise!"

I sighed, leaning back on my heels. "You said Prince Edric—"

"He is wise and fair," the jeweler said with a nod. "And our savior."

"The fae—"

"The fae! They haven't been seen in these parts for a while. We're too well hidden for them to find us. Prince Edric has made sure of that. Have you met him yet?"

I could've probably spent the entire evening trying to wheedle information out of him, but all I was getting was out-of-context snippets. And Riona was still out here somewhere, too. She was the most important thing right now.

With a sigh, I pushed open the door and walked out onto the street, but I stopped short. The square was empty, save a single troll standing in the center, his arms crossed over his chest.

"Lynton." I nodded. I still didn't know whose side he was on. Rutley and Elodia were back at the castle, so I had no backup if this went sideways. But Lynton didn't look ready for a fight. Then again, it was hard to tell what he was ready for. "I'm looking for Riona. Have you seen her?"

"No, but she couldn't have gone very far," Lynton said. "I take it she's finally decided to use her magic?"

I nodded. "Did you know?"

"Of course. Unlike your wizard friend, there were no restrictions placed on her."

"Why didn't you say anything?"

"I don't concern myself with the politics of fae and humans. Whatever her reasons for keeping her power under wraps, they were her own. I had one job."

He spoke evenly, as if he didn't care at all, but I remembered his words to Edric. *I brought those humans here at great personal risk.* The anger on his face. The way he seemed a man—troll—out of patience. Had he finally reached his limit?

"You won't find her by asking these people," Lynton said. "They don't remember the last five minutes, let alone a halfling girl."

I hesitated, unsure if he'd answer me. "What's wrong with them? Are they under a memory spell?"

To my surprise, he nodded. "They've been stuck living without their memories for the past thousand years."

"So they grow old and die without knowing anything else?" I asked, horrified.

"No. They're…" He sighed. "What I mean is: this is all that's left of the troll army that marched on the *aos sí* against Laughlan a thousand years ago."

I was sure I misheard him. "Are you trying to tell me that everyone here, yourself included, is…over a thousand years old?" He nodded, and I ran a nervous hand over my hair. "Trolls aren't supposed to live that long, are they?"

Lynton actually cracked a smile. "No. Edric didn't tell you, but the scholar *was* able to pull something out of our piece of the *seod croí*. He was able to pervert our control over memories. Instead of retaining them, Edric now has the power to make people forget. Forget their lives, their names…" His throat tightened. "Those they love. Even forget to grow old and die."

"But…why?"

"When the *seod croí* was split, Edric stole a piece of it and brought his army here, intending to use it for revenge against the Erlking, who he blamed for the death of his father and the trolls during the battle of the *aos sí*," Lynton said. "He was hoping for more than just retaining and losing memories. He wanted to be able to wield magic like the greater fae so we would be able to fight on equal footing." He almost spat the words. "What began as days turned into weeks, turned into months...then years..." He sighed. "As time dragged on, the army became restless, eager to return to their lands and give up on this ridiculous idea. So Edric and Avram cast a memory spell to keep them...placated until Avram could finally crack the stone's power and take their revenge."

I turned toward the village, amazed that vengeance could fuel all that.

"I was aroused from my eternal slumber to fetch you," he said. "When I realized what he'd done...how long it had been since..." He swallowed hard, the first bit of emotion showing on his face. "I had a family before the *aos sí*, a wife and daughter left behind. I don't know what happened to them. My other daughter was in the battle with us. She's here, but she has no idea who...who I am." He gripped his hands. "Edric said if I brought you back here, he'd rouse her too, so we could be together. But he hasn't made good on his promise."

I took a step forward. "What does Edric want with us? Why has he decided to bring us here? Risk being seen by the fae?"

"Because he has something he didn't before."

"The Pennlan stone?"

Lynton snorted. "We have no use for such things. I'm talking about the halfling girl."

"Riona?" I took a step forward as my heart sank to my stomach. "What have you done with her?"

"She's alive," he said, which didn't give me much confidence.

"You didn't answer my question," I snarled. "What does Edric want with her? Are you going to compel her like Eoghan did? Force her to use the stone?"

"I told you, we have no use for the Pennlan stone," Lynton said.

"That was merely a ploy to get the princess here. Edric doubted she would've been allowed to come on her own without Queen Ayla."

My head was spinning. "I don't understand. Why do you need Riona if you don't need the stone?"

"We..." He furrowed his brow. "What was I saying?"

My stomach dropped as I recognized that glassy-eyed expression. "Lynton, stay with me. What does Edric want with Riona? Where is Riona?"

"Who is Riona?" His eyes glazed over for a moment. "Who are you, for that matter?"

"Damn. Lynton. Don't lose focus now." I took a step toward him but couldn't walk any further. My feet were cemented into the ground. I yanked at them, but they just sank deeper into the ground.

"Can't trust anyone these days, can you?" Edric said, appearing from nowhere as Lynton turned on his heel and walked into the village. "But I'm sure you knew that, didn't you?"

"Where," I yanked at my feet, "is Riona?"

"Safe, for now." He tilted his head. "Lynton wouldn't lie to you."

"But you can," I said. "You meant to kill us in the cave, didn't you? And you sat and *lied* about it to our faces. Have you always had that ability or is that new?"

He lifted a shoulder. "I was surprised to find you *all* alive. I'd hoped to pare off at least your two little soldiers, but no. Riona happened to decide to use her magic to save them." He sighed. "But that's neither here nor there. We've now got everything we need to take the next step in our plan."

The ground beneath my feet moved, and I nearly toppled over as I slid forward. I reached for my sword, but the stone bubbled up to encapsulate my hands as well.

"I should probably just kill you and be done with it, but you might be useful in keeping the queen in line." He smiled. "Come along."

Before I could say another word, the ground moved to follow the troll king, and I went with it.

Chapter Forty-Seven

Cade

I was actually a little grateful Riona was missing; it gave me something else to focus on. Otherwise, I'd return to the nonstop moping, replaying Ayla's… Ayla. Even saying her name was like a hammer to my heart. How I could've misread our entire relationship for so long was beyond me. I couldn't even pinpoint how long I'd loved her, how I'd been so *sure* she loved me back.

The way she'd lit up when I'd come home from the fae realm. How she'd cuddled up next to me on the climb up the mountain, wanting *me* to stay with her instead of anyone else. It was easy to be angry with her, to blame her for making me feel one way when she clearly didn't.

But some part of me still hoped there was a chance for us. That maybe *now* she didn't love me, but she could one day. Especially if I managed to recover Riona, repair that relationship, bring things back to normal. Maybe then…then Ayla would see me as more than her best friend.

Doing so would require me to quit moping and find Riona. So as I stood in the middle of the staircase, I closed my eyes and let the world fall away. The rushing water noise came back with a vengeance, clouding all my senses until there was nothing left. But I focused on the scent that had become familiar, the sweet mead-like taste of Riona's magic. Unique in the fae realm, unique because of her human blood. Unique because she was.

Then…I thought I sensed it.

I began walking slowly, stopping every few feet to let my senses fall away again. The scent was light, but definitely there. I kept moving down the stairs until I reached the landing then continued to the left, toward Edric's wing of the castle. It wasn't as if her scent lingered if she wasn't around, so sensing it now meant she was close.

It seemed to be growing stronger the farther I went until I was standing in front of a doorway. Avram's observatory. I didn't love the idea of Riona alone with the creepy scholar, but perhaps she'd stopped in on her way out.

"Hello?" I called, opening the door. "Anyone home?"

The observatory was empty, but the experiments were bubbling and steaming in their glass vials as they moved through the tubes. I leaned down to peer at them closer, watching the red liquid ooze from place to place as slow as sludge. It was mesmerizing.

Finally, I pulled myself away, turning to look at the rest of the room. There was a cracked door on the other side I hadn't seen before. But as I pushed it open, revealing a long hallway, I realized I'd seen it before—this was the path to the memory stone room.

I kept my footfalls light, knowing that if Avram had left this door open, he hadn't meant to. The gas lamps were off, so I dragged my fingertips along the hallway to keep my bearings. I walked into the room, and the light came up, as if triggered by my presence.

The memory stones sat on a shelf on the other side of the room. I picked one up, examining it. They weren't just baubles—there was something alive inside them. Memories, life, stories…even with my muted abilities, the magic was visceral.

It probably took a little troll magic to pull the memory from the stone, but it wouldn't hurt for me to try. There was a small indentation in the center of the floor where Avram had placed the stone the last time we were in here.

To my surprise, as soon as I placed the small rock in the divot, the memory stone sank into the floor and the lights disappeared in place of a vision from the past. This was an old battle, but it didn't appear to be the one that happened in the *aos sí*. The trolls were fighting other fae—perhaps the *sidheog*, but it was hard to tell.

I kept an eye on the door, hoping the sound didn't travel. The battle was bloody, and although the trolls were victorious, they suffered heavy casualties. The memory was shorter than the one we'd seen earlier, and when it finished playing, the stone popped out of the floor. I replaced it on the shelf, glancing at the others. Perhaps they were, like Edric had said, all about old trolls. But I wanted to try one more before I continued my search for Riona.

I walked to the center of the room and placed another in the hole, standing back as the room darkened once more. But this was a familiar sight—Aoibheann, the Pennlan king, and a new *fuath* queen were sitting around a table in a dim light, the whole *seod croí* in the center of the table. Even dormant, it shimmered and moved with raw power that I could sense from a thousand years in the future.

"We need to destroy it," the Pennlan king said. "It needs to be wiped from this earth."

"It's not that simple," Aoibheann said. "It was made to be indestructible. To withstand any and all magical attacks. You can't just… destroy it with a spell."

"Then several spells."

She waved her hand impatiently. "That won't work."

"Then what do you propose? No one can be trusted with this thing," the *fuath* queen said, her bulbous eyes darting to Aoibheann. "Not even those who created it."

Aoibheann picked up the stone, staring at it as she thought. "The only thing that could possibly destroy it is itself."

The *fuath* scoffed. "That makes no sense. How can an object be used to destroy itself?"

"Not as it is," Aoibheann said, seeming more confident in her thoughts. "But if we… If we split it, we might be able to use the pieces to destroy each other." She glanced up, her golden eyes shining with faint hope. "It's worth a shot."

"And what do we do if that fails?" asked the human king.

"Let's hope it doesn't."

The memory faded away and I jumped to my feet to snatch the stone from the ground and grab another. I could only guess what happened next. They succeeded in splitting the stone, but before they could destroy it, the trolls took off with their piece, and the others walked off as well.

I stopped short. If *we* were to get all four pieces, we could finish what Aoibheann had started. We could eliminate the *seod croí* and the threat Eoghan posed to this world once and for all. Then we'd just have an incredibly dangerous wizard to contend with…but not an incredibly dangerous wizard *plus* the most powerful object ever created.

I swiped the next stone off the shelf and ran back to place it in the spot, holding my breath that this would tell me the next phase in the plan.

Instead, it was…Avram.

"I don't trust him. Not even a little."

"He promises he has something to offer us." Edric's voice filtered in around me, but he wasn't visible. He must've been the source of the memory. "It's been a long time since we've had any hope."

"But what he's asking of us. It would mean giving up our only source of magic—and trusting…trusting a stranger. A powerful stranger."

"If what he says is true," Edric said, "then we won't need that useless trinket anymore. We will have all the power we need at our fingertips. And so will our army."

"But—"

"There's enough magic in the water to sustain us for at least a year. That should give you plenty of time to concoct this potion he describes. Then, we will awaken our army."

"Do you think they will forgive you?" Avram asked.

"Once we march on the fae and reclaim what is ours, they will sing legends of my name."

The memory moved forward, as if Edric were walking down the hall. I recognized the castle, the city outside. This must've been a recent memory, because everything looked more or less the same. Even Avram's wrinkles.

Edric walked down a long stairwell to a part of the castle I hadn't been in before. It was a dungeon of sorts, dark and dank and empty. I doubted they had many prisoners here, what with their city being so insulated. Whoever had arrived had caused a stir.

A dark cell was visible in the dim light, and Edric walked up slowly. "Are you finding your accommodations to your liking?"

"I am, thank you."

My stomach dropped to the floor as my eyes widened.

"Tell me of your proposition," Edric said. "The exact ingredients."

"Well, the list begins with the blood of a half-fae…"

The lights in the room came up, and the memory disappeared. Avram stood in the doorway, his face a mask of fury.

"What are you doing in here, wizard?"

"You…" I turned to him, still not believing what I'd seen. "You betrayed us."

Avram glanced at the floor where the stone was still sitting and licked his lips slowly. "So the curtain has risen."

"I'm going to…" I didn't know what I was going to do. My magic was still unreliable. Avram was clearly in control of his. Riona…

It was then that I realized the strong scent of Riona I'd been following was coming from the scholar. It was as if she were standing right in front of me.

"Where is she?" I demanded, my gaze growing dark. "What have you done with Riona?"

"She's none of your concern anymore," he said.

"She is if—"

The ground rose around me, encircling my legs and my arms, knocking the staff from my hand. I yelped in surprise, a twist of fear running through my veins. But Avram's stone magic held it gently, even as it kept me glued in place.

"I would much rather just dispose of you, as I find wizards distasteful, but His Majesty would like you to join the others." He turned his back on me. "Come along."

I could say nothing else as the floor moved under me, dragging me away.

Chapter Forty-Eight

RIONA

For not the first time in the past few days, I awoke with a splitting headache, feeling as if my body were full of sand. My limbs weren't working right, and neither was my mouth as I opened and closed it. My tongue felt like sandpaper, and I desperately needed a drink. Slowly, my mind caught up with the rest of me, and panic jolted through my body. Edric. He'd done something.

But even as my heart pounded, my body wouldn't move. It could, but it was like pulling teeth to even open my eyes. But I did, taking in the sight of bars to my left.

I was in a cage.

I sat up as quickly as my body would allow, which wasn't very fast at all. My head moved slowly as I scanned what I could of the room outside the stone bars. There weren't any windows I could see, and there was a table full of glass vials and tubes. Along with…

I gulped. Was that my blood?

It was hard to ignore the red liquid sloshing around in a canister, slowly being siphoned into a tube. But it certainly explained the bruises on my arm and why I felt like I was moving through mud.

I followed the tube across the round table to where it dripped into a large cauldron over a blue flame. I couldn't see what was inside, but it felt vaguely…like me. Like a piece of myself had been ripped from my body. Even from this distance, I couldn't shake the eerie feeling.

Slowly, I got to my feet and walked to the bars, holding onto them for support as I continued looking around the room. My cage was in one corner of the long room, and a slender table ran the length. There were smaller vials numbering more than I could even start to count. Perhaps a hundred of them had been filled with a purple liquid…and me. My blood was in there.

What were these trolls up to?

The door opened, and I braced myself as Avram came walking down, muttering to himself. I caught the word "wizard," and my stomach bottomed out. I'd been fairly clear that I was leaving the troll kingdom, and now…I doubted any of them would look for me down here. And even if they did, the trolls seemed to know how to move things around. They could hide me forever if they wanted.

"Oh. You're awake." Avram frowned as he walked to the large cylindrical vial with my blood in it. "I suppose I can take more next time. It's so hard to gauge these things."

"What do you need my blood for?" I snapped, covering the wounds in the crook of my arms with my hands. "Is this some kind of weird troll thing? Do trolls drink fae blood?"

"Don't be ridiculous," he scoffed, walking to the cauldron to inspect it. "This is a complex potion that can be used to transfer magical powers from one individual to another." He lifted the spoon out of the cauldron and sniffed the liquid. "Normally, it's an impossible feat to extract magic like this. But your human blood acts like a carrier. It's the perfect blend."

I made a face. "I'm not a vintage."

"No, but you are powerful."

To my horror, the troll conjured one of my purple butterflies on his fingertip. I watched it drift up toward the ceiling before dissipating into thin air. I swallowed hard.

"Why do you want my power?" I asked, my voice hollow. "What possible reason could you have?"

He stared at me then walked to my cage. Despite my best efforts, I stepped back nervously, hoping he wouldn't reach inside and draw more from me.

"Do you know that the trolls were conscripted to fight in the battle of the *aos sí*?" he asked. "We had no choice. Every able-bodied troll was dragged from their homes and forced to fight by our *greater* cousins. We were expendable, you see. The *daoine maithe* and *sidheog* were not."

"That was hundreds of years ago," I whispered.

"Not for us," he said, straightening. "When Prince Edric took the stone, he had great plans for it. We'd hoped we would find our salvation hidden within the depths, but…all we found was more of the same. I'd thought we would remain in this purgatory forever. Until he came."

My pulse skipped. There was only one *he* I could think of who could promise the trolls the world.

"Now, I suppose I'll see to it that you're fed. We have much more to accomplish here," he said. "An entire army to supply with this potion. So you'd better rest up."

I wasn't sure I'd be able to close my eyes. "What about my friends? What will you do to them?"

"Oh, King Edric must play nice with your…" He gave me a once-over. "The queen. Her stone is a wildcard. We don't know if she's capable of using it. But I have a feeling that the entire charade is about to end, especially now that we know we can make what we need." He smiled. "Fear not. You'll see your homeland again. We'll need to keep you around for future generations."

>–» >–» >–» >–»

I was afraid to fall asleep, though I desperately wanted to. I kept pinching myself and pacing the cage as much as my frail body would allow. I trusted them when they said they wouldn't let me die—it looked like they had a lot of vials to fill, after all. But that didn't mean I wanted to give them an opportunity to take more of what was mine.

They'd also done something to my magic—perhaps the same spell that had kept Cade under control this whole time. I could only manage sparks, not even enough to move a strand of hair. It didn't help that my entire essence felt drained, either.

The irony of my situation wasn't lost on me. Here, I'd spent almost a fortnight pretending I had no magic and now…now all I wanted was to summon a flicker. But there wasn't time to focus on that. I needed to escape, to find my friends, to warn them before any more of Edric's web of lies unraveled.

But before I could attempt anything else, the door opened again and hope ignited that it might be Ward, or even Cade. But it wasn't— just Avram followed by two of the townsfolk and Edric bringing up the rear. The two civilians had dreamy looks on their faces, following Avram without a word.

"Sit here." Avram pointed to two chairs in the corner.

The two sat without a word, resting their hands on their laps.

"Are you ready?" Edric asked.

Avram nodded. "Remove the spell."

Edric pressed his hands to the trolls' faces, and his hands lit up for a moment. When he removed them, their eyes lost that dreamy expression as they blinked heavily.

"W…" The shorter troll was on the left and began rubbing his eyes. "What happened?"

The taller one stared at Avram with confusion. "Where are we? What is this place?"

"Fear not, dear warriors," Avram said softly. "You've been slumbering for a long time, but we've awoken you for a very important job. For our King Edric."

The name seemed to snap them into reality, and they turned to stare at their king, who remained a few paces away, his arms folded across his chest.

"Your Majesty." They fell to their knees, bowing their heads.

"It's an honor to be in your presence."

"Please, tell us how we can be of service to our great king."

"The savior of the troll race!"

It was all I could do to keep from rolling my eyes.

"You see, Avram? There is no danger of them turning against me," Edric replied with a kind hand on both their heads. "You soldiers are the next in line to receive a gift. The gift we've been waiting for these many, many years."

Edric turned to the table and plucked two vials, handing them to the soldiers.

"Drink. And see what your king has given you."

They did as instructed, and I held my breath, praying that maybe this time the potion wouldn't work. But magic hummed in my veins, reaching out from the gaping hole in my soul.

"Conjure," Edric commanded.

The shorter one held out his hand and formed a purple butterfly. My heart shattered as I watched my beautiful magic in the hands of another person. This was worse than when Eoghan had had his hold on me—then, at least, I could fight him. I could make a stand. But now, my power had been all but cleaved from me and handed to a complete stranger.

"I want every one of these vials gone by this evening," Edric said, turning back to his soldiers. "Gather up every troll you can get your hands on until they're all gone. Then you must all practice with your newfound powers. The fae will put up a masterful fight, I'm sure. But they're weak and lazy. And we will be victorious."

"What are you talking about, Your Majesty?" the taller soldier said.

"Avram will explain it all to you," Edric replied with a look to his scholar. "Take them to the city. Build them an arena to practice in."

"But what about the queen?" Avram asked.

I held my breath.

"She will be handled in short order. We have everything we need to keep her in line. She's weak and indecisive, as he said."

I gripped the bars. "She's stronger than you think."

"And she made it very clear she wants nothing to do with you, little fae," Edric replied, looking over his shoulder. "You should be thanking me for saving you from her. With any luck, you'll never have to see her again."

Chapter Forty-Nine

Ayla

I chewed my thumb, watching out my window for any sign of Ward, or Cade…or anybody. I prayed they'd catch up with Riona, and some part of me hoped they wouldn't be able to get out of the cave. Then I could at least try to make right what I'd broken. But that was me being selfish again, I supposed.

After I'd nibbled away my nails, I left the windows, leaving my room for the landing. I rapped on the door and waited, hoping Elodia or Rutley were there. But when I cracked open the door, the room was empty—even their gear was gone. Cade's was, as well.

I exhaled a shaky breath, fear coursing through me. Had *everyone* abandoned me? Would I have to walk the length of the mountain alone? The whole journey back to Pennlan?

Don't panic.

I brushed my sweaty palms on my skirt and left the room, forcing myself to inhale and exhale with every step down the staircase. They couldn't have left me. Ward was angry with me, but he'd explicitly told me Elodia and Rutley would remain behind.

I reached the landing and heard unfamiliar voices, so I started toward them to see what the activity was. But I didn't get very far before a silver stream zoomed through the stone veins on the floor then materialized into the troll king.

"Ah, Ayla," he said with a confident smile. "I'm glad I caught up with you."

"Have you seen any of my…traveling party?" I asked.

"Not lately," he said with a small twitch of his eye. "But I have something to show you. Will you come with me?"

"Of course."

I took his arm, but something felt off. He couldn't lie, but that twitch… Not only that, but Edric's smile wasn't generous or kind. It was more cunning. Dangerous, even. I did my best to keep a passive face, but my heart skipped nervously in my chest—especially when he walked me into what was very clearly a dungeon.

"What are we doing here?" I asked quietly, dropping his arm.

"I told you, I need to show you something."

I thumbed the stone at my neck, praying it would decide to show itself again should I need it. "I'd like to know what you're showing me before I take another step."

The dark cavern shrouded his face, but to my left, the blue lights came up brighter. And that was when my soul nearly left my body.

Ward, Cade, Elodia, Rutley—they were…*enmeshed* in the stone. With only their chests and heads visible. They were all unconscious, hanging like rag dolls in the prison.

"W-what are you doing?" I gasped. "Let them go!"

"In due time, Ayla." He turned to me. "But first, I need something from you." He held out his hand. "Your stone."

"Don't be idiotic," I snapped. "You can't use it. You aren't of the Pennlan line."

"No. But I don't want you using it against me," he said. "And so I need you to hand it over. Or else…"

A flash of light snaked through the rock under our feet, crawling along the floor until it came up around the four entrapped people. At once, they awoke, screaming in pain as the stone crept farther around them. I gripped the stone harder, praying it would come to life for me in my hour of need. But it stayed dormant, the bastard.

"Just hand me the stone," Edric said. "And your friends will live."

"How do I know you aren't lying?" I snapped. "As clearly, you can do that now."

"You don't really have much time to consider that option." The screaming grew louder, and my pulse was so fast I was getting dizzy. I looked back and forth, holding the stone, torn.

"I told you the stone doesn't work," I said, panic raising the volume of my voice. "It's broken. I only used it the once."

"How can we be sure of that?"

"Because if it *worked*, I'd use it to blast you into next year," I snarled, tears falling down my face. "Please, just *let them go!*"

The screaming lessened, and Edric sighed, as if *he* were the one being pained by his own actions. "I don't *want* to kill them, Ayla. It's not necessary, nor is it necessary for us to fight. I *would* like to open trade between our lands, too. But you see…there's something much more important at stake. Something a very long time in the making. And I need…" He took a step forward. "I can't chance your stone coming to life and ruining everything."

"Swear to me you'll release them if I hand this over." I watched Ward, his face growing purple as he gritted his teeth. "*Swear*."

"You know I can lie. What good is swearing the truth?"

I watched Cade's head bob as he came in and out of consciousness. My last words to him had been so hurtful. I couldn't live with myself.

"*Swear* on your father's life," I snarled.

Edric sighed, as if I were the most petulant thing he'd ever had to deal with. "*Fine*. If you give me your stone, I swear that your friends' lives will be spared—as will yours."

"Fine."

I pulled the stone off and threw it at him before I could stop myself. In an instant, the rock surrounding the four drew back and they fell to the ground. I ran forward as the bars opened and landed between Cade and Ward, gripping them to me tightly. I didn't care that they hated me. I was just glad to hear them draw breath.

"Are you all right?" I whispered.

"Why did you do that?" Ward whispered, wincing as he gripped his chest.

"Now, of course, you'll have to stay with them," Edric said as the bars shut behind me. "But you'll be well taken care of. I doubt what we have to do is—"

"You son of a… *You're working with Eoghan*," Cade growled, his voice hoarse as he scrambled to his feet.

My blood went cold as I stared at the back of Cade's head. "What?"

"Our partnership was very brief," Edric said, thumbing the stone in his hand. "He had some demands I'm not quite sure we need to acquiesce to. Namely…" He lifted my stone into the air. "This plus the halfling. But we have our own need for her."

"You *lied*," I snarled. "You swore to me—"

"Your friends are alive. That's all I promised," he said. "This isn't personal. But we've been waiting a very, *very* long time to finally move forward with this plan. Up until now, we didn't have all the tools necessary. But your sister…" He put his hand to his chest. "Excuse me, I know how you feel about her. *Riona* is going to play a key part in the execution of this plan."

"And what plan is that?" Ward said, coming to his feet. "What could you possibly need her for, if not to hand her over to Eoghan?"

Edric turned to us, a curious look on his face. "A thousand years after we took our piece of the *seod croí*, we were no closer to taking its power for ourselves than when we started. But then, fortuitously, we happened upon a man wandering our mountain, looking for trolls. A wizard." He tilted his head toward me. "You are familiar with him."

I balled my fists.

"Of course, our protections on the mountain were complete, and he could do as much as your friend Cade here. But he didn't seem to want to fight. Rather, he wanted to barter." Edric paused, looking at the stone. "He listened to our story and offered a solution. A potion, made with the blood of a half-human, half-fae that could transfer fae magic to a troll. I thought him absolutely mad, but he happened to have a vial of the blood on him."

My stomach twisted. Poor Riona.

"The potion he made did what he promised—it faded, of course, but it was enough to prove to us that he wasn't telling tall tales. So in exchange for this potion, he asked us to give him our stone."

"Tell me you didn't," Ward said, almost in a whine.

"What use did we have for it now? Once we make enough potion for our army, we will leave our mountain prison and march on the fae realm," Edric said. "We are a few thousand strong, and the Erlking has become complacent. With our numbers, we will easily overpower him and take our rightful place at the helm of the fae realm."

"Then what?" Ward asked. "You're going to wake up the town and take them to war with the fae? Do you think they'll want to after they find out you've been keeping them prisoner for the past thousand years?"

"Prisoner?" Edric barked a laugh. "I've saved them. We were less than dogs in the fae realm. Forced to do whatever the greater fae wanted. The soldiers here didn't even have a choice but to fight against that monstrous wizard. And what was left of our army, I led away into the mountains to protect them."

"So this is all about taking the fae realm for yourself?" Cade asked. "Eoghan won't allow it. If he gets all four pieces of the stone, he'll... It'll be like Laughlan all over again."

"Well, that would require him to have this one, wouldn't it?" Edric twisted it in his hand. "And I'm not keen on giving it to him just because he asks. If we can overpower the Erlking, we can overpower a simple wizard." He gestured to Cade. "You're proof of that."

"Eoghan isn't to be underestimated," he said. "Give us the Pennlan stone back, and we can protect it."

"Like I said, I need it for insurance," he said, walking toward the door. "But I promise to be a benevolent warden. I'll be sure to send food and water. For now, though..." He tossed the stone in the air and caught it before pocketing it. "I thank you for your cooperation."

Chapter Fifty

Ward

Nobody spoke for a few minutes. Ayla stared at the stone bars of our prison, her lips parted in surprise, anger, disgust—it was hard to pick one emotion on her face. Cade was seething. Rutley and Elodia were still catching their breaths.

And me...I was furious.

"Why the hell did you give him your stone?" I snapped.

Ayla's head spun toward me. "Excuse me?"

"You could have lit it up and blasted him into oblivion," I said, waving my hand.

She came to her feet. "I *tried*, you insufferable moron. But it doesn't just come on when I want it to." She shook her head. "It hasn't *done* anything since Eoghan tried to kill me, in case you didn't know."

"Well, maybe we should try to kill you and see what it does," Elodia muttered.

"The *most* important thing was keeping that stone in *your* possession," I seethed. "And you just gave it away like it wasn't a *six-week journey to find the damn thing*."

"I gave it away because you were *dying*," she said. "What did you expect me to do? Let him kill the lot of you?"

"*Yes.*"

"Hey..." Rutley began, but I held up my hand to silence him.

"Our lives don't matter, Ayla. *Yours* does. *You* hanging onto that stone is the *most* important thing. Especially now that Eoghan..." I didn't even want to say the words. All this time, all this work, and he'd managed to outsmart us yet again. And he had a head start on looking for the third stone, too. "This was a disaster from the moment you left Pennlan."

She rolled her eyes. "Don't even start with the *I told you sos*."

"And if you'd listened to me, you'd be safely back in the castle, the stone wouldn't be in the troll's hands, and—"

"And Eoghan would still have *their* stone and you'd still be in danger," Ayla barked at me.

"Got you there, boss," Elodia muttered under her breath.

"We don't have time to argue," Rutley said. "What we know is that the king has the stone, Riona, and potentially we're looking at that evil wizard showing back up."

"And they're going to war against the Erlking," Cade said.

"Do they have a chance?" I asked.

"I don't know," Cade whispered. "Aldrick is strong, but he's the only one. There aren't a lot of training matches happening these days. No army to speak of. And I don't know… Riona's powerful when she wants to be. An army of Rionas… I don't know if the fae realm has a chance. Especially because I doubt the Erlking would see it coming."

"We have to get out of here," I said. "Cade, any luck with your magic?"

He shook his head.

"Rutley, Elodia, any ideas?"

Elodia inspected the stone bars closely. "They're solid, boss. I'm sure you need some troll magic to open them."

I ran my hand over my face. "And I don't think any of us have any weapons. Edric stripped us of everything."

Ayla gasped and her hand went to her skirts. To my surprise, she lifted them, almost to the point of indecency, and revealed a small knife. The one I'd given her on our journey after we'd come across the wolves— I'd completely forgotten about it.

"Can you do anything with this?" she asked, handing it to Elodia.

"I can try."

Elodia took the weapon and began chipping at the stone. It was probably hopeless, but it was something. Cade rose to stand next to her, his staff pointed at the stone as he struggled to conjure. Ayla watched him go with a sad sort of stare before those piercing green eyes turned to me.

"Look, Ward," Ayla began quietly. "I'm... I'm sorry. Sorry for everything. All I wanted was... I was trying to do the right thing for Pennlan. But..." She shook her head sadly. "I guess I still have no idea what that is." She gave me a furtive look. "You were right. I had no business leaving Pennlan. And I'm sorry... I'm sorry I've just made a mess of things. I was desperate to find answers."

I glanced at her. "Your stone really hasn't worked since Eoghan? Why didn't you tell me?"

"Because admitting it would make it real," she said. "I didn't even tell Captain Gabhann."

I didn't quite understand that logic. "You shouldn't keep secrets from your captain. Especially about stuff like that."

"I've done... I've been doing a lot of avoiding the truth lately." She met my gaze again.

Elodia let out a curse. The knife handle had broken off the blade. "Well, anyone else got anything hidden under their skirts?"

"Uh..." Cade pointed to the bars. "What's happening?"

The stone melted away until the bars were completely gone. Movement in the shadows put me on my guard, until I recognized the long, silvery hair—and that his arms were laden with our weapons.

"Lynton!" I cried, jumping to my feet. "You're okay. Are you all right? Do you have your memories back?"

"Edric's magic isn't as potent as it used to be," he said with a rueful smile. "Giving away the stone was a mistake."

"He has the Pennlan stone now," Ayla said. "And my..." She straightened. "My sister. He's making a potion with her blood."

Lynton nodded. "He has made several vials and is already bringing the villagers in to take it. I don't know where he's keeping her, though."

"If you'll give me my magic back, I can find her," Cade said.

"I would if I could," the troll replied with a grimace. "But your binding comes from Avram and the king."

"Then we take them out, and you'll get it back," I said, standing.

"Don't kill Edric," Lynton said, his eyes flashing at me. "I don't have any love for the king, but it's his magic that keeps this mountain from collapsing. If you kill him, it will be the death of every troll in this city." His golden eyes met mine. "They're innocent."

"You have magic. Can't you hold up the mountain?" I asked.

"I'm not as powerful as my cousin," he said. "I'd prefer not to test my own abilities if we can."

"Fine." I turned to the group, feeling like it was yet again up to me to come up with a plan. "Our priorities are getting Riona to safety and getting the stone back. Cade, go with Elodia and Rutley. Your magic may not be working, but your staff will leave a bruise if you swing it hard enough."

"Right, and they'll just put us back here in this prison," Cade drawled. "Or worse."

"Then don't let them put you back in prison," I said, as if that were the obvious answer. "Lynton, you're with me. We need to find Edric and get the stone back."

"What about me?" Ayla asked.

"You stay here. Out of sight, out of trouble." I turned to the others. "That goes for all of you. We're outmatched here, and we need to be clever. They'll underestimate us, and that's where we take our advantage." I nodded. "Now go."

Cade and the soldiers jumped to their feet, grabbing their weapons before running out.

Ayla watched them go with a worried sort of look before turning to me.

"I'm not staying."

I looked at the ceiling, inhaling a little. "Ayla."

"If you get the stone back, it needs to come to me," she said. "I'm the only one who can use it."

"And you *just* admitted—"

"Maybe it'll come to life," she snapped. "But me staying here isn't going to help anyone. At least…" She swallowed. "If I'm with you, I have a chance of doing something useful."

"Time is of the essence," Lynton drawled. "The longer we wait—"

"Fine." I didn't like the idea. "Let's go."

>–» >–» >–» >–»

We climbed the stairs, Ayla keeping pace with us, but staying behind Lynton and myself. My mind swirled with options, hoping inspiration would come to me in the heat of the moment. Praying the others wouldn't get tripped up. And wishing my queen had stayed behind where it was safe.

"Lynton," Ayla said softly. "Did you know that Edric had given away the stone?"

"No. Not until… Not until I came back. That was his design. I could tell you he'd taken it, not that he'd lost it."

"They're tricky, the fae," I said. "When they want to be."

"I just don't understand," she whispered. "He *showed* us his stone when we first got here."

"He showed us *a* stone," I reminded her. "That you vociferously admitted was the real one."

She glowered, muttering to herself. "Foolish, *stupid* girl."

"Shh," I whispered, hearing voices ahead.

I motioned for us to flatten ourselves against the wall. Five trolls came walking by wearing whole-body armor, the same they'd worn in the vision from the *aos sí*. They carried no other weapons, but perhaps they felt they didn't need any with Riona's magic pumping through their veins.

When they were gone, we continued.

"I apologize for my part in this," Lynton said. "I had one…one goal in mind."

"Your daughter?" I asked.

He nodded. "All I care about is keeping her safe. That's why—"

A loud groaning stopped him, and Ayla grabbed my arm as the room spun and the three of us wobbled. When we stopped, what had once been a landing had turned into another prison.

"I guess Edric knows we're out," I said, craning my neck. "Lynton, can you get us out of here?"

He walked to the wall and pressed his hands against it, closing his eyes. The stone rippled then calmed without moving. "He's more powerful than I am."

"You said all you care about is keeping your daughter safe, right?" Ayla said softly. "And she's out there? Part of Edric's army?"

Lynton nodded.

"When you use your magic," she said, "think of your daughter. Think of what it will feel like to lose her."

He stared at her for a moment, and I almost felt like pulling Ayla away from the intensity of his stare. But after a moment, he returned to the wall and closed his eyes, furrowing his brow.

The stone rippled again and groaned as it moved. I held onto Ayla's arm as we both nearly lost our balance, but soon the movement stopped —and we had a path out of the landing.

"Let's go," Lynton said, his face a mask of fury.

"What was that?" I whispered to Ayla.

"Eoghan would… He said emotion is part of magical intensity," she said softly. "I used to sit in on lessons with Cade. I thought it might be worth a shot."

"If—*when* you get the stone back," I said, "maybe listen to your own advice."

"I've tried," she said. "But even when Edric was about to crush you,

I couldn't make it work. Not even when we were in the cave." She shook her head. "No matter how desperately I wanted to."

I reached down and grasped her hand. "We'll figure it out. Together."

"So you're un-resigning?" she asked, hopefully.

I snorted. "I'll think about it."

CHAPTER FIFTY-ONE

CADE

I led the way, feeling a little like a lamb to slaughter. I had nothing to offer, except, as Ward had so nicely pointed out, that my staff was hard when I swung it. Still, Elodia and Rutley followed with grim, determined expressions. So from them, I took a little courage. Riona needed us.

We stopped at every corner to make sure the coast was clear then continued. Every so often, I'd get the faintest whiff of that sweet, mead scent, but I was sure I was imagining it because it seemed to be coming from all sides. But where it tasted strongest, I led us.

"Do you know where you're going?" Rutley asked.

"Kind of," I said, as we crept down a hall. "Edric's been busy. I'm picking up Riona's scent all over the place. It's hard to discern what's her and what's…"

What was just her blood. Her essence. The thought of someone draining *me* of my magic was horrifying. Using Riona's to take up arms against her own people? It shook me to my core.

"The good news is that the potion seems to wear off after a while," Elodia said. "So if we can keep them at bay until it goes away…"

"That still leaves them with their troll magic," I said, glancing up at the rock around us. "Which is going to be a problem." I looked over my shoulder. "What's your plan when we find Riona?"

"Hack, slice, the usual," Rutley said. "We aren't planners."

"Speak for yourself," Elodia said. "What are you thinking, wizard? You have a history fighting the fae."

"I don't have any insight. The most I've seen of troll magic is what they've done to this city," I replied.

"Didn't you just spend six months training with the fae?" she asked, quirking a brow. "Can't be that different."

"Their magic flies through the air," I said. "Not through the rock."

"Strategy, man. I'm talking strategy. Is it just throwing spells at one another or is there some thought behind it?"

I slowed my gait, thinking. "It's a bit of instinct and strategy. The fae are as tricky in a fight as they are in speaking. They won't let you have an inch. The only way to win is to find the upper hand, whatever that is."

"Then let's find the upper hand," Elodia said. "Ward said they'd underestimate us. So let's use that to our advantage."

I didn't have a clue how we'd do that, but as we turned another corner, we stumbled into the open-air garden I'd seen before when I'd run into Edric.

"Wow," Elodia whispered, walking up to one of the emerald bushes and touching it. "What artistry. Did Edric make this?"

"Seems like it," I said. "Suppose he didn't have enough to do in the past thousand years. Must've been…"

"Lonely," Rutley said. "Each of these leaves is intricately carved."

"A thousand years is a long time," I replied.

I tensed as footsteps and voices approached. The others heard it, too and jumped to hiding spots. I dashed away, crouching low behind a bush studded with giant red rubies shaped like roses.

"Come along. The king wants us to start training immediately."

Avram walked out of the castle, followed by ten trolls decked out in armor, but no weapons. Not that they needed any, especially as one of them conjured a familiar purple butterfly.

A strong scent of Riona crossed my tongue, and I balled my fists then released my anger. The trolls were more or less innocent in this. Avram and Edric, they were the ones who needed to be stopped.

They filed out of the garden and after a beat, the three of us popped up from our hiding spots and gathered in the center of the garden.

"Where are they going?" Elodia asked.

"I don't know," I said, inhaling. "But I'm getting a strong whiff of Riona from that direction. Maybe if we follow them, we'll find her."

⤐ ⤐ ⤐ ⤐

We kept a healthy distance, but my curiosity was getting the better of me as we left the castle. Part of the city had been flattened, the buildings gone in favor of a large plain. There were at least fifty trolls already there, seemingly waiting for instruction. As we drew closer, I realized that the strong scent of Riona wasn't coming from her—but from all the trolls that now had her magic. I cursed silently. We'd gone the wrong way. Riona wasn't here; her stolen magic was.

"What is this?" Elodia asked. "What kind of…"

"It's a training arena," I replied. "There was one at the Erlking's castle. Was this here before?"

Rutley shook his head. "This is new. Terrifying and new."

"We need to—"

Light moved through the stone veins at our feet, and before I could say another word, we were surrounded by trolls—this time *with* weapons. Stone spears pointed within inches of our eyeballs, and I doubted swinging my staff would help us.

"How in the world did you escape the prison?" Avram asked, a safe distance from us.

"Ingenuity," Elodia replied.

"It doesn't matter," Avram said. "You're all expendable now. His Majesty has your Pennlan stone, and your magic is…" He smirked. "There's nothing you can do to stop us."

"Eoghan will come back, looking for that stone," I said, thinking quickly as the spears drew closer. "He will destroy everything you've built for your treachery."

Avram scoffed. "We're not afraid of a wizard."

I gripped my staff, an idea coming to mind—a last option. "Why don't you test that theory? If you think yourselves invincible, if you think you can fend him off," I gripped my staff, "set your army against a wizard."

"Cade, what are you doing?" Elodia muttered.

"Why not release me from this spell you've got me under and see how strong your army really is?"

It was a shot in the dark. Avram would've been smarter to kill us. But he'd struck me as a proud man, a man who seemed to believe he was better than he was. I just hoped I'd read him right.

"You are nothing compared to Eoghan," Avram said, and my stomach sank. "But it's an intriguing proposition. Very well..." He clapped his hands, and the spears retracted a few inches. "Let's put your wizard magic against our army of fae and see how well you fare."

We didn't get a full reprieve, as the spears led us down into the training ring. But it did give us a chance to talk.

"You know if you start winning, Avram's going to take away your magic again," Rutley muttered, keeping a wary eye on the trolls.

"I'm counting on it," I said with a look to them. "Remember what Ward said."

Elodia nodded in understanding.

We reached the training ring, and I took my place on one end, stretching my arms and planting my feet. On the other side, fifty trolls took their positions—and Avram stood to the side. Elodia and Rutley had just one troll guarding them. A good sign. I was acutely aware that he could pull my magic at any moment and I'd be obliterated. So I needed to be careful and appear to be losing. At least until Elodia and Rutley could get into position.

"Are you ready?" Avram asked, holding up his hand.

"My magic, if you please," I said.

He rolled his eyes and stomped his foot on the ground. Something invisible slid from my body and in its place, a rush of the familiar, like my very soul being returned to my body. Tears welled in my eyes as I became whole once more, magic filling every nook and cranny. Before I even knew what I was doing, I gathered and shot a spell at a nearby boulder, obliterating it into a million pieces.

"Much better," I said, adjusting my shoulders. "Now, shall we?"

Riona's purple magic barreled toward me, and suddenly, I was back in the fae realm, fighting against Darragh. I conjured a shield spell, watching for something to come sideways or above. But it never came. The trolls were worse at fighting than I thought—it was going to be difficult to pretend.

But just as I had that thought, a ripple of the stone beneath my feet drew my attention, and I just barely dashed out of the way of a barrage of rock that would've crushed me. So perhaps a little effort would be required…

Another flash of purple, more rock, and it was all I could do to keep one step ahead. Clíodhna's voice echoed through my ears.

"You think too much."

I took a breath, clearing my mind, and fell into the warmth of magic. My movements became instinctual, sensing the magic humming through the air and ground before it came within striking distance, conjuring a shield for this, a block for that. I closed my eyes, letting my magic see for me. The world slowed down, and like mist clearing, I saw the opening to obliterate them all.

I released a barrage of magic, but not through the air—through the rock. It split the rock as it traveled, spreading green light everywhere.

Then it was gone—along with my breath—as the rushing sound returned. I fell to my knees, clutching ears as I saw the return fire out the corner of my eye. But I was helpless—and I wouldn't survive. My limbs were frozen as I prepared for the pain.

Almost too late, something big and bulky knocked me to the ground, and the spell missed us by inches.

"Duck, man," Rutley grumbled, pushing himself off me.

"You shouldn't have—"

Avram let out a strangled cry, an arrow through his chest. He turned, weakly, to where Elodia's bow was still singing, before toppling over.

As before, the deafening sound was gone, and my magic was back in my body. I gaped at the scholar, blood dripping from his mouth as he gasped for air until he finally went still.

"Cade," Rutley barked, elbowing me. "The others?"

I felt the magic before I saw it and slammed my staff into the ground, creating a shield around Rutley, Elodia, and myself against the barrage of butterflies and rock magic.

"Hold your fire!" I called. "We aren't here to hurt you!"

But there was no getting through to them. Elodia had killed their beloved scholar, and I was a wizard—and the last one they'd seen had almost destroyed the continent. Their attacks on my shield increased, and a couple butterflies got through the cracks.

"Cade," Elodia said, wincing as a pebble pelted her. "Take them out!"

I couldn't, not when I could hear Lynton's voice in my mind, begging me to spare them. They *were* innocent, trapped here by a mad king and his equally mad scholar, asleep for a thousand years. So, instead, I put my staff to the ground, locating the veins of magic, and cast a simple sleep spell. One by one, they toppled to the ground, still.

"Did you kill them?" Rutley asked.

"No," I said.

"Why the hell not?" Elodia asked. "They're going to—"

"We'll let Lynton deal with them," I said, turning to them. "But for now, they'll stay asleep until I wake them. We need to get back to the castle and find Riona before they make any more of them—or Edric does something drastic."

CHAPTER FIFTY-TWO

RIONA

I studied the bars, searching for any sign of weakness. But they were solid stone, formed with troll magic, and could only be dismantled by magic. I reached deep within me, searching for the magic I'd been so desperate to ignore, and dragged it to the forefront. But all I could conjure was a faint butterfly, not nearly enough. I released my effort, exhausted but not deterred. I had to keep trying. I couldn't let them take any more of me.

Staring at my hands, I wondered what was going on in the castle above. Did they know I was gone? Did they care? Cade and Ward probably did, as did Elodia and Rutley. But Ayla... Ayla was glad to be rid of me. A tear dripped down my cheek, and I wiped it away hastily. No more crying over someone who didn't want me.

I closed my eyes and balled my fists, digging deep again. Searching for my butterfly magic, or even that secondary...that other magic that seemed to be dying to be useful. But since I'd woken up in this cage, the voices in my head had been silent.

The door opened, and everything in me tensed, ready to fight. Edric came downstairs, taking the steps quickly. He was agitated, fury on his face.

"You. Come with me."

He stomped his foot, and the bars around me melted to the floor. I backed up an inch, going nowhere, as he reached down and yanked me to standing. I was still reeling and woozy from the blood loss, plus whatever other potions they'd put in my body, and my legs wouldn't work right as he dragged me across the room.

"Walk, you stupid halfling," he barked.

"You took all my blood, you stupid troll," I shot back, my words slurred.

"Fine."

He released me and I fell into a cradle of rock he'd conjured that followed behind him. I moved, my hands and legs free, and held onto the sides as he walked the staircase. He was muttering to himself.

"Trouble with your master plan?" I asked.

"Shut up."

A small flicker of hope lit in my chest. Maybe my friends hadn't left me yet. "What's your next step? Drag me to the fae kingdom?"

"Perhaps just threaten to crush you," he said.

"Then how will you use my blood to make your army?" I replied. "You need me alive."

"Then I'll just *crush* them."

"Seems like you're having trouble with that," I said with a smirk. "Or else—"

The cradle shook violently, and I had to grab onto the edge to keep from falling out. But it wasn't because of what I'd said. Our path was blocked.

"Edric."

Ward stood in the center of the receiving hall, his sword bared. Ayla was behind him, clutching her chest where her stone should've been. Lynton stood behind them, his hands on the ground as if ready to fight.

"Riona!" Ayla cried. "Are you all right?"

I couldn't speak. Was that relief in her eyes?

"Let her go," Ward demanded. "And we'll let you live."

"You can't do anything against me," Edric said.

As if to prove a point, magic zoomed from his feet toward them. I cried out in warning, but Lynton was faster, easily knocking whatever it was away.

"This isn't necessary, cousin." Lynton rose slowly "The Erlking who conscripted us is long dead. The fae there now would—"

"What do you know of the fae there now?" Edric said, pointing at him. "They're all the same. Given the chance, they'll kill us all as punishment for stealing the stone. At least with this magic, we have a *chance* against them."

"The fae aren't your enemy," Ayla said.

"That's rich, coming from you," Edric replied with a snort. "Weren't you the one who said you don't trust them?"

"I was wrong," she said. "Projecting my own… It doesn't matter. I was wrong, that's all that's important." She squared her shoulders. "Let my sister go."

"Now she's your sister?" Edric said as the cradle rippled, rock covering my hands and legs. "That's not—"

"Quit talking," Ward said, inching closer.

"Good idea."

I saw the magic above them before they did and cried out in warning. But it was too late. Big hunks of rock fell from the ceiling, intent on crushing those below. Lynton scrambled, but he couldn't do anything when they were in mid-air. I reached for my magic and—

The chunk of rock fell onto a circle of green that surrounded Ward, Ayla, and Lynton. It took me a split second to recognize the magic and my hopes lifted to the sky as Cade, Rutley, and Elodia came running up the hall from the other side, Cade's staff glowing bright green.

"Oh, that's not happening," Edric said, stomping his foot again— and Cade's magic was gone. But there was fear on the troll's face now. "What… Where is Avram?"

"Met the business end of my arrow," Elodia said, nocking another. "Shall I make it two for two?"

"Elodia," Ayla said, stepping forward. "Edric, please listen to reason. Let Riona go, and we can bring your people to Pennlan. Or even back to the fae kingdom. We can release them from their spell and—"

"*No!*" Edric said as the rock crept up my body, firming and squeezing. "I have come *too* far to turn back now. The Erlking throne is *mine*. We *earned* it from the blood spilled in the *aos sí.*"

"We'll see—" Ward tried to walk forward, but his feet had sunk into the floor. Everyone's had. And the rock surrounding my body crept higher, surrounding my stomach, arms, and crawling toward my neck.

"W-what are you doing?" I said, panting as breathing became hard. "You need…my blood."

"I'll just have to take what I can and move quickly," Edric said, his golden eyes wild with fear. "It'll be enough."

"Riona!" Ayla yelled, pulling at her legs. "Lynton, *do something*!"

"I'm trying! But he's too strong."

"*Help!*" I was now covered with stone from my neck down with stone as the breath and life was squeezed out of me. I found my sister's gaze, seeing the horror in her eyes. There was apology there, too, and regret. Then nothing.

⇥ ⇥ ⇥ ⇥

The air was cold as snow crunched under my feet. The pain I'd felt was gone, and all that was left was peace—except not wholly. I couldn't take a deep breath, couldn't feel my body. I was walking and yet standing still, moving toward something I shouldn't have been seeing.

Riona…

I froze, fear shooting through my body. That voice, that familiar voice. He was here. He was coming to take me.

Riona, do not fear me.

No, I had to fight. I had to… I couldn't let myself be taken by him again. I wasn't…

I'm not your enemy. I can help you win.

I opened my mouth to scream, but nothing came out. I fell to my knees in this world, but the other side of the world was drawing ever closer.

In the distance, beyond the garden trellis, movement. I reached for it, grasping at nothing and making no progress. It was as if something were firmly planting me in this garden, no matter how much I wanted to walk to the other side. And I wanted it—for all my grousing about not wanting to kill myself, it was the simpler solution. That monster wouldn't have control over me. Edric wouldn't be able to use my blood to attack my homeland. Everything would be better if I could just *go…*

Riona, it's not your time.

I stopped abruptly. What I'd thought was the wizard was actually… a female voice. Garbled, but becoming clearer. It wasn't Leandra's voice, either. Yet still familiar.

I stopped fighting and let the stillness overtake me as the figure came into view.

Aoibheann.

She was as beautiful and formidable as she'd been in the vision. But the edges of her form were blurred, almost like she wasn't fully in this world. Her lips moved but made no sound. There was concern on her face—fear. She spoke louder, but it was like the cool blast of wind.

"Help me," I whispered. "I don't know what to do…"

There was pity in her eyes, and she reached into her pocket, pulling out white magic in the palm of her hand. My magic. But why would she have it? And what did she want me to do with it?

"…help her…"

"What?" I wanted to say, but my lips wouldn't move. I was walking backward, out of this in-between place, back to the pain and misery.

"…help your sister…"

"…only you…"

>↠ >↠ >↠ >↠

I opened my eyes and regretted it. Ayla was screaming my name, Ward and Cade cursing Edric's name, and I was slowly being crushed to death. But there was something else now. The magic that had been resting dormant in my veins was stirring. Not enough to free me, but enough.

Ayla's stone was in Edric's pocket. I didn't know how I knew that, but I did. It almost called to me, the way it had in that lake. It was all I could do to keep myself awake, but I found that white magic, the same Aoibheann had held in the palm of her hand. As Edric focused on the others, I used that magic to slide into his pocket and surround the Pennlan stone, pulling it out gently and floating it over to my sister, resting it in her hand.

Then I went back into the darkness.

CHAPTER FIFTY-THREE

AYLA

My voice was hoarse from screaming, but it was the only thing I could do as I watched my sister grow redder and redder as Edric's stone magic squeezed her. Lynton was doing what he could, but it was clear the king was the king for a reason. I pulled at my feet.

"You don't need this," I said, knowing my words would do no good but trying anyway. "You don't need Riona's magic. There's no enemy for you to fight anymore. The fae aren't going to treat you like they used to."

"You can't be sure of that," Edric said. "You don't know what they're capable of."

"I—" Something small and cold slipped into my hand and I gasped, opening my palm.

My stone.

As soon as relief had coursed through me, dread took its place. What good was this stupid thing when it wouldn't work?

"I'm so sorry, Riona," I whispered, bringing the stone to my lips. "I'm not worthy of—"

The world before me vanished, bathed in blue light, and my heart pounded. Voices spoke to me, and I reached out to them as if they were the only thing that mattered in this world. I apologized for my actions, my unworthiness, and thanked them for giving me another chance to be the sovereign who could wield this stone.

A woman with thick rope braids nodded at me and whispered words I couldn't understand. Aoibheann. She wore a smile on her face as if I finally understood some mystery she'd wanted me to solve. I wasn't exactly sure what that was, but I did know…this time I would not fail.

Edric met my gaze, fear in those golden eyes as he realized the stone was bright in my hand. I felt pity for him, sensed his desperation. His fear. But it wasn't for his people; it was for himself. Fear that when his army found out what he'd done, what he'd *stolen* from them in pursuit of his own selfish desires…they would turn on him as Lynton had. Fear that his thousand-year vendetta had been for naught.

I pitied him. But I wouldn't make the same mistake twice.

The magic was powerful and absolute, but so very…so very delicate as it surrounded Riona, releasing her and passing through it to Edric. And when it reached its target, it left nothing behind.

I exhaled as I came back to myself, realizing I'd been floating a few inches off the ground. There was stunned silence as the sound of my magic echoed off the stone.

"Ayla…" Ward whispered. "You…"

"You did it," Cade said, walking as if he wasn't sure he knew how anymore. "You used the stone."

I barely heard them, rushing across the room to where Riona lay on the ground. She was pale, bloody, but her chest rose and fell faintly.

"Riona," I whispered, cupping her face—the face so similar to mine. "Wake up. Please."

"Here." Cade waved his staff over her, a haze of green magic falling across her body.

The color immediately returned to her cheeks. Slowly, she stirred and mumbled, wincing hard and rolling onto her side. Then, as if realizing she had the ability to move, she sat up and looked around.

"What happened?"

"Edric—" Ward started, but whatever he had to say was lost as I crushed my little sister to me.

"Riona, I'm so sorry," I whispered, tears leaking down my face. "I'm so… I should never have said what I said to you. It wasn't fair. I hope one day you can forgive me for my weakness, for being so—"

"I forgive you."

"Really?" I sat back. "That easily?"

"You're my sister," she said with a lift of her shoulder. "And…I think I have you to thank for saving my life…" She rubbed her head. "I had the weirdest dream, though. I—"

A loud, ominous boom echoed from somewhere above the castle. Almost like something had cracked.

"Oh no…" Cade said, staring at the ceiling. "We have to get out of here."

He jumped to his feet and started conjuring a portal when a large piece of rock appeared in front of him, nearly knocking the staff from his hand. All eyes went to Lynton, whose face was a mask of fury.

"You will not leave the trolls here to die," he said. "You promised they would live."

"Of course we won't," I said, giving Cade a meaningful look. "Lynton, can you keep the mountain up long enough for us to get everyone out?"

"Not long. I'm not…" The troll swallowed. "I don't have the magic Edric did. I will need help."

"Then we'll help," Riona said, which was met by a chorus of dissent.

"You barely have your magic back," Cade barked.

"You nearly died," Ward said. "Cade, get Ayla and Riona back to Pennlan—"

Another ominous crack—this one followed by a loud *boom*.

"We don't have time for that," Lynton growled. "The mountain is collapsing now. I suggest, *Your Majesty*, that you use that stone to keep you and your sister safe until all the trolls are."

"No time for arguing," I snapped, helping Riona to her feet. "We have to move!"

>→ >→ >→ >→

We ran outside the castle and, to my horror, sunlight was streaming in from the top of the cavern—and a large piece of the mountain had landed in the middle of the city. Lynton made a sound and knelt to the ground, closing his eyes. Magic poured from his body, sliding through the streets and up the sides of the mountain. The rumbling ceased, but it seemed the damage was done.

"Hurry," he said with a whimper. "I can't hold it long."

"I'll help," Cade said.

"No," Lynton said. "Create one of those portals to Pennlan. Unless you can do both."

Cade hesitated. "I'll try. But—"

"Portal is more important," Ward said. "Elodia, go south, Rutley, go east. I'll go north. Riona, if you're up for it, go west. Ayla, stay here with Cade—"

"Riona stays here," I said. "She's not yet recovered."

Ward opened his mouth to argue, and I waved him off. "If I die, she'll carry on the Pennlan line. We have to get everyone to safety."

"Quit arguing and *go*," Lynton barked.

"Fine," Ward seethed. "Be careful."

I ran as fast as I could toward the western part of the city. I tried yelling at the trolls, telling them they needed to get to safety, but that was met with curious looks and surprise that there was a human walking amongst them. So I had to resort to alternate methods—physically dragging the troll back to where Cade was waiting.

"Well, this is fascinating," the troll said. "A human in our parts!"

"Yes, very interesting," I grumbled as I pulled him along. Luckily, he was docile, if not a little obnoxious.

We ran up the hill, and I slowed, my heart soaring to the skies. Cade had conjured a portal and just beyond was...

"Home," I whispered. Just a few feet away. But I couldn't relax yet, not when there were so many people in danger.

Ward was dragging two trolls, much the same as I had, and

unceremoniously tossed them through the portal before turning and running back into the city. So I followed suit and kept at it.

It felt like it was taking an eternity, and I'd only gotten through the first block and saved maybe ten trolls. Every time I returned, Lynton looked more exhausted. I didn't know how long he could hold the mountain—and somehow, I knew that if we left *one* troll behind, he would never forgive us.

So I ran back into the city again and again, dragging befuddled and confused trolls out of their homes and tossing them into the green grass of Pennlan. The only thing I kept thinking was the ticking clock, and how all these trolls were innocent. That they deserved to have a life after spending a thousand years imprisoned by their own king.

I'd completed one block and was onto another when another crack echoed above our heads. And to my horror, a boulder the size of a city block fell from the ceiling, headed straight for the castle. Cade was too busy focusing on casting spells into the city to notice.

I stepped forward, confident in my abilities now. The stone lit up exactly as it was supposed to, and a blast of blue light zoomed toward the boulder, obliterating it and showering Cade with small pebbles. He caught my gaze, surprise and relief on his face, and I half smiled.

"Don't stop now," Ward grunted, passing me with two trolls over his shoulder.

"Ward, we… This place is coming apart," I said, holding the stone in my hand. "Maybe…maybe we just blow the top off. Then we won't have to worry about keeping the mountain from collapsing."

"Do you think you can do that?"

I stared at the front of the castle. "With my sister, I bet I could." He gave me a sideways look, and I blew air between my lips. "Saying it is the first step toward believing it. Leave me alone."

He smirked and ran back toward the city. "Be quick!"

"Riona," I called, beckoning her over. "I have an idea, but I need your help."

I told her my plan and she gave me a worried look. "If we don't do this right, we could make things worse."

"Lynton can't hold on for much longer," I said, reaching out my hand. "C'mon. Let's give it a try."

As soon as her hand slipped into mine, the stone lit up more brightly than it had before. She smiled at me, perhaps feeling the magic as well. And together we turned toward the mountaintop that was shaking and cracking.

"Lynton, be ready," Cade called as he readied his staff.

"Can you…wield it?" I asked Riona. "I'm not sure I have the aim yet."

"Me neither."

"You're better at it than I am."

She offered me a small smile and tightened her grip. The magic in my chest increased as she pulled it toward her. The voices sang in my mind again.

"Can you hear that?" I whispered.

"Hear what?"

I cracked an eye. "Never mind."

And like a sunbeam, the magic exploded upward from her body. Everything was white and didn't fade—for a moment, I thought we might've died. But it was just…just the sun falling on us for the first time in days. I blinked until my eyes adjusted and a burst of cold air hit my face. The blue sky was cloudless above, punctuated by the sound of rocks falling harmlessly away.

"Well, I think that did it…" Cade said with a clearing of his throat. "You did promise to blow a hole in the mountain, Riona…"

CHAPTER FIFTY-FOUR

WARD

With the mountain a bit sturdier, or at least with less strain on Lynton, I sent Ayla and Riona back to the castle to make preparations for the trolls now milling about in the plains just outside. The sun would be harsh on their skin, and Cade was too busy to conjure any sort of shelter, so Riona would have to think of something.

"Just make sure they're comfortable," I said to Riona, who nodded.

Elodia, Rutley, and I stayed behind to scour the city for the remaining trolls. It took most of the day and was exhausting, tedious work. But finally, when the sun set behind the mountain, I found no more trolls hiding in the city.

"That's it," I said, putting my hands on my hips. "That's everyone."

"It's not," Lynton said, watching the city. "We're still missing someone."

I was about to argue until I saw the look on his face. His daughter. "Maybe she's already gone past..."

"She hasn't. I would've seen her. I..." His face went slack as Elodia came walking over the hill dragging a protesting teenager.

"Let me go!" the troll girl said, kicking at Elodia. "I will destroy you, human!"

"I'm guessing that's—"

"Aniline!" Lynton ran forward, and immediately, the mountain trembled. He skidded to a halt, looking up as the remaining pieces of the mountain wobbled and fell inward. "*Run!*"

Elodia grabbed the girl and yanked her forward, and luckily, she complied. And as the mountain collapsed, the four of us, along with Cade, dashed through the portal. The sound of the mountain crumbling vanished as Cade closed the portal behind him, the only evidence of the chaos the puff of dust that had made it through.

We stared at the plain beyond us, breathing heavily. Then I became aware of activity behind us. I wasn't sure what I'd expected, but it warmed my heart to see that Ayla had gone to Gabhann and rounded up my soldiers to start feeding and providing blankets and other items to the bewildered trolls. As the memory spell wore off, some were confused, others angry, and still others were stuck under the spell and seemed content where they were.

Ayla and Riona were amongst them, seemingly helping Bronwen dispense soup from a large cauldron in the middle of the field. Ayla's hair was pulled up away from her face as she walked bowls of soup to the trolls. Riona was using her magic to make more of everything and hand them out. Every so often, they'd bump into each other and smile.

"I don't know what we do now," Lynton whispered as a purple butterfly flitted by his face. "Where do we go?"

"Tonight, you rest," I said, patting him on the back. "Tomorrow, we'll visit the Erlking and find you a permanent place. Perhaps back in the wildlands, if you want."

His mask slid. "How can you be sure he won't enslave us again?"

"He won't," Cade said, walking up beside him. "Because you'll have me to protect you. And Riona."

"And me," I said then added sheepishly, "for what that's worth."

Lynton stepped up to the group and stomped on the ground weakly. Magic flowed from his body, but much less robustly than it had before. Still, it wasn't intended to do more than get the trolls' attention.

"My…my siblings," he said, his voice hoarse. Cade tapped his staff on the ground and when he spoke again, the volume was amplified. "We have a lot to discuss. Our king… Edric is dead."

A gasp of horror rose from the crowd, but Lynton held up his hands.

"He wasn't the sovereign we hoped he'd be. He enslaved us these past thousand years, kept us in stasis while he readied his own plans for his own desires. Meanwhile, our loved ones back in our lands perished." He turned to his daughter, who gave him a soft smile. "We have a chance at a new beginning, thanks to the queen of Pennlan and her compatriots. These are our friends—we owe our continued existence to them."

I felt a swell of pride as the trolls looked at us—at Ayla, at Elodia and Rutley, Riona. Even Cade, with his staff.

"Tonight, we rest. Tomorrow, we venture back to our ancestral home to find… Find a new home. Any who wish to stay behind may do so. You are free to make your own choices." He paused. "Finally free to do what you wish. But I'm going home. And you are all welcome to join me."

And that was all he said to them, as he turned to us, reaching for my hand.

"Thank you," he said, squeezing it then turning to Cade. "And you, wizard. I'm sorry we treated you so—"

"Bygones," Cade said. "Now, how about we get some of that stew? It's been months since I've had Bronwen's legendary recipe."

>-» >-» >-» >-»

I had two bowls, having forgotten what a good meal tasted like in the fortnight we'd been gone. I sat down, my feet aching from running all over the troll kingdom, and savored it, watching the soldiers and taking a break for the first time in what felt like ages.

"So. This is what it'll be like when you're captain."

Platt was behind me, arms crossed over his chest. "What? Bringing magical creatures into our kingdom?" I shrugged. "I try not to make it a habit."

He snorted. "Gabhann is making a mistake. As is Her Majesty. But I suppose—"

"You know," I cut him off, "you could be off doing something useful, like making sure our guests have bedrolls and enough food and water."

He stormed away, and I couldn't help but feel like *that* was a harbinger of things to come. But I'd solve that problem later. I wasn't captain yet anyway.

"He seems mad."

Ayla stood in front of me now, a bowl cupped in her hands—this time with a piece of crusty bread perched on the side.

"Do you want to make *him* your captain?" I asked.

"Absolutely not," she said, making a face. "He's too much of a butt kisser. I need someone who'll call me out when I deserve it." She cleared her throat. "Are you still hungry?"

I waved her over, not that I was famished, but that bread was tempting. "Can't believe Bronwen was able to whip all this up so quickly."

"Riona helped," Ayla said, sitting down beside me. "And Cade, when he returned." She looked at me. "You got everyone out?"

I nodded. "Now how we'll get them to the fae realm, I haven't a clue."

"They could stay here," Ayla said. "I wouldn't mind having an army of trolls just outside my doorstep... You know, just in case."

"They don't belong here," I said softly. "They deserve to go home."

"I know. Just...wishful thinking," she replied with a sigh. "They're handling it well, I suppose. The last thing most of them remember was the battle of the *aos sí*. Just unimaginable horror and bloodshed, only to wake up a thousand years in the future. Everything they knew is gone."

"They'll figure it out," I said. "They're alive, aren't they?"

"Thanks to you."

"Thanks to *you*," I added, nudging her. "So you've figured out that stone, huh?"

"Somewhat." She looked at it curiously. "It seems to work better when Riona's around."

Her gaze moved out into the trolls until it landed on Riona, who was talking with Lynton's daughter and offering her another bowl of soup.

"How is it going with your *sister*?" I made sure to emphasize the last word.

"We haven't had a chance to really talk," Ayla said. "I owe her a few thousand more apologies."

"Probably not necessary," I said, watching her as she handed a bowl of stew to Lynton with a smile. "She's got quite the forgiving heart."

"Too forgiving," Ayla said. "More than I deserve." She turned her stone over a few times. "I've been thinking a lot about what I said. And why…" She glanced at me from beneath her lashes. "Not that there's any excuse, but—"

"Go on."

She dropped the stone. "To accept that Riona is my half-sister is to accept everything that Eoghan did. To believe that the man I thought had raised me, had *loved* me like his own, was really…" Her voice cracked. "But it's more than that, too. Because if Eoghan really wasn't who I thought he was, that means he's really…*gone*. And I'm all alone on this big throne I'm not prepared to…." She swallowed. "If I make a mistake, if I make the wrong call…there's no one who'll save me." A tear leaked down her cheek. "None of which is Riona's fault, of course."

I watched her play with a blade of grass, her vulnerable words echoing in the silence between us. "I get it. You've been through a lot. But there's one thing you're wrong about: you aren't alone. You have Captain Gabhann, Cade—"

She snorted. "Not sure about him anymore."

"He'll come around," I said. "Riona, too. And…" I glanced at her hand sitting next to me and gently covered it with mine. "And you have me."

"Does that mean you're staying?" Ayla asked.

I watched her, a little smile teasing the corners of my mouth as I squeezed her hand. "I suppose I could stay behind. After all, we..." All the levity left my body. "We have to find the other two stones before Eoghan does."

She deflated. "I can't believe Edric just *gave his away*. Now we're even. One to one. Unless..." She shook her head. "I don't want to think about it."

"We'll send someone to the south as soon as we get these trolls settled," I said.

"You?" She met my gaze with a frown.

It should've been me. But I shook my head. "I have to stay and protect my sovereign. You know, in case he comes back. And we have to kick some sense into these other kingdoms, too, so they'll start trading with us again."

She groaned. "Why'd you have to remind me? I'm sure... The merchants are going to be furious with me when they find out I went on an adventure instead of solving their problem."

"To be fair, you *were* trying to solve their problem. Just in a roundabout way."

She stared off into the distance, defeated.

"You know," I began, clearing my throat, "if you start firing off beams of light from that stone, they might not be so eager to mess with you. And since you and Riona are on speaking terms now, you might just have the opportunity to show off some real power. Cow them into opening the borders."

"I don't know if I have it in me to..." She swallowed hard. "In about three days, I'll realize that I ended Edric's life and have a complete breakdown about it."

I sat back on my haunches. "Edric had a hundred lifetimes to do the right thing. He wasn't the hero."

"But he could've been saved. I could have saved him." She rubbed her hands together. "I only... I didn't want to risk making another mistake."

I looked out at the trolls, watching their tired smiles and nervous conversations. "You saved them, Ayla. They're free to live however they choose. All thanks to you."

She didn't look convinced as she rose slowly, removing her hand from under mine. "I'm going to do another sweep and make sure everyone's taken care of. Get some rest."

But I took her hand again, pulling her back down to sit next to me. "You need your rest, too."

She smiled, glancing at our joined hands, and settled back down.

CHAPTER FIFTY-FIVE

CADE

I watched Ward and Ayla talk, ignoring the burn of jealousy as I turned away. Ayla had made her choice—for now—and it wasn't me. They looked cozy and happy. I supposed Ward had forgiven Ayla. They would probably…

I couldn't think about it.

The trolls had gathered around small firepits or were sleeping on bedrolls that Riona had conjured. She seemed to have better control over her magic than she had in the past, and I couldn't help but be a little proud of how far she'd come. Something must've shifted in her mind, and I was grateful for it. She was far too powerful to keep herself under wraps.

"Wi… Cade," Lynton called, walking up to me. "May I have a word with you?"

He and I walked off to the side, away from listening ears.

"I would like to visit the Erlking now," he said. "I want to know sooner rather than later if we will not be welcome back in our own lands."

"Of course," I said. "But you will be."

He made a noise of distrust.

I tapped my staff to the ground, sending a bolt of magic to Riona. I was starting to like this new way of casting magic. It seemed a bit more controlled than flinging spells through the air. Riona turned, a frown on her face, and disappeared into a flock of butterflies, appearing next to us.

"What's up?"

"Lynton would like to go see Birch now," I said. "Just in case things don't go our way."

"Conjure the portal where no one will see you," Lynton said. "I don't want an audience."

"What about Ward?" Riona said. "He should—"

"Leave him," I snapped, forcing myself not to look in their direction. "He's busy anyway."

We walked back toward the castle, disappearing around the side, and I cast the portal, placing it in the hall just outside the Erlking's receiving room. Lynton made a sound of fear as he gazed past the green circle, but he straightened his shoulders and stepped through.

And just like that, we were in the fae realm. The sound of the Erlking's receiving room echoed down the hall, and I could only imagine the creatures assembled there. Lynton craned his neck as he looked around, in awe of the palace and all that was here.

"I've never..." he began.

"C'mon," Riona said with a look at me. "Let's push our way in there."

As predicted, the room was filled with all manner of creatures. Lynton stood agog, and it occurred to me that he perhaps hadn't seen so many different types of creatures assembled in one room before. At least, not clamoring for the attention of the Erlking.

But just as she'd done with me, Riona grabbed his hand and yanked him forward, and I followed, casting a little magic to move the creatures out of the way. They argued, but as soon as they saw who was walking by, surprise replaced derision. And the room fell silent—but it didn't seem to be magic.

"What is..." Birch stood and his eyes widened. "Granddaughter, what have you brought...?"

She cleared her throat. "Your Majesty, I present to you L..." She paused. "*King* Lynton of Gwyllion."

"Gwyllion is no more," Lynton said. "But I am king of the trolls."

He said it almost like a dare, expecting the Erlking to strike him down where he stood. But Birch was silent, watching him as if he wasn't quite sure what to make of him.

"Why don't you tell me what happened?" Birch said.

Riona took the lead, providing a winding summation of our journey up the mountain and inside the castle. When she came to the part about Eoghan and that the trolls had given up their stone in exchange for a potion that used her blood, Birch jumped to his feet and a cry of horror rose from the audience.

"Treachery!" he bellowed. "How dare you stand before me—"

"It wasn't him," Riona said, holding up her hands. "It was Edric. Lynton was under a spell." She waved her hands around. "I'm fine. I promise."

Birch narrowed his gaze then sat down. "This is a fantastical tale, granddaughter. What would you ask of the Erlking?"

"There are a few thousand trolls on the greens outside Pennlan castle," Riona said. "We'd like permission to resettle them in their former home in the wildlands."

A rumble of curiosity came from the audience, and Birch rubbed his chin. "Why should we offer quarter to those who betrayed us? Those who would steal blood from their fellow creature?"

"It wasn't them," Riona said, a little exasperatedly. "It was—"

"Be that as it may. These creatures still imbibed the potion. They still have knowledge of it."

"No, we don't," Lynton said. "The only troll who did was killed by an arrow. And the only memory of the potion buried by the mountain." He stepped forward and put his hand to his chest, bowing. "We have spent these past thousand years asleep while our lives weren't ours. I ask…" He swallowed. "I ask the Erlking's forgiveness for the brazenness of our late king. I only seek a safe place for my people to rebuild their lives after they were so unfairly taken from them."

Birch watched him for a moment then stood. I held my staff, though I didn't know what to expect.

"Forgiveness granted," he said with a tense smile. "You may return to your former lands and make them what you will, with my blessing." He paused and narrowed his gaze. "*As long as* you keep to your lands and forget all designs on this throne of the Erlking."

"Of course, Your Majesty," Lynton said.

A ripple of magic moved through the room, and the back of my neck burned. Lynton winced as if it were a new feeling for him, but then he fell to his knees, relief on his face.

"Thank you, generous Erlking," he whispered. "Thank you for your mercy."

"Rise, King Lynton," he said as the conversation dulled around us. "You are king of a people in need of leadership. Do not show weakness in front of these bloodthirsty creatures or they will eat you alive."

Lynton nodded and rose, wiping his face and straightening. "Thank you."

"You will, of course, need help." He looked at Riona. "You, granddaughter. Resettling them will be your charge. Since you are *so familiar* with the wildlands."

"But what about Aldrick?" she asked, nervously. "Shouldn't I continue my training?"

The old fae beamed. "From the sounds of it, you are doing just fine on your own."

>→ >→ >→ >→

"I can't believe it," Lynton said, holding his chest. "The Erlking's generosity knows no bounds."

"I'm sure he'll want something in return, eventually," Riona replied, looking back into the room we'd exited. "But for now, you're safe."

"As safe as any of us are, with Eoghan wandering about with one stone," I said, looking out as we passed a window. It was easy to feel like we'd secured a victory, but in the grand scheme of things, all we'd done was waste six months looking for a stone that had already been given away.

"Lynton, can you give us a second?" Riona asked, and the troll nodded as he gave us space. "Why the sour face?"

"I saw another memory, before I was captured by Edric," I said. "Aoibheann said that in order to destroy the *seod croí*, it had to be split into pieces…and each piece needed to be used against the others."

Riona opened and closed her mouth. "So if we got all four pieces, *we* could destroy it?"

"Theoretically," I said.

"Well, first we'd have to get all four pieces," she said. "And so far, we just have one."

"I'm going in search of the third piece of the stone," I said. "Now."

"W… Now? Now-now?" She looked at Lynton, standing at the end of the hallway, staring at a painting. "What about him?"

"He has you," I said with a smile. "Ayla has her stone—and Ward. And you, of course. But I can make it to the southern part of the continent now and continue until I find it." I heaved a heavy breath. "Assuming he hasn't beaten us to the punch again."

She swallowed. "Aren't you at least going to say goodbye?"

"What do you think I'm doing?"

"Not to me," she said with a frown. "To Ayla."

I probably should've. It would've been the mature thing to do. But I couldn't bear to hear her say those words again, to tell me she didn't love me *like that*. And perhaps some part of me hoped, as it had six months ago, that if I brought back another piece of the stone, if I helped us get closer to our goal… She might look at me the way she was looking at Ward around that firepit.

"Cade, she'll be heartbroken," Riona said with a click of her tongue. "You're her best friend."

"And that's all I am to her," I said hotly. "I don't expect you to understand—"

"You told her you loved her and she turned you down," she said pointedly.

I frowned as my cheeks warmed. "How did you—"

"I can read a room," she said with a hearty eye roll. "Regardless of how she feels, you owe it to her to at least talk about what happened before you disappear for who knows how long."

"I can do whatever I want. I'm a wizard," I snapped. "And you shouldn't be defending her."

"She's having trouble dealing with her trauma. It's... She's not the only one," Riona replied. "She needs you to stay around and protect her in case Eoghan comes back."

"Why does she need me when she has you?" I asked with a smile. "You have more magic than you know."

"Cade..."

I pulled her into a hug. Her head barely reached my shoulders. "I'll write her a letter."

"See that you do." She wrapped her arms around me and closed her eyes. "Thank you."

"For what?"

"Believing in me," she said, stepping back to look up at me. "You're the first one who ever has."

I stepped back. "Take care of yourself, Riona."

And with that, I conjured a portal to the farthest point south on the continent and stepped through.

Acknowlegments

I thought writing a book while pregnant was difficult, but writing a book with a newborn is a whole 'nother level, y'all. Especially a newborn who flat-out stops sleeping for eight weeks and who must be on or near Mom every second of the day. So while this book took twice as long from first word to final draft, it got finished. Eventually.

But it would not have gotten this far without the help from my village—starting with my husband, who supports everything I do and write with aplomb. Doing this alone would've been absolutely maddening, and with you, it's only half-maddening and a whole lot of fun. Next, big thanks to my mom and my mother-in-law, who would do the awful thing and take their precious grand baby twice a week so I could have time to focus on the book and make progress. I'd also be remiss if I didn't thank Scrivener for iOS and Dropbox, because half of this book was written on my phone in a dark nursery.

As usual, my book-related village came through as well: my beta readers Chelsea and Kristin, my editor Danielle, and my QA checker Lisa. Thank you for helping this jumbled mess of a plot shine.

Finally, a special thanks to the little nugget who made finishing this book all the more difficult: You are my sunshine, even when skies are gray. I can't wait to see who you grow up to be.

ALSO BY THE AUTHOR
THE PRINCESS VIGILANTE SERIES

Brynna has been protecting her kingdom as a masked vigilante until one night, she's captured by the king's guards. Instead of arresting her, the captain tells her that her father and brother have been assassinated and she must hang up her mask and become queen.

The Princess Vigilante series is a four-book young adult epic fantasy series, perfect for fans of Throne of Glass and Graceling.

Available in ebook, Paperback, and Hardcover

ABOUT THE AUTHOR

S. Usher Evans was born and raised in Pensacola, Florida. After a decade of fighting bureaucratic battles as an IT consultant in Washington, D.C., she suffered a massive quarter-life-crisis. She decided fighting dragons was more fun than writing policy, so she moved back to Pensacola to write books full-time. She currently resides there with her husband and kids and frequently can be found plotting on the beach.

Visit S. Usher Evans online at:
http://www.susherevans.com/